VALENTINE
CANDY
MURDER

LESLIE MEIER

KENSINGTON
PUBLISHING CORP.

www.kensingtonbooks.com

KENSINGTON BOOKS are published by

Kensington Publishing Corp.
119 West 40th Street
New York, NY 10018

Compilation copyright © 2019 by Kensington Publishing Corp.
Valentine Murder © 1999 by Leslie Meier
Chocolate Covered Murder © 2012 by Leslie Meier

All Kensington titles, imprints, and distributed lines are available at special quantity discounts for bulk purchases for sales promotion, premiums, fund-raising, educational, or institutional use. Special book excerpts or customized printings can also be created to fit specific needs. For details, write or phone the office of the Kensington Special Sales Manager: Attn. Special Sales Department. Kensington Publishing Corp., 119 West 40th Street, New York, NY 10018. Phone: 1-800-221-2647.

The K logo is a trademark of Kensington Publishing Corp.

ISBN-13: 978-1-4967-2701-5
ISBN-10: 1-4967-2701-0
First Kensington Trade Edition: January 2019
First Kensington Mass Market Edition: January 2021

ISBN-13: 978-1-4967-2230-0 (ebook)
ISBN-10: 1-4967-2230-2 (ebook)

10 9 8 7 6 5 4 3 2 1

Printed in the United States of America

Contents

VALENTINE MURDER

Prologue

*Once upon a time there was a poor
kitchen maid named Cinderella . . .*

On the day she died, Bitsy Howell didn't want to get out of bed. Her bedroom was cold, for one thing. It was always cold, thanks to her landlady, Mrs. Withers, who turned the heat down to fifty-five degrees every night to save money on heating oil. It didn't matter one bit to Mrs. Withers that it was the coldest winter in twenty years.

And if the cold bedroom wasn't reason enough to stay in bed, well, the fact that it was Thursday made getting up especially difficult. Bitsy hated Thursdays.

Thursday was story hour day at the Broadbrooks Free Library where she was the librarian. Just thinking about story hour depressed Bitsy. She found it practically impossible to keep ten or fifteen preschool children focused on a storybook. Thanks to TV and video games, they had no attention span whatsoever. They fidgeted and wriggled in their seats, they picked their noses, they did everything except what Bitsy wanted them to do, which was to sit quietly and listen to a nice story followed by a fingerplay or song, or maybe a simple craft project.

This Thursday, however, happened to be the last Thursday in January. That meant the library's board of directors would meet, as they did on the third Thursday of every month. Bitsy would not only have to cope with story hour, but with the directors, too.

Bitsy had come to the tiny Broadbrooks Free Library in Tinker's Cove, Maine, from a big city library. One factor in her decision to leave had been her poor relationship with her boss, the head librarian. Little had she known that she was swapping one rather difficult menopausal supervisor for seven meddlesome and inquisitive directors.

Bitsy sighed and heaved herself out of bed. She padded barefoot around her rather messy bedroom, looking for her slippers. She found one underneath a magazine and the other tangled in a pair of sweat pants. One of these days, she promised herself, she would get organized and pick up the clothes that were strewn on the floor. Not today, of course. She didn't have time today.

On her way to the bathroom she raised the shade and peered out the window, blinking at the bright winter sunlight. Shit, she muttered. It had snowed again.

Arriving at the library, Bitsy studied the new addition which contained a children's room, workroom, and conference room. It was undeniably handsome, and badly needed, but it had been a dreadful bone of contention.

When she had first come to Tinker's Cove the library was a charming but antiquated old building that was far too small for the needs of the community. Getting the board to agree to build the addition, and then raising the money for it had been a struggle, one Bitsy wouldn't want to repeat. Now, if she could only get them to take the next step and buy some computers so the library could go online.

"Tiny baby steps," she muttered as she unlocked the door. Flicking on the lights as she went, Bitsy headed for her office. She had an hour or so before the library opened and she wanted to have her facts and figures straight before the board meeting.

Pushing aside a few of the papers that cluttered her desk, she set down a bag containing a Styrofoam cup of coffee, with cream and sugar, and a couple of sugary jelly doughnuts. She draped her coat over an extra chair and took her seat, flicking on the computer. Soon she was happily immersed in numbers and percentages, all the while slurping down her coffee and scattering powdered sugar all over her desk.

At ten minutes past ten she heard someone banging at the main entrance and realized she hadn't unlocked the doors.

"I'm so sorry," she apologized as she pulled open the heavy oak door. "I lost track of the time."

"No problem, my dear," said Gerald Asquith, smiling down at her benignly. Tall and gray-haired, dressed in a beautifully tailored cashmere overcoat, he was the retired president of Winchester College and one of the members of the board of directors. "I know I'm a bit early, but I want to go over the final figures for the addition before the meeting."

"Of course," said Bitsy. "I'll get the file for you."

Bitsy had hoped Gerald would seat himself at the big table in the reference room, but instead he hung his coat up on the rack by the door and followed her into her office. When she gave him the file he sat down at her desk, displacing her, and began studying it.

Bitsy gave a little shrug and headed for the children's section. She had to come up with something for story hour anyway; it was in less than an hour, at eleven.

She was leafing through a lavishly illustrated edition of *Cinderella* when she felt a presence behind her. Turning, she greeted Corney Clarke with a polite smile. Corney, an attractive blonde of indeterminate age, ran a busy catering service and called herself a "lifestyle consultant." She was also a member of the board of directors.

"Can I help you?" asked Bitsy, mindful of her status as an employee.

"No. I came a little early to see the new addition. It's a big improvement, isn't it?" said Corney, walking around the sunny area, admiring the low bookshelves and child-sized seating.

"It sure is," agreed Bitsy. "We must have been the only library in the state without a children's room."

"It must be fun doing story hour, now, in such nice surroundings," surmised Corney.

"Oh, yes," said Bitsy, attempting to sound enthusiastic. "Today we're reading *Cinderella*."

"Oh." Corney wrinkled her forehead in concern. "I don't want to tell you how to do your job, but are you sure that's a good choice?"

"The children like it . . ." began Bitsy.

"Well, of course they do. But does it send the right message?"

"It's just a fairy tale." Bitsy bit her lip. Personally, she didn't think every story had to have a socially redeeming message, and she wasn't sure Corney was the right person to decide what was suitable for young children, either. After all, she was childless and never married, though not from lack of effort.

"Well, we don't want our little girls growing up and thinking life is a fairy tale, do we? We don't want them to wait for Prince Charming to rescue them from the kitchen—we want them to become self-actualizing, don't we?" Corney gave Bitsy an encouraging smile, and patted her hand. "I'm sure you can find something more suitable." She paused for a moment and came up with a suggestion. "Like *The Little Engine that Could*," she said, turning and striding off in the direction of the office.

Bitsy rolled her eyes and replaced *Cinderella* on the shelf. Pulling out one volume after another, she dismissed them. Children's literature was so insipid these days. Everything had to have a positive, meaningful message. She wanted something with a little bite. Something exciting. She opened a battered copy of *Hansel and Gretel* and began turning the pages. This ought to keep the little demons' attention, she thought, admiring a lurid illustration of the tiny Hansel and Gretel cringing in terror as the grinning witch opened the oven door.

"Say, Bitsy, do you know where those figures for the addition are?"

Bitsy closed the book and turned to face Hayden Northcross, another member of the board of directors. Hayden was a small, neat man who was a partner in a prestigious antiques business that was known far beyond Tinker's Cove.

"Gerald's got them, in my office," said Bitsy.

"I'll see if he's through with them," said Hayden, turning to go. "Say, what's that?"

"Hansel and Gretel. For story hour."

"Oh, my dear! Not *Hansel and Gretel!"* exclaimed Hayden, throwing up his hands in horror.

"No? Why not?" inquired Bitsy, tightening her grip on the storybook and starting a slow mental count to ten.

"Not unless you want to traumatize the poor things," said Hayden. "I'll never forget how frightened I was when Mumsy read it to me. I think it may have affected my entire attitude toward women." He cocked an eyebrow and nodded meaningfully.

Bitsy wasn't quite sure how serious he was. Hayden and his business partner, Ralph Love, had also been domestic partners for years. Hayden thought it great fun to shock the more conservative residents of Tinker's Cove by flaunting his homosexuality.

"It's just a story," said Bitsy, defending her choice. "I'll be sure to remind them it's make-believe."

"I'm warning you. You're playing with fire," said Hay-

den, waggling his finger at her. "That book contains dangerous themes of desertion and cannibalism—the mothers are
sure to object."

"You're probably right," said Bitsy, putting the book back
on the shelf.

"You know I am," said Hayden, flashing her a smile.
"See you at the meeting."

The meeting, thought Bitsy, biting her lip. That was another sore point. The fact that the board met at the same time
Bitsy was occupied with story hour was not coincidental.
She was convinced it was their way of letting her know she
was not a decision maker. She was just the hired help, allowed to join the meeting only for the last half hour to give
her monthly report.

It hadn't always been like that. When she first took the
job, the board had sought her advice, and had adopted her
suggestion that the library be expanded. But as time passed
they seemed to grow less receptive to her views, and began
easing her out of their meetings. They'd also become increasingly intrusive, always poking their noses into her
work.

Bitsy checked her watch and resumed her search. She
had better find something fast; it was already a quarter to
eleven and little Sadie Orenstein had arrived. She was
slowly slipping a big stack of books through the return slot
in the circulation desk, one by one, while her mother studied
the new books. The Orensteins were ferocious readers.

Pulling out book after book, she shook her head and
shoved them back on the shelf. It seemed as if she had read
them all, over and over. Absolutely nothing appealed until
she found an old favorite, *Rumpelstiltskin*.

She smiled at the picture of the irate dwarf on the cover.
The kids would like it, too, she thought. She would have
them act it out and they could stamp their feet just like
Rumpelstiltskin. Tucking the book under her arm, and telling Sadie she'd be right back, she hurried to the office. She'd

just remembered that she had left a file open on the computer and wanted to close it.

There she found Ed Bumpus, yet another member of the board of directors, busy disassembling the copy machine. Ed was a big man and when he bent over the machine his shirt and pants parted, revealing rather more of his hairy backside than she wanted to see. She stared out the window at a snow-covered pine tree.

"We want copies of the addition finances for the meeting, but the danged machine won't work," explained Ed. He was a contractor and never hesitated to reach for a screwdriver.

"That's funny. It worked fine yesterday. Maybe it's out of paper. Or needs toner. Did you check?"

"What kind of idiot do you take me for? Of course I checked!" snapped Ed, growing a bit red under his plaid flannel shirt collar.

"We'll have to call for service, then," said Bitsy, leaning over Gerald to ease open her desk drawer. "You can make copies at the coin machine by the front desk. Here's the key."

"Could you be a doll and do it for me?" Ed gave her his version of an ingratiating smile.

Still leaning awkwardly over Gerald, Bitsy reached for the mouse and clicked it, closing the file. Then she took the report from Ed. More children had gathered for story hour— she could hear their voices. They would just have to wait a few minutes. She was not going to risk being insubordinate to one of the directors, especially Ed.

When she returned she found him lounging in the spare chair, sitting on top of her coat, and joking with Gerald, who was still sitting at her desk. What a pair, she thought, annoyed at the way they made themselves at home in her office.

"Here you go," she said, handing him the papers and turning to go. She really had to get story hour started.

"So you're reading *Rumpelstiltskin* to them today?" inquired Gerald, who was still sitting at her desk. His tone was friendly—he was just making conversation. Now that he was retired he had all the time in the world.

"I think they'll like it," said Bitsy, eager to get out to the children. Unsupervised, there was no telling what they might get up to.

"Well, I don't think it's a very good idea. It's a horrible story," said Ed. "It used to make my little girls cry."

"Really?" Bitsy kept her voice even. She was determined not to let him know how irritated she was.

"In fact, I don't even think it belongs in the library. With all the money we spend on new books I don't know why you're keeping a nasty old book like that. Just look at it—it's all worn out."

"I guess you're right," said Bitsy, who knew the acquisitions budget was a sore spot with Ed, who favored bricks and mortar over books. His objection, however, reminded her of a box of new material that had arrived the day before but hadn't been opened yet.

"I'm just going down to the workroom for a minute," she said, more to herself than the directors. Grabbing the box of art supplies and taking a pile of red construction paper from the corner of her desk, she quickly left the office and hurried through the children's room, giving the assembled mothers and children a cheerful wave.

"I'll be right with you—we're making valentines today," she called, opening the door to the stairs that led to the lower level. She rushed down, hearing her footsteps echo in the poured concrete stairwell, but caught her foot on the rubber edging of the bottom step. She fell forward, twisting her ankle and bumping her head painfully on the doorknob. The sheets of red paper cascaded around her; the coffee can containing child-safe scissors clattered to the concrete floor and crayons rolled in every direction.

Groaning slightly, she pressed her hands to her forehead and sat down on the next to last step, waiting impatiently for the blinding agony to pass. Using a trick she'd picked up in a stress management workshop, she concentrated on her breathing, keeping her breaths even. Gradually, the pain receded. She unclenched her teeth and blinked her eyes. Grasping the handrailing, she pulled herself to her feet, only to feel a stabbing pain in her ankle. Conscious that she was already late for story hour, she tried putting her weight on it even though the pain made her wince. The ankle held and she limped through the dark and empty conference room and on into the brand-new workroom. The workroom, unlike the conference room, had windows and she squinted her eyes against the bright sun. She bent over the box, which was sitting on the floor, and yanked at the tape.

Hearing the outside door open, she raised her head.

"Oh, it's *you*," she said, recognizing the figure outlined against the bright light streaming through the windows. Of all the nerve, she thought angrily. This was just too much; the morning was spinning out of control. She'd had enough. She took a deep breath, preparing to give vent to the emotions she had been suppressing for so long, but she never got the chance to say what was on her mind.

Bitsy Howell's last words were rudely interrupted.

Chapter One

*That country was ruled by a wise king
and his beautiful and kind queen . . .*

In the big kitchen of her restored farmhouse on Red Top Road, Lucy Stone sang a little song as she tucked the last of the breakfast dishes into the dishwasher. She couldn't help feeling cheerful. Today, after what seemed like a solid month of cloudy skies and snowstorms, the sun was finally shining. The sky was a cloudless, bright blue. The pine trees in the woods bordering the yard were deep green, frosted with white. Mounds of snow covered her car, the shed, the garden fence; everything sparkled in the sunlight. It was so bright that she had to squint when she looked out the window.

Inside, it revealed crumbs and dust that had gone unnoticed in the dim, cloud-filtered daylight of recent weeks, along with a few dried-out pine needles from the Christmas tree. As the dishwasher hummed she wiped off the counters with a sponge and straightened the mess of papers that had collected on the round golden oak table.

Looking at the now neat but ever-growing pile, she gave

a big sigh. It was her "to-do" list. Bills to pay, car insurance renewal forms to file, bank statements to balance, income tax forms to complete. A partially completed feature story she was writing for the local paper, *The Pennysaver.* The latest issue of *Maine Library Journal.*

She glanced at the clock—it was a few minutes past eight. A peek in the family room revealed that her four-year-old daughter, Zoe, was happily playing a game on the family computer. She was the only one home besides Lucy. Lucy's husband, Bill, a restoration carpenter, was already at work. The older children were all in school: Toby, sixteen, and Elizabeth, fourteen, attended high school, and ten-year-old Sara was in third grade at the Tinker's Cove Elementary School.

No time like the present, decided Lucy, sitting down and picking up the magazine. The board meeting wasn't until eleven; she had plenty of time to read it and become familiar with library issues. It was her first meeting as a director and she wanted to make a good impression.

An hour later, her head was buzzing. What had she gotten herself into? Being a library director was a bigger responsibility than she thought. Budgets. Maintenance. Circulation. Employee relations. Acquisitions. Censorship. Information technology. Not to mention security.

She had no idea security was a big issue for libraries, but it was. Thanks to the journal she now knew that seven librarians in New England had been the victims of brutal attacks in the last year, and one had been raped. "Librarians, generally women, often work alone at night, so they are natural targets," explained the state library commissioner. "Libraries often contain valuable artifacts and rare books, not to mention an increasing amount of computer equipment. We have to be more vigilant about security, something we have tended to take for granted."

Poor Bitsy, thought Lucy, resolving to ask her fellow board members if the new addition had been equipped with an alarm system. If it hadn't been, it should, and the older part of the building should be included, too.

The dishwasher clicked off and Lucy checked the clock. Already past nine and she wasn't dressed yet. Neither was Zoe, she realized.

"Come on, sweetie," called Lucy, standing in the doorway. "We have to get dressed. It's story hour day."

Zoe didn't move from the computer. Lucy repeated her request.

"Zoe, time to get dressed."

"I don't want to."

Surprised at this answer, Lucy crossed the room and peered over her daughter's shoulder at the brightly colored screen, where lime green robots were chasing a little brown bunny. "Is it a good game?" she asked.

Zoe didn't answer. Her attention was fixed on the screen; her chubby fingers were busy pushing buttons on the control pad.

"I'll tell you what," said Lucy, in a cheerful but firm voice. "You can play a little longer, while I get dressed. But then we'll have to turn off the computer. Okay?"

She looked expectantly at Zoe, waiting for an answer, and thought she detected a little nod. Good enough. She hurried upstairs, wondering exactly what a library director should wear.

Returning to the family room a half hour later, Lucy was pleased with her choice. She was wearing her good wool slacks, a turtleneck jersey, and the extravagantly expensive designer sweater Bill had given her for Christmas. She had added a simple gold chain and a pair of pearl earrings.

Now for the next challenge, she thought, surveying the family room where Zoe was still absorbed in "Bunny Beware." Another gift from Bill, but Lucy wasn't sure she approved of this one.

"Zoe, honey. Remember our bargain? Mommy's all dressed. Now it's your turn."

"I'm busy," said Zoe. The computer game had apparently rendered her immobile. Powerful electronic forces, emanating from the screen, had seized control of the little girl's mind and body. Something had to be done.

Lucy switched off the machine.

"Whaaaaaaa!" shrieked Zoe.

"It's time to get dressed," said Lucy. "You don't want to miss story hour, do you?"

"Story hour's dumb and Miss Howell's mean!"

"Zoe, that's enough," said Lucy, firmly taking her daughter's hand and leading her to the stairs. "What do you want to wear today? How about your turtleneck with the hearts? It's only two weeks 'til Valentine's Day, you know."

It was well after ten when Lucy and Zoe, bundled against the single-digit weather in bulky down parkas and snow boots, left the house. Bill and Toby had shoveled a path to the driveway earlier that morning, but they hadn't cleared the snow off the car. With a gloved hand Lucy scraped the snow away from the door handle and pulled. It didn't budge. It was frozen shut by a layer of ice that had formed underneath the snow.

"This is going to take a while," Lucy told Zoe. "Why don't you make some snow angels for Mommy?"

It was a quarter to eleven when Lucy and Zoe finally got under way in the old Subaru station wagon. Thank goodness for four-wheel drive, thought Lucy, as they made steady but slow progress over the snow-covered roads. In Tinker's Cove the DPW plowed, but set the blades high, leaving an inch or two of snow to protect the expensive asphalt.

If you didn't like snow, thought Lucy, you shouldn't live in Maine. At least not this winter with record low temperatures and unusually heavy snowfalls. Fortunately, she loved cold weather and always felt a sense of excitement when the flakes began to fall. As she drove along, she was enchanted by the way last night's storm had turned the bare winter trees into a glistening fairyland.

Turning onto Main Street, she thought that Tinker's Cove, with its red brick storefronts and tall-steepled white church, was truly a picture-perfect New England town. Today, however, Main Street seemed deserted; few people were out and about in the bitter cold. She spotted Mr. Ericson, the postman, bundled up in a red and black buffalo plaid jacket and a checked wool cap with black fur earflaps. She gave the horn a friendly toot as she passed him.

Turning into the library parking lot, she saw there were a number of cars. No wonder, she thought; she was late. It was already ten past eleven. Story hour was bound to attract a crowd of mothers and kids tired of being cooped up at home. The directors would also have gathered for their meeting. She parked the car and helped Zoe out of her seatbelt and booster seat and they hurried up the narrow path between the snowbanks.

"We're late, we're late," she began.

"For an important date!" exclaimed Zoe, completing the rhyme and stamping her purple Barbie boots on the cocoa fiber mat.

"For my first meeting," fretted Lucy, as she pulled open the door.

Chapter Two

When Snow White awakened from her nap,
she was surprised to see the Seven Dwarves . . .

As they entered the library, Lucy's eyes were drawn as always to the softly gleaming pewter tankard that sat in a locked display case in the entry. A neatly printed label identified it as "Josiah's Tankard" and noted it had been presented to the library in 1887 by Henry Hopkins, the last surviving descendent of Josiah Hopkins, who was the first European to settle in Tinker's Cove. The tankard, which had been handed down through the family, was said to have been brought from England by Josiah.

If one looked closely, and the light was right, an elaborate design featuring a flowering shrub with a bird perched on one of the branches could still be discerned in the tankard's worn and battered surface. The initials "J" and "H" were somewhat easier to see, along with the date, 1698.

Lucy thought the library was a fitting place for the tankard, which represented the long history of the little town that was first incorporated in 1703. Whatever drew Josiah Hopkins to this rugged spot on the Maine coast was a puzzle, considering the brutally cold winters and the stony soil unfit for farming, but the homestead he built had stood until just a few years ago when it had burned to the ground in a spectacular fire that had claimed the life of Lucy's friend, Monica Mayes.

The homestead was gone, but the tankard had survived, safe in the library. Lucy found that comforting, just as she believed it was a privilege to live in a house that had sheltered many generations before her family had moved in. Living in a place that had ties to the past gave her a sense of security; she liked knowing that she was yet another link in a long chain of mothers and fathers and children connecting the unknowable future to the past.

Today, however, Lucy and Zoe didn't have time to admire the tankard. Instead, they pushed open the second set of doors and greeted Miss Tilley, who was seated at the circulation desk.

"I see they've put you back to work," said Lucy.

Miss Tilley had been the librarian for years, until she retired and Bitsy took her place. With her white hair and china blue eyes, Miss Tilley looked like the very image of a sweet old lady. Lucy knew better, and enjoyed her old friend's tart wit and sharp tongue.

"There should be a volunteer on duty, considering that Bitsy has story hour today, but nobody has shown up yet," said Miss Tilley, who only allowed her very dearest friends to call her by her first name, Julia. She was holding the "Date Due" stamp as if she couldn't wait to use it.

Lucy knelt to unfasten Zoe's pink parka, and gave her a little pat in the direction of the children's room. "See you later, sweetie," she said, watching as Zoe went to join her friends.

"We never had these problems when I was in charge," said Miss Tilley, leaning forward and whispering loudly to Lucy. "The volunteers knew that they were expected to come on their assigned days."

"Well, Bitsy has had a lot on her mind with the new addition and all." Lucy looked around, noting how well the new construction meshed with the older portions of the building. "It looks great, doesn't it?"

"Hummph," snorted Miss Tilley. "I just hope the heating bill doesn't bankrupt us."

"I doubt it will. Nowadays they use lots of insulation." Lucy looked around. "So where does the board meet?" she asked.

"We've always used the reference room, but I expect that will change now that we have that conference room. Why they put it in the cellar is something I'll never understand. Cellars are for storage—they're not fit for human habitation."

"Is that where everyone is?" asked Lucy, smiling at Miss Tilley's stubborn resistance to change.

"Not yet. I think they're still in Bitsy's office," said Miss Tilley, taking a pile of books that a young mother was returning. "That will be seventy-five cents," she said, sounding awfully pleased to have caught the overdue books.

Lucy went around the desk and down the dark little hallway leading to Bitsy's office. She smoothed her sweater nervously and took a deep breath, then pushed open the door.

"If it isn't our newest member," exclaimed Gerald Asquith, greeting her warmly. "Welcome! Everybody—this is Lucy Stone, who's made quite a little reputation for herself as a writer for our local newspaper, *The Pennysaver.*"

"A very little reputation," said Lucy, blushing. She enjoyed freelance writing for the paper, but was rarely able to manage more than one or two feature stories a month.

"I'm Ed Bumpus," said Ed, leaning forward in his chair to shake her hand. "I know your husband, Bill. We're in the same business."

"I've heard him speak of you," said Lucy, giving him a friendly smile. She looked around at the others, searching for familiar faces. "I know Corney, of course, but you probably don't remember me. I've attended some of your workshops. I enjoyed them very much."

Lucy extended her hand but Corney ignored it, merely nodding vacantly and murmuring, "Oh, yes."

"Hayden Northcross, here," said Hayden, promptly filling the void and taking Lucy's hand with both of his. "I must say it's nice to have some new blood on the board."

"I guess we're all here then, except for Chuck," said Ed. Lucy couldn't decide if he was grumbling, or if his voice always sounded that gruff.

"You know he tends to run late," said Corney, leaping to the absent member's defense. "After all, he's a lawyer. He'll be here."

"It's well after eleven—shall we go down?" suggested Gerald.

There was a murmur of assent, and the directors began moving toward the door.

"You know, Bitsy seems to have less and less control over those children every week," said Corney, hearing the noise from the children's room.

"She's not there," said Lucy, observing the group of lively preschoolers and a handful of chatting mothers. "Where could she be?"

"I think she said she was going down to the workroom," offered Gerald.

"Maybe she's lost track of the time. I'll run ahead and remind her," volunteered Lucy, eager to be helpful.

"Young legs," said Gerald, nodding approvingly as Lucy headed in the direction of the stairway.

"I'll see if Miss Tilley's free," said Corney, as if to remind everyone that she used to be the youngest person on the board and, even though she now had to share that distinction, was still no older than Lucy.

Corney was just approaching the circulation desk when Chuck Canaday made his appearance, bursting through the doors with his unbuttoned coat flapping about him, bringing a wave of cold air.

"Ooh—it's cold out there," said Corney, wrapping her arms across her chest and greeting him with a smile.

"It's invigorating," said Chuck, giving his thick mop of gray hair a shake. "Makes me wish I had more time for skiing."

"Me, too," agreed Corney. "I had a great time at Brewster Mountain last weekend."

"Really? How was the snow?"

"Fresh powder."

"Uh-hmm." Miss Tilley interrupted their little exchange. "Everyone's waiting for us. It's time we joined the meeting."

"Who'll watch the desk?" asked Corney.

"Bitsy will have to do it—there's no one else," said Miss Tilley. "It's not very busy, and she can leave story hour if the need arises."

Chuck and Corney's eyes met; Corney gave a little shrug, and they followed Miss Tilley toward the waiting group.

Having left the others at the office, Lucy hurried across the children's room where she was happy to see that Zoe was busy chatting with her friend, Sadie Orenstein. Whatever do four-year-olds talk about? she wondered, as she pulled open the steel door to the stairs. As she thumped down in her snow boots she noticed the mess of paper and art supplies spilled at the foot of the stairs, and quickly picked them up, wondering what had happened. She set the box down in the corner and pulled open the door to the conference room, flicking on the lights.

"Bitsy?" she called. "Are you down here?"

Receiving no answer, Lucy went on through to the workroom door. She gave a little knock and pulled it open.

It took a moment or two for her to register the sight: Bitsy was lying flat on her back, legs and arms awkwardly akimbo, like one of Zoe's discarded dolls.

"Oh, my God," exclaimed Lucy, rushing toward her. She bent over the fallen woman, noticing her eyes were wide open and there was an odd look of surprise on her face. Lucy instinctively stepped back, and saw a hole in Bitsy's cardigan sweater, just above her heart. It was then she noticed the puddle of blood seeping beneath Bitsy's body.

Repulsed, Lucy forced herself to search for a pulse and reached for Bitsy's wrist with trembling hands, hoping to find a flutter of life. Her arm felt heavy, like a dead weight, and Lucy knew it was futile. It was obvious Bitsy was dead.

Lucy's heart was racing and she felt dizzy and sick to her stomach as she backed away from the body. This was no longer Bitsy; this was something horrifying and frightening. She was shaking all over, and her teeth were chattering. She had only one thought: she had to get away. She turned and fled, running out of the workroom, across the conference room, and up the stairs. Throwing open the door, she ran smack into the group of directors. Suddenly speechless, her mouth made a noiseless little "O."

Chapter Three

*The Gingerbread Man was afraid to cross
the stream, but along came a clever fox . . .*

"What's the matter?" asked Gerald, taking her hands in his. "It's B-b-b," said Lucy, her eyes darting wildly at the group clustered around her. Their faces seemed distorted, as if they were reflections in a convex mirror. She suddenly felt woozy and the room began to whirl around her.

"Lucy, get a grip on yourself," scolded Miss Tilley.

She turned toward the voice, and her eyes settled on her old friend. Then, looking beyond the group, she saw the mothers and children waiting for story hour to begin. She watched as Zoe settled beside Sadie and opened a book for them to look at together. It was all so normal, so peaceful. Nothing like the awful thing downstairs.

"Is Bitsy hurt? Has she fallen?" Gerald peered over her shoulder, at the stairs.

Lucy straightened her back and took a deep breath. "She's dead."

"That can't be," insisted Miss Tilley.

"There must be some mistake," added Corney.

"I'd better take a look," said Ed, stepping to the front of the group.

"I don't think you should," protested Lucy, as the group surged past her and hurried down the stairs. "At least not until the police get here," she added, leaning against the wall for support. She was still dizzy and trembling with shock.

The police, she thought. I've got to call the police. But she found herself hesitating, reluctant to move. Instead, she watched Zoe, who was pointing at something in the book. It must be funny—the two little girls were giggling.

Somewhat shaky on her feet, Lucy stepped away from the wall, determined to get control of herself. Now that she was back upstairs in the sunny new addition, she could hardly believe what she had seen in the basement. She felt a little surge of hope. Maybe she'd been wrong. Maybe it wasn't too late for Bitsy. The rescue squad had defibrillators and all kinds of lifesaving equipment.

Walking carefully so as not to alarm the mothers and children, she went to the office. There she picked up the receiver and, using all her concentration, punched in 9-1-1 with a trembling hand.

"Tinker's Cove Rescue. This is a recorded line."

"There's a . . . we need help . . . fast. No, I think it's . . ." stammered Lucy, furious at herself because she still couldn't seem to form a simple sentence.

"Take it easy," said the dispatcher, trained to handle emergencies. "What's your name?"

"Lucy Stone."

"Where are you, Lucy?"

"The library."

"What's the problem?"

"Bitsy Howell—I think she's been shot."

"I'm sending an ambulance and I'm notifying the police. Have you been trained in CPR?"

"I can't," said Lucy, thinking of Bitsy's bloody body.

"That's all right," said the dispatcher. "Just stay calm. Help will be there in a few minutes."

"I can already hear the sirens," said Lucy, remembering that the police and rescue station was just around the corner from the library.

"Can you open the doors? Make sure they can get in?" asked the dispatcher.

"I can do that," said Lucy, who had clung to the dispatcher's calm voice like a lifeline. "Thank you."

She went to the front door and hailed the paramedics, who were stepping out of the ambulance. She held the door open for them and they hurried in, carrying cases of equipment. Lucy pointed them to the stairs.

As they rushed through the children's room the mothers and children looked up in surprise.

Oh, dear, thought Lucy. I'll have to give them some sort of explanation. She crossed the circulation area and leaned against one of the low children's bookcases for support.

"We've had an accident. There won't be any story hour today. I think we'll have to close the library."

"What is it?" asked Juanita Orenstein, Sadie's mother. "Can I help?"

The others looked at Lucy expectantly, curious about the sudden change in plans.

"I think it would be best if everyone just left," said Lucy, thinking of the children.

"That's too bad," said Anne Wilson, who was firmly holding each of her three-year-old twin boys by the hand. "We'll have to wait 'til next week, fellas."

"That's right, come back next week," Lucy told the mothers, who began gathering up their belongings and zipping their children into snowsuits.

"Lucy, you look terrible," said Juanita, wrapping an arm around her shoulder. "What's going on?"

"Bitsy's badly hurt," Lucy whispered.

"Oh, no!" Juanita's big brown eyes were full of concern. "What happened?"

"I'm not sure." Lucy was already regretting giving in to the impulse to confide in Juanita and arousing her curiosity. "Could you do me a favor and take Zoe home with you? I don't know how long I'm going to have to stay here."

"Sure," said Juanita. "Take as long as you need—I don't have any plans for today."

"Thanks," said Lucy. "I really appreciate it." She went over to Zoe and Sadie in the corner. "Guess what? You're going to have lunch at Sadie's today," she told Zoe.

The girls turned to face each other, and they raised their eyebrows in happy surprise before dissolving into giggles.

"Let me know if there's anything else I can do," offered Juanita, zipping up her jacket.

"Thanks," said Lucy, watching as the mothers and children began leaving.

She wondered if she ought to have some record of who was present at the library, so she went over to the circulation desk and found a piece of paper.

"Before you go, would you mind putting your names down here?" she asked, as the group started to file past the desk. When everyone was gone she took out a second sheet of paper, wrote "Library Closed Today" on it, and went outside to tape it to the door. The cold made her shiver, and her teeth began chattering. She hurried back inside, automatically glancing at the tankard. Only when she saw it was still safe in its locked case did she think to wonder if Bitsy had been shot because she interrupted a robbery. She was about to lock the door, when she heard someone pounding up the granite steps outside. She opened the door a crack and saw Officer Barney Culpepper.

Barney was a big man with a face like a Saint Bernard and a belly that hung over his belt. Lucy thought she'd never been so glad to see anyone. Barney was an old friend ever since the days when she'd been a Cub Scout den mother and they'd served together on the pack committee.

"What in heck's goin' on here, Lucy?" he asked, wiping his size thirteen boots on the mat and removing his hat.

"I think Bitsy was shot." Even as she said it she could hardly believe it.

Barney's eyes widened in surprise, but otherwise he remained as unflappable as ever.

"I guess I better see for myself. Where is she?"

"Downstairs."

She started to follow him, but decided against it. She couldn't face seeing Bitsy's body again. She took a seat instead and looked around the empty library, trying to think if there was anything else she should be doing. A minute or two later the board members began returning to the upper level, apparently on Barney's orders.

"Who does he think he is?" fumed an indignant Corney. "I've never been spoken to in that tone by anyone!"

"He's right," said Chuck. "We should never have gone down there. We may have destroyed important evidence."

"We didn't know that," said Hayden. "She could have been hurt and needed help."

"The poor woman is past help now," said Gerald. He sat down opposite Lucy, on one of the child-sized seats. He looked pale and shaken.

"Barney Culpepper—I remember when you were a little boy with dirty hands. Don't think you can tell me what to do!" Miss Tilley burst through the door, with Culpepper close on her heels.

"I'm sorry, Miss Tilley. I'm just doing my job. Now I want you to sit down and wait. When the state police get here I'm sure they'll have some questions for you." He paused and surveyed the group. "That goes for all of you. Just make yourselves as comfortable as you can."

"This isn't very comfortable," said Gerald, rising stiffly to his feet. "I propose we all move to the conference room."

"No can do," said Barney, shaking his head and planting himself in the doorway. "Nobody goes downstairs."

"The reference room," suggested Miss Tilley, leading the way.

The other board members followed her and seated themselves in the captain's chairs at the big table in the center of the paneled room. From his perch above the fireplace, an abundantly whiskered Henry Hopkins looked out from his portrait with his usual expression of smug satisfaction.

"What do we do now?" asked Gerald, who was president of the board. He looked toward Chuck, naturally relying on his legal expertise. "Is there some action we should take as a board?"

"Not yet," replied Chuck. "All we can do is wait for whoever will be in charge of the investigation to get here." He paused and shook his shaggy head slowly. "I can't believe this."

"It's terrible," said Hayden, his face still white with shock.

"We may have to close the library for a while," said Chuck, scratching his chin thoughtfully. "It's a crime scene, after all. The police may insist."

"Crime scene? Couldn't it have been an accident?" asked Hayden, fidgeting nervously with his watchband.

"She was shot! Any idiot could see that!" thundered Ed, regarding Hayden with a scowl. Lucy suspected he didn't much like Hayden under the best of circumstances.

"Shot? I didn't hear a shot," insisted Hayden.

"Who could hear anything? Those kids were making such a racket," said Corney. She seemed rather put out at this unexpected turn of events.

"I can't believe it," said Lucy, echoing Chuck. "Just this morning I was reading that seven librarians were attacked since last July. Now it's eight."

"I read the same article," offered Chuck. "It said libraries are targeted because of the computers and other valuables."

"The tankard!" exclaimed Miss Tilley. A bright red splotch appeared on each of her crepey cheeks.

"It's all right," said Lucy, hastening to reassure the old woman. "It hasn't been touched."

"I guess that means we can rule out theft as the motive," observed Gerald.

"Maybe it was something personal," offered Corney. "A boyfriend, maybe."

"I wouldn't doubt it," sniffed Miss Tilley. "These girls today just beg for trouble."

"Poor Bitsy," sighed Hayden. "Somehow she seems a very unlikely victim."

"What's that supposed to mean?" challenged Ed.

It was like a reflex, thought Lucy, becoming interested in the dynamics between the board members. If Hayden spoke, Ed had to respond negatively.

"I just can't imagine why anyone would want to kill her," mused Hayden, undeterred by Ed's hostility. He sighed. "Poor Bitsy."

"I can't help but wish this had happened someplace else," said Gerald, drumming his fingers on the table. "I mean, it shouldn't have happened at all, of course, but why did it have to happen here?"

"If you want my opinion, it seems all too typical," said Corney. "We might as well admit it: Bitsy was disorganized. Her office was a disgrace—papers and dirty cups everywhere. She was so messy it's a wonder she got anything done." Corney shook her head. "Her life was probably a mess, too."

"She sure was messy," agreed Ed.

"She ran the library very poorly," sniffed Miss Tilley. "The volunteers weren't properly organized, the new acquisitions were not shelved promptly, she was always late with circulation figures—I could just go on and on. In fact, I was planning to give her a very poor evaluation."

Listening to the others, Lucy was shocked. The woman was dead, after all. Truth be told, if she had been killed by an intruder as Lucy suspected, they all had to bear some responsibility. As the library's board of directors, they were her employers.

"Well, hell," said Chuck, slamming his fist down hard on the table. "I liked Bitsy and I think this is a damned shame. She had her faults—we all do, for that matter—but she didn't deserve to die. She was just doing her job the best she could and now she's dead." He pulled out a handkerchief and blew his nose noisily. "All I can say is I hope they catch the bastard who did this!"

"I certainly intend to."

They all turned in surprise to look at a slight, pale man with a long upper lip, rather like a rabbit, who was standing in the doorway.

"Let me introduce myself. I'm Detective Lieutenant Horowitz. I'm with the state police, and I'm in charge of the investigation." He paused, studying the group. "So, who wants to go first?"

Chapter Four

"Gingerbread Man, climb on my back and
I will carry you safely across the stream,"
said the clever fox.

"**A**s president of the library, I suppose that honor falls to me," said Gerald. He glanced at Chuck in a silent plea for support and received a little nod. "What do you want to know?"

"Let's start with the introductions," said Horowitz, pulling a notebook out of his pocket. As Gerald named each member of the board, Horowitz made a notation in the book, jotting down that person's address and phone number.

Lucy wondered if Horowitz would acknowledge her; after all, she first met the state police detective years before when she had been working at Country Cousins, the giant catalog retailer, and discovered the owner, Sam Miller, dead in his car. When her turn came, however, he didn't show the slightest flicker of recognition and treated her exactly like the others. Maybe her appearance had changed, she thought. After all, she wasn't getting any younger.

When Horowitz had finished getting all the names he looked up from his notebook and studied the group, letting his gaze rest on each of the directors. As he studied them, Lucy noticed a slight shifting of chairs, as if the individual members were joining together to present a united front against this outsider. Their reaction made her feel oddly isolated. She wasn't really part of the group yet, and after hearing them talk about Bitsy, she wasn't sure she wanted to be. Finally, Horowitz spoke.

"Let's go through the events of the morning—who got here first?"

"That would be Bitsy," said Gerald. "The victim."

"When was that?"

"I'm not absolutely certain of the time, but she was supposed to begin work at nine. I arrived at ten, when the library is due to open, and found the doors locked. I knocked and she let me in. She said she had been working and forgot the time."

"If the library doesn't open until ten, why did she come in at nine?" asked Horowitz.

"To prepare for the day, to do paperwork, that sort of thing," said Gerald.

"What was she doing when you arrived?"

"Something at the computer, I think," said Gerald. "It was on when I came in but the screensaver program had started. Flying toasters or some such nonsense."

Horowitz consulted his notebook. "And you were here for a meeting?"

"That's right. We're all members of the board of directors."

"And what time was the meeting supposed to start?"

"At eleven," said Gerald.

Horowitz looked sharply at Gerald. "You came an hour early? What for?"

Gerald looked a bit uncomfortable. "Well, I wanted to go over the agenda."

"Anything special on that agenda?"

"Not really. Everything was pretty much routine." He

paused and studied his hands. "We had received the contractor's final bill for the new addition and needed to authorize the last payment. That was the only new business."

"Any problems about that?"

Gerald waved a hand in the direction of the new children's room. "I think the addition pretty much speaks for itself—everyone's delighted."

A small "hmmph" of dissent could be heard from Miss Tilley's corner of the table, but everyone else nodded agreement, eager to show support for their leader.

"Any conflicts among the board members? Problems with Bitsy?"

"Oh, no," said Gerald. He couldn't resist glancing furtively toward Chuck, who gave him the slightest nod.

"All one big, happy family?" asked Horowitz.

"Absolutely," said Gerald, his voice a bit too loud.

Horowitz nodded. "Okay—who came next?"

"I guess that would be me," said Corney, who had prepared her explanation. "I came early because I wanted to see the furniture in the new addition."

"And what time was that?"

"Let me see," said Corney, producing a leather agenda and opening it. She ran down a list of things to do with a neatly manicured finger. "I stopped at the post office and the florist shop on the way, oh, and I stopped in at the garage to make an appointment to have my tires rotated. It must have been about ten-fifteen when I got here."

"Thank you," said Horowitz with a tired little sigh. "What did you do when you arrived?"

"Well, first I took off my boots and put on my shoes—I do so hate to track snow onto the carpeting. It's really bad for the fibers and it's no bother to bring shoes if you have an attractive tote. They're available in a variety of fabrics and coordinate with almost any outfit."

Lucy was suddenly self-conscious about her snow boots, which she hadn't thought to remove, and was glad they were hidden beneath the table.

"And then I hung up my coat in the closet," continued Corney, who seemed determined to turn every answer into a lifestyle lecture. "Good clothing is an investment, you know, and it lasts so much longer if you take proper care of it. After that I went to see the new children's room and I chatted a bit with Bitsy. I looked around some more and then I joined the others in the office. Maybe it was ten-thirty or so."

"What was Bitsy doing then?"

"I believe she was choosing a book for story hour," said Corney.

"When is story hour?"

"At eleven."

"The same time as the meeting?" Horowitz sounded doubtful. "Isn't that kind of unusual?"

"Not at all," said Miss Tilley, eager to clear up the confusion. "As directors, we felt our valuable paid staff was better employed elsewhere during meetings. We wished to avoid any duplication of effort."

Horowitz shook his head and frowned. "Wouldn't it be more usual to include her—for input?"

"We found Bitsy's input most valuable," said Chuck. "She always came for the last half hour or so, after story hour, to give a report and answer questions."

"I see," said Horowitz, dropping the matter. "Okay—let's summarize. It's ten-thirty. Mr. Asquith is in the office, and the victim is in the children's room with Ms. Clarke. Is anybody else here?"

"I was," said Hayden. "When I arrived I saw Corney and Bitsy talking." He nodded nervously. "I went to join them but Corney had wandered off, so I spoke with Bitsy."

"What did you talk about?"

Hayden shrugged. "Books. Nothing of consequence."

"All right," said Horowitz impatiently. "How long did you talk about nothing with the victim?"

"A few minutes. Then I asked her about the addition figures. She told me Gerald had them in the office and I went there."

Horowitz narrowed his lashless eyelids. "You were concerned about these figures?"

"Not at all," Hayden hastened to assure him. "Just curious. This was a big project and I wanted to know if it came in under budget."

"Did it?"

"You're darn tootin' it did," said Ed, leaning back in his chair and propping one ankle on his knee. "If Ed Bumpus says it's gonna cost so much, that's how much it costs."

"You were the contractor?" Horowitz raised his pale eyebrows.

"Not for this job, no. But I've got the experience and I took charge of things for the board. Made sure it got done right. And under budget."

"And what time did you arrive this morning?"

"Lemme see—I guess around ten-thirty. Maybe later. I saw him," he stabbed a finger toward Hayden, "talking with Bitsy when I came in. I went straight to the office, to make copies for the meeting. Danged machine didn't work."

"When you got to the office, who was there?"

"Just him," said Ed, pointing to Gerald with a thick finger. "Nobody could get the machine to work, so when Bitsy came she went off to the front to make the copies on the coin machine. That's when he came in and her, too," he said, pointing to Hayden and Corney.

"That's right," said Miss Tilley in a clear, precise tone. "I came as I always do at a quarter to eleven. The volunteer responsible for the circulation desk had not shown up, something that unfortunately is not all that unusual. I noticed that quite a few books had been returned, and someone was waiting to check one out, so I took charge temporarily. While I was at the desk two directors came in—Lucy and Chuck." Miss Tilley clucked her tongue. "They were both late."

"I was late," admitted Lucy, with an apologetic little smile. "It was ten past when I arrived. I greeted Miss Tilley, sent my daughter over to the children's section for story hour, and went into the office to join the others. They were ready to begin the meeting, but Bitsy hadn't started story hour, so I went downstairs to get her."

Horowitz held up his hand. "Whoa. When did Bitsy go downstairs? And why?"

"It must have been close to eleven by then," said Gerald, looking to the other board members for confirmation.

"I think that's right," agreed Corney.

"And why did she go downstairs?"

"To get something, I guess," said Ed, scratching his chin. "She kinda ran off."

"As if she'd just remembered something?" asked Horowitz.

"Yeah," said Ed.

"Let me get this straight, now," said Horowitz. "Mrs. Stone went downstairs to get Bitsy sometime after eleven-ten. Where are the rest of you?"

"Well, we were leaving the office, on our way to the conference room," said Gerald.

"All of you together? As a group?"

"No. I went to the front to get Miss Tilley," said Corney. "That's when Chuck arrived."

"Okay. Mr. Canaday, Miss Tilley, and Ms. Clarke are in the front by the desk. Mr. Northcross, Mr. Asquith, and Mr. Bumpus are leaving the office. Mrs. Stone is downstairs. Is that right?"

They all nodded.

"And all this time nobody was alone? You were all in each other's company all the time?"

The directors exchanged uneasy glances.

"There was quite a bit of coming and going," admitted Corney, looking around the table. "I certainly couldn't say that for sure."

"I admit it—I made a pit stop," said Ed. Seeing Horowitz's puzzled expression he added, "You know—the men's room."

Horowitz nodded.

"And I went into the reference room," added Gerald. "I went to get the gavel. It's stored in a closet there."

"Before this goes any further I'd like to know what you're getting at," said Chuck. "You seem awfully interested in our movements. Is one of the directors under suspicion?"

"At this point of the investigation everybody's a suspect," said Horowitz.

"That's ridiculous!" exclaimed Gerald. "None of us killed Bitsy. It must have been someone from outside—the workroom has an outside door, you know."

"I know," said Horowitz. "That was one of the first things I checked."

"And?" inquired Chuck, taking over from Gerald.

"Nobody came in that way."

"How can you be so sure?"

"It was locked."

"Of course," agreed Chuck, nodding thoughtfully.

The directors avoided each others' eyes, and carefully studied the small section of table directly in front of each of them while Horowitz went on.

"Whoever killed her either came in through the main door—or had a key to the outside workroom door."

Lucy felt the room begin to swirl around her as the image of Bitsy's body came back to her. She tightened her grip on the arms of her chair.

"That doesn't mean one of us did it. The library's a public building. Anyone can come in," said Gerald.

"That's true," said Horowitz. "Did you see anyone who seemed suspicious?"

"No," volunteered Lucy. "The only people here besides us were the mothers and children for story hour." She paused and added helpfully, "I had them all write down their names before they left."

"Did any of you see anyone else?" asked Horowitz.

The directors shifted uneasily and shook their heads.

"Just because we didn't see anyone doesn't mean that someone didn't come in," insisted Chuck. "Perhaps someone who had a personal score to settle. And with all these bookshelves, it would be easy for someone to remain unnoticed."

Horowitz nodded. "I'll keep that in mind. Thank you all for your cooperation. I know it's past lunchtime and you must be hungry. You're free to go now, but I'd like you all to remain available to assist in the investigation."

"What does that mean?" asked Hayden.

"It means don't leave town," said Ed. "Right?"

"Not quite," said Horowitz. "If you plan to go on vacation in the near future, please let me know. That's all."

There was an audible sigh of relief from the board members when Horowitz turned to leave, pausing in the doorway to consult with a uniformed trooper.

"Well, this is quite a new experience," said Corney, turning her big blue eyes on Chuck. "I've never been a suspect before."

"I can't believe he really thinks one of us did it," protested Hayden. "It's absurd."

"Well, I don't think he could suspect me," said Lucy. "After all, I found Bitsy."

There was a murmur of sympathy from the board members, and Hayden reached across the table and gave her hand a little squeeze.

"By the way, Mrs. Stone," said Horowitz, turning to face the group. "I ought to mention that you will be of particular interest to the investigators."

"Me?" squeaked Lucy. "Why?"

"Precisely because you found the body." He paused. "Studies show that the person who reports a murder quite often turns out to be the murderer. You found the body, you made the call—that makes you the prime suspect."

Chapter Five

There was an old woman who lived in a shoe,
She had so many children she didn't know what
to do.

"What?" exclaimed Lucy, jumping to her feet and following Horowitz out of the reference room. She was slightly out of breath when she caught up with him by the circulation desk. "You don't really think I killed Bitsy, do you?" she asked. "You know who I am, don't you? Don't you remember me?"

Horowitz took his time answering. "I remember you, all right," he said, tilting his head and studying her with his pale eyes. "And I think we ought to get one thing straight right from the start: I don't want you playing detective. Got it?"

"I have no intention of doing any such thing," Lucy announced indignantly. "And why did you say I was the prime suspect, in front of everybody?"

"Just stirring the pot a bit," he said, scratching his chin thoughtfully as he watched the directors beginning to leave. Miss Tilley was the first to go, leaning on Hayden's arm. "So tell me, was anything they said in there the truth?"

"Don't ask me," said Lucy with a toss of her head. "I'm

not supposed to play detective, remember? Besides, I'm new. Today was my first meeting."

"Some first meeting," said Horowitz with a sardonic little grin. Out of the corner of his eye he was watching Ed Bumpus, who was apparently disagreeing with Chuck about something.

"It was awful." Lucy looked down at the floor, then raised her eyes to meet Horowitz's. "I can't believe anybody would want to kill Bitsy. She was nice to everybody. She was always willing to help you find things. She sure changed the atmosphere in the library—not that Miss Tilley wasn't wonderful in her own way. But Bitsy made it a fun place to be. I came in at least once a week. She had all the new books, and you always ran into somebody you knew."

"Well, somebody sure didn't like her," he said. "And they did a pretty neat job of killing her."

"Were you really serious when you said it was one of the directors?"

Just then Lucy heard the door slam, and looked up to see that Ed had left and Chuck was deep in conversation with Gerald. Corney was standing a little apart, probably waiting for Chuck.

"Seems likely."

"Well, if that's so, why didn't you question us individually? And why didn't you check our hands? I thought there's some chemical test that tells if you've fired a gun."

"There is," said Horowitz with a long sigh, "but I don't think your good buddy Canaday was going to let me administer paraffin tests to the board members, do you? First thing he'd do is give a little speech about how everybody wants to cooperate with the investigation, but of course, they also need to protect their rights, so they'll be happy to cooperate after they've retained legal counsel. I'm not going to be able to get anything from that crew, believe me."

"I really think I could be helpful," offered Lucy. "Maybe they'd talk to me since I'm a member of the board."

"Oh, no," said Horowitz, holding up his hands. "The way you can help is by minding your own business and leaving the investigation to the experts."

His gaze shifted and Lucy turned to see Chuck approaching them; Gerald and Corney had left.

"Lucy, I don't think we've been formally introduced. I'm Chuck Canaday." He reached out his hand to shake hers.

"It wasn't much of a morning for formalities," said Lucy, taking his hand. "Of course I know who you are. I've seen you around town."

"Same here, and I've heard nothing but good things about you. I'm glad you've joined the board." He paused and gave her a half smile. "Our meetings are usually a lot quieter—you had a terrible shock this morning. I really think you ought to go home now and get some rest. And just for your information, Gerald has asked me to represent the board in the investigation," he said, giving Horowitz a pointed look, "but if you wish to retain your own attorney please feel free to do so." He gave her hand a final squeeze of dismissal. "Will you be able to get home?"

"I'll be fine," said Lucy. "Thanks for your concern."

He was already turning away from her, however, and draping an arm around Horowitz's shoulder.

"Now. Lieutenant," he was saying, "I want to assure you that the board will do everything it can to facilitate your investigation . . ."

Lucy went to retrieve her coat from Bitsy's office, where she had left it. She hesitated for a moment, then pushed open the door and stood in the doorway, struck with the way Bitsy's personality had filled the little room and trying to comprehend the fact that she would not be using it anymore. Her fingers would never pound the computer keyboard again, she would never reach for the pens and pencils stuffed in the English marmalade jar.

The office, of course, was just as she had left it. Little yellow stickies adorned the perimeter of the computer screen, the desk was covered with a sea of papers, and the window-sill was stacked with books and bound reports. Pictures and notes had spread far beyond the confines of the bulletin board, nearly covering one entire wall. Lucy paused and studied them.

There were postcards sent by authors and publishers announcing new books, nametags from conferences such as the New England Bookseller's Association's annual meeting in Boston, and clippings from book reviews. There were lots of notecards, too, mostly thank-you notes from grateful patrons who appreciated Bitsy's efforts to get them hard-to-find information and obscure books. There were even drawings made by the children who attended story hour, including one by Zoe.

Lucy reached out to unpin it.

"What do you think you're doing?" demanded an authoritative male voice.

Lucy jumped and turned to see a youthful state trooper holding a roll of yellow crime scene tape.

"My daughter made this drawing—I wanted it as a keep-sake," she explained.

"I'm sorry—my orders are that nobody is to touch anything."

"I hardly think this qualifies as evidence," argued Lucy, withdrawing a push pin from the corner of Zoe's crayon portrait. "Besides, I'd be happy to sign a receipt or something."

"I'm sorry," he said. "I was just about to seal this room. You'll have to go. Please put the pin back just as it was."

"May I take my coat?" snapped Lucy, angry with the trooper's inflexible attitude.

He nodded and Lucy snatched it up, feeling like a criminal for attempting to take her own daughter's drawing. She glared at him as she left, then marched across the circulation area to the door, shrugging her arms into the sleeves as she went. She flung the doors open, hardly noticing the collection of official vans and police cars parked in front of the li-

brary, and ran down the stairs and along the path to the parking lot. She yanked the car door open and sat down hard in
the driver's seat. She fumbled in her purse, looking for the
ignition key and when she couldn't find it, burst into tears.
She sat there, gripping the steering wheel and sobbing out
loud, feeling both relieved and utterly ridiculous. When the
tears finally stopped, she wiped her eyes and checked her
coat pocket for the car keys. Finding them, she started the
engine.

Driving more slowly than usual, she followed the familiar streets to Juanita's house. As she rolled down Elm Street
she spotted a police cruiser parked in front of a large Victorian mansion that had seen better days. The original clapboard had been replaced with asbestos siding that was
showing its age despite a coat of paint. A rickety metal fire
escape was tacked to one side, indicating the house had been
cut up into apartments. That must be where Bitsy lived, she
thought, slowing the car.

She remembered Bitsy complaining about her landlady,
and dredged her memory for the woman's name. Willoughby?
Wetherby? Withers! That was it! A honk from behind prompted
the realization that the car had practically stopped, so Lucy
pulled over to the side and gave the puzzled driver a wave.
She sat there for a minute, observing the house and wondering if she dared pay a visit to Mrs. Withers.

There were some questions she'd like to ask her. Had
Bitsy had any visitors lately? Had she seemed upset? Was
she involved in a relationship?

Lucy was just about to get out of the car when she spotted
a police officer coming around the side of the house. He
climbed the steps to the front door and rang the bell, then
stood waiting for the door to open. After his second ring the
door did open and Lucy got a glimpse of Mrs. Withers, who
was dressed in a bright orange sweater and garish brown and
green plaid pants.

Disappointed at this lost opportunity, Lucy pulled out

from the curb and drove on to the Orensteins' house. Juanita
was obviously bursting with curiosity when she opened the
door, but tactfully restrained herself from questioning Lucy
about the morning's events.

"Are you all right, Lucy? You still look a little shaky. Can
I give you a cup of tea or some lunch?" she asked, taking
Lucy's arm and drawing her into the warm living room
where Zoe and Sadie were playing with Barbie dolls. Rows
of the leggy creatures were sitting on the sofa, and more
were carefully arranged on bright pink plastic doll furniture
set out on the carpeted floor.

"No, thanks. I'm really okay. I just want to get home."
She sighed. "Zoe, it's time to go. Can you help clean up the
toys, please?"

"Never mind," said Juanita. "Sadie can do it later. Come
on, Zoe. Let's find your coat."

"Thanks for everything," said Lucy, when Zoe was suited
up against the cold and ready to go.

"It was nothing," Juanita told her. "Sadie always enjoys
having Zoe visit."

As they trudged through the snowy yard to the car, Lucy
noticed that the bright sunlight of the morning was gone.
The sky was filling up once again with heavy gray clouds.
She sniffed the air.

"I smell snow," she told Zoe, helping her climb into her
booster seat and snapping the seatbelt.

"You can't smell snow," said Zoe, laughing.

"Oh, yes, you can," said Lucy, once again starting the car.

As she drove, her mind kept going back to the moment
when she found Bitsy's body. It was as if her thoughts were
a broken videotape that kept replaying the same image over
and over. She kept trying to get past it, just as she tended to
fast forward a rented movie through the violent parts, but
her mind would not cooperate. It was stuck on Bitsy's murder.

Tears pricked at her eyes, and she tried to blink them back as she came to the steep climb up Red Top Road. She downshifted for the climb, and the Subaru obligingly chugged up the hill toward home.

The house was empty. Lucy glanced at the clock and was shocked to see it was only two-thirty. She would have guessed it was much later.

"I'm hungry," said Zoe, pointedly eyeing the cookie jar.

"Good idea," said Lucy, remembering that she hadn't had any lunch. She put the kettle on to heat and set a plate of chocolate chip cookies on the kitchen table. Then she scooped some hot chocolate mix into two mugs and waited for the water to boil.

Damn Horowitz, she thought. What business did he have accusing her like that in front of all the others? Even if it was a little joke. And why was he joking anyway about something as terrible as murder? It was just a job for him—he didn't know or care about Bitsy. It didn't matter to him who the killer was so long as he caught him. Or her. The thought gave Lucy pause. Of course it could be a woman—a woman could shoot a gun just as effectively as a man.

She jumped as the kettle shrieked, and filled the mugs. Sitting down at the table opposite Zoe, she stirred her hot cocoa. Thank goodness the other kids were still at school— she wasn't ready to deal with the noise and confusion they brought home with them.

"Careful—it's hot," she warned Zoe.

"I know, Mom."

"Good."

Lucy lifted the mug to her lips. It felt heavy and she used two hands so it wouldn't spill. This is ridiculous, she thought, feeling that all her energy had somehow drained from her body. The little chores she ought to be doing seemed impossibly difficult. All she could do was sit.

This is depression, she decided. Shock and depression, compounded by low blood sugar. She made herself take a sip of cocoa, and then another.

If only she didn't feel so responsible. She knew it was absurd. She was the newest person on the board; she hadn't had time to do anything. But still she couldn't help feeling that she should have done something to prevent Bitsy's death. How could such a thing happen? And in the library, of all places?

They should have had a security system. But if one of the directors did kill Bitsy, as Horowitz seemed to think, it wouldn't have made any difference. Lucy put her head in her hands. How could she go back? How could she ever face those people, wondering all the time if one of them was a murderer?

Horowitz and his "mind your own business" be damned, she thought. There was only one way she could get through this, and it was by finding the murderer as soon as possible. She couldn't wait for the police to muddle their way through the case——that could take months, especially if the board members retained lawyers as she expected they would. The police wouldn't get very far unless they found some hard physical evidence, like the gun. She was the first one on the scene, however, and she hadn't seen anything.

That meant they would have to depend on questioning the suspects, but she didn't think these particular suspects were likely to submit themselves to that. They had nothing to gain and everything to lose; it was far safer to say nothing.

Of course, they would talk among themselves——that was human nature. They would have plenty to say to each other that they wouldn't want to share with the police. She drummed her fingers on the table. Tomorrow, she decided, she'd make a point of paying a visit to Miss Tilley. Horowitz could hardly call it meddling—after all, she would only be doing what any good neighbor would do. Paying a friendly visit to an elderly neighbor and having a nice little chat.

"Mom, can I have some more cocoa?" asked Zoe.

Lucy heard the roar of the school bus as it began the slow climb up the hill. Sara and Elizabeth and Toby would be home any minute.

"I guess I better heat up enough for the whole gang," she said, giving Zoe a little hug and tickling her tummy. "There's nothing like cocoa on a cold day."

The door flew open and Toby and Elizabeth jostled each other, each trying to be the first one in. Sara brought up the rear, her plump, round face red with anger.

"It's not fair! I never get to use the computer!" she screamed hoarsely at her older brother and sister.

Elizabeth and Toby weren't there to hear her. They had already vanished into the family room, shedding hats and scarves and coats as they went.

Lucy followed, and found them huddled over the computer, eyes fixed on the screen.

"Come on, come on," chanted Toby impatiently. "This thing takes forever to boot—I don't know why they didn't get a Pentium 90."

"Too cheap," commiserated Elizabeth. "I'm amazed they got anything at all."

"Don't you want some cocoa?" asked Lucy. "How was school?"

"Later, Mom. We're busy." Toby's eyes didn't waver from the screen as he clicked the mouse with his enormous hand. He was a junior in high school and already topped six feet; Lucy had trouble finding clothes and shoes big enough for him.

"Look at the mess you've made—aren't you going to hang up your coats and things?"

"Sure, Mom," said Elizabeth, brushing her short, dark

hair out of her eyes, which were also fixed on the screen. "We'll do it later—we want to do this first."

Lucy was dismayed but right now she didn't have the energy to make them behave in a civilized manner. "Okay, just don't forget," she muttered, returning to the kitchen. It could be worse, she thought. They could be experimenting with drugs or sex or vandalizing some building. At least the Internet was supposed to be educational, even if it didn't do much for one's social graces.

"Mom, it's not fair," insisted Sara, who was pouring herself some cocoa. "I never get to use the computer. Elizabeth and Toby won't let me."

"We'll have to figure something out," said Lucy. "Why don't you take Zoe sliding when you finish your cocoa?"

"That's no fun," grumbled Sara, stuffing her chubby cheeks with cookies. "I want to play 'Zoroaster.'"

"One cookie at a time, please, and don't forget to chew," reminded Lucy, reaching for the ringing phone.

"Hi, Ted," she said, recognizing his voice. Ted Stillings was the chief reporter, editor, and publisher of the local weekly newspaper, *The Pennysaver.* "I guess you must have heard."

"Gosh, Lucy, you might've given me a call," he complained.

Lucy occasionally worked at the paper, filling in for Ted's assistant, Phyllis, in addition to writing features on a freelance basis.

"I knew it was too late for this week—the paper came out today."

"Yeah, but I would've liked to get some on-the-scene coverage for next week."

"No chance of that, I'm afraid. The state police got right there."

"Well, you were there. What can you tell me?"

"Not much," said Lucy. "Like the other directors, I'm shocked and saddened by this dreadful event."

"Come on, Lucy," coaxed Ted. "You can't do this to me. You're a reporter, for God's sake."

"I'm a freelance feature writer," she corrected him. "And besides, I've already been warned by Horowitz to mind my own business."

"You know you're not going to let a little thing like that stop you. Come on, tell me what you know."

"Well," drawled Lucy, yielding to Ted's coaxing, "Horowitz definitely thinks one of the directors is the murderer, but I just can't see it."

"Because they're all such upstanding citizens?"

"No—because they were more or less all together all morning. I don't think anybody had enough time. I think it must have been somebody from outside. Bitsy must have had a personal life away from the library. It could have been a jilted boyfriend, somebody like that. What have you heard?"

"I haven't talked to too many people yet. I did get some background stuff—I had her résumé in my files, from the selectmen's meeting when she was hired."

"Where'd she come from?"

"Massapequa, Long Island. She worked in a library there."

"Does she have family there? An ex-husband?"

"You know, I just don't know. I interviewed her for a profile piece when she first took the job. I pulled it out but it didn't really have much information. When I thought about it, I remembered being kind of frustrated because she wouldn't answer any personal questions. Just talked about all her plans for the library, how much she liked living in Maine, stuff like that."

"Maybe she had something to hide," suggested Lucy. "Maybe that's why she was killed."

"Could be," admitted Ted, "but so far I haven't found out much. I hope I can turn up something for next week's paper."

"At least you've got plenty of time."

"Yeah," said Ted. "So where's that story on gambling that you tell me you're working on? Can I expect it anytime soon?"

"Soon," hedged Lucy.

"Like when?" pressed Ted.

"Next Friday?"

"Can't you do it in time for next week's paper?"

"No way," said Lucy.

"Okay, but I'm counting on you, Lucy. Friday at the latest."

"I won't let you down," promised Lucy.

"Sure," said Ted, sounding skeptical.

As Lucy replaced the receiver she heard a commotion in the family room. Sara had evidently attempted to gain access to the computer, prompting outraged protests from Toby and Elizabeth.

"Enough!" she announced, marching over to the machine and turning the power switch off.

"You're not supposed to do that!" screamed Elizabeth. "You'll wreck it!"

"She's right, Mom," added Toby.

"I don't care," Lucy said through clenched teeth, placing her hands on her hips. "It's been a very long day and I want some peace and quiet. I want you to pick up your coats and hats off the floor and then go outside and have some good old-fashioned fun in the snow. Do you understand me?"

"Do we have to?" groaned Toby, looking at her as if she were completely mad.

"Yes, you do," insisted Lucy. "And have a good time, too!"

The kids clattered out obediently; Lucy suspected they'd be sneaking back into the warm house before long. She had better enjoy the peace and quiet while she could. She piled a few pillows at one end of the couch and lay down, closing her eyes and trying to empty her mind of all thoughts.

After a few minutes, she realized it was futile. Her mind was buzzing with questions. Why had Bitsy left Massapequa? Why did she choose Maine, of all places? Did she have a special reason for coming to Tinker's Cove? And if she hadn't come to Tinker's Cove, would she have been murdered? Why did she die?

Before she realized what she had done, Lucy was back on her feet and heading for the kitchen. It was too late today; she had to get supper started. But tomorrow, she decided, she was going to start looking for some answers.

Chapter Six

*Little Red Riding Hood decided to pay
a visit to her grandmother.*

On Friday morning Lucy looked out the window and saw a snow squall. The wind was tossing some fine little flakes around, but there wasn't enough snow for school to be closed. Lucy sent up a little prayer of thanksgiving when the school bus carried the three older kids off in the morning, then she started tidying up the kitchen. She was just wiping off the counter when Bill came in looking for his lunchbox before leaving for work. A skilled restoration carpenter, he had been hired by a nearby church to reconstruct a wineglass pulpit that had begun to wobble dangerously, putting the minister on decidedly shaky footing when he gave his sermon.

"What's on the menu today?" he asked, opening the lunchbox and taking a peek.

"A meatloaf sandwich and a thermos of vegetable soup." Lucy always tried to include something hot. She knew that the congregation's budget didn't provide for heating the sanctuary on weekdays and Bill's space heater couldn't begin to warm the entire church.

"Mmmm," said Bill, snapping it shut and setting it on the kitchen table so he could zip his jacket. He looked at her thoughtfully. "Lucy, are you all right about this Bitsy thing?"

"As all right as I can be, I guess," said Lucy. "It isn't as if we were close friends."

"That's right," said Bill. "She must have been hanging around with some pretty desperate characters to get herself killed. It's no business of yours, and I hope you'll leave it to the police."

Lucy started to protest but he grabbed her hand and pulled her to him, folding her in his arms.

"I couldn't stand it if anything happened to you."

Lucy looked into his eyes and stroked his beard, now tinged with gray. "Don't worry," she said, placing her hands on his chest and gently pushing him away. "Horowitz has already warned me to mind my own business."

"Sounds like good advice," said Bill, putting on his gloves. "I hope you'll take it."

"I intend to. Besides, I don't have time to investigate— Ted's after me to finish a story for him," said Lucy, reaching up to pull Bill's watch cap down over his ears. "It's cold out there—stay warm, okay?"

"Okay." He gave her a quick kiss and was gone.

A glance at the kitchen clock told Lucy it was a few minutes past eight. If she was lucky, she thought, she might just catch Horowitz at his office.

Before she had time to think better of it, she punched in the number of his direct line. As she listened to the rings she chewed her lip nervously.

"Horowitz."

"Umm, Lieutenant, uhh, this is Lucy Stone," she stammered.

"Ah. Good morning, Mrs. Stone."

"You can call me Lucy," she invited, wondering what his first name might be.

"That's all right, Mrs. Stone. Is there a reason for this call?"

"Actually, there is. There's something I forgot to tell you yesterday."

"And what's that?"

"Well, when I went to find Bitsy, a whole box of art supplies was spilled on the stairs. It looked as if she was going to have the kids make valentines—there were lace doilies and red construction paper and scissors and crayons all over." She paused. "Do you think it's important? Maybe she encountered the killer on the stairs?"

"Or maybe she just tripped," said Horowitz.

"In that case, wouldn't she have picked up the mess?"

"I doubt it," sighed Horowitz. "From what I've seen of her, she never cleaned anything up that could be left for later."

"Have you searched her apartment?" probed Lucy, determined to take advantage of Horowitz's unexpectedly chatty mood.

"We're working on it," he admitted, before catching himself. "Mrs. Stone, didn't I tell you to leave this investigation to the police?"

"I just thought you ought to know about the spilled art supplies," said Lucy, sounding hurt. "I was trying to be helpful."

"Well, thanks."

The line was dead; Horowitz had hung up.

Lucy replaced the receiver and finished tidying the kitchen, then pried Zoe away from "Bunny Beware" and got her dressed for Kiddie Kollege. As a four-year-old she attended three mornings a week, on Mondays, Wednesdays, and Fridays.

After leaving Zoe in her basement classroom at the town's

recreation center, Lucy stopped in at the day care center just down the hall where her friend, Sue Finch, worked.

When she entered, Sue was helping a little boy out of his winter jacket. She looked up and gave Lucy a big smile.

"I was hoping you'd stop by," she said, tucking her glossy pageboy behind her ears.

"I guess you heard," said Lucy. "That's a cute sweater," she added, noticing the embroidered design that showed Mary coming to school with her little lamb.

"It's not really my style," said Sue, who preferred tailored, sophisticated clothing. "But the kids love this kind of stuff." She propped her hand on her hip and cocked her head. "So, tell me all about it. Did you really discover Bitsy's body?"

"Don't remind me," groaned Lucy.

"Was it awful?" asked Sue, stepping closer and whispering so the children wouldn't hear.

"What do you think? She was shot!"

Sue patted her shoulder. "Poor thing. It must have been quite a shock." She thought for a minute. "How did the kids take it?"

"Zoe was with me—but she didn't see anything. Actually, she didn't seem bothered at all. In fact, she said Bitsy was mean and story hour wasn't much fun anyway."

"Kids can be so . . ." Sue looked for a word to finish the sentence.

"Honest?" suggested Lucy.

"That wasn't exactly the word I was looking for, but it will do. Poor Bitsy didn't have a clue about kids." Sue surveyed the bright and homey day care center, where a dozen little ones were happily occupied.

"I always liked her," said Lucy. "She was a breath of fresh air after Miss Tilley. She started bringing in new books—the kind people like to read. Bestsellers and popular authors. And she was friendly. Didn't make you feel like a thief for borrowing a book." She fiddled with the zipper tag on her jacket. "I can't imagine why anyone would want to kill her."

"She must have had a life outside the library," said Sue. "I'll bet it was a boyfriend or something." She narrowed her eyes mischievously. "Isn't it usually the boyfriend? You're the expert, after all."

"I'm no expert—and I don't think Bitsy had a boyfriend."

"Well," said Sue slowly, turning her attention to two little boys at the sand table. "Sand isn't for throwing, Peter. Why don't you see how many shovels it takes to fill the truck?" She turned back to Lucy. "You know, she might have gone just a bit too far with the wrong person."

"What do you mean?" Lucy was mystified.

"You know—all the personal comments she made. Like when I took out a book about gardening. It was August and Sidra had just gone back to college. Bitsy concluded I was suffering from empty nest syndrome. 'Looking for a new hobby now that your baby has left home?' she asked. 'No,' I told her. 'My daylilies are looking kind of straggly.'"

"They need to be divided."

"I know that now," said Sue, keeping an eye on the sand table. "That's exactly what the book said. And I followed the directions and I expect I'll have outstanding daylilies this summer." She looked out the window at the lightly falling snow and added, "If summer ever comes."

"I don't see how something like that could get her killed," said Lucy. "She just liked to make conversation."

"Peter—I'm warning you. If you keep throwing sand at Justin you'll have to go to time-out." Sue turned back to Lucy and nodded knowingly. "Everybody's got secrets, and this is a very small town. It wouldn't be hard to hit a nerve— somebody looking up bankruptcy information or stuff about divorce . . ."

"A book about poisons, maybe?" asked Lucy, but Sue didn't answer. She was headed for the sand table.

"I'll call you later, Lucy," she said, raising her hand in a wave.

Lucy thought about what Sue had said as she headed over to the Quik-Stop. Maybe she had a point. Bitsy loved to make conversation but her friendly questions could be misinterpreted, especially by somebody who had something to hide.

Pulling into the parking lot at the combination gas station and convenience store, she wondered if Bitsy had been less popular than she had thought. She braked and climbed out of the car, noticing a fresh scattering of discarded lottery tickets mixed in with the falling snow that was blowing about. She wondered how many more worthless tickets were buried in the accumulated snow that covered the ground.

A bell on the door tinkled when she went inside and a pretty girl at the cash register looked up.

"What can I do for you today?" she asked politely.

"I'm not here to buy anything," Lucy apologized. "I write for *The Pennysaver* and I'm working on a story about gambling, especially the state lottery. Can you answer some questions for me?"

"Sure." The girl gave a little shrug.

"First, I need your name," said Lucy, getting her notebook out of her shoulder bag and uncapping her pen.

"Lois Kirwan."

"Oh, I know Dot," said Lucy. In fact, everybody knew Dot, who worked as a cashier at Marzetti's IGA. "Is she your mother?"

"Mother-in-law," said the girl. "I'm married to Tommy."

"That's nice," said Lucy, getting down to business. "Well, what I wondered is how big a business are these lottery tickets? Do you sell a lot of them?"

Lois nodded. "We must sell hundreds, even thousands."

"Is that in a week?"

"No." Lois chuckled. "That's in a day."

"I had no idea," said Lucy.

"I've seen people spend their entire paychecks on scratch tickets." She paused and leaned across the counter. "I'm not supposed to—the owner would have a fit if he knew—but I tell them it's a waste of money. You can't beat the system. These tickets come in rolls of five hundred and sell for a dollar apiece. On average, the winning tickets total three hundred dollars. It's a losing proposition. It has to be or the state wouldn't make any money."

"How much of the store's business is lottery tickets?" asked Lucy.

"Most of it—I'd guess at least half. Then there's cigarettes— that's probably the other half."

"What about milk and bread?" That was all that Lucy ever bought at the Quik-Stop herself.

"Hardly anybody buys anything here without buying at least one lottery ticket, too. Lots of times, if they have a five or a ten dollar bill, they'll take the change in scratch tickets."

Lucy was shocked at this extravagance. "Is there a typical buyer?" she asked.

"Everybody buys them. Except kids—we can't sell them if you're under eighteen."

"What about the people who buy a lot at one time?"

"They tend to be older—and mostly men. There's one man—he's really distinguished looking. Like he's rich. Nice overcoat. Beautiful leather gloves. Drives a big Lincoln. He comes in at least once a week and buys a lot of tickets. Fifty minimum, sometimes a lot more. At least he can afford it. A lot of them, well, you know they're emptying out their wallets and poking around under the car seats to scrape together enough change to buy a ticket. It's sad. It's such a waste of money."

"They're hoping they'll get lucky and strike it rich," said

Lucy. "Have you had any big winners who bought tickets here?"

"I've never had a big winner on a scratch ticket but we've had some pretty big Lotto winners." She pointed to a picture frame on the wall behind her that contained three Lotto stubs. "I think one was a hundred thousand dollars. We never had a million dollar winner. George—he's the owner— keeps telling me we're due." She shook her head in disapproval. "He tells the customers that, too. He thinks the lottery is the greatest. He's always putting up the signs the lottery commission sends." She paused and rolled her eyes, indicating the large number of colorful advertisements stuck up all over the store. "Like we don't have enough already. And if the Lotto pot is bigger than usual he wants me to mention it to all the customers."

"Do you ever play?" asked Lucy.

"Me? No way. I've got a jar at home I put all my spare change in. Last year I had enough to buy a new sofa."

"You're a smart girl."

"Yeah, too smart to stay in this job. I've got my name in at the bank. As soon as there's an opening, I'm outta here." The bell jangled and she turned to help a customer.

"Thanks for all your help," said Lucy, concluding the interview so Lois could get back to work. "Good luck with the bank job."

"Hey," said Lois, turning to tear off a handful of scratch tickets. "You make your own luck, know what I mean?"

Lucy gave her notebook a satisfied little pat as she left the store. Thanks to Lois she had gotten some good quotes she could use in her story. She'd love to talk to the owner, George, to find out exactly how much of his business came from the lottery but doubted he'd cooperate. In her experience, small-business owners tended to be close-mouthed when it came to facts and figures.

She climbed in the car and started the engine. If only she knew someone who was a compulsive gambler, she thought, or a recovered compulsive gambler. That would give the story a face, someone the readers could identify with.

At least she had a good start, she thought, backing the car around and turning onto Main Street. The next step was to get some information from the lottery commission. But before she tackled that, she wanted to pay a little visit to Miss Tilley.

It was the least she could decently do, she rationalized. After all, she had been friends with the former librarian ever since she and Bill first moved to Tinker's Cove nearly twenty years ago. Furthermore, both she and Miss Tilley were members of the library board of directors. Paying a visit to a fragile and elderly colleague who was undoubtedly distressed by this violent turn of events could hardly be construed as attempting to investigate Bitsy's murder.

"I suppose you're investigating Bitsy's murder," said Miss Tilley, when Rachel Goodman admitted Lucy to the little antique Cape Cod house. Rachel worked mornings for Miss Tilley, taking care of the housekeeping and laundry and preparing a substantial midday meal for her.

"Can you stay for lunch?" asked Rachel. "I'm making fish chowder." Rachel's son Richie was good friends with Toby, and she and Lucy were well acquainted.

"It smells delicious," said Lucy, inhaling the rich fragrance. She guessed that Rachel would welcome some relief from Miss Tilley. "But I can only stay for an hour or so. I have to pick up Zoe at twelve."

"How about some tea, then?" offered Rachel, taking Lucy's coat.

"I'd love it. Thanks."

"Sit right down," invited Miss Tilley, who was ensconced in her favorite wing chair by the fireplace. She made a cozy picture, sitting beside the glowing fire with a colorful crocheted afghan warming her legs. "It's about time you got here. You have to get to the bottom of this."

"I've been told not to meddle," Lucy informed her dutifully. "Lieutenant Horowitz doesn't want me interfering in his investigation."

"Nonsense. You're in a far better position to discover who killed Bitsy than anyone else."

"I don't know about that," demurred Lucy, taking the tea from Rachel.

"I have work to do in the kitchen, so I'll leave you two to visit," said Rachel. A cloud seemed to pass over her usually sunny face. "It's just awful about Bitsy. I can hardly believe it really happened." She dabbed at her nose with a tissue and returned to the kitchen.

"I can believe it," said Miss Tilley. "I would have liked to strangle her a few times myself."

"Well, thinking about it and actually doing it are two separate things. There are times when we'd all like to do away with someone . . ."

"Bitsy asked for it," said Miss Tilley, smoothing the afghan with gnarled fingers. "Right from day one."

"I'm really surprised to hear you say that," said Lucy. "I always thought she did a great job."

Miss Tilley threw up her hands in disgust. "Hardly. She was so disorganized. It was a scandal. Things were always such a mess."

"Her style was different from yours, but you have to admit that she did some good things." Lucy wanted to say that Bitsy was friendly and welcoming, but was afraid Miss Tilley would be insulted. "A lot of people liked the way she ran things—more people than ever were using the library."

"Oh, she was Miss Nicey-nice to the patrons, I'll give you that. Never bothered with overdue fines, never even made the children wash their hands before they handled the books."

Lucy couldn't help smiling. She knew a lot of Tinker's Cove natives remembered Miss Tilley's insistence that they wash their "little finger bones" as soon as they entered the library.

"I know people think it was silly, but the library has always had a limited budget," continued Miss Tilley. "Making the children wash their hands saved quite a bit of wear and tear on expensive books. But that's neither here nor there." She waved her blue-veined hand back and forth. "The point I was trying to make is that she talked about people behind their backs."

"You're not the first person I've heard say that."

"Oh, yes," nodded Miss Tilley. "For instance, if you took out a book on, oh, say sexual dysfunction, Bitsy would notice. And she'd talk about it. She'd mention it to the next person who came along, and the next. And each time she'd embellish it. First it would be 'Guess who took out a book on sexual dysfunction.' Then it would be 'I guess Lucy Stone is having some problems with Bill.' Before the day was out she'd have you considering divorce because you and Bill were sexually incompatible!"

"Did she really say those things about me?" said Lucy, feeling rather sick.

"Oh, I don't know. I was just using you as an example." She took a sip of tea and looked at Lucy over her teacup. "But I don't see why not you, too. She talked about everybody."

"After Zoe was born I took out a book on abnormal psychology and she asked me if I was suffering from postpartum depression," recalled Lucy.

"I heard about that," volunteered Rachel, returning with the teapot.

"I never had post-partum depression!" exclaimed Lucy.

"Everybody thought you did," said Rachel. "I was so relieved when I saw you'd gotten over it."

"I never had it," insisted Lucy.

"Okay. I believe you," Rachel said diplomatically. "More tea?"

"No, thanks," said Lucy, furrowing her brow thoughtfully. "I don't know—this seems kind of a stretch. What kind of secret could she have found out that would be damaging enough that somebody would have to kill her? Besides, she's done a lot of good. Just look at the new addition—that would never have happened without Bitsy."

"That's the most ridiculous thing I've ever heard, Lucy Stone!" Miss Tilley was quivering with rage. "That is absolutely untrue! I don't know where you got an idea like that! The board decided to build the addition, and the board raised the money. Bitsy had nothing to do with it!"

"I'm sorry," said Lucy, hastening to make amends. "I must have misunderstood."

"You certainly did. In fact, all Bitsy contributed to the fundraising effort were some harebrained ideas. She proposed using the endowment fund, said it was too little money to bother about keeping, and she even suggested we sell Josiah's Tankard to buy computers. As if computers will ever replace books! But she wouldn't hear it—all she ever talked about was computer-this and computer-that! I don't know what people see in those newfangled machines anyway."

Lucy thought of her struggle to disengage Zoe from the computer earlier that morning and smiled. "They're certainly not all they're cracked up to be. Sometimes they're more trouble than they're worth."

"My thoughts exactly," said Miss Tilley. "And most of the board members agreed with me."

"So Bitsy was out of favor with the board?"

"She certainly was. In fact, I had suggested taking steps toward dismissing her. It's tricky these days, you know. People sue for wrongful dismissal. Chuck told us we had to be very careful and begin documenting all the reasons why we were unhappy with her." She paused and smacked her lips.

"Now we won't have to bother with all that. Looks like whoever killed that creature did the board a big favor."

"That's a terrible thing to say." Lucy was truly shocked. "Maybe you didn't like her, but she didn't deserve to die!" She paused a moment. "And she wasn't a 'creature'—she was a person."

"I have a right to my opinion," the old woman said stubbornly. "And I can call her a creature if I want to."

"Well, not to me, you can't," said Lucy. She was appalled at her old friend's attitude. She got to her feet and placed her cup and saucer on Miss Tilley's antique tavern table, then looked straight at the old woman. "You're really going too far. I'm not going to listen to talk like this."

Rachel, who had overheard them in the kitchen, hurried out and got Lucy's coat out of the closet. She held it up and whispered in Lucy's ear as she slipped her arms into the sleeves.

"Don't pay any mind when she says things like that—she's just getting old and she doesn't like it."

Lucy squeezed Rachel's hand. "You're a saint to put up with an old witch like her," she said, not bothering to lower her voice. "Thanks for the tea."

From the doorway, Rachel called after her, "Take it easy, Lucy."

As she walked to the car, Lucy heard Miss Tilley's quavering voice.

"I don't know what she's got so high and mighty about!" she declared as Rachel closed the door.

Chapter Seven

Three little kittens,
They lost their mittens,
And they began to cry . . .

The snow squalls had stopped when Lucy left Miss Tilley's, and the sun was making a halfhearted attempt to break through the clouds. It didn't look as if it had much of a chance, Lucy thought glumly; the slim opening between the clouds was getting narrower by the minute. She shivered and pulled her hat down over her ears and got in the car.

She turned the key in the ignition and pushed the heater controls up to maximum. Then she pulled away from the curb, neglecting to check for traffic. The loud honk of a horn as a pickup truck swerved to avoid the Subaru made her jump.

Why am I so upset, she asked herself as she carefully checked her mirrors. Driving slowly along the snow-packed road, she wondered why she had found Miss Tilley's attitude so disturbing. She hadn't been especially good friends with Bitsy, after all, and Bitsy certainly hadn't minded spreading rumors about her. Still, she couldn't help but be saddened by her death. It was horrible and shocking, but, she realized, dwelling on it wasn't getting her anywhere. She had a few minutes before she had to pick up Zoe, so she decided to stop at the IGA.

The automatic door opened for her and she took a shopping cart. The fluorescent lights made the aging store look dreary; it was nothing like the shiny new superstore that had opened out on the interstate. Nevertheless, it offered a change from the gray monotony of winter in Maine.

Lucy stopped at the magazine rack and leafed through one of the women's magazines but decided she didn't want to get organized and wasn't interested in perking up her wardrobe or spicing up favorite family meals. What she really wanted to know was who killed Bitsy, and why, information she wasn't going to find in *Family Circle*. She replaced the magazine and slowly pushed the cart along, pausing at the meagre display of fresh flowers and potted plants.

Why didn't they ever have anything but those ghastly carnations? The red color was an unpleasant reminder of Bitsy's blood, spreading out on the gray industrial tile of the workroom. She picked up a little polka-dot plant in a pink pot and examined it; it didn't look worth three ninety-nine so she put it back.

Dispirited, she pushed on to the produce department, wishing that she hadn't gotten so angry at Miss Tilley. She shouldn't have reacted the way she did; half of what Miss Tilley said was for effect. She loved to shock people, and she had certainly succeeded this morning. Lucy had found the old woman's callousness toward Bitsy's death shocking, but sometimes it seemed to her that old people didn't react in quite the same way to death as younger people. She remembered her own grandfather checking the obituaries every morning and his satisfaction when he occasionally discovered he'd outlived a younger acquaintance.

"Never touched a drop and wouldn't eat red meat," he'd comment. "Didn't do him much good, did it?"

She smiled to herself, remembering a spry old fellow in a plaid flannel shirt neatly topped with a bow tie, and khaki pants held up by suspenders. He certainly enjoyed an occasional glass of whiskey, and insisted on meat and potatoes for dinner every night. Grandma's occasional experiments with spaghetti and Spanish rice had not been successful. He had lived to be eighty-five even though he never ate a raw vegetable and considered fruit unfit for human consumption unless it was baked inside a pie crust.

Lucy reached for a bag of oranges and, on further consideration, added a bag of grapefruit. Even if the board members had favored Bitsy, she thought, they would have been thoroughly dismayed by her proposal to sell Josiah's Tankard. An idea like that would have lost her some friends, that was for sure.

She stopped, resting her forearms on the handle of the cart, and considered a display of cereal. Now that she'd had time to think it over, Miss Tilley's attitude toward Bitsy wasn't really all that surprising. Miss Tilley had devoted her life to the library; she had worked there for fifty years or more. It was much more than a job to her. The library contained everything she held dearest in life, including Josiah's Tankard. She must have been deeply hurt when she was forced to retire and her job was given to Bitsy. And it certainly didn't help matters that Bitsy's attitudes were so radically different from hers.

If Miss Tilley was entitled to dislike Bitsy, if she regarded her as an enemy, Lucy guessed she couldn't blame her for taking some satisfaction in her demise. Putting it that way made it seem better, she decided. "Demise" was a much nicer word than "murder."

Miss Tilley was just reacting in a very human way. Queen Elizabeth I probably indulged in a chuckle or two

when she succeeded in detaching Mary, Queen of Scots'
head from her neck.

And besides, she was never going to get to the bottom of
this without Miss Tilley's help, she decided. Miss Tilley
knew everything about everybody in town, and who had
what skeletons hidden in which closet. She also knew a lot
about Bitsy, even though that knowledge was tainted with
disapproval. There was no way around it, Lucy concluded,
pushing the cart to the checkout: she was going to have to
apologize to Miss Tilley.

As she stood in line, Lucy regarded the woman in front of
her. She was wearing a bright pink parka that certainly
didn't complement her green-and-brown plaid polyester
pants.

"Mrs. Withers!" exclaimed Lucy.

"Yes?" The woman turned, revealing a round face with
narrow lips, brightly outlined in fuchsia lipstick.

"You don't know me," began Lucy. "I'm Lucy Stone. I
was the one who found Bitsy Howell yesterday."

"The police said she was shot." Mrs. Withers looked
doubtful. "That so?"

"Oh, yes." Lucy nodded. "Do you have any idea who
might have done it? Did she have a fight with her boyfriend
or anything like that?"

"Not likely. She didn't have no boyfriend. No friends at
all, far as I could tell. Kept herself to herself." Mrs. Withers
began unloading her cart onto the checkout conveyor.

"That was a terrible thing," added Dot, the cashier.

"It's really quite a loss for me," confessed Mrs. Withers
sadly.

"You were close?" inquired Lucy.

"She was my tenant." Mrs. Withers's penciled eyebrows
shot up. "The police have sealed the apartment! I don't

know when I'm going to be able to move out her stuff and get it rented again."

"That's just normal procedure," said Dot, ringing up a box of cookies.

"What will happen to her things?" asked Lucy.

"I spoke to her family, in New York someplace. I asked when they were coming and what to do with it all, and you know what they said? They said just give it all to the Salvation Army!"

"Everything?" Lucy was shocked.

"Everything! Imagine that." Mrs. Withers's numerous chins quivered in indignation.

"Don't they want anything of hers? Something to remember her by?" asked Dot. "That'll be eight dollars and sixteen cents."

"Not a thing—said I should just get rid of it all," said Mrs. Withers, pulling her wallet out of her imitation leather purse. "Doesn't seem like they've got much family feeling, if you ask me."

"Poor Bitsy," sighed Lucy, reaching into her basket for the bag of oranges.

Back in the Subaru, driving down Main Street on her way to Kiddie Kollege, Lucy passed Hayden's antique shop, Northcross and Love. In the window she noticed a tavern table, similar to Miss Tilley's, with a couple of pewter tankards displayed on it. That was an idea, she thought. Miss Tilley might enjoy having a tankard similar to Josiah's Tankard. Of course, she couldn't afford one as old and valuable as Josiah's Tankard but she might find something that was less expensive. Even a reproduction. She resolved to come back to the shop when she had more time.

When she and Zoe got home, Lucy cut up some of the oranges and grapefruit and sprinkled a little dried coconut on top.

"It's called 'ambrosia,'" she told Zoe.

Starved for vitamin C and sunshine, the two of them finished the entire bowl. Then Zoe scampered off to the family room, and Lucy got out her gambling notes. She put in a call to the state lottery commission for information and learned most of what she wanted was on the commission's website. Then she made a second call and left a message with Gamblers Anonymous. After that she called Ted to discuss the illustration for the story.

"We need some good art," she told him. "I was thinking of a photograph of discarded lottery tickets in a parking lot or something."

"I'll see what I can come up with," he said. "Any luck getting some quotes from a problem gambler?"

"I've got a call in to Gamblers Anonymous, and I'm waiting for some info from the lottery commission. It's coming along. It would be a lot easier if I knew a compulsive gambler." She paused and studied the dirty lunch dishes that were still on the kitchen table. "What have you heard about the murder?"

"Not much. They're keeping a particularly tight lid on this one."

"Anything about the funeral arrangements?"

"Her family's made arrangements to have her cremated. There'll be a memorial service at a later date."

"That's about what I expected."

"Is the library board going to do anything?"

"I don't think so," said Lucy. "What I hear is that the board members weren't happy with Bitsy and at least some of them wanted to fire her."

"Bitsy?" Ted was astonished.

"I was surprised, too. I thought everybody loved her." Lucy heard the school bus, down at the bottom of the hill. "I've got to go—the kids are home. But you know, I heard something funny today, and it might be a motive for whoever killed her. It seems that Bitsy liked to gossip about the books people took out of the library. You know, like if you took out a book about alcoholism she would start telling other people."

"So what?"

"Well, from what I heard, she would start with the fact that you borrowed the book but pretty soon you would be a full-fledged alcoholic."

"Oh," said Ted, grasping the possibilities. "That would be a very dangerous thing to do in a town like this."

"I know," agreed Lucy as the kitchen door flew open and the kids blew in. " 'Bye."

She hung up the receiver and faced her offspring, a no-nonsense expression on her face.

"Boots on the newspaper under the radiator, please. Coats on hooks. Bookbags, well, anywhere except the kitchen floor. Got it?"

"Aye, aye!" said Toby, giving her a mock salute.

"Unnnh!" grunted Sara, tugging at her boots without bothering to untie them.

"You'd think we were idiots," grumbled Elizabeth. "It isn't as if we didn't know to hang up our coats."

Lucy decided to let that one go and started putting the lunch dishes in the dishwasher. The kitchen gradually emptied as the older kids finished taking off their snow gear, and Zoe appeared in the doorway.

"Toby made me stop playing computer," she complained.

"Well, you've been playing for hours. It's time to give somebody else a turn. Why not help me make some fruity Jell-O for dessert?"

After they had finished filling a mold with lemon-flavored gelatin studded with orange pieces, Lucy decided to see if one of the kids would help her access the lottery commission on the computer.

When she went into the family room, she found Toby, Elizabeth, and Sara huddled together over the keyboard. For once, they weren't fighting—whatever they were looking at was equally fascinating to all three. Lucy stood behind them and peered over their shoulders, but all she saw was line after line of text.

"Type in: I'm 18, I have long blond hair, and I have a 36-inch bust," prompted Elizabeth.

"Better make it 39 inches," said Toby, prompting peals of giggles from the girls.

Wow! appeared on the screen. *I'd reelly like to meet you.*

"Stop it!" exclaimed Lucy. "He's probably some pervert."

"Mom, he's just some hopeless computer nerd in Chicago or somewhere," said Elizabeth with a toss of her short black bangs.

"It's fun to get him going."

"He thinks we're a gorgeous blonde," said Sara, giggling.

"Well what if he finds out our address or something? He might even come here—what about that?"

"The only address he knows us by is B.Boobs." Toby was laughing.

"Are you sure?" Lucy was suspicious. "He doesn't know where we live?"

"No, Mom. This is cyberspace. For all he knows, B.Boobs lives in Norway." Toby clicked away at the keyboard. "That's a good idea—I'm going to put in something about fjords."

Lucy watched as the reply appeared on the screen: *Do girls in Norway wear bras?*

No, typed Toby, sending the girls into gales of laughter.

"Stop it! Right now! I can't believe your father and I spent thousands of dollars on a computer just so you can talk dirty with some weirdo," complained Lucy. "Anyway, I want you to find a website for me."

"Sure, Mom. What do you want?"

"I've got it here." Lucy consulted a slip of paper. "Three 'w's, a period, then 'm-e-l-o-t-t-o,' another period and 'c-o-m.'" Toby clicked the mouse a few times and typed in the letters. "Here it is."

"Just like that?" Lucy was impressed.

"Sure. Here, take the mouse. You can click around and find what you want, okay?"

"What if I make a mistake?"

"You can't," shrugged Toby. "Just keep clicking. I'm going to get something to eat."

Lucy took his seat. Hesitantly, she tried moving the mouse. A little arrow zoomed across the screen. She pointed it at "About the Maine Lottery Commission" and clicked. Nothing happened.

"It's not working."

"Put the arrow on the letters," advised Sara.

Lucy adjusted it and clicked. A picture of lottery headquarters appeared.

"Look at that!" Lucy was impressed again, and waited for more. Nothing happened. "Is this all I get? Just a picture?"

"See the little arrow in the corner? Put the mouse there and hold it down."

Lucy followed Sara's instructions and text appeared, explaining the lottery's creation by a vote of the state legislature. Soon she was pulling up tables of sales by towns, average return to vendors, prize awards by town and county. She grabbed a pencil and started noting the information down on a piece of paper she extracted from the printer.

Toby returned and stood beside her, chewing on a sandwich. Lucy smelled peanut butter.

"You don't have to do that," he said. "You can print it out."

"I can?"

"Sure." Toby clicked the mouse a few times and the printer began humming and spewing out sheets of paper.

"Wow," Lucy said, awestruck. "I didn't know it could do this. This is amazing."

Toby patted her shoulder sympathetically. "You'll be okay, Mom. It's just 'future shock.'"

Future shock . . . that was a good term for it, thought Lucy. Pleased as she was with the results of her Internet research, thanks to the kids she'd discovered that there was a definite downside to computers. Thinking of the various board members, she didn't think they would be as enthusiastic about putting the library online as Bitsy was. While she thought the kids' explorations of the Internet were harmless enough, even if they were a waste of time, she didn't think Ed or Gerald or Miss Tilley would agree. They certainly wouldn't want the town's youth to have access to the uncensored information available on the web.

But, she thought as she collected the sheets of paper from the printer, computers weren't the sort of issue that led to murder. Or were they?

Tomorrow, she decided, she'd pay a visit to Hayden's shop and see about those tankards. And since she was going to be there anyway, she might as well ask Hayden about Bitsy's relations with the board members.

Chapter Eight

Jack Sprat could eat no fat,
His wife could eat no lean,
Together
They licked the platter clean.

It was almost three o'clock on Saturday afternoon before Lucy got away for an hour or two of antiquing. But when she pulled open the heavy pine door, she discovered that Northcross and Love was not the type of antiques shop she was used to. There was no clutter of dusty, mismatched objects covering every available surface, no display cases crammed with bits and pieces of china and glassware and jewelry. Instead, a few highly polished pieces of furniture, carefully spotlighted, were arranged to suggest a homelike setting. A Queen Anne dining table stood on a tastefully faded Oriental rug with a Canton soup tureen serving as a centerpiece. Above it, a gleaming brass chandelier held at least a dozen hand-dipped candles. It had not been converted to electricity; that would undoubtedly be considered heresy by the shop's clientele, who apparently took their antiques very seriously indeed.

Lucy turned the tag on one of the chairs arranged around the table and gasped when she saw the price was fifteen thousand dollars.

"Can I help you?"

Lucy looked up and saw Hayden standing in a doorway that led to the back of the store.

"Lucy—I didn't recognize you! This is a nice surprise." He was smiling warmly and seemed genuinely glad to see her. "I didn't know you were interested in antiques."

"I am, but I'm afraid you're a little bit beyond my price range," she said.

"We cater to serious collectors," said Hayden. "In fact, most of our business is through the computer and our customers are scattered all over the country."

"I had no idea," said Lucy. "I do most of my buying at flea markets and auctions."

"You can still find nice things, but it's getting harder. Are you interested in anything in particular?" He cocked his head, and looked at her over his half-glasses. In a Harris tweed sport coat, bow tie, and tasseled loafers, Hayden was the very picture of a country gentleman.

"Yesterday I saw two pewter tankards in the window, but I notice that they're gone."

Hayden was crestfallen. "I just packed them up—they're going to California. If I'd known you were interested I would have let you know."

"I probably couldn't have afforded them, anyway. Do you mind telling me . . . ?"

"Not at all." He smiled sympathetically. "The pair went for twenty."

"Twenty dollars?" Lucy's hopes revived.

"Twenty thousand."

"Oh."

"You're new to pewter?" inquired Hayden.

"Very new—I don't know much about it at all. It's not for me. I'm looking for a gift. For Miss Tilley, in fact. I thought she might like having something like Josiah's Tankard."

"That's a lovely idea." Hayden nodded in approval, and his bald head shone in the intense light from the overhead spots. "Is it her birthday? I should send a card."

"No." Lucy couldn't resist the urge to confess to this pleasant man. "I had a disagreement with her, about Bitsy. I want to give her the tankard as an apology."

"Miss T. never approved of Bitsy." He clucked his tongue. "It was classic, really. She ran the library for more than thirty years. She didn't want to retire—the board really had to force her out. It was very difficult." He gave a little shudder. "It was obvious that the job was getting to be too much for her, but she simply would not admit it."

"I know. I remember when she had that awful accident and nearly killed Jennifer Mitchell. She kept insisting it wasn't her fault—she wanted to keep on driving!"

Hayden shook his head, amazed at this example of the foolishness of the older generation. "Lucy, my partner and I usually have a coffee break around now—will you join us?"

"Sure," agreed Lucy with a big smile. "I never say no to coffee."

He led her to a surprisingly modern and efficient office area in the rear of the store where a tall, lean man in a plaid shirt and jeans was pounding on the buttons of a fax machine.

"Ralph, stop abusing that machine," said Hayden. "There's someone I want you to meet."

Ralph turned, revealing a ruggedly handsome face that reminded Lucy of Gregory Peck in his early movies.

"Ralph, this is Lucy Stone. She's a fellow sufferer on the library board."

"I'm pleased to make your acquaintance," drawled Ralph, brushing a lock of black hair out of his eyes and extending a huge hand to Lucy.

"Same here," said Lucy, grasping his hand and finding it pleasantly warm and strong.

"Take a seat," invited Hayden, setting cups on a Formica table. "How do you take your coffee?"

"Just black."

"Good for you. I can't resist adding cream, even though I shouldn't." Hayden patted his round little tummy.

Lucy sat down and shrugged out of her coat.

"Let me take that," said Ralph, hanging it up on a coat rack and then taking a seat beside her.

Hayden joined them, setting a plate of homemade blueberry muffins in the center of the table. Ralph helped himself to a huge one and passed the plate to Lucy, who shook her head and passed it along to Hayden.

"You're missing something special," said Ralph with a wink as he spread a generous pat of butter on his muffin. "Hayden makes great muffins."

"I wouldn't bother, except Ralph enjoys them so. And he never gains a pound, lucky devil."

"Not me," said Lucy, who had struggled to lose the twenty extra pounds she had gained when she was pregnant with Zoe and wasn't about to put back on. "I have to watch every calorie."

Ralph shrugged and reached for another muffin. "You know, you haven't made popovers in a dog's age," he said, turning to Lucy and indicating Hayden with a glance. "His popovers are even better than his muffins."

"I'm awfully glad he didn't," said Lucy, taking a sip of coffee. "I can never resist popovers."

"With homemade strawberry jam . . ." began Ralph.

"Stop!" yelped Lucy in mock distress. "I can't stand it! I guess I will have a muffin."

"So, Lucy," began Ralph, his tone now serious. "What do you think of all this business at the library?"

"I don't know what to think," admitted Lucy. "I've only been to one board meeting."

"Heck of a meeting," he said, busying himself with buttering another muffin.

"Now, Ralph, don't discourage Lucy," said Hayden. "That's the first time we've ever actually had a murder—although I must admit we've come close a few times."

Lucy smiled at his joke. "I heard that the board was planning to fire Bitsy—is that true?" asked Lucy, nibbling on her muffin.

Ralph snorted and Lucy looked up sharply in surprise.

"I'm afraid Ralph doesn't have a very high opinion of some of the board members," explained Hayden. "But this is the first I've heard of any plan to fire Bitsy. I mean, I know Miss Tilley loathed her, but I don't think she could get the necessary votes. Staff changes take a unanimous vote. I wouldn't have voted to fire her, and neither would Chuck." He paused and looked at Lucy. "What about you?"

"No." Lucy's voice was firm.

"Maybe that's why she was killed," drawled Ralph.

Lucy's eyes met Hayden's. "Do you think one of the board members is the murderer?" she asked.

"It's crossed my mind," admitted Hayden, "especially after Horowitz gave his little speech. What I can't figure out is when any of them had the opportunity. She must have been killed just minutes before you discovered her, and we were all together then."

"That's not quite true," Lucy reminded him. "It would only have taken a minute or two, you know, and both Ed and Gerald told Horowitz they left the group."

"What did I tell you?" demanded Ralph, pounding the table with his fist. "I told you my money was on Ed."

"Don't pay any attention to him," Hayden told Lucy. "He and Ed have never seen eye to eye. They have some . . . uh, philosophical differences."

"Right," agreed Ralph. "I'm civilized and he isn't."

Lucy smiled. "He is pretty crude, but that doesn't make him a murderer. And Gerald may be every bit the gentleman, but he was also away from the group for a few minutes."

Hayden nodded. "He said he went into the reference room to get the gavel for the meeting," he explained to Ralph.

"Ah-ha!" exclaimed Ralph. "But did either of you actually see him holding the gavel?"

"I didn't," said Lucy.

"Neither did I," said Hayden.

"Well, there's your suspect," announced Ralph.

"He's just joking, you know," Hayden hastened to tell Lucy. "I've been on that board for a long time. I know them all pretty well, and I honestly can't picture any of them shooting her. No matter what Ralph thinks, they really are a pretty decent bunch. They've all donated hours and hours of time to the library. I really think it must be something to do with Bitsy's personal life—after all, we knew very little about her except as the librarian."

"The problem with that is that she doesn't seem to have had any sort of a life at all. Kept herself to herself. At least, that's what her landlady said."

Ralph looked doubtful. "Everybody has some sort of private life. Everybody."

"Maybe we're overlooking the obvious here," said Hayden. "I finally got to read that article you and Chuck were talking about, about violence against librarians, and it said most of the violence was related to a robbery, either computers or some valuable artifact or other."

"But nothing was taken," protested Lucy.

"Maybe she discovered someone attempting a robbery. They killed her and then got frightened."

"That could be," agreed Lucy. "When I went downstairs all the art supplies were spilled, as if she'd been startled, or maybe even in some sort of struggle."

"That's awful," said Hayden, looking rather pale and turning his mug around in circles. "I didn't know that. Bitsy must have been terrified."

The three fell silent, staring at the table. Finally, Ralph voiced what they were all thinking.

"Winter in New England. It looks beautiful but it's brutal. And this winter's been especially bad. Right about now a lot of people are probably getting pretty desperate. The little they managed to save over the summer is gone and they don't have money for heating oil and food . . . and there are still a couple of months of cold weather ahead."

It was true, thought Lucy. Poverty was prettier in the country, where it was hidden away in the woods and tucked behind weathered clapboards, but it was every bit as terrible. She remembered the days when it had been a struggle to pay the bills and keep the children warm and fed. One winter, when there was no work, she and Bill had borrowed money from his folks. They were lucky. Without the elder Stones to help them out, they would have had to accept welfare and go to the food pantry in the cellar of the community church, like so many others. And now, welfare reform was literally leaving a lot of people out in the cold, forcing them to do whatever they could to survive.

"A robbery—that's probably what happened," she said, reluctant to pursue such a depressing subject further. A change of subject was definitely called for. "Now, before I go," she asked brightly, "where can I find a tankard?"

"Lucy was interested in those pewter tankards we had in the window," said Hayden. "She's looking for a gift for Miss Tilley."

"Not that I could have afforded those," Lucy hastened to add.

"They are extraordinary," Ralph told her. "A matched pair, impeccable provenance, superior craftsmanship, great age. They're worth every penny."

"I'm sure they are," said Lucy. "I had no idea pewter is so valuable. I guess I'll just send flowers."

"You could," agreed Ralph, with a shrug. "Not that they'll last very long. The poor things will simply wither under her gaze."

"You're probably right," said Lucy, laughing. "Pewter would definitely be more durable."

"You can find nice pewter around here quite reasonably," offered Hayden. "I saw an interesting piece at that place— the Treasure Trove. I meant to go back and check it out."

"He's right," agreed Ralph. "Good stuff does turn up now and then around here. You know how the town got its name, don't you?"

"Tinker's Cove? Actually, I don't."

"It used to be a place where tinkers, you know, tinsmiths and pewterers and peddlers, spent the winter. They gathered here and worked all winter making the wares that they ped-dled to farms all over the state."

"I didn't know that," said Lucy.

"It means that every so often something really nice turns up. You know, that funny old ashtray of Grandpa's turns out to be a priceless, two-hundred-year-old porringer."

"I should be so lucky," said Lucy, rising to go. "I think I will check out the Treasure Trove."

"Happy hunting," said Ralph, shoving back his chair and standing up.

"Thanks for the coffee."

"The pleasure was all ours," said Ralph.

"We don't get to meet too many suspected murderers," agreed Hayden, holding her coat for her.

"Did I miss something?" asked Ralph.

"The police detective announced to the board members

that I'm his prime suspect because I found Bitsy's body," said Lucy, blushing.

"I can't believe that," said Ralph.

"Of course not," said Hayden. "I was just joking."

"So was Lieutenant Horowitz—we happen to be old acquaintances," explained Lucy, pausing at the door. "At least I hope he was joking. Otherwise I'm in big trouble."

Chapter Nine

The Ogre guarded his treasure fiercely . . .

Lucy checked her watch when she left Hayden and Ralph and discovered she had at least an hour before she had to be home. She decided she might as well stop in at the Treasure Trove and see if they had any pewter.

The Tinker's Cove Treasure Trove, originally a gift shop built in the shape of a pirate's chest, had seen better days. It was located on Route 1A, the old state highway which used to be the major road to the coast. When the superhighway was built, however, tourists no longer had to spend hours creeping along on the old two-lane road and business declined. Once freshly painted every spring, the Treasure Trove's dark brown siding was now faded and peeling, and owner Frank Ford supplemented his shrinking stock of new items with so-called antiques and collectables sold on commission. When the yard sale was over, the Treasure Trove was only too happy to accept the leftovers.

When Lucy turned into the parking lot she didn't have any difficulty finding a space, even though only a small area had been plowed. Hers was the only car.

The dim afternoon light was already fading as she made

her way carefully across the ice and clumped snow and reached for the doorknob. The door stuck and she had to yank hard before it finally opened. When she got inside, she was greeted with a welcome blast of heat from the coal stove Frank had constructed from an oil drum. Nobody seemed to be watching the store, so she began browsing among the cluttered counters, careful not to trip on any of the items that crowded the narrow aisles.

The place was an incredible jumble: pressed glass goblets and Depression glass plates were set on old cans of motor oil and stacks of *Life* magazines; boxes and boxes of old yellow *National Geographic* magazines; old-fashioned push lawnmowers and sets of rusty painted metal breadboxes and kitchen canisters; chipped plates and blue and green glass insulators from electrical poles. Nothing was organized—it was the sort of place where you could look for hours, finding worthless bits and pieces that brought back long-forgotten memories of childhood. Lucy picked up a clear glass pitcher painted with red and blue stripes and bright yellow lemons that was just like the one Aunt Helen had at the lake, except Aunt Helen's still had its matching tumblers, and remembered Sunday afternoon visits and grown-up conversations that seemed endless to a little girl who wanted to go swimming. She stroked a bright orange pillow crocheted from synthetic yarn that was just like the ones Mrs. Pilling had on her avocado green sofa, and recalled the day Mr. Pilling fell down dead in his yard from a stroke. His little beagle dog sat on the spot for days, waiting for Mr. Pilling to return.

Shaking her head to clear out the cobwebby images of days long past, Lucy picked up her pace and marched purposefully along, searching for the dull gray gleam of pewter. She poked in boxes of old pots and mismatched china and found a sugar bowl with no lid and a modern Scandinavian-style pitcher, rather dented. There were quite a few small trays, all modern and clunky looking, engraved with "Our

Daily Bread" in gothic letters. She was just about to give up, fearing it was getting awfully late, when she stumbled over a box of cans and tins containing screws and assorted hardware—clearly discarded from someone's garage or workshop. She grabbed the corner of a glass display case to catch her balance and spotted a little tankard, hidden behind a plastic figure of Fritz the Cat.

The display case was locked, so she looked around for Frank. Not finding him, she gave a yell, and he came through the curtained doorway behind the sales counter. He was one of those thin, wizened people who never seemed to age, looking much the same at sixty as at forty. His hair was salted with gray and he was wearing his usual brown cardigan over a worn flannel shirt.

"Can I please see this old mug? The case is locked." One thing Lucy had learned from previous negotiations with Frank was never to use any word that might imply value to describe a desired object. It might be a pewter tankard but she would call it a mug, she resolved, as Frank bustled over with a bunch of keys attached to his belt with a chain.

She tapped her foot impatiently as he tried key after key, finally finding one that worked.

"This what you want?" he asked, lifting a rather lumpy piece of amateur pottery.

"No, that metal one," said Lucy, pointing.

"Oh," said Frank, lifting it up and examining it. "This is nice."

"I just need something for pens and pencils—how much do you want for it?"

"I think this might be a genuine antique," said Frank, peering through his bifocals and stroking the white stubble on his chin. He glanced quickly at Lucy. "A hundred dollars."

"What?" Lucy made her eyes very wide, indicating her shock and surprise at this outrageous demand. "For that old thing? You're crazy. I wasn't planning on spending more than fifteen."

"I couldn't let it go for that," he said, shaking his head mournfully. "How about seventy-five?"

Lucy adjusted the strap of her shoulder bag and looked toward the door, as if she were preparing to leave. "Twenty-five, and that's my absolute limit."

"Fifty?" whined Frank.

"Done," snapped Lucy, whipping out her checkbook.

Leaving the store, Lucy encountered a woman struggling to carry a heavy cardboard box, and held the door for her. As if embarrassed, she gave a quick bob of her head in thanks and scuttled past.

Lucy noticed her turquoise jacket, a color that hadn't been fashionable for a number of years, and her boots, which were worn down at the heel. She guessed the poor thing was trying to raise a few dollars by selling her bits and pieces to Frank.

As she crossed the parking lot, carefully watching her footing in the waning light, she passed a big old sedan with patches of rust and a peeling vinyl roof. A heavy man with a big, bushy beard sat at the wheel and the back seat was filled with a squirming bunch of children.

She was opening the car door when she heard his voice. "I've had it with you," he growled. "Shut up, all of you!"

She glanced at him and he looked up at her. "What are you looking at?" he demanded.

She didn't answer, but ducked inside the car and shut the door. She started the engine, already feeling a little pang of guilt for spending so much money. While the car warmed up, she began unwrapping the tankard in order to take a closer look at it. Fifty dollars was more than she had planned to spend; she was already regretting the impulse that made her agree to such a high price. And as if to emphasize the waste, here, right next to her, were people who obviously had more need of that money than she did.

She turned to look at the crowded car once again, and saw the woman returning, still carrying the box. Apparently her things weren't even good enough for Frank. She had barely gotten back in the car before the man started the engine and, giving Lucy a glare, spun out of the parking lot at high speed, spraying bits of ice and gravel.

Who could blame him for being angry, thought Lucy. He and his family were wanting in the land of plenty and they weren't the only ones. Unfortunately, poverty was just about as common in Tinker's Cove as the rocks that lined the coast or the pine trees that stood in long-abandoned pastures. She remembered her conversation with Ralph and Hayden, and thought that a robbery was probably the reason for Bitsy's death.

With that thought came the discouraging realization that it was unlikely the murder would ever be solved. Without a motive, the police would only identify the murderer when, or if, something turned up in connection with another crime. A similar modus or someone willing to talk in exchange for a plea bargain.

Remembering the package in her hand, she took the little piece of pewter out of the crumpled newspaper Frank had wrapped it in. It was hard to see clearly in the dim light of late afternoon, but the tankard had a nice feel to it, she decided. It felt substantial in her hand but not too heavy. The shape was attractive, and even though pewter was a soft metal and dented easily, the straight sides were smooth. She wrapped her fingers around the handle and discovered they fit easily without pinching. Flipping it over, she examined the bottom and found it was smooth, with no identifying marks.

Lucy didn't know a great deal about antiques, but she felt confident that she had a good eye. She had visited museums and historic homes and studied the contents and frequently attended auctions, noting which items attracted the highest bids. And the more she studied the tankard, the happier she was with her purchase. She couldn't exactly say why, but something about the tankard made her suspect it was older and more valuable than she had originally thought.

Even so, thinking of the family in the car, she still felt guilty about spending such a lot of money so frivolously. She resolved to make a substantial contribution to the food pantry, and to go through the closets. The kids had plenty of outgrown but still serviceable winter clothes that could go to some less fortunate children.

Feeling somewhat better, she smiled as she flicked on the headlights and shifted into gear. Fifty dollars. It was a lot to her, but it was a far cry from the twenty thousand that Hayden had gotten for his matched pair.

What if, she thought as she pulled onto the dark road, she had discovered a truly valuable tankard, one that was worth thousands? It wasn't that ridiculous—after all, Ralph had said that good things turned up all the time, their value unrecognized until discovered by a knowledgeable collector or dealer. Maybe, she thought, hugging the happy thought to herself as she sped toward home, maybe she had found a real treasure at the Treasure Trove.

On Sunday afternoon Bill took the older kids to a benefit basketball game—the firefighters and police had teamed up against the teachers to raise money for a family that had lost their home when they tried to heat it with an old kerosene stove—and Lucy settled Zoe in front of the TV with a stack of videos and sat down at the computer to work on the gambling story. While she clicked away at the keyboard, she periodically looked away from the screen to admire the tankard. Here she was feeling guilty about spending fifty dollars for a gift for Miss Tilley, and at the same time Tinker's Cove residents were spending well over five hundred dollars per person, per year, on the state lottery.

At least she had something to show for her money—a useful and attractive object that she hoped would please her old friend. If she had spent that money on scratch tickets, she thought, all she would most likely have would be a pile of worthless cardboard.

It was odd, she thought, how quickly people had accepted the lottery. When she was a girl, she remembered, her mother had often criticized a neighbor who played the illegal numbers game. "It's a waste of money that could buy milk and bread for his children," she used to say. "He might as well throw it away."

It had been quite a surprise to Lucy when her mother began including lottery tickets in the children's Christmas gifts, and had also begun tucking them into birthday cards. What had happened to make her change her mind? After all, gambling was gambling, whether it was sponsored by the state or the mob. And with the chance of winning in the state's Big Big Jackpot at something like 55 million to one, the mob offered better odds.

Of course, the state lottery not only promoted their games with glossy advertising that promised wealth and happiness but it also was supposed to provide money for education. Funny, thought Lucy, giving a little snort, that taxpayers would resist a one or two percent increase in the property tax amounting to ten or fifteen dollars a year at the same time they would spend hundreds on the lottery.

"It's practically un-American not to play," she quoted the man from Gamblers Anonymous she had interviewed by telephone earlier that afternoon. "After all, Bingo supports the church and the lottery helps education. It's the new American Dream—you don't work hard to get rich, you just play the lottery."

Finishing up the story, Lucy picked up the tankard. She'd

love to know how much it was worth. Had she lost money? Was it really worth only the fifteen dollars she had originally wanted to spend? Or was it a bargain at fifty? How could she find out? Tomorrow, she decided, she'd stop by the shop and ask Ralph to take a look at it. Maybe, she thought hopefully, she had a winner.

Chapter Ten

After they had been wandering in the woods
for a very long time, Hansel and Gretel came
upon a cottage made of gingerbread and candy.

On Monday morning, Lucy wasted no time in making good her resolution to make a donation to the food pantry. After leaving Zoe at the rec building for nursery school, she headed straight for the IGA. There, armed with the flyer that came in the Sunday paper, she took advantage of all the buy-one-get-one-free promotions, and filled her cart with boxes of pasta and jars of spaghetti sauce, cans of tuna fish and soup, and bags of rice and beans. All nutritious, filling stuff. She also bought a box of confectioners' sugar and a bag of conversation hearts; Valentine's Day was just around the corner, and she always made pink-frosted cupcakes trimmed with heart candies for the kids.

When she arrived at the community church, Lucy saw she wasn't the only one making a delivery. Ed Bumpus was unloading a box from the back of his gargantuan pickup truck, a glossy black model perched on oversized tires and trimmed with lots of shining chrome. Lucy didn't feel very friendly toward Ed—she hadn't liked his attitude at the board meeting—but she could hardly ignore a fellow member.

"That's quite a truck you've got there," Lucy said, admiring the cab, which was trimmed with a sun visor and topped with a row of roof lights. A big, black Lab dog was sitting inside.

"My wife says I'm no better than a little kid—I gotta have my toys," he said, hoisting the heavy box onto his shoulder.

"What have you got in there?" asked Lucy, following him down the path to the church basement.

"Moose," grunted Ed. "I give 'em one every year."

"Did you shoot it yourself?" asked Lucy, remembering the shotgun rack inside Ed's truck.

Ed turned to face her, his puffy face even redder than usual. "Usually, I do, but this year, I struck out. My cousin got this one, but don't tell the pastor, okay?"

"You've got a deal."

The basement door popped open as they approached, and the minister, Clive Macintosh, greeted them. He was new to the job, having arrived in Tinker's Cove only last summer.

"Well, well, what's all this?" he asked, rubbing his hands together.

"Moose. Wrapped and frozen and ready to cook," said Ed, dropping the box on a table with a thud and heading back out to get another.

"Terrific," said Clive, professing enthusiasm but looking somewhat doubtful.

"It's a Maine thing," Lucy hastened to reassure him. "Trust me—people will really appreciate it."

Clive looked at the box suspiciously. "How do you cook it?"

"Just like beef—it's not gamey," Lucy said, placing her bags of groceries on the table, too. She wished she'd thought to buy something a little more interesting. "These are just the usual nonperishables. Macaroni. Tuna. That kind of stuff."

"We can sure use it," said Clive, his eyes widening as Ed

appeared with another box. "We're having a hard time keeping up with the demand. The committee members tell me it's the worst they've ever seen."

"It's the weather," said Lucy. "It's been so cold that people are using more heating fuel than usual—that means there's less money for groceries."

"Well, we're certainly very grateful," said Clive as Ed set the box on the table.

"Think nothing of it. It's my pleasure," said Ed, panting a little from the exertion. "See you get this in the freezer, now."

"I will, and thanks again," said Clive as Lucy and Ed went through the door.

"He's a funny little guy," said Ed as they made their way up the walk to the parking lot.

"He's from some posh town in Connecticut," said Lucy. "I don't think they eat moose there."

"Can't be much of a place, then," said Ed, thoughtfully propping his elbow on the side of his truck. "Say, have you heard anything more about this Bitsy mess?" He wrinkled his forehead, jamming his bristly eyebrows together in concern. "Has that cop been botherin' you?"

"Oh, no." Lucy waved her hand dismissively. "That was just a joke. I've known him a long time. I'm not really a suspect."

"Wish I could say the same," muttered Ed. "He's been nosin' around my crew, gettin' in the way and askin' a lotta questions."

"He's just doing his job," said Lucy.

"Well, I wish him doin' his job didn't keep me from doin' mine."

Lucy nodded. She knew how much Bill, and most contractors, hated interference on their job sites. "Did you find out what he was asking about?"

"Lot of stupid stuff, if you ask me. I don't think he's got

any more idea of who killed Bitsy than my dog here." He jerked his head toward the cab. "I heard you're kind of a detective yourself. Whadda you think?"

"Me?" Lucy didn't like the way Ed was staring at her with those beady eyes of his. She felt a bit like that poor moose, caught in the sight of one of his shotguns. "You heard the pastor—it's no secret how desperate people are this winter. I think Bitsy must have interrupted a robbery, something like that. Whoever did it is probably scared and laying real low. I don't think they're going to solve this anytime soon."

"Yeah," grunted Ed. "I think you're right." He opened the door to his truck and reached across the seat, giving the dog a pat on the head. "Say hi to Bill for me," he said, hoisting himself into the seat.

"Sorry, Lucy, but Ralph's not here," said Hayden, a few minutes later when Lucy stopped by with the tankard. "He's over in Gilead, checking out an estate sale."

"That's too bad—I was hoping he could tell me if I had found a treasure or not," said Lucy, unwrapping the tankard and setting it on the table in the shop. "What do you think?"

"Very nice," said Hayden, examining the tankard. "I think it's lovely. Excellent craftsmanship. Nice patina. How much did you pay?"

"Fifty dollars."

He nodded approvingly. "That's a steal."

Lucy beamed with pride. "You really think so?"

"I do," affirmed Hayden. "But I ought to warn you—I'm no expert on pewter." He turned the tankard over and checked the bottom. "Interesting."

"What's interesting?"

"I don't want to get your hopes up, but you see how smooth it is? Josiah's Tankard, the one at the library, is like that, too. It means the piece was made in a mold. Later pieces were worked on a lathe and have finishing marks on the bottom. That means this tankard has quite a bit of age."

"Are you sure?" Lucy couldn't quite believe her luck.

"Yeah. Miss Tilley asked Ralph and me to examine Josiah's Tankard a few months ago so we could write a description for the insurance policy. It was quite an experience—very hush-hush. After dark. The library was closed, of course. She even had a police officer standing by when we opened the case."

Lucy chuckled. "I can just imagine." She paused. "Then you think it's good enough to give to her as a present?"

"I'm pretty sure, but if you want to be extra safe, why not check with Corney? She has quite a nice pewter collection, you know."

"I didn't know," said Lucy, "but that's a very good idea. Thanks."

Lucy was hesitant to drop in on Corney unexpectedly, whom she barely knew, so she stopped first at the Quik-Stop to call. When she pulled the car up to the pay phone, she pulled in beside a dark blue Chevy sedan with its engine running. Climbing out of the Subaru, she noticed the sedan was occupied. Probably someone waiting for a companion who had dashed into the store.

She didn't waste time making the call—the temperature was well below freezing. Corney was home, testing a recipe, and said she'd love to see the tankard. Lucy was encouraged at her reaction. Not only would she learn more about the tankard, but she might be able to pick up some more information about Bitsy. Hurrying back to her warm car, Lucy glanced at the occupant of the Chevy.

He was hunched over the steering wheel and for a moment Lucy thought he might be sick. When she looked closer, however, she saw he was busily scratching away at a lottery ticket. Not a single ticket, she realized with a shock, but a stack of tickets at least an inch thick. He was so absorbed in this activity that he didn't even notice her.

Embarrassed, as if she had seen him doing something obscene, she quickly turned away and got into her own car. She started the engine and backed out too fast, skidding a bit on the icy parking lot. Regaining control of the car, she turned onto Route 1 and headed for Corney's place on Smith Heights Road, the most expensive section of Tinker's Cove, where enormous seaside mansions belonging to wealthy summer people clung to stony perches overlooking the sea.

How much did a stack of tickets like that cost, wondered Lucy as she drove along. Fifty dollars? A hundred dollars? Why would anyone spend that much money and then spend the morning sitting in a freezing parking lot? It didn't make any sense. You'd have to be crazy to do something like that. Or, she realized, possessed by an uncontrollable urge to gamble. An urge that was every bit as strong as an alcoholic's desire for a drink, or a drug addict's need for a fix.

Lucy shivered and made the turn onto Smith Heights Road. There, she was hardly warmed by the oceanfront view; cold surf was pounding the ice- and snow-covered rocks far below the road. A few black ducks were bobbing about in the waves and Lucy wondered how they could survive in such inhospitable conditions.

Corney said she wouldn't have any trouble finding the house, and she didn't. The jumbo-sized mailbox was clearly labeled "Corney Clarke Catering," but the topiary shrub in the shape of a chef was also an indication she was in the right place.

Corney's lengthy driveway was clear of snow right down to the blacktop and Lucy wondered how this was accomplished. Her own driveway contained a good deal of packed snow, despite Bill and Toby's best efforts. It had snowed practically every day since Christmas and shoveling walks and drives clear was a constant problem for most people, but apparently not for Corney.

Knocking on the door, Lucy noticed the Christmas wreath was already gone, replaced with a gilded wood pineapple. The pineapple, she knew, was a symbol of hospitality.

"Hi, Lucy, come on in," said Corney, opening the door. She was dressed in jeans and a sweater, topped with a spotless white chef's apron.

"Excuse my mess," she said, waving a hand at a breathtakingly attractive living room. Two white sofas draped with brightly colored quilts faced each other in front of a fireplace, moss green carpeting covered the floor, and brass accent pieces caught the fitful morning sunlight. The windows were filled with blooming narcissi and their sweet, heady scent filled the air. How come they didn't flop, wondered Lucy, who had started many a gravel-filled bowl of bulbs with the children. And how come they were all in bloom at the same time? All Lucy ever managed to grow were thin, straggly leaves that had to be propped up until they grudgingly produced a sickly blossom or two.

"Let's go in the kitchen," said Corney. "I'm baking and I need to keep an eye on things."

Lucy hesitated for a minute, reluctant to risk soiling Corney's floor with her boots. She needn't have worried, she realized; the hallway to the kitchen was paved with terra cotta tiles. She followed Corney on into the kitchen, where a huge, black, professional-style stove radiated a gentle warmth. A center island was covered with trays of scallop-shaped cakes and the aroma of butter and almonds was almost intoxicating.

"Boy, those smell good," said Lucy, climbing up onto an oak stool. Corney hadn't offered to take her coat, so she unzipped her parka and slipped her gloves into the pockets.

"They do, don't they?" agreed Corney, opening the oven

and extracting a baking sheet. "Everyone loves madeleines and I think they're a nice alternative to those pink-frosted cupcakes everyone makes for Valentine's Day."

"I tried them once, but they stuck to the pan," admitted Lucy, refusing to think of the sugar and candy hearts sitting in her car, destined to be made into pink-frosted cupcakes.

"You have to butter the tins generously, and be sure to flour them, too," advised Corney. She gave the sheet a quick twist, and a dozen madeleines obediently popped out of their shell-shaped depressions. Corney slid them onto an antique wire rack and then faced Lucy. "So, what brings you here? I hope you don't want to talk about Bitsy—that was too awful. The sooner I can forget, the happier I'll be."

"I won't be able to forget until we know who killed her and why," said Lucy, somewhat self-righteously. She quickly added, "But I'm not here to talk about Bitsy. I wanted to ask your opinion about a tankard I bought. It's a gift for an old friend, and I want to be sure it's a good piece. Hayden told me that you collect pewter."

"I do," said Corney, waving her hand at an English pine dresser generously filled with assorted pieces of pottery and pewter.

"That's a lovely display," said Lucy.

"People often make a mistake with pewter," said Corney. "They'll think that just because a piece dates from the eighteenth century and costs the earth, that it belongs with their fine mahogany sideboard. It doesn't, of course. Mahogany really requires silver, and it makes pewter look drab. But here with country-style pottery and baskets and pine and oak—well, I think the result speaks for itself. It's spectacular."

"So it is," said Lucy, feeling rather humble as she produced the tankard and unwrapped it for Corney's inspection.

"Isn't that cute!" exclaimed Corney, taking it and looking it over. "I hope you didn't pay too much for it."

"Fifty dollars."

She nodded. "You didn't exactly get a bargain, but you didn't get rooked, either."

"Really?" Lucy was disappointed. "Hayden thought it might be quite old."

"Oh, no," said Corney, shaking her head. Even after a morning of baking, Lucy noticed, she looked neat and fresh and when she shook her head every hair fell right back into place. "See how the bottom is smooth? That means it's something called Brittania. It was kind of a new, improved pewter that was introduced in the nineteenth century. It was lighter, and instead of using molds the craftsmen could shape it on a lathe."

"But wouldn't that have left marks?"

"You'd think so, but the opposite is true. The very old pieces, the ones made in molds, have the marks. They're also much heavier."

"I must have misunderstood Hayden," said Lucy. "I thought he told me the opposite."

"I'm sure I'm right," said Corney, with a little nod. "I know my pewter."

"I'm sure you do," said Lucy, rewrapping the tankard. She felt her stomach rumble and realized she was hungry. Her eyes were drawn to the madeleines and she ran her tongue over her lips, wishing that Corney would ask her to stay for coffee. "These look so delicious," she said. "Did you use Cousin Julia's recipe?"

"All my recipes are original," said Corney, raising her eyebrows. "Besides, how would I have your cousin's recipe?"

Lucy laughed. "That's just what I call Julia Child."

"Julia Child is your cousin?" Corney was definitely interested.

"No, no," Lucy said and shook her head. "It's kind of an inside joke. When I was first married I used the Fannie Farmer cookbook a lot, and I happened to read the introduction by Fannie Farmer's niece. In it she calls Fannie Farmer 'Aunt Fannie.' After that, I started calling the book 'Aunt Fannie.' Then, when I got my Julia Child cookbook, I started calling that book 'Cousin Julia.'" Noticing Corney's somewhat puzzled expression, Lucy finished lamely. "It's kind of stupid, I guess. In those days I hadn't done much cooking and it made me feel better to think I had a family of helpers."

"No, no. It's interesting," said Corney, who didn't sound interested at all. She started to pack the cooled madeleines in a tin lined with waxed paper.

Lucy sighed. It didn't look as if she was going to be offered a single one. "So you don't use cookbooks? All your recipes are original?" Lucy looked past Corney, at a row of strikingly beautiful amaryllis plants in full bloom that were sitting on a windowsill.

"They have to be—my reputation depends on it. I can't put someone else's recipes in my column."

"But isn't that difficult? I mean, most recipes are pretty similar. How can you come up with a new pie crust recipe, for example?"

"Oh, you add something to make it unique. A pinch of nutmeg." Corney waved her hands impatiently.

"I guess I really ought to be going," said Lucy, taking the hint and sliding off the stool. "So you start with a recipe by Aunt Fannie, but you change it a little? Is that how it works?"

"Sometimes." Corney's face was getting flushed. "Sometimes I have an idea for something new, like my Cheesy-Zucchini bread."

"But that's really just a variation, isn't it?" They were standing by the door.

"Not at all." Corney practically spit out the words as she opened the door. "It's my own recipe. It's original. Nobody else makes Cheesy-Zucchini bread."

"Okay, if you say so," said Lucy, shrugging. This didn't

seem to be the right time for a lengthy good-bye and she hurried to zip up her parka. "Well, thanks for your advice about the tankard." She gave a little wave and stepped through the doorway. The door thudded shut behind her, and the gilded pineapple rattled against the glass panes.

Lucy stood on the farmer's porch a minute to pull on her gloves. Then she walked to the car, wondering why Corney had been so brusque. You'd think the recipe police were watching what people cooked, or something. Good thing, thought Lucy as she pulled open the car door, that she hadn't told Corney about that zucchini variation for the Cheddar Cheese Bread recipe that was printed right on the cornmeal box.

But as she drove down the snow-rutted streets to the rec center, where she was due to pick up Zoe, she wondered exactly how important this question of recipe authorship really was. She had certainly touched some sort of nerve with Corney.

And what if, she wondered, Bitsy had done the same thing? After all, Bitsy knew who took what books out of the library and didn't hesitate to jump to conclusions. If Corney had borrowed some cookbooks and then used the recipes in her column, claiming them as her own . . .

Lucy braked slowly at a stop sign and carefully turned the corner, pulling up in front of the rec building. She sat for a minute, tapping the steering wheel with her gloved hand.

"What am I thinking?" she muttered to herself. "That's just crazy," she added under her breath as she unstrapped the seatbelt and climbed out of the car. After all, nobody would kill somebody over a stupid recipe.

Chapter Eleven

*The princess closed her eyes tight and kissed
the ugly frog. When she opened her eyes she
saw a handsome prince sitting in his place.*

That evening, after the kids had settled down, Lucy joined Bill in the family room where he was exploring the Internet on the computer.

"That's disgusting!" she exclaimed, when she looked over his shoulder at the image on the screen. It was a rather grainy photograph of two women and a man engaged in sexual acrobatics.

"I think it looks like something we ought to try," said Bill, clicking the mouse. A dialog box appeared, inviting him to view more exotic pictures for the "low, low price" of nineteen dollars and ninety-five cents. All he had to do was type his credit card number in the box below.

He started to reach for his wallet, prompting a cry of protest from Lucy.

"Just teasing," he said, chuckling.

"It's a good thing I'm here to keep an eye on you," she said, settling herself on his knee and stroking his beard. "I had no idea this sort of stuff was in there." She let her head fall on his shoulder. "Can the kids find this stuff?"

"Sure."

Lucy watched as another picture gradually filled in the screen. It was a photograph of a naked woman in a dog collar on her hands and knees, lapping water from a bowl.

She clicked her tongue in disgust. "This explains a lot," she said.

"What do you mean?" Bill clicked the mouse and the picture disappeared, to be replaced by one of a bare-breasted dominatrix brandishing a whip.

"I couldn't understand why some of the library board members were giving Bitsy such a hard time about going online. Now I know why—can you imagine Gerald Asquith giving the go-ahead to something like this?"

"Oh, you never know," drawled Bill, clicking the mouse again. "Maybe Gerald enjoys a good spanking."

"Bill!" Lucy gave his hand a little slap. "Maybe you're the one who needs a spanking."

"Anytime," he said, winking and adding a growl.

"But seriously," began Lucy, "isn't it funny how you think you know people but you really don't?"

"What do you mean?" Bill gave the mouse another click to shut down the computer, and it began the usual series of squeaks and groans.

"Well, I've gotten to know some of the board members a little bit better and they're not quite what I expected. Take Hayden. I'd always kind of avoided him because I wasn't all that comfortable with his lifestyle, you know, the way he lives with Ralph. But I was over there the other day and they were terrific. I really like them."

"What were you doing over there?" Bill asked suspiciously, as he reached around Lucy to turn off the power switch.

"I saw something in the shop and I stopped in to ask the price—boy, that place is expensive! Anyway, after we'd established that I couldn't possibly afford anything in the place, Hayden gave me a cup of coffee."

"Hmph."

"Stop it. They're very nice. Both of them. You'd like them, too."

"I'm sure," said Bill. "But that doesn't mean I have to approve of them."

"Whatever," said Lucy, not willing to argue. "And you know who I ran into at the food pantry? Ed Bumpus! He gave them a ton of moose meat."

"Ed's a good guy."

"Yeah, he is. What I can't figure out is why he's on the library board. He doesn't really seem like much of a reader."

"Ain't that the truth." Bill smiled. "He probably got finagled into it by somebody. He's one guy who can't say no."

"Not like Corney," mused Lucy. "She's one tough cookie."

"Really? I thought she was Ms. Bountiful, bringing the good life to one and all."

"Ms. Stingy is more like it," Lucy pouted. "I dropped in today while she was baking and she must have had hundreds of little cakes sitting there on her kitchen counter. Cooling, you know. Smelling absolutely divine. And it was getting on to lunch time and I was positively starving. I mean, actually drooling over the darned things, and do you think she gave me even one?" Lucy shook her head. "No way."

"Poor Lucy," said Bill, giving her a squeeze. "Come out to dinner with me on Valentine's Day at the Greengage Cafe and you can eat as much as you want. You can stuff yourself with crab ravioli and that terrific salad of theirs and all the tiramisu you can possibly eat."

"Are you serious?"

"Absolutely."

"Then you've got a date," said Lucy, giving him a long, lingering kiss.

* * *

The next morning, Lucy was humming as she fixed breakfast. After the kids departed, rushing out at the last minute to catch the bus, and Bill had given her a rather less perfunctory goodbye kiss than usual, she sat down at the computer.

"Mom! I want my bunny game!" complained Zoe.

"I want to check something—you can have the computer in a minute," said Lucy.

She leapfrogged her way through the World Wide Web and in a few minutes had e-mailed a message to S. Maddox Bailey, the curator of pewter at the Museum of Fine Arts in Boston. Confused by Hayden and Corney's conflicting advice about the tankard, she had decided to consult an expert.

She then played a few games of "Bunny Beware" with Zoe. She was surprised at how entertaining the game was; no wonder Zoe was addicted. After she finally won, she checked her e-mail and was disappointed to find no reply.

"I don't think this e-mail is all it's cracked up to be," she said, turning the computer over to Zoe.

Sitting down at the kitchen table, she unwrapped the tankard and examined it in the bright morning sunlight that was streaming through the windows. She could not find any evidence of finishing marks on the tankard's smooth bottom but just to be sure she used the magnifying glass she'd started keeping in the telephone book. Even then she could find no trace of any scratches.

According to Hayden, that meant the tankard was probably about the same age as Josiah's Tankard, which didn't have finishing marks, either.

Corney, on the other hand, had been quite certain that the tankard wasn't even made of pewter but of something called Brittania. How could she be so sure, Lucy wondered. That was the really irritating thing about Corney—she was such a know-it-all.

She set the tankard down on the oak table and got up to take something out of the freezer for dinner. When she turned back from the refrigerator she noticed that the kitchen was growing darker; the morning light was already being driven out by thick clouds. Her eyes fell on the tankard, and she smiled. The dimmer light suited it, she thought. It had a quiet, muted presence all its own that spoke of the long, gray winter, icy ponds, and the black, bare limbs of trees.

Corney must be wrong for once, thought Lucy. The tankard really was lovely. It would look wonderful on Miss Tilley's tavern table, filled with a few branches of winterberry. In early spring it would be perfect with pussy willow branches, then forsythia, and a bit later, lilacs. Come summer it could hold bright orange and red and yellow zinnias.

She carried it into the dining room, where she tugged open the bottom drawer of the big old pine dresser she used as a sideboard and began looking for a box and a bit of wrapping paper. There wasn't much there except for Christmas wrap; she would have to make do with plain white tissue paper.

That would be fine, she thought; somehow a gaudy pattern didn't seem quite right for Miss Tilley. Fortunately, she had saved a gift box that was just right for the tankard. She tucked it in and wrapped it, finishing the package with a narrow maroon ribbon.

Maybe it wasn't quite as fancy as something Corney would do, but it looked very nice, she thought, setting it on the table. She put away the wrapping things; it was time to think about lunch.

Passing through the family room to the kitchen she noticed Zoe had abandoned the computer; she was lining up her Barbies against the couch. Lucy gave the e-mail another try, but there was nothing.

Shivering, she checked the thermometer outside the kitchen window. Five degrees; now that the sun had disappeared the temperature was dropping. She went into the pantry for a can of soup and heard the furnace, down in the cellar, turn on.

She plopped the tomato soup into a pot and added water. As she stirred, she wondered how two experts like Corney and Hayden could have such different opinions on the tankard. Maybe Corney had been confused for some reason or other. If Josiah's Tankard didn't have finishing marks, and her tankard didn't either, they must both be about the same age.

While the soup heated, Lucy made sandwiches and poured two glasses of milk. Then she called Zoe for lunch, and ladled the soup into bowls.

"Careful, it's hot," she warned, sitting down opposite the little girl.

"I know, Mom. I'm not a baby."

"You're right, you're growing up," agreed Lucy, taking a bite of her sandwich. "What would you like to do after lunch? Do you want to invite one of your friends over to play?"

"Can I call Sadie?"

"Sure."

When they finished eating, Lucy checked the computer while Zoe made her phone call. This time, she had a response.

This is a question that I am frequently asked by beginning collectors. Oddly enough, the answer is different from what you might sensibly expect. Brittania, which is worked on a lathe, does NOT have finishing marks. Older pewter which was cast in a mold DOES have finishing marks. Hope this helps you.

So, Corney was right. She always was. Old pewter had finishing marks—that was what the curator at the museum had said. But hadn't Hayden told her that when he examined Josiah's Tankard a few months ago he had found no finishing marks?

Stunned, Lucy slid into a chair. Could that be right? Had she somehow misunderstood? No, she clearly remembered Hayden telling her that old pewter, like Josiah's Tankard, had a smooth bottom.

Lucy felt her chest tighten. This was important. She drummed her fingers on the computer table. If Hayden was right, Josiah's Tankard was a fake. It had to be a relatively modern reproduction that had been substituted for the original.

Was that why Bitsy had been killed? Lucy found herself on her feet, heading for the phone. What if Bitsy had discovered the theft? That could be the motive for her murder. She didn't even need to know that the tankard was a fake to be a danger, realized Lucy, pushing open the swinging door to the kitchen. Simply suggesting that the tankard could be sold to raise money would have put the thief in jeopardy.

After all, only a few people had access to the tankard. Once the theft was discovered it would be easy enough to figure out who had taken it.

Zoe looked up as her mother approached the telephone. "Sadie's not home," she said, shaking her head sadly and replacing the receiver on its hook.

Lucy didn't reply, but started to snatch the phone, determined to call Horowitz. Suddenly, her hand in midair, she stopped. Hayden, she thought, feeling her heart sink. Oh, no. It had to be Hayden. He had told her himself that he had been the last person to handle the tankard.

But he'd said the examination had been supervised. Miss Tilley had been there, probably a few others besides. And a policeman. Lucy gladly seized on the idea. Hayden couldn't have taken it then. He had been watched far too closely. And besides, she thought, her mind whirling, the substitution could have been made earlier.

It must have been, Lucy realized. In fact, it could have been switched anytime in the last hundred years. She heaved a great sigh of relief and started once again to pick up the phone. Just then it rang.

"Lucy—Julia here."

"Julia? Oh, Miss Tilley! I didn't recognize your voice."

"Lucy," she began, her voice more quavery than usual. "Something terrible has happened."

"Are you all right?" Lucy's first thought was that the old woman had had an accident. "Have you fallen?"

"No, no. I'm fine," Miss Tilley said, impatiently brushing away her concern. "It's the tankard. It's gone."

"Gone?"

"Gone. Stolen. When I got to the library I found the case smashed to smithereens."

"Oh, no." Lucy tried to absorb this new information. "When did this happen?"

"I don't know. I just discovered it."

"Are you in the library now?"

"Yes."

"Who's with you?"

"No one."

Lucy was suddenly fearful for her elderly friend, bird-thin and frail, possibly alone with a thief in the closed and deserted library.

"I'll be right there," she said.

Chapter Twelve

*Snow White took a bite of the poisoned
apple and fell to the ground.*

Getting right there seemed to take forever. Lucy had to pry Zoe away from her Barbies and hustle her into her outdoor clothes. Then she had to throw on her own parka and boots, and scrape the ice-covered windshield of the car. All the time she was busy with these frustrating details, she was distracted, worrying about Miss Tilley. What if the thief was still in the library? And why had she called her—why hadn't she called the police?

When Lucy finally pulled up in front of the library, she automatically began to unstrap Zoe from her booster seat. Then she stopped and refastened the seatbelt. There was no way she was going to take her little girl into a potentially dangerous situation.

"I'm just going to run in for a minute," she told Zoe. "Don't you dare move, okay?"

"Okay, Mommy." Zoe's eyes were big and round; like a little fawn, she was alert to her mother's unease.

"I'll be right back," promised Lucy, closing the car door and locking it.

She dashed up the library steps, observing the fact that the big oak door showed no sign of a break-in. But when she entered the vestibule, she couldn't help gasping when she saw the smashed glass case. The recessed alcove that had contained Josiah's Tankard was now empty, filled only with a few shards of broken glass.

Proceeding on into the library proper, Lucy found Miss Tilley sitting glumly at the circulation desk.

"Have you called the police?" asked Lucy.

"Of course," snapped Miss Tilley. "What do you take me for? An idiot?"

"Why aren't they here?"

"I don't know. They said there was some sort of emergency and they'd get here as soon as they could. You got here pretty quickly—I hope someone is keeping an eye on that sweet little girl of yours."

"Actually, I left her in the car," said Lucy.

"You did? What were you thinking? Go and get her immediately!"

"I thought you might be in some sort of danger," said Lucy, defending her actions. "I thought she'd be safer in the car."

"Well, there's no danger here. I wouldn't have called you except for the fact that they're taking so long to get here. I was getting bored."

"I see that," said Lucy, biting her tongue. "I'll go and get Zoe now."

As she hurried back to the car, Lucy figured it must have taken her at least twenty minutes to reach the library. That was a long time to wait for help, considering that the police station was just around the corner. What could have happened, that they couldn't have responded more quickly?

Taking Zoe by the hand, Lucy hurried back up the steps. In the vestibule, the little girl planted her feet, stopping suddenly.

"It's broken," she said, pointing at the glass case with her pink mittened hand.

"I know. A bad person broke it and took what was inside."

"A bad boy?"

"Maybe," said Lucy, unable to resist smiling. "We don't know who did it."

Lucy pushed open the interior doors.

"That's my girl," cooed Miss Tilley. "If you pick out a book, I'll read it to you."

"Go ahead," said Lucy, giving her an encouraging shove in the direction of the children's section. "I wonder what's holding up the police?" she said, turning toward Miss Tilley.

"That's what I'd like to know," fumed Miss Tilley.

Lucy had expected her old friend to be distraught and upset, perhaps even ill with shock, but Miss Tilley seemed to be just plain mad. Her jaw was set and her teeth were clenched, and she was drumming impatiently on the desk with her knobby, blue-veined hand.

"When did you discover the theft?" asked Lucy, unzipping her parka.

"When I got here this morning—it must have been about eleven-thirty. We finally got permission from the police to reopen—it certainly took them long enough to look for that gun or whatever they were doing in here. I called Gerald this morning and he told me." The old woman cackled. "I don't think he was planning on calling me. He made a great point of telling me that I didn't need to concern myself about the library and he had found a temporary librarian. Well, I wanted to make sure the police had left things in good order. I had planned to do some errands with Rachel anyway, so I had her drop me off here and she went on to the IGA.

"Of course, I noticed the theft as soon as I opened the door. I tried to call her back but she had already gone. So I called the police. And you."

Lucy reached out and patted her hand. "I'm glad you called me. I know this must be very upsetting for you."

"Of course it is." Miss Tilley's expression seemed to imply that Lucy was mentally deficient. "I feel a great responsibility for the safety of the tankard. It represents the history of our town."

Lucy decided to keep her suspicion that the tankard was not genuine to herself for the time being. "It seems an odd thing to steal," observed Lucy. "Is it worth a lot?"

"Similar tankards have gone for twenty-five thousand or more at auction," said Miss Tilley. "But I don't imagine it's the sort of thing you can get quick cash for like a TV or a computer or something like that."

"That's true," agreed Lucy, a little surprised at her old friend's understanding of criminal behavior. "Can I make you some tea or something?"

"Might as well. It doesn't seem as if the police are in any hurry." Miss Tilley was beaming at Zoe, who was climbing up onto a chair beside her. "You picked one of my favorites, you clever girl . . . *Blueberries for Sal*."

Lucy went off to Bitsy's office to heat up some water and when she returned with two steaming mugs she found that Lieutenant Horowitz had arrived. Much to her surprise he had only one officer in tow, and was unaccompanied by the usual crowd of crime scene technicians. He was carrying a small bundle and placed it in front of Miss Tilley.

"I think we've solved your robbery," he said. "Would you take a look at this and identify it if you can?"

Miss Tilley unwrapped the brown paper bag with trembling hands and drew out a tankard encased in a plastic bag. "This is Josiah's Tankard," she said, emitting a shaky sigh of relief. "This is wonderful. I can't tell you how pleased I am."

Lucy gave her a big smile and a hug. "Do you mind if I look at it? I've never seen it up close."

Receiving a nod of permission from Miss Tilley, Lucy

picked up the tankard and placed it under the desk lamp. Examining it through the clear plastic, Lucy could see the primitive design of the tree and bird, and the crude date and letters. The tankard appeared to be authentic, but when Lucy examined the bottom she found it was smooth, just like the tankard she had bought. It also seemed lighter than she would have expected, given the shape and size of the piece. "It's lovely," she said, handing it back to Miss Tilley.

"Well, that's that," said Horowitz. "Crime solved."

Just then the double doors burst open and Rachel rushed in, breathless from running up the stairs.

"What's going on?" she demanded, panting to catch her breath. "I saw the police car outside . . . and the broken glass . . ."

"Everything's under control," Lieutenant Horowitz informed her.

"The tankard was stolen," added Lucy.

"But it's been recovered," concluded Miss Tilley, giving the tankard a proprietary little pat.

"Well then, if the lieutenant has no objections, I think I ought to get you home," Rachel told Miss Tilley. "You've had quite a morning."

"No objections," said Horowitz, as Rachel helped Miss Tilley to her feet. "We have to keep the tankard for evidence for the time being, but I give you my personal promise that it will be returned to the library as soon as possible."

"I understand," agreed Miss Tilley, slipping her arms into the sleeves of the coat Rachel was holding for her. "Besides, it wouldn't be safe here until we have repaired the case."

She then took the younger woman's arm and made her shaky way to the door. The morning had definitely taken a toll on her, thought Lucy.

But when she removed her coat and Zoe's from the coat rack, preparing to leave, Horowitz stopped her.

"I'd like a word with you, Mrs. Stone," he said, causing Miss Tilley and Rachel to glance at her curiously.

"I'm afraid you can't stay here," said Miss Tilley. "I have to lock up."

"You can just give the key to me," said Horowitz.

"I'm afraid that won't do," said Miss Tilley, standing her ground. "I am responsible for locking the library."

"All right," said Horowitz, taking Lucy's elbow and steering her through the doorway. He stopped on the steps and they waited while Miss Tilley locked the door with trembling hands. He gave the officer a nod, and the young trooper gave Miss Tilley his arm. Slowly, the trio descended the steps toward Rachel's car.

A gust of wind hit them and Zoe huddled close to her mother, wrapping her arms around Lucy's hips. Lucy shivered and turned up her collar, waiting for Horowitz to speak. She sensed from the way he was tapping his foot on the stone step while he waited for Miss Tilley to get out of earshot that he was angry with her but she didn't understand why.

"I warned you not to mess around in this investigation," he began, glaring at her.

"I haven't been," said Lucy, her eyes opening wide with surprise. "Really."

He waved the plastic-wrapped tankard at her. "So why were you asking Hayden Northcross about this?"

"I was only asking his advice. I wanted to buy a tankard as a gift for Miss Tilley."

"And was he helpful?"

"Not really. He gave me the wrong information." Lucy paused. "That's not the real Josiah's Tankard."

"What?" Horowitz looked at her skeptically.

"It's a fake."

"Hayden told you that?"

"No, but he was wrong." said Lucy, struggling to keep her teeth from chattering in the cold. "It doesn't have any finishing marks on the bottom."

"That means it's a fake?"

"According to the curator of pewter at the Museum of Fine Arts."

"This is very interesting," said Horowitz. His breath made a cloud in front of his face.

"I think this might have something to do with Bitsy's murder," suggested Lucy, wrapping her arms around Zoe.

"Oh, yes. Yes, it does." Horowitz was rapidly tapping his foot.

"Well, I don't know anything about that," said Lucy, defending herself. "I was only trying to find out if a little tankard I bought in a junk shop was worth anything."

"And was it?"

"No." Lucy shook her head and picked up Zoe, hugging her tightly. "Just about what I paid for it."

"Not like this one. It may be a fake, but it cost two people's lives."

"Two lives?" Lucy's face was white. "Bitsy and who?"

"Hayden Northcross. He shot himself this morning."

"Oh, no!"

"It looks like he murdered Bitsy. The suicide gun is the same caliber as the murder weapon but we still have to test it to be sure."

"Oh, my God. Hayden. I can't believe it," said Lucy. Zoe was suddenly very heavy in her arms and she let her slide back down to the ground.

"I'm guessing he switched the tankards a while ago. Something like that isn't easy to fence, but as an antiques dealer he was in the perfect position to sell it."

"He told me he was asked to examine it a few months ago." Lucy's voice was flat and expressionless. She didn't want to believe her earlier suspicions about Hayden were true.

"He may have taken it then. Or earlier. It doesn't matter. I think Bitsy discovered the switch, and that's why he killed her. Then you come along, asking questions about tankards and he panics and offs himself."

"Are you saying he killed himself because of me?" Lucy was astonished.

"I am." Horowitz nodded his head sharply and glared at her. "If you hadn't gone around asking questions you had no business asking, he'd be alive today and I'd have Bitsy's murderer instead of a whole lot of guesses and suppositions and a case that will never be closed."

"I had no idea . . ."

"That's right. You have no idea. You just go poking around, sticking your nose in places you have no business. Well, I'm warning you. The next time you start messing around in one of my investigations I won't hesitate to slap you with charges of obstruction. So from now on you better just mind your own business, okay? And as for your suspicions about that tankard you'd better keep them to yourself. Understand?"

Horowitz was angry, but his gray face didn't pick up any color. The long lines between his nose and mouth simply hardened, like fast-setting concrete.

"Okay," said Lucy meekly.

She watched as Horowitz snatched the tankard and marched down the steps and climbed into the cruiser, giving the officer behind the wheel a nod. He accelerated, driving off in a cloud of exhaust vapor.

"I'm cold, Mommy," whined Zoe. "Let's go."

Moving on automatic pilot, Lucy descended the steps, carefully holding Zoe's hand so she wouldn't slip on the ice. She helped her get settled in the booster and then climbed into the driver's seat, turning on the ignition and pushing the heat to high.

She didn't put the car into gear, though; she just sat there, sorting through her emotions. Hayden was dead. It was all wrong. He wouldn't have killed himself, and he certainly wouldn't have killed Bitsy.

She felt a surge of anger. How could Horowitz accuse her of driving Hayden to kill himself? She hadn't had anything to do with it. Or had she? A sense of guilt stole over her. Maybe she had blundered onto something, asking questions about the tankard. Clutching the steering wheel, she rested her forehead on her hands.

"Mommy! Let's go!" demanded Zoe from the back seat.

She was right, thought Lucy. This wasn't accomplishing anything.

"In a minute," she said, rummaging in her shoulder bag for the cell phone she carried in case of emergencies. She punched in the number for *The Pennysaver* office.

"Ted? It's Lucy."

"Hi, Lucy. You got that story on gambling for me?"

"Uh, no," said Lucy. "I do have something, though. Have you heard about Hayden?"

"Hayden Northcross? No. What?"

"He's killed himself."

"No way—are you sure of this?"

"Horowitz just told me."

"Thanks, Lucy. I'll get right on it."

Lucy pushed the button to end the call and replaced the phone. Then she pulled away from the curb, not quite sure where she was going.

Lucy took Zoe to McDonald's, partly to reward her for being such a good girl all morning and partly because she didn't want to go home. The bright colors and shiny surfaces of the fast-food restaurant seemed preferable to the quiet house.

Zoe chomped on her cookies and slurped down a cup of hot chocolate, but Lucy found that once she had her apple pie she couldn't eat it. She sipped her coffee instead, trying to put the morning's events in perspective.

Hayden was dead. She still couldn't believe it. She didn't want to believe it. She liked Hayden. She wouldn't have hurt him for the world. She felt a flush of anger and resentment against Horowitz. How could he think she would have pushed Hayden into a corner, leaving him no option but suicide?

And she didn't believe for one minute that Hayden had killed Bitsy. After all, he had genuinely seemed to like her. Lucy ran a finger up and down the side of her coffee cup. This just didn't add up. After seeing Hayden and Ralph together, she was convinced Hayden would never have killed himself. Through the years she had learned something about human relationships, and she would have bet the house that they were truly devoted to each other. Horowitz was definitely on the wrong track.

She turned the empty Styrofoam cup in circles on the Formica table and watched Zoe pop the last cookie into her mouth. More than anything she wanted to get to the bottom of this and Horowitz wasn't going to stop her. She wanted to know who killed Bitsy, and Hayden. Because the more she thought about it, the surer she was that Hayden hadn't killed anyone. Not Bitsy, and not himself.

Noticing that Zoe was finished, Lucy crumpled up the food wrappers and squeezed them into a tight ball. Then, rebelliously leaving the tray on the table instead of carrying it over to the trash container, she took Zoe's hand and led her to the car.

Chapter Thirteen

The Seven Dwarves placed Snow White's body
in a glass casket and covered it with flowers.

The reference room was the same as always. The rich patina of the pine paneling glowed softly in the light of the wall sconces, the portrait of Henry Hopkins glowered down from above the unused fireplace, and the big oak table and captain's chairs were in their usual place. But the group of directors gathered at an emergency meeting the next morning were stunned and shocked.

Or doing a good job of appearing that way, thought Lucy, as she studied the faces of her fellow directors.

"First Bitsy and now Hayden," said Corney. "I can hardly believe it."

"When I heard the news on my car radio last night I nearly went off the road," said Chuck. He shook his head slowly. "I just don't understand it."

Lucy wished she knew a little more about Chuck. He seemed like such a nice guy; she wondered if he really was.

Corney certainly thought he was. She had reached across the table and was giving his arm a consolatory squeeze. Her expression was one of sincere sympathy. Oh please, thought Lucy.

"It's most distressing," agreed Miss Tilley in a matter-of-fact tone. "But at least the tankard has been recovered."

That damn tankard, it seemed to Lucy as she studied the old woman's face, was far more important to Miss Tilley than Bitsy and Hayden's lives.

"He was always an odd duck, if you get my drift," said Ed, hoisting one of his bristly gray eyebrows and twisting his mouth into a leer. He was nervously jiggling his leg and fidgeting with his big, callused hands. He looked around abruptly. "Where the hell's Gerald? I don't have all morning, you know. I've got work to do."

"He's making copies," volunteered Lucy. She'd liked Ed when she ran into him at the food pantry but today she wanted to scream at him, telling him to get out and leave the meeting if he had such important business. She didn't want to hear his nasty innuendos about Hayden, or his sexist comments about Bitsy. They were dead and they deserved a minimum of respect and a few minutes of his time. She didn't say anything, however, but sat quietly, twisting her wedding ring round and round her finger. She looked up when Gerald bustled into the room and began distributing copies of the agenda.

"I guess you've all heard the news," he began. "Our fellow director, Hayden Northcross, took his own life yesterday. I spoke with the police officer in charge of the investigation, Lieutenant Horowitz, and he told me that he believes Hayden was responsible for Bitsy's murder, also." His voice faltered, but he cleared his throat and continued. "Apparently overcome by remorse, he committed suicide."

For what seemed to be a very long time, no one said anything. The directors' eyes were downcast; they all appeared to be studying their agendas intently. Finally, Corney broke the silence.

"Hayden killed Bitsy?" she asked. "That's incredible."

"Did the lieutenant give you any idea *why* he killed Bitsy?" asked Chuck.

"No." Gerald sighed. "He wouldn't give me any details, just told me that as far as he is concerned the case is closed."

There seemed to be a lessening of tension in the room, thought Lucy, as if a general sigh of relief had been expressed.

"I don't suppose we'll ever know," volunteered Ed. "So let's get on to item two, if you don't mind."

"I mind," said Lucy, surprised to hear her own voice. "Two people are dead, two people who cared about this library. Aren't we going to do something in their memory?"

"Absolutely." Gerald nodded. "I'm open to any suggestions you may have."

"The obvious thing would be to name the new wing after them. We could announce it at the dedication ceremony," offered Lucy.

"That could turn out to be embarrassing," cautioned Chuck. "After all, we don't know all the details yet."

"I quite agree," said Miss Tilley in a firm voice. "I understand Bitsy's family is planning a memorial service in Massapequa. I suggest we send flowers. I don't know if plans have been made yet for a service for Hayden, but we could also send flowers when it is announced."

"I think that's the best course of action, at least for the time being," said Gerald. He looked around the table and everyone nodded agreement.

"Now that that's out of the way, can we move on?" demanded Ed.

Gerald looked at him sharply, then consulted his agenda. "The next order of business is the reopening of the library. I would like to propose we hire Eunice Sparks as interim librarian—I have her résumé here and, as you can see, she is well-qualified and I can personally recommend her. She can start immediately, and I propose we reopen on Monday."

Gerald passed out copies of the résumé and the directors bent their heads over them.

"There's no question that she's a qualified librarian," observed Miss Tilley. "However, in a situation like this it might be preferable to have someone who is familiar with our library. I would be more than happy to serve in the interim, on a volunteer basis."

"We certainly appreciate your offer," said Gerald, quickly. "However, it would not be fair to take advantage of your generosity. You are far too valuable to the library as a member of the board, and as you know, it is against our policy to include employees as board members." He had expected this reaction from Miss Tilley and had prepared for it, realized Lucy, impressed despite herself.

Heads bobbed around the table; the others were relieved to have this matter dealt with so neatly. Ed shifted restlessly in his seat.

"There is just one remaining matter and then I'll adjourn the meeting," said Gerald. "We now have a vacancy on the board, and we also need to find a permanent librarian. We already have a nominating committee to suggest new board members—it includes me, Chuck and," here he paused before adding, "Hayden."

"I'll take his place," offered Lucy.

"Any objections?" Gerald looked around the table. "Very well then."

"I'll head the search committee for a new librarian," volunteered Chuck.

Predictably, Corney also volunteered.

"I suggest Miss Tilley," said Ed. "She knows the job better than anyone."

"That's settled then," said Gerald, bringing down his gavel.

But he was wrong, thought Lucy, as she buttoned her coat. Nothing was settled at all.

Chapter Fourteen

*Then one day, Bambi's mother told him that
hunters had come to the forest.*

After the meeting Lucy hurried out to her car. She
had no inclination to linger and chat with the
other board members. She no longer felt comfortable in
the library; she just wanted to get away. When she pulled
open the door to the car, yanking hard because it was stiff
in the cold, she spotted a foil-wrapped package she had
left on the back seat and paused.

With a sinking heart she remembered she had another errand—she had planned to make a condolence call at
Ralph's, bringing a sour cream coffee cake she had baked
especially for him.

She was tempted to skip it but her conscience got the better of her and she drove across town to the house he had
shared with Hayden. She paused before knocking on the
door, wondering briefly if she could just leave the cake. Instead, she raised the knocker and pounded it home. It was an
ornate knocker, hanging on one of a pair of carved oak
doors, with huge black wrought-iron hinges and a dangling
iron circle instead of a traditional doorknob. That was be-

cause Ralph and Hayden had converted a church, abandoned when the Methodists joined the Congregationalists to create the Tinker's Cove Community Church, into a home.

Hearing the click of the lock being unlatched, Lucy braced herself to face Ralph. Even so, she was shocked when the door finally opened, revealing his ravaged face. The dark shock of hair that had reminded her so much of the young Gregory Peck hung limp and greasy today and there were deep hollows under his cheekbones.

"I wanted you to know how sorry I am about Hayden," Lucy began. "I baked this coffee cake for you."

"Thanks." Ralph took the foil-wrapped package and stood looking at it. "Would you like some coffee?" he finally asked. "I know I should eat but I can't face sitting at the table alone."

"Of course," said Lucy, swallowing hard. It would be easy enough to make an excuse and flee back to the comfort and security of home, but that would mean abandoning Ralph to his grief and loneliness. "I'd love some coffee," she said.

Ralph led her through the spacious living room, formerly the sanctuary of the church, which was now furnished with Victorian sofas and Oriental carpets. They went downstairs, where the old church hall now served as an elegant dining room and the spacious kitchen had been modernized with top-of-the-line appliances and cabinets. While Ralph filled the coffee pot, Lucy sat herself at the huge antique refectory table and sliced the cake.

"This is good," said Ralph, taking a huge bite and showering brown sugar and nuts onto the table. Embarrassed, he brushed them away. "I haven't eaten much, lately."

"I wanted to make popovers for you—I remembered you saying how much you like them—but they didn't come out."

He nodded. "That happened to Hayden, too, until he started using four eggs." He sighed, and his voice quavered. "He swore by the *Moosewood Cookbook*."

"That must have been it," said Lucy, content to talk about comforting trivialities. "I only used two. Fannie Farmer can be a bit stingy with eggs."

"Yankee thrift." He swallowed hard. "We used to argue about it. I said it was a result of the rocky soil and the hard climate. Hayden said it was just meanness of spirit."

"There was nothing mean about Hayden—he had a generous spirit," said Lucy, accepting a cup of fragrant Kenyan blend. "It must have been an awful shock."

"It was—it still is," said Ralph, sitting down opposite her and spooning sugar into his cup. "I know he's gone—there's no doubt about that—but somehow I can't believe it. I keep expecting him to walk in and say it was all a mistake."

"That's natural. Everybody feels like that. It's unthinkable, so it can't be true." She reached out and patted his hand. "After a while, when you feel up to it, maybe you could try one of those support groups that help you cope with loss."

Ralph snatched his hand away. "I don't know how welcome I'd be, given the circumstances." He paused. "I think I have to do this my own way."

Lucy chewed her cake thoughtfully. He was right, of course. As a homosexual grieving the loss of a same-sex partner, he would certainly be the odd man out with the widows and widowers. "It must be terrible," she said, thinking of how lost she would be without Bill.

"It is. It's indescribable. It hurts physically, you know. I feel like I've been hit by a truck and had my insides ripped out. Even breathing hurts. And the worst part is what the police said. That he killed himself. That he killed Bitsy. That can't be true."

Lucy looked around the kitchen, the kitchen that had been Hayden's. Gleaming copper pots hung from a rack above the stove. A row of potted herbs stood on the windowsill above the sink. Cookbooks were tucked away, yet ready at hand, in a shelf built into the work island. It was so like Hayden, she thought. Simple. Attractive. Practical.

"I don't think anybody who knew him believes the police theory," said Lucy.

"I'll never believe he would hurt Bitsy," insisted Ralph. "He'd never hurt anybody—especially not me. We had all kinds of plans for the future—we'd just bought tickets for a cruise next month. Not to mention the plans we had for the business, and the house. We were going to set up a website and buy new carpet and redo the bathroom. Someone who's going to kill himself doesn't sit up half the night looking at wallpaper books, does he?"

"I don't think so," said Lucy.

"And that business about stealing the tankard—that's nonsense. He wouldn't do that—he has . . ." Ralph's voice broke as he corrected himself. "He *had* too much respect for antiques. They were his life. He would never do something like that." He shrugged. "He didn't need to. The business is successful—we were making plenty, believe me."

"What do you think happened?"

"I don't know." He ran his fingers through his hair and propped his elbow on the table, resting his head on his hand. "I think it had something to do with the library. First Bitsy and now him." He picked at a crumb of brown sugar. "I should never have gone away that day—I blame myself. We were both going to go to an estate sale in Lewiston, but he said he had some library business he had to clear up. Told me to go to the sale without him. 'Make a killing' he said. Those were his last words to me."

Lucy felt rotten when she left Ralph. She felt completely inadequate in the face of such raw grief. As a mother, she was used to patching up boo-boos with Band-Aids, giving a kiss and making it all better. There was nothing she could do to help Ralph—her healing powers could not cure his pain.

"What's the matter, Lucy? You look as if you lost your best friend!" exclaimed Sue, who was just leaving the recreation building when Lucy arrived to pick up Zoe.

"I just took a cake to Ralph," explained Lucy. "He's having a real hard time."

Sue was serious. "We're all going to miss Hayden. He was some character." She sighed. "I was going to ask his advice about slipcovering the couch. I was going to have him over for lunch one day—he was always fun, and he would have had some terrific ideas." She tucked her glossy black hair behind her ear. "Say, do you have any plans for lunch today?"

"Nothing beyond peanut butter and jelly and chicken noodle soup," admitted Lucy.

"Come on over to my house. We can cheer each other up."

"Thanks," said Lucy, smiling for the first time that day. "I'll get Zoe and I'll be right over."

Sitting at the table in Sue's gleaming, streamlined kitchen, Lucy thought how nice it was that she and Sue were able to spend more time together. After Sue had started the day-care program in the community center she had been working full-time, determined to make the project a success. Thanks to her determination and hard work, skeptical town meeting voters were now convinced of the once controversial center's value, and generally approved annual funding without a murmur of opposition. Now convinced that the center's future was secure, Sue had recently cut back her hours and only worked mornings.

"I want to have some time for myself," she had told Lucy. "I want to be able to take a walk, or curl up with a good book, or take an afternoon nap. That's not a crime, is it?"

"Certainly not," agreed Lucy, who had fallen into the habit when the children were little and always seemed to find herself growing sleepy after lunch.

"So, tell me what you think about these sudden deaths," said Sue, interrupting her thoughts and giving her a handful of silverware to set the table. Zoe was happily ensconced in the living room with a sandwich and a pile of carrot sticks, watching a Disney video.

"I don't know what I think," confessed Lucy. "The police theory is that Hayden stole the tankard some time ago and replaced it with a fake. Bitsy discovered the substitution and confronted him and he killed her. Overcome with remorse, he killed himself."

"But you don't believe that," said Sue, tucking a covered dish into the microwave.

Lucy thoughtfully laid a fork down on the table. "No. You knew Hayden better than I did. Do you think he was a thief? That he would murder Bitsy? I just can't believe it."

"Me, either," agreed Sue, ripping apart a head of lettuce to make a salad.

"I do think this all has something to do with the tankard." Lucy folded a napkin and placed it on the table. "I think whoever stole the tankard killed Bitsy and framed Hayden."

Sue sliced a radish into neat circles. "But wasn't the tankard found with Hayden's body?"

"It's fake," said Lucy, opening the cupboard and taking out two plates.

"So the real one is still missing?" Sue's voice was muffled; she'd stuck her head in the refrigerator.

"I just hate myself for thinking this but it must be one of the directors," blurted Lucy. She paused, remembering how flattered she had been to be asked to join the board and how she had agonized over what to wear to her first meeting. "That probably sounds ridiculous—they're all such respectable, hard-working, civic-minded people."

"Oh, I don't know about that, Lucy," said Sue, setting the salad bowl on the table. Hearing the microwave ding, she turned away. "They always seemed like a pretty difficult bunch to me. Bitsy was always complaining about them."

"Miss Tilley certainly didn't like her much," volunteered Lucy.

"Yeah, but she's a little old to be a murderer."

Sue set the casserole on the table and lifted the cover, releasing a wonderful herb-filled fragrance.

"That smells delicious," exclaimed Lucy. "What is it?"

"Cassoulet." Sue was smug.

"Wow. Isn't that hard to make?"

"It is complicated, but now that I have more time, I enjoy cooking things that are a little special."

"It's great," said Lucy, her mouth full of beans and sausage. "Perfect for a cold winter day."

Sue sat down and filled her plate. "If you think about it, none of those directors are exactly paragons of virtue. Take Chuck, for example. He's quite a ladies' man, at least that's what I hear. What if he had some kind of relationship with Bitsy? He wants out, she doesn't. It could get messy. Or Corney? Bitsy knew that her so-called original recipes weren't original at all. They came from cookbooks in the library—at least that's what I've heard."

"Face it—you'd love it to be Corney," said Lucy.

"You're right," agreed Sue, taking a bite of salad. "I hate that column of hers. It just infuriates me, the way she latches onto something and pretends she thought it up in the first place. Like at Christmas, she was writing about Yorkshire pudding as if she invented it." She paused to chew. "Gosh, my grandmother made Yorkshire pudding every year for Christmas, my mother made it, and I make it. We were making it for years before Corney ever heard of it."

"Golly, I guess I touched a nerve here," said Lucy, smiling. She glanced around Sue's stripped-down kitchen, which had evolved during the years she was working so hard at the center. The charming clutter of collectables was gone; it was now an efficient meal-preparation center. "I think you're just jealous."

Sue snorted. "Trust me. There's some sort of deep, dark,

disgusting secret there. Nobody is as perfect as Corney pretends to be." She paused, helping herself to seconds of cassoulet. "And she's not the only one. Take Ed, for example. Sid had quite a laugh about that. Said the board would pick the one contractor in town who had a reputation for shoddy construction." Sid was Sue's husband.

"Bill says people are always saying things like that about contractors and it's hardly ever true," said Lucy, loyally defending her husband's chosen trade. "Besides, that new addition speaks for itself. It's beautiful, and it doesn't detract from the original building. That's a hard trick to pull off, believe me."

"Okay," said Sue, amused at her reaction. "But there's still what's-his-name, the college president."

"Gerald?" Lucy asked in surprise.

"Yeah, Gerald. Newly retired from a prestigious job—that can be a very stressful time. All of a sudden he's got a lot of time on his hands. People aren't jumping to answer his every beck and call. It's something to think about."

"Gerald's above reproach," insisted Lucy. "Everybody knows that."

"Those are the worst kind," said Sue, smiling as Zoe came into the room. "Is the movie over already?"

"No." She shook her head sadly. "Bambi's mother died."

"That's a sad part." Sue was sympathetic. "Tell you what. The movie gets better. How about if I come and watch it with you? You can sit in my lap—would you like that?"

Zoe nodded.

"Okay." Sue got up and took the little girl's hand. "We'll let your mom clean up the lunch dishes, okay?"

"That's not fair!" protested Lucy, pretending to be outraged.

Zoe giggled.

"Don't make too much noise with those dishes," advised Sue. "We want to hear the movie and we don't want to be disturbed. Isn't that right, Zoe?"

"Right!" agreed Zoe, delighted to be telling her mother what to do.

"Well, I guess I'd better get to work then," Lucy said, her voice resigned. Actually, she didn't mind clearing up one bit; she enjoyed the way Zoe and Sue delighted in each other's company.

She scraped the few dishes and gave them a quick rinse, preparing to load them into the dishwasher. Moving automatically, she was wondering how long ago Josiah's Tankard was stolen. Perhaps there were photographs that could establish when the substitution was made.

She opened the dishwasher door and pulled out the wire rack, preparing to load it, but the subtle gleam of a piece of pewter caught her eye. She picked the piece up and held it in front of the window, amazed. It was a perfect copy of Josiah's Tankard, except for the fact that the bird in a bush design had been replaced with the seal of Winchester College.

"Sue!" she yelled, hurrying into the TV room. "Where did you get this?"

Sue looked up from the couch, where she was snuggling with Zoe. "What? That? We've had it forever."

"But where did you get it? When did you get it?"

"Calm down, Lucy. It's not original."

"I know that—it's got the Winchester College seal, for one thing."

"Right. That's it. They made them when the college had its centennial. Sid was doing some work over there, and they gave him one. They were giving them out to everybody."

"What year was that?"

"It was a long time ago—is there something on the tankard?"

Lucy looked closely at the seal on the tankard, and made out the numbers. "It says 1878. That means the centennial was 1978—just before Bill and I moved here."

"That sounds about right," agreed Sue. "But I don't see

why this is so important. I bet most houses in Tinker's Cove have at least one of these things."

"I didn't know that," said Lucy. "Don't you see? This must be how the switch was made. It wouldn't be very hard to get rid of this seal—it's stamped very lightly."

Sue nodded. "It would be easy enough to copy the design from Josiah's Tankard—it was made with a punch. All you'd need is a tenpenny nail and a hammer."

"That's one mystery solved," said Lucy, giving the tankard a little pat.

"Yeah—but I don't think it's going to be much help," said Sue, sitting back down on the couch beside Zoe. "Now you've got a whole town full of suspects."

"You're right." Lucy sat down in the rocking chair and glumly studied the tankard. "You know," she finally said, "the more I find out about this mess, the less I seem to know."

Chapter Fifteen

*The littlest Billy Goat Gruff was afraid of
the troll who dwelled beneath the bridge.*

On the way home, Lucy stopped at the Quik-Stop to
pick up a gallon of milk. Much to Zoe's disappointment, she left her in the car. If she allowed her in the store,
the little girl would insist on choosing a treat and Lucy had
no intention of getting involved in the endless negotiations
such a purchase required. Besides, she could keep an eye on
her through the store window.

In the parking lot, she noticed with disapproval the familiar litter of lottery tickets. Guiltily, she thought of the story
she was supposed to be writing for *The Pennysaver.* She had
to get it finished; Ted was expecting it in two days, on Friday.

Lucy yanked open the door, intent on dashing over to the
dairy case and getting out of the store and back to the car as
quickly as possible. Instead, she ran right into Gerald
Asquith, trim and distinguished as ever in his camel hair
coat.

"I'm sorry!" exclaimed Lucy, growing rather red in the
face. "I wasn't watching where I was going."

"Lost in thought, no doubt, thinking about your next writing project," he said, smiling down at her benignly. "No harm done, I assure you."

"I'm glad I ran into you, no pun intended," began Lucy, with an apologetic little smile. "There are a couple of things about the library that I'd like to discuss with you."

Actually, Lucy wanted to find out more about those Winchester College tankards, but didn't want to come right out and say so.

"I can certainly understand that," said Gerald. "You must be wondering why you ever agreed to join the board. I hope you're not thinking of resigning."

"Oh, I wouldn't do that. After all, I just agreed to join the nominating committee. In fact," she continued, improvising, "that's what I'd like to talk about with you."

"Well, why don't we get together for an hour or so?" He withdrew a leather-covered calendar from his breast pocket and opened it. "I'm free tomorrow morning. How would that be?"

"Fine," said Lucy, a little surprised at his promptness. He seemed almost eager to schedule the meeting. "About ten?"

"Ten's fine. Now where shall we meet? Would you like to go someplace for coffee?"

Lucy was flummoxed. She really wanted to get a peek at his house in hopes of learning a little more about him. The way things were going, she wanted to know as much as possible about her fellow board members.

"Oh," she sighed. "I'm trying to lose a few pounds—I'm afraid I gained some weight over the holidays. But I have no will power at all, so I've been avoiding coffee shops." She lowered her eyes as if sharing a shameful secret. "I can't resist the muffins—especially the chocolate chip ones."

He responded just as she hoped he would and chuckled indulgently. "Well, we can't expose you to temptation, can we? How about my house—I have an office there."

"That's fine. I'll see you at ten." agreed Lucy.

As he turned to push open the door, she added, "And remember—no muffins!"

He turned back, gave her the high sign, and left.

Lucy looked past him, checking that Zoe was behaving herself, and was relieved to see the little girl was sitting quietly in her regulation car seat, no doubt hoping that her good behavior would be noticed and rewarded. Finally completing her errand, Lucy joined her a minute later.

"Did you get me something?" Zoe's voice was hopeful.

"I sure did," said Lucy, handing her a foil-covered chocolate heart. "That took longer than I thought it would, but you waited very patiently."

"Thank you," said Zoe, taking the candy and unwrapping it. "Who was the man?"

"Mr. Asquith, from the library."

As Lucy started the car and slipped it into gear, her thoughts returned to the murders. That's how she thought of them—murders. After talking to Ralph and Sue she was more than ever convinced that Hayden had not committed suicide but had been killed, most likely by the same person who killed Bitsy.

Horowitz thought he had the case all wrapped up—Bitsy was murdered by Hayden because she somehow discovered the theft of the tankard. Fearing discovery when Lucy began inquiring about the tankard, Hayden had killed himself. It was all nonsense, of course, just like his allegation that she had been instrumental in Hayden's decision to kill himself. It was so unfair. So frustrating. And worst of all, Horowitz would consider the case closed and the real murderer might never be discovered.

She glanced in the rearview mirror, checking on Zoe. The little girl was chewing contentedly, studying the bright red wrapper. Returning her eyes to the road, Lucy noticed that snowflakes were starting to hit the windshield.

"Uh-oh," she said out loud. "I think it's starting to snow again."

"Yay!" exclaimed Zoe, kicking her heels against the seat.

Lucy couldn't quite share her daughter's enthusiasm. "Haven't you had enough snow yet this winter?" she asked.

"Nope." Zoe shook her head. "I like snow."

"Well, maybe we won't get too much," said Lucy hopefully, thinking aloud. If this turned out to be a big storm, she might not be able to keep her appointment with Gerald. The flakes were falling more thickly now, and she looked at the sky but its whiteness gave her no clue. This could be just a flurry, or a blizzard. She flicked on the aging car radio, hoping for a weather report, but today was not one of its good days and it just buzzed. The uncertainty was driving her nuts, she realized. She wanted to know what to expect.

And that wasn't all, she realized. More than anything she wanted to know who killed Bitsy and Hayden, and why, but if she tried to investigate she ran the risk of angering Horowitz even more. She had no doubt he would file charges against her if he thought she was meddling in the case.

The thought gave her pause. Certainly Horowitz couldn't construe her meeting with Asquith as meddling in the investigation. She was a director, after all, and was responsible for the library. She had every right to talk with the other directors about library business. And there was plenty of business that needed to be settled. Who was going to replace Bitsy? Not to mention Hayden. And what about that security system? The theft of the tankard was even more proof that such a system was needed.

No, she concluded as she turned into her own driveway, there was no way Horowitz could object to her meeting with Asquith. She had plenty of legitimate reasons for the meeting, even if she did nurture the hope that she would discover something that would shed light on the deaths.

Gerald lived in one of the big old sea captain's houses lining Main Street, and Lucy was conscious of the aged condition of her Subaru as she drove between the imposing brick pillars on either side of the circular driveway and parked. The bright sun was merciless; yesterday's dusting of snow had melted, revealing every dent and bit of rust.

The brick steps were wet with the melting snow as Lucy climbed up to the door that was exactly in the center of the Federal-style mansion and tapped the shiny brass knocker. She didn't have time to admire the handsome pinecone wreath before the door opened and she was admitted.

"So nice to see you," said Gerald, taking her hand and drawing her into the center hall. Lucy had a general impression of Oriental rugs, gilt mirrors, and a sweeping stairway before she was installed in Gerald's study. The study, tucked under the stairs, was a cozy, book-lined room featuring a huge, leather-topped desk. She sank into one of the over-sized armchairs and wished that she could spend the entire day here, immersed in one of her favorite mystery novels.

"This is a lovely room," she said. "It's a wonderful place to curl up with your favorite book."

"I suppose it is," said Gerald, brushing some crumbs off his desk. "I'm afraid I don't really appreciate it. My wife tends to shoo me in here during the day—she's not used to having me home, you see. I only retired a few months ago."

"I'm awfully glad you could see me," began Lucy. "I've been terribly upset about all this business with the library."

"I really feel that I should apologize—what a terrible time to take up the duties of a director. This is all most un-usual, of course. Nothing like this has ever happened before, at least not in the twenty-odd years I've been on the board. First Bitsy, and now Hayden," he said, looking rather bleak. "It's overwhelming."

"I know," said Lucy, staring out the window at the snowy trees. "Do you really think Hayden killed Bitsy?"

"The police think she discovered he'd stolen the tank-ard," said Gerald.

"You know, something's been bothering me about the

tankard," Lucy began slowly. "I'm no expert on pewter, but I don't think the tankard that was found with Hayden is really Josiah's Tankard."

Gerald's jaw dropped. "You don't?"

"No. I had a chance to look at it quite closely, and it seemed awfully light in weight for a really old piece. And then I learned about the commemorative tankards the college had made, and it seemed a substitution could have been made."

"The college tankards had the Winchester seal . . ." began Gerald.

"I know, but the seal could have been rubbed off easily enough, and replaced with the design. That's why I wanted to ask you about the tankards . . ."

"Have you told anyone about this?" demanded Gerald, cutting her off.

"Only Lieutenant Horowitz."

"Good." Gerald nodded, and once again brushed at the papers on his desk. "I don't think you should tell anyone else. Not until we know for sure."

"Didn't Horowitz tell you about this?" Lucy was puzzled.

Gerald looked at her blankly with his pale blue eyes, and his Adam's apple bobbed. "Maybe he did," he finally decided. "It may have slipped my mind." He attempted a little chuckle. "One of the penalties of old age—I don't seem to remember things as well as I used to."

Lucy smiled sympathetically. "The other thing that's been bothering me is whether the library has an alarm system. In light of everything that's happened I really think it ought to be a priority."

"I must say that I agree with you. Some of us wanted it included in the new addition, but we were told it was unnecessary."

"Who said that?" Lucy's interest was piqued.

"Well, a few members wanted to keep costs down, anyway, and Ed Bumpus assured us the building would be virtually intruder-proof. Something like that." Gerald gave a little nod and brushed his hand across the desk.

Lucy wasn't sure if it was a nervous habit, or if some sticky crumbs were indeed clinging to the papers.

"Will the library be opening soon?" inquired Lucy. "If you need volunteers to staff the desk, or anything else, for that matter, I'd be happy to help."

"Thank you, but that won't be necessary. Eunice is a thorough professional. She was one of the college librarians until she retired a few months ago and I asked her if she would take over temporarily. Actually, she jumped at the chance."

"That's wonderful," said Lucy enthusiastically. Then an unwelcome thought struck her. "You are sure she'll be safe?"

"Of course. Why not?"

"Well—two people are dead," said Lucy, feeling that she was restating the obvious.

Gerald pursed his lips and drummed the table with his long, slender fingers. He touched the latest issue of *The Pennysaver,* just out that morning. "According to this, the police say the investigation is closed. They're the experts, and they're satisfied. I think it's time to move on."

"You're right," conceded Lucy. "The most important thing we can do right now is to get the library up and running again." Gerald opened a folder, taking out a sheet of paper. Once again, he brushed it off. "We were planning on dedicating the new addition in a few weeks, but I think we ought to postpone it until all this has died down."

"That's probably best," said Lucy, standing to go. "Thanks for taking the time to meet with me."

"No problem at all," said Gerald, taking her hand in his.

Lucy was shocked. His hand was icy cold, and his grip was unpleasantly tight.

"Please remember," he said, his eyes meeting hers. His usual smile was gone and his jaw was set in a hard line. "Investigations of this sort are best left to the police. You have a family to think of. If, as you suspect, the murderer is still at large, well, I wouldn't want to see you become the next victim." His lips twitched, almost as if he was attempting a smile but couldn't quite manage it. "Take care."

"I will, I certainly will," said Lucy, stumbling slightly as she left the room.

In the hallway she encountered a tall woman with gray hair, neatly dressed in a blue twin sweater set and a wool tweed skirt. "You must be Lucy Stone," she said, smiling warmly. "Gerald told me you would be coming. I'm Lucretia Asquith."

"It's nice to meet you," stammered Lucy. "I was just leaving."

"I'll see you to the door, then. I hope you'll come back again soon so we can get to know one another."

"Me, too," said Lucy, hurrying out the door. She knew she was being rude, but she couldn't help it. She had an irrational urge to flee, to get away from that house and Gerald Asquith as fast as she could.

Chapter Sixteen

*The Snow Queen lived in a beautiful
castle made of ice.*

Once she was safe in her car, driving over to the Orensteins' to pick up Zoe, Lucy considered her reaction to
Gerald's comment. She must have misunderstood his meaning, she decided. He wasn't the sort of man who went
around making threats; he had probably just been warning
her not to get involved in a dangerous situation. He was
probably sincerely worried about her.

Worry, as she well knew, wasn't always entirely rational.
And the situation at the library would have to be especially
distressing to the older, more conservative board members,
like Gerald. Nothing like this had ever happened before. It
must seem to Gerald that his formerly sedate and ordered
world had suddenly turned topsy-turvy.

What she needed, what they all needed, she decided as
she turned into the Orensteins' driveway, was time to gain a
little perspective on the situation.

"You're here already?" exclaimed Juanita, as she opened
the door. "I had no idea it was so late."

"No problems, then?"

Juanita waved her hand, dismissing the very idea. "Not with these two—they get on like a house afire. They've been playing in Sadie's room all morning."

"That's terrific," said Lucy. "It's our turn next—maybe Sadie can come over one day next week?"

The fine weather continued to hold as Lucy and Zoe drove home. There wasn't a cloud in the sky and the temperature was a balmy thirty degrees according to the revolving sign in front of the bank. After lunch, she decided, they'd have to get outside for some fresh air. It would do them both good.

Lucy noticed the blinking light on the answering machine when she got the plates out of the cupboard, and listened to her messages while she made tuna sandwiches for herself and Zoe.

"Hey, Lucy, Ted here. I'd like to use your gambling story in next week's paper—let me know when it will be ready, okay?"

Jeez Louise, thought Lucy guiltily. With everything that had happened lately she had forgotten all about the story. The research was all done—she just had to write the darn thing. Maybe she'd have a chance to work on it later this afternoon.

"Lucy, it's me," began the next message and Lucy recognized Sue's voice. "I got a flyer from the Portland Galleria—it's that time of the year again. How about shopping 'til we drop this weekend? Either Saturday or Sunday is fine with me. Give me a call, will ya?"

Lucy smiled. She always enjoyed shopping with Sue, who was an expert at sniffing out bargains. And this was a terrific time to find them, now that the stores were holding their big clearance sales.

She began a mental list as she set the plates on the table and poured two glasses of milk. Bill needed some new long underwear, Elizabeth needed pajamas and hadn't gotten any for Christmas, Toby needed socks. They could use some new towels, and she'd love to have a new dress to wear for her Valentine's Day dinner with Bill at the Greengage Cafe.

"Did you have a nice time at Sadie's this morning?" she asked Zoe.

"Sadie has Diamond-Dazzle Barbie. She has a crown. And the matching Ken has a shiny silver jacket."

"Wow," said Lucy, who could just imagine the total effect. "They must be . . . beautiful."

"Not Ken," Zoe corrected her. "He's handsome."

"Handsome is as handsome does," recited Lucy. "Does he behave himself?"

"He does whatever Barbie says."

Lucy couldn't help chuckling at this glimpse of Zoe's ordered imaginary universe, in which the newest, most glamorous Barbie was the indisputable queen of all she surveyed.

"Next week when Sadie comes you can play with your new Barbie—what's she called? Extremely Emerald?"

"No, Mommy. She's Emerald Elegance." Having straightened up that little misunderstanding, Zoe slid down from her chair and trotted off to the family room to save Funny Bunny from the evil electronic elves.

Standing at the kitchen sink, Lucy looked out the window at Red Top Hill. Thanks to the strong sunlight and the mild temperature, a few bare patches of asphalt were beginning to appear on the icy road. The steep hill just beyond the driveway was still covered with snow, however. They were the last house on the road and hardly anyone drove past this time of year; even the school bus turned around rather than following the hilly twists and turns that led past Blueberry Pond and eventually back to town.

For a moment, as she regarded the snowy hill, Lucy was a little girl again, tucked safely between her father's arms as he guided their speeding six-foot Flexible Flyer past the snow-mounded cars lining the still city street and took her swooping down Reservoir Road. She screamed all the way, she remembered, and he thought she had been frightened.

No, she told him, she was screaming because it was so much fun.

Shutting the dishwasher door, Lucy decided that Funny Bunny would be there tomorrow and every other day, but the conditions on Red Top Road were rarely this ideal for sliding.

"Come on, Zoe," she called. "We're going to see just how fast we can get my old sled to go."

The paint had worn off the old Flexible Flyer years ago, and the rope was frayed, but the runners were still bright silver, thanks to the coating of oil Lucy rubbed on them every time she put the sled away.

"Won't it be dangerous in the road, Mommy?" asked Zoe.

"I don't think so," said Lucy, standing at the top of the hill and surveying the situation. As she thought, yesterday's light snowfall on top of the tightly packed snow beneath it would provide an ideal sliding surface. The fresh snow was just beginning to soften up and it would give them just the slippery surface they needed for maximum speed. "Nobody's been along here all day, and even if somebody comes they'll have to drive pretty slowly," said Lucy. "We'll have plenty of time to see them."

"Okay," said Zoe, with the solemnity of an Olympic contender. "I'm ready."

"Me, too," said Lucy, settling herself on the sled and tucking Zoe between her legs. Unlike her father, she preferred to go down feet first. She pushed off with her arms, and the sled inched along, gradually picking up speed until they were flying down the hill so fast that the snow-covered trees seemed to whizz by them. At the bottom, Lucy pushed the steering bar with her feet, hoping to brake into a neat circle. Instead, they rolled off into the snow, shrieking and laughing.

Lucy heard her joints creak as she got back on her feet and knew that her muscles would undoubtedly be sore the next day. That's what they invented ibuprofen for, she thought, as she brushed the snow off her face.

"Again?" she asked Zoe.

"Yes!" screamed the little girl, her eyes sparkling above apple red cheeks. She took off, running up the hill, while Lucy followed more slowly, towing the sled.

An hour or so later, Lucy and Zoe were extracting themselves from some scratchy blueberry bushes when they heard the familiar groan of the gears on the school bus as it prepared to climb the other side of the hill. They ran up to meet it, waving at Moe, the bus driver.

"Mother, don't tell me you've been sliding," said Elizabeth, twisting her lips into a scowl and rolling her black eyeliner-lined eyes. "Thank goodness none of my friends are still on the bus."

"What friends?" Toby asked predictably. "You don't have any friends."

"Do, too."

"Who? Lard-face Lance?" teased her older brother, referring to Elizabeth's on-again, off-again boyfriend.

"You're disgusting," said Elizabeth, turning her back and trudging off toward the house.

"Come on, Toby," begged Sara. "Let's go sliding, too. It looks like fun."

"It is fun," said Zoe. "Lots of fun."

Toby cast an expert eye at the hill. "You know, if we made a little bank of snow at the bottom, we wouldn't go into the bushes."

"That's a good idea," said Lucy, wondering why she hadn't thought of it herself. "I'll get the shovel and start while you get out the sleds and stuff."

Soon Toby and Sara were spinning down the hill in snow saucers, and eventually even Elizabeth appeared, trying out the snowboard she got for Christmas.

Realizing that she was soaked to the skin, Lucy decided to go inside to warm up. Zoe wasn't ready to come in yet, and as Lucy climbed wearily up the hill one last time she smiled to see her littlest one whirling past on a saucer, safe in her big brother's arms.

Back inside the warm kitchen, she tugged off her snow-encrusted hat and mittens and laid them on top of the radiator. Then her boots went in the tray by the door; she unzipped and peeled off her snowsuit, hanging it up in the pantry, next to the water heater. In the powder room, she brushed out her damp hair, hardly recognizing herself in the mirror. With her hat hair and red cheeks, she looked, she realized with a shock, just like the aging photographs of that little girl who went sledding with her father so many years ago.

She put a big pot of hot chocolate on the stove and opened the door to call the kids. Hearing the unfamiliar sound of an engine—a souped-up one at that—she stuffed her feet back into her boots and went out to investigate, drawing her sweater tightly across her chest.

As she ran down the driveway she heard the engine coming closer; it sounded to her like one of those pickup trucks with oversized tires. It seemed to be coming from the direction of the pond, along the part of the road that wound through the woods.

She waved at her kids and called to them, but they weren't paying any attention. They didn't seem to be aware of the approaching truck. Toby was seating himself in one of the saucers and Zoe, she saw, was jumping in his lap. He had just pushed off with his arms, and began sailing down the hill, when the truck appeared on the other side, at the bottom of the hill.

Horrified, Lucy saw that it was going way too fast; the driver was probably hoping to build up enough speed to make it up the hill. Sara, standing at the crest, spotted the truck and began waving her arms, trying to warn the driver to slow down. Either he didn't see her, or decided to ignore her and sped up the hill right past her, directly toward the saucer.

Lucy covered her mouth with her hand and held her breath; there was nothing she could do but pray. Toby must have seen the truck by now, and realized the danger he and Zoe were in, but the saucer was impossible to steer. Once started down the hill, there was no way he could change its direction.

It was up to the driver of the truck to do something. "Stop! Stop!" she screamed, knowing there was no possibility that he could hear her. He must see the saucer, though. Why wasn't he stopping?

If only Toby could push the saucer out of the truck's path—but it was spinning toward it. It was only feet from the huge black tires of the truck, she realized, and tears sprang to her eyes. A horrible sound came from her throat, a high-pitched, keening scream.

Then, miraculously, she saw the saucer tip and curve away from the truck, spilling Toby and Zoe into the snow on the side of the road.

Never stopping, the truck hurtled past her, a roaring blur of black and chrome. Furious, she spun around and tried to make out the license plate, but it was covered with crusted ice.

Clenching her fists, she pounded them once against her thighs, then turned to the kids. They were fine, stamping their feet and shaking the snow out of their hats.

"Come on in," Lucy called to them in a shaky voice. "I've made some hot cocoa."

She stood there in the cold and growing dimness, watching as they plodded up the hill, towing their sleds and saucers. She wasn't chilled at all; she was furious. How could the driver of that truck have been so irresponsible? Could it be possible that he didn't see them?

Lucy didn't think so. There had been plenty of light and the kids were dressed in bright clothes; they were out in the open on the snowy hill. They were highly visible. In fact, she realized with a shock, it had almost seemed as if the driver had been driving directly toward them. But that was absurd, she thought. Nobody would do a thing like that.

Trudging back to the house, Lucy resolved to ask Barney if any of the local youths had a particularly reckless reputation, and a fancy truck to go with it. He would probably know who the driver was; he might even have a word with him.

Then again, perhaps she shouldn't report it. She wouldn't like to get some kid in trouble over some cold-weather high-jinks.

That was ridiculous, she decided, marching along the driveway. She had her family to think of. She stopped dead in her tracks. Where had she heard that lately? From Gerald Asquith?

Oh, no. She brushed the thought away. This was an accident. A near miss by some kid with more horsepower than sense. There was no way Gerald could have had anything to do with it. No way at all.

Chapter Seventeen

*Every time he told a lie, Pinocchio's
nose grew a little longer.*

When the alarm went off the next morning, Lucy confused it with the scream of an ambulance. She had a brief, terrifying image of a black-and-chrome truck hurtling through the snow and crashing into the Subaru. But when she opened her eyes, she was safe in bed beside Bill.

She rolled over, reaching for the alarm clock, and moaned in pain. She was getting a bit old for sledding, she decided. Everything hurt: arms, back, and most painful of all, her thighs.

"I'm not as young as I used to be," she moaned, cautiously pulling herself to a sitting position.

"Why don't you lie in for a bit," suggested Bill. "I'll bring you breakfast in bed."

"Oh, no," said Lucy. "I don't dare. If I lie down, I might never get back up." She sighed, and groped for her slippers with her feet. "There *is* one thing you could do for me."

"Sure. What is it?"

"Put my slippers on for me," she asked plaintively.

* * *

After the kids had left for school, Lucy sat at the kitchen table, nursing a cup of coffee. She had filled Bill's lunchbox and was waiting to say good-bye to him. But when he appeared, reaching over her shoulder for the box, she held his arm.

"Do you know anybody who has a black-and-chrome pickup?" she asked.

"Probably. Why do you want to know?"

"One came tearing up the road yesterday, when the kids were sledding. It was a close call. We were lucky."

Bill sat down, scratching his bearded chin. "Ed's got one like that, I think."

"That's right. I saw it at the food pantry. It could've been that truck."

"He's a pretty careful driver, though," said Bill, shaking his head. "Doesn't sound like him."

"Maybe someone who works for him?"

"If I see him, I'll ask him." said Bill, standing up. He stroked her cheek with his hand. "If the kids want to slide, have 'em stay in the yard, okay?"

If confession is good for the soul, Lucy figured her soul must be in tip-top shape this morning. She thought she'd handled telling Bill about the kids' near miss pretty well. She'd told him just as he was getting ready to leave the house, his mind already on the day ahead. And by asking him about the truck, she'd neatly positioned him as her helper, not her critic.

A psychological masterpiece, she decided, having left Zoe at Kiddie Kollege and heading over to *The Pennysaver* office. If only she could manage Ted as well.

The little bell on the door tinkled as she pulled it open, causing Ted to look up from his desk.

"Hi, Lucy. Have you got the story?"

"No."

"No?"

"Please don't yell. I'm in a lot of pain."

"What happened?"

"I was in kind of an accident yesterday. I was sledding with the kids and a big truck . . ."

"Are you all right?" Ted hopped to his feet and began clearing files off a chair. "Sit down."

"Thanks," said Lucy, allowing herself to groan as she lowered herself onto the seat. "I'm just sore all over."

"What about the kids?"

"They're fine. It was just a near miss, but I was too upset to work on the story."

"Take all the time you need," he said, magnanimously. "Actually, I have some features left over from this week that I didn't use. What a week—murder, suicide, theft all tied up in a neat little bundle. It doesn't get much better than this." He paused and shook his head regretfully. "If only they'd been lovers."

"Who? Bitsy and Hayden?" Lucy raised an eyebrow. "Not much chance of that."

"I know, I know," Ted hastened to say. "I was only saying that it would have been a nice touch."

"Well, it would have made the whole thing more understandable," admitted Lucy. "I can't for the life of me think what would possess Hayden to do these things."

"Horowitz is pretty definite about it—he was quite chatty, in fact. Pretty unusual for the great stone face."

"He thinks he's got a nice, tidy case, all tied up with a bow," fumed Lucy. "He isn't going to go looking for loose ends, is he? He wants the case closed. He didn't know Hayden—he doesn't know how ridiculous this whole thing is."

"Oh, no," mused Ted. "So you don't agree with the official solution?"

"Not by a long shot," admitted Lucy. "Hey, thanks for being so nice about the story. I absolutely, positively promise I'll have it for you next week."

"I've heard that before," said Ted, looking doubtful.

It was barely ten when Lucy left *The Pennysaver* office, walking carefully down Main Street to her car. The sidewalk was clear but there were icy patches and the last thing she wanted to do was fall. The way she felt, she'd never get up again. The ibuprofen she'd taken earlier was helping, but her arms and legs still ached.

In the car, Lucy considered her options. Zoe wouldn't be out of Kiddie Kollege until twelve. She could spend that time in a hot tub; the only problem was she didn't know anybody who had one. Besides, she wouldn't be able to relax— not even in a hot tub—until she sorted out her emotions, still unsettled from yesterday's near tragedy. She couldn't shake the feeling that Gerald was somehow involved, ridiculous as that seemed. Nevertheless, he had no sooner given her a clear warning to mind her own business than the frightening incident with the truck had occurred. Besides, she had definitely gotten the sense that Gerald was hiding something, but how could she find out what it was?

She put the key in the ignition and adjusted the rear view mirror, catching sight of the gift she had wrapped for Miss Tilley. With everything that had been happening, she had forgotten all about it. No time like the present, she decided, slipping the Subaru into drive and turning up the heater.

Rachel greeted her warmly when she opened the door.

"Lucy! What a nice surprise! Come on in out of the cold—I've got the kettle on."

"That sounds great," said Lucy, with chattering teeth.

"Why is it that the car heater doesn't kick in until you're wherever it is that you're going?"

"Just one of those things, I guess," said Rachel, taking her coat. "Sit down by the fire."

Miss Tilley was seated in her usual rocking chair on one side of the fireplace, a brightly colored, crocheted afghan covering her legs.

"Don't you make a cozy picture," began Lucy, holding out the present. "This is for you. To let you know how badly I felt about quarreling with you last week."

"There's no need for an apology," said Miss Tilley, as she took the present. Her eyes were bright with amusement. "I'm a quarrelsome old biddy. Such behavior shouldn't be rewarded, should it, Rachel?"

"Absolutely not," said Rachel, as she carried in the tea tray. "You'll undo all my efforts to civilize this old witch."

"I could take it back . . ." began Lucy.

"Never mind." Miss Tilley flapped her hand, shooing her away. "Since you've gone to all this trouble, I don't want to disappoint you."

"All right, then," said Lucy, taking a cup and cautiously seating herself in the comfortable armchair on the other side of the fireplace. "I'll let you keep it. I hope you like it."

Miss Tilley's fingers trembled as she unwrapped the present, another sign of her increasing debility. Lucy didn't watch her struggle, but studied the bright flames dancing in the fireplace and concentrated on relaxing her painful, tensed muscles.

"This is lovely! Thank you," exclaimed Miss Tilley.

Lucy looked up and smiled at her. "I thought it might remind you of Josiah's Tankard."

"It does—it's very similar, isn't it?" She ran her fingers over the smooth surface and wrapped them around the handle. "You really didn't need to do this, you know."

"I know," Lucy said, smiling. "I wanted to."

"Where shall we put it?" asked Rachel. "On the mantel?"

Before Lucy could suggest the tavern table, Miss Tilley pointed to it. "Over there, I think. In the light from the window."

Rachel carried the tankard across the room and placed it on the little round, pumpkin-colored table. It seemed to sit happily there, quietly glowing, as if it had found a home.

"Perfect," said Rachel, and they all nodded in agreement, admiring the effect. "Well, it's back to the kitchen for me—I've got to keep an eye on my pudding or it will burn."

Lucy took a sip of tea, but spluttered when Miss Tilley abruptly posed a question.

"Have you got to the bottom of this business at the library yet?" the old woman asked.

"Not quite," admitted Lucy. "But Horowitz thinks he's got the whole thing wrapped up."

"That's ridiculous. Hayden wouldn't have hurt a fly." Miss Tilley's tone was definite.

"You know," began Lucy, determined to confess yet another sin, "when I decided to get you a tankard I asked Corney and Hayden for some advice about pewter. Horowitz said Hayden may have misunderstood my interest—he said it might be my fault that he killed himself."

"That's the most ridiculous thing I've ever heard."

"This is just a theory," began Lucy, "but what if Josiah's Tankard isn't genuine? What if Hayden had switched it? That would be quite a motive for suicide."

"I've had my doubts for a while," admitted Miss Tilley, surprising Lucy with her complacency. "I didn't want to alarm the board unnecessarily, but I was going to suggest having it appraised by an expert. Something about it isn't quite right—but I don't for one minute think Hayden made the switch."

"When did you first notice it?"

"When we had it out the last time—it seemed lighter than I expected."

"When was it last authenticated?" asked Lucy. "Is there documentation of any kind?"

"There is, and I tried to check it, but the file was missing. I meant to pursue it, but I came down with the flu and I never got around to it. Gerald probably knows where it is."

"Of course," said Lucy, leaning forward and reaching for the teapot. "More for you?"

Miss Tilley shook her head, and Lucy refilled her own cup. Settling back in her chair, she decided to ask Miss Tilley about her old friend. "How is Gerald these days? He seems to be managing so well as president of the board, but all this must be taking a toll on him."

"Oh, Gerald's used to managing crises—he used to be president of Winchester College, you know. He faced down mobs of protesting students in the sixties—he'd only been on the job a couple of weeks when they staged a huge demonstration. And since then it's been one thing after another. Why, just before he retired the college trustees voted to ban alcohol on campus—poor Gerald had to tell the fraternities!" Miss Tilley cackled merrily. "I guess if he could handle that, he could handle anything."

"He must have been glad to retire," ventured Lucy.

"I don't know about that." Miss Tilley was suddenly solemn. "I hated having to retire, and I suspect Gerald felt the same way. It's hard to give up something you love."

"I'm sure it is." Lucy's voice was soft. "But he seems quite busy. I suppose he's on a number of boards. He must have investments to manage. And then there's golf and traveling. I've heard retirees say that they're busier in retirement than they were when they worked."

"I don't think that's quite the case with Gerald." Miss Tilley folded her hands in her lap and looked out the window at the bird feeder where a blue jay had suddenly alighted, scattering the chickadees and titmice that had been gathered there. "Blue jays are such bullies," she said. "I wouldn't allow it, if they weren't so handsome."

"Lunch is almost ready," said Rachel, appearing in the doorway. "Will you stay, Lucy?"

"No, thanks. I have to pick up Zoe. I didn't realize it was so late."

"Well, come back anytime," said Rachel, pulling Lucy's coat out of the hall closet. "You're always welcome."

"Especially when you bring presents," added Miss Tilley, nodding toward the tankard.

"Honestly, she's no better than a five-year-old," clucked Rachel.

"I'm no better than I ought to be—and neither are you!" shot back the old woman.

"I'm afraid that none of us are," said Lucy, giving a little wave as she went out the door. "And some of us are a good deal worse," she muttered as she climbed into the car. She started the engine, shifted to drive, and carefully checked for traffic before pulling away from the curb. It wasn't something she'd care to admit, even to herself, but she didn't want to risk another encounter with that black-and-chrome truck.

Chapter Eighteen

The Fairy Godmother waved her magic wand and
Cinderella's rags became a beautiful ball gown.

Saturday morning found Lucy sitting at the kitchen table, enjoying a second cup of coffee and reading the morning paper while she waited for Sue to pick her up. The house was unusually quiet; Bill had taken the younger kids ice skating on Blueberry Pond, and Toby and Elizabeth were still sleeping.

Hearing Sue's horn, Lucy struggled painfully into her coat, grabbed her gloves and bag, and hobbled out to Sue's brand-new car, an enormous sport utility vehicle guaranteed to be virtually unstoppable.

"What's the matter with you?" asked Sue, as Lucy hauled herself up into the passenger side seat. Her muscles were still sore and she couldn't help groaning as she strapped the seatbelt on.

"I'm stiff and sore from sledding with the kids."

"About time you acted your age," teased Sue, who avoided exercise like the plague. "Serves you right. You should have been sipping tea and nibbling scones safe indoors."

"You're probably right," agreed Lucy. "Let's have lunch someplace nice, okay? No fast food."

"Fine by me," said Sue, carefully maneuvering the enormous four-wheel-drive vehicle, complete with a rhino guard, out of the driveway.

"I always feel so safe in your car," said Lucy, observing the mounds of snow that lined the road. "It's good to know that if a wild rhino should decide to charge, we're ready."

"You never know," said Sue. "It's good to be prepared. Say, are you going to Hayden's funeral tomorrow? I heard Ralph hired Corney to do the food. No expense spared."

"I guess I should—being on the board and all."

"Don't give me that—you wouldn't miss it for the world." Funerals were major social events in Tinker's Cove, and were discussed for months afterward.

"I wonder what she'll serve?"

"Whatever it is, you can be sure she stole the recipe from somebody," said Sue.

"Are there rules about that? Corney told me that as long as you add something new to a recipe you can claim it as your own."

"Hmmph," snorted Sue. "I think it takes more than a pinch of salt or a dusting of parsley to create a new recipe, and I'm not the only one. Laura Winkle—she works over in the courthouse, you know—told me that somebody was suing Corney for copyright infringement. I don't remember who, but I do know they were planning on calling poor Bitsy as a witness. Of course, they can't do that now. Maybe they'll settle out of court."

"Would something like that be a motive for murder?" Lucy was skeptical.

"Laura said they were asking for half a million in damages."

"Gee, sounds like a motive to me," mused Lucy. "Do you think Corney knows how to use a gun?"

"Sure." Sue chuckled. "Keep watching her column. 'A quick and easy way to clean your chimney.'"

Lucy laughed. "'Exterminating pests—easier than you thought.'"

"Make your own colander."

"Painless pumpkin carving."

"Don't remind me," moaned Sue. Her attempt to follow Corney's directions for a Victorian lace Halloween pumpkin had resulted in a badly nicked finger that became infected and required a trip to the emergency room and an expensive course of antibiotics. "It isn't that I don't think Corney is capable of murder, I just think she would prefer a less direct method."

"Like tossing a few toxic mushrooms into the coq au vin?"

"Exactly."

"But even if she had a motive to kill Bitsy, why did she have to kill Hayden?" asked Lucy, twisting a lock of hair around her finger.

"He could have figured out that she killed Bitsy," speculated Sue. "And don't forget, he knew a lot about cooking, too. Maybe he knew what a phony she really is."

"Oh, my," said Lucy. "Do you think all this animosity might be because you're jealous of Corney?"

"Absolutely not," insisted Sue. "Why would I be jealous of her?"

Lucy didn't answer; she was looking out the window at the dirty wall of snow that lined the highway. The sky was a dark slate gray and a few flakes were beginning to fall. "I wish winter would end," she said.

"Me, too," sighed Sue.

Once they were inside the Galleria, Portland's newest and most elegant mall complete with potted palm trees and fountains, they forgot all about the weather outside. They lingered over lunch in the Parrot's Perch, enjoying glasses of white wine with their salads. Then they ventured into the stores, where the clearance sales were in full swing. Lucy made quick work of her list, and was seriously considering splurging on a designer dress.

"It's a Diane Fish dress—trust me, you can't go wrong," urged Sue.

"But it's ninety dollars."

"A steal. See the tag. It was over three hundred."

"I could wear it to the funeral," rationalized Lucy, who really wanted it for her Valentine's Day dinner with Bill.

"It's a classic. You can wear it anywhere. Trust me. You'll hate yourself if you don't get it."

"You think it's that good a deal?"

Sue rolled her eyes. "Just look at it. The buttons are all different. Handmade, I bet. And it has pockets. Removable shoulder pads. You don't find these features in cheap dresses."

"I know." Lucy sighed. "It's just that I haven't even paid all the Christmas bills yet."

"Hey—I just remembered. I got a coupon in the mail. It's like a scratch ticket—it said you can save up to seventy-five percent on sale prices."

"Really?"

"Probably not," said Sue, rummaging in her purse. "But you could save something. Ah-ha! Here it is!"

"It doesn't say how much you save," said Lucy.

"Right. You take it to the salesclerk and scratch the little gray circle. She'll take off whatever percent is printed under it."

"What if it's only ten percent?"

Sue sighed. "Tell her you changed your mind."

"And you don't want this ticket?"

"No!" exclaimed Sue. "I really want you to get this nice new dress that is an absolutely terrific bargain and would look great on you and you're really beginning to get on my nerves!"

"Okay. Okay," said Lucy, taking the ticket. "But I'm warning you—I'm not going to get it unless it's at least fifty percent off."

"Whatever," said Sue, waving her arm and dramatically collapsing into a chair outside the fitting rooms.

Lucy approached the cash register, which was staffed by a tired-looking woman with swollen ankles. "Cash or charge?"

"Charge," said Lucy, producing her card. As if it were an afterthought, she added, "Oh, I have this coupon."

"Here you go," said the clerk, handing her a shiny new penny. "Just scratch off the gray circle."

Lucy worked at the circle, brushing away the rubbery crumbs produced by the scratching. "Wow!" she exclaimed. "It says seventy-five."

"Good for you," said the clerk. "Most of them are for ten or twenty percent. That brings your total to twenty-two fifty."

"That's great!" enthused Lucy. "That's a three-hundred-dollar dress."

"It pays to shop at Waldrons'," said the tired salesclerk, repeating the store's slogan.

"I guess it does," nodded Lucy. She took her bag and went over to Sue, who was leaning back in the chair with her eyes closed, a mountain of packages piled on her lap.

"How'd you do?" she asked, without opening her eyes.

"Seventy-five."

"Seventy-five dollars? Not bad."

"No—seventy-five percent off."

Sue's eyes popped open. "You're kidding."

"Nope."

"Damn."

"Something the matter?"

"If I'd known, I would have kept it for myself," she muttered. "I'm ready for a break—how about a cappuccino?"

* * *

That night, after doling out her purchases to the kids, Lucy went upstairs to try on the new dress. As she took it out of the bag she noticed that some of the scratch ticket crumbles were stuck to the tissue paper. Thoughtfully, she picked them up and with her thumb rolled them against her fingers. They reminded her of something, but she couldn't quite remember what. Brushing off her hands, she lifted the dress and slipped it over her head. She was standing in front of the mirror when Bill appeared behind her.

"Zip me up?" she asked.

"Okay," he said, with a twinkle in his eye. "If I can unzip you later."

"Deal," said Lucy, turning to face him and wrapping her arms around his neck.

Chapter Nineteen

*The Queen was furious and threw
the Magic Mirror against the wall.*

"God, I hate funerals," said Bill, giving his tie a tug. He was seated beside Lucy in the hushed, flower-scented sanctuary of St. Christopher's Episcopal Church.

Funeral regulars who had come to the earlier visiting hours to gape at Hayden's embalmed body—"Doesn't he look wonderful?"—were certainly disappointed. Not only was there no open casket, there was no casket at all since Hayden had been cremated. Ralph had chosen to have a memorial service, and a very simple one at that. No eulogies. No sharing of personal remembrances of the departed. Just beautiful music played by a string quartet and a simple reading from the *Book of Common Prayer*.

Looking around the church, Lucy noticed that it was filled with unfamiliar faces. This was not the usual Tinker's Cove crowd; these folks were wearing city clothes and their hair, both the men's and the women's, had been styled by hairdressers with more skill than Moe the Barber or the girls at Dot's Beauty Spot. These people were buffed and massaged, stylish and polished, and Lucy was glad she was wearing her new dress.

"I wish they'd get started," complained Bill.

"It has started," whispered Lucy. "It's just music."

"Hunh," grunted Bill. "Who are all these people?"

"Antiques dealers, interior designers, Hayden's clients . . . he was very big in the antiques world."

"Oh," said Bill, unimpressed. In a few minutes his breathing grew regular and Lucy knew he had fallen asleep. He gave a little snort and she elbowed him, afraid he would start snoring. His eyes opened for a second, then closed, and he was off in dreamland once again.

Lucy relaxed against the back of the pew, allowing her mind to drift with the music. There in the front pew she caught a glimpse of Ralph, somber in his black suit. She remembered having coffee with them, and how much they enjoyed each other. Tears began welling in her eyes and she tried to fight them back. Think about something else, don't think about Hayden. Just listen to the music, she told herself, following the soaring notes of a violin solo.

Her eyes roamed around the church and lit on the cross that stood on the altar. It was unusually simple for an Episcopalian church, she thought, realizing it was made of pewter instead of silver. It had to be the tankard, she thought, chewing on her lip. Two people associated with the library were dead, and the tankard was a fake—there had to be a connection. What had Miss Tilley told her? That Gerald had all the documents authenticating the tankard?

What she wanted, she decided, was to take a look at those papers. What she didn't want, however, was another encounter with Gerald. The man gave her the willies.

She looked around the church and spotted him sitting by a stained glass window with Lucretia beside him. She was being ridiculous, she thought, studying his profile. With his gray hair, his strong, angular nose, and his firm jaw, he was still a handsome man—the very image of New England respectability.

Her lips twitched when she remembered Miss Tilley telling her that most of the highly revered New England sea captains hadn't been above smuggling or blockade running, if the profits were high enough. "Pirates, all of them," she'd proclaimed.

There was something of the pirate about Gerald, realized Lucy. He took pains to disguise it, she thought, but she had sensed a tension about him, a certain wariness, that indicated hidden depths. Gerald wasn't entirely respectable.

She would call him tomorrow, she decided, and if he suggested a meeting she would insist that she was too busy. She would tell him to return the documents to Miss Tilley; a good idea, she realized, because it would give her request extra weight.

That settled, Lucy bowed her head and sent up a silent prayer that Ralph would find comfort. The music stopped and the priest stepped up to the lectern. "Please join me in saying the words of Jesus Christ: Our father, who art in heaven . . ."

After the service, Lucy and Bill followed the crowd to the reception in the parish hall. They stood in line and shook hands with Ralph, who looked leaner and handsomer than ever in his dark suit. He, in turn, introduced them to Hayden's parents. Mrs. Northcross was a tiny woman with dyed red hair, dressed in a black suit with a fussy, ruffled white blouse underneath the jacket. Mr. Northcross towered over her, with a bald head and a fringe of white hair. They seemed confused and bewildered by this reversal of the natural order; they hadn't expected to outlive their son.

Lucy took their hands and murmured how sorry she was, wishing she could think of something truly comforting to say. Funerals always made her feel depressed and inadequate.

Bill pressed his hand against her back and steered her toward the buffet set up along the wall on the opposite side of the room. Corney had really outdone herself, thought Lucy, filling her plate with tiny salmon sandwiches, cheese puffs, and stuffed mushrooms.

"Watching our weight, are we?" asked Sue, appearing beside her.

"I didn't have any lunch," lied Lucy.

"Liar," said Sue.

"The dress looks nice."

"Thanks." Lucy took a bite of stuffed mushroom. "When I die I want something like this. Simple and tasteful."

"And no expense spared."

"Absolutely. After all, you can't take it with you," agreed Lucy, watching as Corney refreshed a tray of crudités. "Are you sure about that lawsuit?"

"Not really, it was just something I heard," admitted Sue, sipping a glass of white wine.

"I suppose I could check at the courthouse."

"I suppose you could," said Sue, smiling and nodding to someone across the room. "Don't look now, but your friend the lieutenant is here."

"He is? Where?" demanded Lucy, scanning the crowded room.

"He's staring right at you," said Sue. "From behind the coffee urn."

"Oh, I see him. But he's not looking at me." As Lucy watched, the detective took something out of his pocket and studied it, then carefully replaced it. "I wonder what he's doing here. After all, the case is supposed to be closed."

"Well," said Sue, nibbling on a piece of celery, "I don't think he's here for the food. He's not eating anything."

"That's Horowitz for you," said Lucy. "That man doesn't know how to have a good time." She put down her plate on a nearby table. "Well, that was delicious but now it's time to circulate."

She made her way across the crowded room to a spot between the windows where Bill was talking with Ed Bumpus.

"I should have known I'd find you talking construction," said Lucy, taking Bill's arm. "It's nice to see you, Ed."

"Hayden got quite a turnout," said Ed, popping a tiny piece of toast topped with beef tartare into his mouth. "Even if some of these folks walk a little lightly in their shoes, if you get my drift." He chewed thoughtfully. "I can tell you— I was sure glad to see Bill here. There's no question Bill's a straight-up kind of guy. Not like these here . . . well, y'know what I mean."

"That's Bill," said Lucy brightly. "He's hard-working, reliable, trustworthy. You can count on him."

"I know—and that's why I had him look over the figures for the library addition." He gave Bill a hearty slap on the back. "It means a lot to me to know that if anything is ever questioned I can say, 'Bill Stone said it was all okeydokey.'"

"Has anybody been questioning the figures?" Lucy asked curiously.

"Only Chuck," said Ed, indicating the lawyer, who was chatting with Mrs. Asquith. "That guy gives me a pain in the ass."

"What do you expect? He's a lawyer," said Bill, shrugging philosophically.

"He's probably being extra careful, because of everything that's happened," speculated Lucy.

"I don't care what he is," said Ed, an angry tone creeping into his voice. "He's got no reason to question me. I've got a reputation in this town, y'know."

That's right, Lucy thought to herself, and it's not all that good, from what I've heard. "Hey, Ed," she began. "You know that nice truck of yours? It wasn't out our way lately, on Red Top Road, was it?"

"Not that I know of," said Ed, a note of caution in his voice. "Why?"

"One just like it came tearing down the road the other day when my kids were sledding. It gave me a real scare."

Ed popped a huge stuffed mushroom in his mouth and chewed noisily. "Dunno nuffin' 'bout it," he said, wiping his greasy fingers on his trousers.

"All's well that ends well, I guess."

"That's right," said Bill. "The kids shouldn't have been in the road, anyway."

"Say, Bill," began Ed, turning his back on her, "whaddya think of these new steel two-by-fours?"

No longer included in the conversation, Lucy headed for the coffee table in search of Horowitz, but he was nowhere to be seen. She took a cup and sipped at it, peering over the rim, and spotted the detective striding purposefully across the crowded room. As Lucy watched, he took Gerald by the elbow and led him through the doorway.

Lucy followed them into the hallway, where a uniformed policeman was waiting. She watched, astonished, as Gerald was quickly handcuffed and marched outside to a cruiser which spun off rapidly down the street.

Blinking her eyes in disbelief, Lucy looked around the room to see if anyone else had noticed. But the whole thing had happened so quickly that no one seemed to have seen a thing. No one, that is, except for Lucretia Asquith. Tall and trim as ever, she was pale with shock.

Lucy took her arm and led her out of the crowded room and into an empty office.

"What happened?" she asked Lucy, nervously rubbing her hands together.

"Gerald was arrested," said Lucy, filling a paper cup from the water cooler in the corner and handing it to her. "Do you have any idea why?"

Mrs. Asquith took a sip of water and shook her head.

Lucy noticed a sprinkling of dandruff on the shoulders of her black suit. Suddenly, she remembered the way Gerald had brushed at the papers on his desk.

"He gambled, didn't he?" asked Lucy, thinking of the little gray crumbles she had scratched off the coupon in the store the day before. The words were out before she knew it.

Mrs. Asquith sagged in the chair and Lucy grabbed for the cup before it spilled. She lifted it to the older woman's lips, holding it so Lucretia could take a sip.

"We're going to lose everything," she whispered.

"Everything?" Lucy was stunned. The Asquiths were worth a pretty penny.

"The house is in foreclosure."

"Oh, my God."

Mrs. Asquith nodded grimly. "He always gambled a little bit, but never enough to matter. Then he retired. He couldn't control it anymore. The lottery, scratch tickets, even casinos."

Lucy chewed her lip. "But gambling's not illegal," she said. "Why did they arrest him?"

Mrs. Asquith studied her hands in her lap.

"Did he steal?" asked Lucy.

Mrs. Asquith suddenly jerked back in her chair, and her hands flew to her head. She yanked at her hair and then dissolved into tears.

"There, there," said Lucy, trying to calm her. She was terrified Mrs. Asquith was becoming hysterical.

"I hate him!" she hissed, pounding her hand on the desk. "I hate him for doing this to me."

"Just hang on," said Lucy, patting Mrs. Asquith's shoulder and handing her a tissue. She looked nervously toward the door. "I don't think anybody saw but us. Wait here and I'll get my husband. We'll drive you home."

A shudder ran through the older woman's body, and she began twisting and shredding the paper hankie.

Lucy left, closing the door, and hurried down the hall to the parish room. The crowd had thinned, she noticed. She caught Bill's eye and he came across the room to her.

"I've been looking for you—where've you been?" he asked.

"You won't believe it," she whispered. "Horowitz arrested Gerald Asquith, just a minute ago. I've got a hysterical Mrs. Asquith in the church office. Can you help me get her home?"

"I'll drive her car—you follow, okay?"

"Thanks." Lucy was truly grateful; she could always count on Bill.

She surveyed the coat rack and decided a black cashmere with a fur collar and a light dusting of dandruff was probably Mrs. Asquith's. She pulled it off the hanger and led Bill to the office. There, he gently drew Mrs. Asquith to her feet and Lucy draped the coat over her shoulders. Then, Mrs. Asquith's keys in his hand, he hurried off to bring the car around. Lucy slipped into her coat and waited with Lucretia in the hallway until he pulled up in a black Lincoln town car.

He opened the door on the passenger side and waited as Lucy escorted the older woman down the icy pathway and helped her into the car. Lucy watched as they drove away slowly, and then went to get the Subaru.

Alone in the car, she flipped up the visor and leaned forward so she could see the sky. It was the blank, milky white that often signaled a snowstorm. She started the engine and switched on the radio, searching for a weather report.

All she got, though, was varying tones of static as she drove past the big, substantial clapboard houses that lined Main Street. On one big, snow-covered lawn a group of children, togged out in bright red and blue and green snowsuits, were making a snowman. The scene reminded her of a Christmas card.

If only life was like the paintings, she thought. She loved

living in New England—the small towns, the rugged indi-
vidualists, even the annual town meetings. Self-reliance.
Hard work. Thrift. Common sense. Common crackers. She
loved it when the kids came in with rosy cheeks, looking
like the children in Tasha Tudor books. What had gone
wrong, she wondered, pulling up and parking behind Mrs.
Asquith's car and watching as Bill helped Lucretia into the
house.

She was so absorbed in her thoughts that she never once
looked in the rearview mirror, never noticed that she had
been followed.

Chapter Twenty

*The Giant was furious when he realized
Jack had stolen his treasure.*

On Monday morning the radio announced Gerald's arrest
for the theft of Josiah's Tankard:

"Former Winchester College President Gerald Asquith
was arrested by state police who allege he stole an antique
pewter tankard from the Tinker's Cove Library, placing a
copy in its place.

"State police say the theft went unnoticed for years, and
was only discovered when the copy was found with the
body of Hayden Northcross, who committed suicide last
week. A subsequent investigation revealed that Asquith sold
the tankard at Sotheby's auction house in New York City,
and received more than forty thousand dollars for it."

Stunned at the amount, Lucy dropped the knife she was
using to make peanut butter and jelly sandwiches for the
kids' lunches, spattering jelly on the floor. She bent down to
wipe it up with a paper towel, eagerly listening for more details about the arrest. All she learned, however, was that Gerald would be arraigned that morning.

As Lucy finished packing the lunches she decided she would spend the morning finishing up the gambling story. Ted would undoubtedly want to run it as background for the story about Asquith.

"Bill?" she called up the stairs. "Do me a favor and drop Zoe off at Kiddie Kollege this morning?" She checked the clock, and sent a second message echoing up the stairs: "You've got five minutes 'til the school bus."

"We're always way too early," said Toby, clattering down the stairs and stuffing his lunch into his backpack.

"You always rush us out there," complained Elizabeth, "and then we have to wait in the cold."

"It wouldn't be quite so cold if you wore gloves and a hat and zipped your jacket." Lucy could hear the bus, down at the bottom of the hill. "If you don't get out there this minute, you're going to miss it and I really don't want to drive you this morning. Sara! Get down here! It's the bus."

"You don't have to yell, Mom. I'm right here."

Lucy gave her middle daughter a kiss on the cheek, and a shove toward the door. Then with a sigh of exasperation she watched the three go down the driveway: Toby strode along on his long legs, Sara ran, and Elizabeth did her very best imitation of Tyra Banks on a fashion runway.

Turning back to the sink, Lucy loaded the breakfast dishes into the dishwasher. Then she zipped Zoe into her snowsuit, handed Bill his lunchbox, and gave them each a good-bye kiss. Finally alone in the house, she went straight to the computer.

It was eleven when she was finished; she just had time to drop the story off before she had to pick up Zoe.

"Lucy! I knew you wouldn't let me down," exclaimed Ted, when she pushed open the door to *The Pennysaver* office.

"It's all here," she said, handing him a computer disc. "The greed, the compulsion, the desperation, and the shame."

"Sounds like a B-movie," said Ted.

"Isn't that what this is?" asked Lucy. "What's happening to nice, quiet Tinker's Cove?"

"I don't know, but I'm not complaining," said Ted. "This sure beats writing about the Cub Scouts' Pinewood Derby."

"I guess," chuckled Lucy, who well remembered long, noisy Sunday afternoons in the church basement when Toby and the other boys in his den raced the little wooden cars they had carved out of blocks of wood. "Did you go to the arraignment this morning?"

"Yeah. It was pretty awful. Gerald looked terrible. He hasn't got a lawyer, yet. The judge entered a not guilty plea for him. No bail, of course."

"They think he'd skip town?"

"Worse. I think they're worried he might kill himself."

Lucy studied the counter between herself and Ted. "Was his wife there?"

"No."

"Poor Gerald."

"Poor Gerald! I'm surprised at you, Lucy. The man stole the town's most valuable artifact—actually pretended he was selling it on behalf of the library—and you feel sorry for him?"

"I do. He couldn't help himself any more than an alcoholic or a drug addict can. Read my story and you'll understand."

"That doesn't make what he did right," said Ted. "And besides, if he had been on drugs or booze he would've been caught a lot sooner."

"True enough," said Lucy, turning to go. At the door she paused. "Did you talk to Horowitz?"

"He gave the usual press conference."

"I just wondered, did he say anything about Bitsy or Hayden?"

Ted smiled and shook his head. "Not a word, kiddo. Just the contrary. He made a big point of saying that this did not change the status of the Howell and Northcross cases, which are both closed."

Lucy shook her head in disbelief. "I don't get it. We have this little town library and all this stuff is going on: murder, suicide, theft, for Pete's sake, and he's saying there's no connection. That just doesn't make sense." She pushed open the door and marched out, leaving the little bell attached to the top of the door tinkling in her wake.

Once she was out on the sidewalk, Lucy felt as if she needed to burn off some steam. Instead of driving, she decided to walk over to Kiddie Kollege. It was only a few blocks and the fresh air would do her good.

The sun wasn't shining and the sky was still full of clouds, but the temperature was unusually mild. The thermometer outside Slack's Hardware read thirty degrees, a heat wave.

The next shop was the Carriage Trade, a shop that sold expensive, tasteful clothing for women. The four dress forms in the window were bare, except for sandwich boards with the letters S-A-L-E. Lucy smiled, thinking that Sue would no doubt be checking out the bargains if she hadn't already done so.

Maybe she should stop in, too. After all, she loved the sweater Bill had bought here and given her for Christmas. The thought gave her pause; she had last worn the sweater at her first meeting of the library board when she had been so worried about making a good impression.

She smiled grimly at the thought. If only she'd known then what she knew now. The board members weren't quite the upstanding citizens she had once thought. Ed Bumpus was gruff and rude, Corney was plagiarizing recipes for her column, Gerald was a gambler. Who else had a secret, she wondered, a secret that was important enough to kill for?

There was still one board member, she realized, who she hardly knew. It was about time, she decided, picking up her pace, that she got better acquainted with Chuck Canaday.

Chapter Twenty-one

*Bambi and all the other animals fled in terror
from the flames that were consuming the forest.*

As much as Lucy had enjoyed her brisk walk over to Kiddie Kollege, the walk back to retrieve the car convinced her it hadn't been such a good idea. Zoe dragged her feet and dawdled, stopping every few feet to poke a stick into the snow piled alongside the sidewalk.

The balmy temperature didn't seem quite so balmy, either, thanks to a smart breeze. The sign in front of the bank may have read thirty degrees but the wind chill made it feel more like twenty. When Zoe plopped down in the slushy snow to make a snow angel, Lucy lost her temper.

"Zoe! You're going to get soaking wet!" she scolded, lifting the little girl to her feet and carrying her the remaining few feet of sidewalk to the car. "It's lunchtime. We have to get home."

Lucy strapped her into her booster seat and started the engine, pushing the heater up as high as it would go. It was times like these, she thought, when she wished she lived a bit closer to town.

She drove the familiar route down Main Street on automatic pilot, thinking of what she was going to make for supper, and not paying much attention to the car. She had reached Route 1 and was speeding along when she first noticed wisps of smoke or steam slipping out from the side of the hood.

Not quite believing what she was seeing, she rubbed her eyes and checked the gauges. The engine temperature was normal, the oil light wasn't on. She slowed down a little bit but that only seemed to make things worse; the smoke was really pouring out now and a car coming the other way flashed its lights and honked at her.

Seeing the turnoff for Red Top Road ahead, she pulled over to the side and stopped the car. She got out to investigate and was horrified to see little orange tongues of flames licking up through the crack between the hood and the fender.

"Oh, no," she exclaimed, yanking open the back door. With shaking hands she struggled to unfasten Zoe's seat belt, then grabbed the little girl by the upper arms and dragged her out of the car.

"Ow! That hurt!"

"I'm sorry, baby," she crooned, clutching the little one to her breast and backing away from the car. It was then she spotted her purse on the passenger seat.

She dropped Zoe to her feet, ordering her to stay put, and cautiously approached the car. She could feel the heat on her face; the flames were a good six inches long now and black smoke was pouring from the engine. She held her breath and reached into the car, snatching her purse and dashing back to Zoe.

Hearing an ominous whoosh, she grabbed her mittened hand and dragged her away from the car. There was a big pop; Lucy turned and saw the interior burst into a ball of flame.

"Oh, my God," she moaned, collapsing to her knees and clutching Zoe to her.

By now the car was totally engulfed in flame and the air

was filling with thick, black smoke. The acrid stink of burning oil and plastic irritated her nose and throat and made her eyes sting. Lucy coughed and backed even farther away, reaching into her purse for her cell phone. When she could breathe a little better she punched in 9-1-1.

"My car's on fire," she told the dispatcher. "I'm at Route One and Red Top Road."

"Is anyone in the car?"

"No. We're out, we're safe," said Lucy, caressing Zoe's cheek and pressing the little girl tight against her hip. She sobbed. "Please hurry."

"They're on the way," said the dispatcher. "Just hold tight and they'll be there in a minute or two."

"Thank you." Tears were rolling down Lucy's face and she was shaking with sobs, unable to take her eyes off the burning car. She was terrified to think what might have happened if she hadn't stopped the car in time. It had all happened so fast; only a few minutes had passed from the moment she first noticed the smoke.

In the distance she could already hear the sirens growing steadily louder as the firetrucks approached. When the engine arrived some of the men immediately began spraying foam on the car and the road; two others approached her.

"Are you all right?" asked the first, a tall man whose face was obscured by the cloth he wore beneath his helmet.

"We're fine," said Lucy, her voice wavering and her face crumpling. "I'm sorry. I just can't seem to stop crying."

"It's shock," said the shorter firefighter, who Lucy was surprised to see was a woman. "It's normal. I'll get you some blankets."

Lucy realized she was shivering, and so was Zoe, and was grateful for the warmth of the orange blankets the firefighters draped over their shoulders. It was only a few minutes later when Barney arrived and bundled them in the back of his cruiser for the drive home.

"What happened, Lucy?"

"I don't know. One minute I was driving home and the next I was standing by the side of the road watching my car burn up."

"Have you had any trouble with it lately?"

"No. I just got the oil changed last month. The mechanic said everything looked fine. It's old, but it's never let me down." It was true, she realized. The Subaru had been like a faithful friend, carrying her and the kids to countless ballet lessons and Cub Scout meetings and swimming classes, hauling tons of groceries home from the IGA, giving her the freedom to come and go in all kinds of weather. "I'm going to miss that car," she said.

"You got a lot of years out of it," sighed Barney.

"Nearly 150,000 miles."

"I guess it deserves a rest, then," said Barney, turning into the driveway. He braked and turned his jowly Saint Bernard face to her. "I've got an accident report to fill out, if you feel up to it."

"Sure," said Lucy, dabbing at her eyes and sniffling. "Actually, I'll be glad of the company. Come on in."

But as she fussed around the kitchen, heating up soup and spreading peanut butter and jelly onto bread for sandwiches for the three of them, Lucy couldn't add much information to what she'd already told Barney. For the life of her, she couldn't figure out what had caused the car to suddenly burst into flames.

After they finished eating, Barney stood up and put on his jacket, then smoothed his hand over his graying crew cut and set his cap on his head. Standing in the kitchen in his regulation black boots, he tapped his clipboard against his leg.

"Listen," he said in a low voice, making sure Zoe couldn't hear, "I don't like the sound of this. Especially with everything that's been going on. I think you should lay low, if you know what I mean."

"What do you mean?" Lucy narrowed her eyes.

"I mean, I think that fire might not o' been an accident. I think it might have been set."

"Oh," said Lucy, suddenly feeling rather weak in the knees and sitting down. It was one thing to harbor a vague suspicion, as she had ever since the near miss when the kids were sledding, but it was another thing altogether to have those suspicions voiced by somebody else, especially if that somebody else happened to be a police officer.

"This is getting really scary," she said, shivering involuntarily and raising tear-filled eyes to Barney. "When I think what could have happened—what if I hadn't gotten Zoe out of the car in time?"

"I didn't mean to upset you," said Barney, who would rather deal with a drunk and disorderly than a crying woman any day. He started to reach for the doorknob, but stopped himself and stood uneasily shifting his weight from one foot to the other.

"All's well that ends well, I guess. But it wouldn't hurt to be extra careful for a few days." He turned and yanked the door open. "Better safe than sorry, right?"

Chapter Twenty-two

*The Fairy Godmother waved her wand again,
and the pumpkin was transformed into a
beautiful coach.*

After Barney left, Lucy dried her eyes and began tidying up the lunch dishes. She appreciated his warning, but at the moment she was concerned with a more immediate problem: how to tell Bill about the car. She was afraid he might not take it well.

But when she finally screwed up her courage to tell him, after making sure he was sitting down with a beer near at hand, he surprised her.

"Lucy, that car doesn't owe us a thing," he said, pulling her down on his lap. "Things are just things, but people are people. All I care about is that you and Zoe are okay." He gave her a squeeze. "It's a good thing you realized something was wrong when you did—it could've been a tragedy."

"I know." Lucy fingered his beard. "But what will I do now? I don't have a car anymore!"

"I'll call the insurance agent tonight," said Bill, patting her knee. "We probably won't get much for the car, but we should get a rental car for a few weeks while we look for something new."

"Really?" Lucy smiled, considering the possibilities.

"Really. Now, where's my supper, woman?"

"It's my morning at the food pantry, so just call the church if you need me." Juanita's breath made a cloud in the frosty morning air as she stood on the doorstep the next morning, dropping Sadie off for a playdate.

"We'll be fine," said Lucy. "Say, can you give me a ride into town when you pick up Sadie?"

"Sure. You've got car trouble?"

"You could say that. The car caught fire yesterday."

"It did? Is everybody all right?"

"Zoe and I got a little scare, that's all."

"You're lucky nobody was hurt. How'd it happen?"

"I wish I knew. The car was going great until I noticed the smoke." She shook her head. "They tell me it's a complete loss. I'm supposed to pick up a copy of the accident report at the police station, and I have to pick up a rental car. The insurance will pay for it—thank goodness."

"Well, that's one good thing," said Juanita brightly, but her big brown eyes were solemn. "I'll take you wherever you need to go. See you later."

After she left and the girls went upstairs to Zoe's room to play, Lucy decided to give Chuck a call. The sooner she got to the bottom of this mess, she realized, the happier she'd feel.

The motherly voice that answered his phone assured her that Mr. Canaday would certainly be delighted to meet with her, but unfortunately he was not in his office. She might be able to reach him at home, the voice said, rattling off the number. Or on his car phone—Lucy should definitely try that. And of course, she could always dial his pager. That would probably be best.

Lucy hung up and looked at the numbers she had scrawled down on her notepad. She dialed Chuck's home number and got his machine: "You know what to do. Leave a message and I'll get back to you."

She left a message, asking him to call her, and dialed the car phone, but couldn't get through. An operator thanked her for trying but said a connection could not be established at this time.

As a last resort she tried the pager. A recorded voice told her to punch in her phone number, and she did, but doubted Chuck would respond to a number he didn't recognize.

That done, there was nothing to do but wait. In the meantime, she could mix up some cookie dough for the girls. She was just putting it in the refrigerator to chill when the phone rang.

"Lucy, it's Chuck, returning your call."

"Thanks for calling back so quickly," began Lucy. "Something's happened and I'd like to get together with you to discuss the library." An odd thought occurred to her and she digressed. "I mean, Gerald isn't still president, is he?"

"Actually, he is," said Chuck. "I checked the bylaws and we have to have a board meeting and vote on a new president."

"Can we do that? Do we still have a quorum?"

"I'm not sure," admitted Chuck. "I think we do as long as everybody comes. There are still five of us, right?"

"Yup. You, Corney, Ed, Miss Tilley, and me . . . but I have to tell you I had a close call yesterday."

"What happened?" He sounded genuinely concerned.

"My car burst into flames."

"Jesus, Mary, and Joseph—are you okay?"

"Yup. The car's gone, though."

"Well, that can be replaced." He paused. "I think we better talk. Can you come into the office?"

"Sure, I'm picking up a rental today. Monday, Wednesday, and Friday mornings are best for me."

"How about ten tomorrow—Wednesday morning? If we don't have that storm they're predicting."

"That's fine with me." Lucy paused, then asked, "What storm?"

"It's supposed to be a big nor'easter—but they've been saying that all winter. I swear they do it just to encourage business—everybody runs to the store and stocks up on batteries and stuff and we just get a few more inches of snow."

"Well, I'm keeping my fingers crossed just in case," said Lucy. "See you tomorrow."

"Wow! Valentine cookies," enthused Juanita when she arrived at a little after one. "Did you help?"

Sadie pointed out a particularly large, lopsided heart thickly covered with bright red icing and silver dragées. "I made that one for you."

"For me? It's beautiful! Thank you!"

Lucy smiled as Sadie, beaming with pride, presented her mother with the cookie. "That one is too beautiful to eat, so you'll have to take some of the others, too." She filled a plastic bag with cookies, glancing at Zoe as she worked. She'd been doing the same thing all morning, she realized. It was as if she had to reassure herself that Zoe was really all right.

She handed the bag of cookies to Juanita. "We'll just get our coats, okay?"

"Take your time. I'm not in a rush."

A half hour later, Juanita dropped Lucy and Zoe at the garage. "I don't mind waiting." she offered. "Just in case."

"There's no need. I called this morning and the car's all ready."

"Okay. See ya later . . . and thanks for the cookies."

"Thanks for the ride," said Lucy, waving.

She and Zoe went into the office, where Lucy rang the bell for service. She was just opening her checkbook when a kid with long blond hair appeared. The name embroidered on his shirt was Gary.

"Hi. I've come to pick up a rental car."

"Okay," he said, flipping through a pile of invoices. "It's Stone, right?"

"Right," she said, holding tight to Zoe's hand so she couldn't wander off in the direction of the vending machines.

"Here we go. It's all set with the insurance company."

"That's great."

"No problem. Hey, that was some fire you had. That car is toast."

"You've seen the car?" asked Lucy.

"Yup. Cops impound all the wrecks with us. DUIs, arrests, they all come here. Want to take a look at it?"

Lucy hesitated, remembering the fear she had felt the day before. "I don't think so," she finally said. "Do you have any idea what caused the fire?"

"Fire marshall's gonna take a look, but I don't think he's gonna be able to tell. There's not much left." Gary grinned at her as he handed over the keys. "You're sure you don't want a souvenir? I pulled the medallion off."

"I guess I would," said Lucy. "Thanks." She took the little chrome ornament representing the constellation Pleiades and tucked it in her pocket, but she kept her eyes straight ahead as she walked to the rental car, a big Buick sedan. She didn't want to see the burned-out hulk of the Subaru.

As she unlocked the car, Lucy thought of what Barney had said. It would be easy enough to set a car on fire; all it would take was a gas-soaked rag thrown onto the radiator. Anybody could do that in a second, especially since she had been using a bungee cord to hold down the hood since the latch had broken a few months ago.

Maybe she was paranoid, she thought as she opened the car door for Zoe, but it seemed as if a lot of things were going wrong all of a sudden. First there was the near miss with the truck when the kids were sledding, and then the fire yesterday. What is it they say, she wondered as she helped Zoe into the back seat—trouble comes in threes?

Not if she could help it, she decided. From now on she was going to have to be more careful. She could no longer take her safety, or the kids' safety, for granted. She was going to have to take precautions, like locking the house and the car, and keeping a closer eye on the kids.

"There's no seat for me!" Zoe complained as Lucy strapped her in.

"That's right. You know, I think you're big enough now that you don't need one. What do you think?"

"I'm a big girl."

"So you are," said Lucy, bending down and kissing her on her head. "Know what? I love my big girl very much."

"I know." Zoe smiled the complacent smile of a secure child who is sure of her parents' love and care.

Lucy gave her knee a little pat and got behind the wheel where she adjusted the seat and the mirrors, then started the motor. The roar of the engine startled her; this car was a lot more powerful than the Subaru. She'd have to drive cautiously or she'd be going far too fast, and without four-wheel drive, she reminded herself as she shifted into drive. She inched her way across the lot to the curb cut and stopped there, checking for traffic. She was glad she did, as a huge dump truck zoomed past, going much faster than the speed limit.

She jumped involuntarily, then gave herself a little shake. Being careful was one thing, but she couldn't go on being terrified all the time. She took her foot off the brake and glided out into the road, accelerating gradually. Tomorrow, she remembered, she'd be seeing Canaday. Maybe together they could get to the bottom of this thing.

Chapter Twenty-three

*The King and Queen decided it was time for
their son, the Prince, to choose a wife.*

When Lucy got to Canaday's office the next morning, after leaving Zoe at Kiddie Kollege, she found it was a modern suite located on the second floor of the outlet mall, right above Liz Claiborne and Van Heusen. Canaday wasn't there.

"I'm sorry," said his secretary, a fiftyish woman with permed gray hair and eyeglasses on a string around her neck, "but Chuck's running late. He said he hoped you'd wait—he'll get here just as soon as he can."

"No problem," said Lucy, taking a seat on a rather battered captain's bench and picking up a copy of *People* magazine. She couldn't help staring at the woman; her polyester plaid vest reminded her of someone. "Are you related to Edna Withers?" she finally asked.

"She's my twin sister. I'm Edith and she's Edna, and we're both Withers because we married brothers." Edith looked at her sharply, over her half-glasses. "And we don't ever swap, so don't bother to ask."

"It never occurred to me," said Lucy, her mind boggling at the thought.

"Well, you'd be surprised how many people it does occur to," insisted Edith. "And they don't mind saying so, either."

"So your sister is, I mean was, Bitsy Howell's landlady?"

Edith nodded. "Wasn't that terrible? Her getting shot like that? Right in broad daylight? Gives you the creeps."

"Sure does," said Lucy.

"And then that family of hers—I never heard of such a thing! 'Just give everything to the Salvation Army.' That's what they told Edna. It doesn't seem as if they cared, somehow."

"Did she do that? Give everything away?" Lucy was wondering if she could get a peek at Bitsy's apartment—maybe she could find some sort of clue there.

Edith nodded, dashing her hopes. "I spent all weekend helping her clear out the place. That Bitsy, poor thing, she wouldn't have won any prizes for neatness, I can tell you that. Stuff everywhere. So many books—I guess you'd expect that, her being a librarian. And papers scattered everywhere, lots of them filled with nothing but scribbles and numbers. We filled bags and bags with nothing but garbage. Then there were the clothes—they had to be boxed up. And there were her little bits and pieces, jewelry and a Bible and little oddments, you know what I mean. Those we boxed up and sent to her family, even though they said not to. We couldn't quite throw them away. We just couldn't."

"I think you did the right thing," said Lucy.

"I hope so." Edith reached for a tissue and blew her nose. "We decided to keep the furniture, after all. I told Edna that she might as well because she could raise the rent a little bit for a furnished apartment."

"Might as well," agreed Lucy.

Hearing footsteps in the vestibule, Edith tilted her head toward the door. "That's him, now," she said.

"Hi, Edith. How's every little thing?" asked Chuck, shaking a dusting of snow off his overcoat and hanging it on a rack.

"Just fine, Mr. C." She nodded toward Lucy. "Mrs. Stone is here."

"Lucy! Thanks for waiting." He picked a stack of letters off the corner of Edith's desk and glanced through them. "Can I offer you something—coffee? Coke?"

"No, thanks."

"Well, come on in my office," he said, opening the door for her. "Edith, no calls, please."

Lucy took a seat opposite Chuck's desk and looked around his office. She'd never seen anything like it—every surface was covered with piles of papers. Folders were even tucked in the bookcases, stuck between the law books, and spilling out of the lower shelf onto the floor.

"Don't mind the mess," he said, waving a hand. "I'm more organized than I look. And I'm awfully glad you called. I'm really concerned about the library. Things were bad enough, and now this business with Gerald . . ."

"It came as a complete surprise?"

"You bet it did. Shock is more like it." He propped his elbow on the desk and rested his cheek on his hand, shaking his head. "Mrs. Asquith wants me to defend him, but I had to tell her that it was impossible. I mean, I can't defend him and represent the library's interests, too." He shrugged. "I gave her some names. I hope the DA's not going to be too hard-nosed about this and is willing to work out a deal with Gerald. They could let him make good the loss and give him a suspended sentence."

"Unless," began Lucy, an unbidden thought coming to mind.

"What?"

"I just thought of it. What if Gerald killed Bitsy and Hayden?" said Lucy. "Maybe they figured out that he stole the tankard."

"Gerald? A murderer?" Chuck snorted. "I don't think so."

"Neither do I," agreed Lucy. "But I didn't think he was a gambler, either. Something's at the bottom of this. I mean Bitsy and Hayden, and well, me, too." She set her jaw, looking at him defensively. "I don't think I'm paranoid but I can't help wondering if my car was set on fire on purpose. Being on this board seems to be awfully dangerous. If it isn't the tankard, what could it be?"

Chuck leaned back awkwardly in his chair and scratched his head, mussing up his hair. "Listen, if you want to quit, I'll understand," he said.

For a second, Lucy was tempted. "No," she said. "If someone's trying to scare me off, they picked the wrong person. I don't like being scared. It just makes me mad."

Chuck grinned. "Well, if you're determined to stick it out, can I ask a favor?"

"Anything."

"Do you think you could ask your husband to look at some figures for me? He's a contractor, isn't he? He knows about construction costs, right? He'd know if something was out of line or not, wouldn't he?"

"I guess so."

Chuck began rummaging through the papers on his desk. "See, I'm having a problem with the figures for the library addition. We all got that final accounting at the meeting, and everything looked fine. But after Bitsy was killed I copied all the files in her computer—just to be safe, you know. Just a precaution. And when I was going through them, well, I noticed that her figures didn't match the final accounting." He stopped shifting the papers around and looked at Lucy. "I'm not saying it means anything. After all, I don't know what her figures were based on. Were they estimates? Were they from invoices? I don't know, and I don't have time to really go into it. But I do know that with Gerald's arrest, Horowitz is going to be asking for the books and I want to know what's in them."

"Bill's not doing much these days," admitted Lucy, "because of the weather. I don't think he'd mind. But you know he's already checked the figures for Ed. Everything looked okay to him."

"I know. I wouldn't even think of asking him except for all that's happened."

"It's worth a try," said Lucy, doubtfully.

Chuck poked through a few more files and shook his head helplessly. "Edith!" he yelled. "Where are those library figures?"

She bustled in and zeroed in on the credenza, deftly producing a thick file.

"What would I do without you?" asked Chuck, taking it from her.

Edith smiled at him and clucked her tongue. "You really need to tidy up this office." She sounded just like a mother telling her son to clean up his room.

"I'll do it tomorrow," he said, leafing through the folder.

"I've heard that before," said Edith, going back to her desk.

Chuck looked up and smiled at Lucy, inviting her to share his amusement. She couldn't resist and broke into a smile, too.

"You know, I stopped in at the library—that's why I was late, in fact," said Chuck. "I thought that with all this upset things might be topsy-turvy. But they weren't. The new librarian has everything running smoothly."

Lucy nodded. "It's amazing, isn't it? The board's a shambles but it's business as usual in the library. Makes you wonder if we're really needed, doesn't it?"

"I guess somebody has to sign the checks," observed Chuck. "Thanks for this." He gave her the folder. "And be careful. We can't keep losing board members at this rate or we won't have a quorum."

She was sure he meant it as a joke, but it rattled her.

Clutching the folder, she hurried out the door and into the hallway, almost bumping into Corney, who was wearing a hat and scarf in a becoming shade of blue that emphasized her eyes, and was carrying a large box, wrapped in a big red ribbon.

"A valentine for Chuck?" asked Lucy, with a big smile.

"Not really," said Corney, her face reddening. For once she seemed embarrassed. "Actually, he did some work for me, saved me from a bad situation and, well, this is just my way of saying thanks."

"I'm sure he'll appreciate it," said Lucy, giving her a little wave and heading down the stairs.

The lingering almond aroma left no doubt in Lucy's mind that Chuck was going to receive a big box of madeleines. Lucy wondered if it was really a thank-you present; hadn't Sue mentioned something about a big lawsuit involving Corney?

Pushing open the door, Lucy saw that snow had started to fall. Forgetting all about her resolution to be more careful, she dashed across the parking lot to the car, never noticing the big, black pickup truck that was just turning in. Never slowing, it rounded the line of parked cars and pulled up behind the Buick, blocking it in.

Lucy's heart leapt to her mouth, but when she looked up she saw it was only Ed.

"Hi, Lucy. How's it going?"

"Fine." Lucy nodded, stepping up to the cab of the truck. "Looks like we're going to get that storm after all."

"Yeah," agreed Ed. "The wind's pickin' up already. S'posed to be one hell of a blow."

"And we've got a high tide and a full moon. There could be flooding."

"Well, you're high and dry there on old Red Top. You don't have to worry." He glanced curiously at the folder she was holding. "What'cha got there? Library business?"

"Oh, no." Lucy found herself reluctant to admit the truth. "It's just some legal papers for Bill—a disgruntled customer."

"Wouldn't expect he'd have that sort of problem," drawled Ed.

"Some people are never satisfied," shrugged Lucy, backing away from the truck. "Do you mind moving? I've got to get to the IGA before the storm gets any worse."

"Sure," said Ed, touching the bill of his cap in a polite farewell. "Didn't realize that was your car. Thought you had a little rice burner. Did something happen to it?"

"I had an accident," said Lucy, unwilling to go into details. "That's too bad." Ed scratched his chin. "Maybe you'd better be more careful."

"I sure will," said Lucy, giving him a little wave and climbing into the Buick. She laid the folder down beside her without a glance and settled herself behind the wheel. It was only when she turned to check that everything was clear, before backing up, that she noticed the big magic marker letters on the folder. They spelled out two words: "Library Addition."

And they must, she realized, have been clearly visible to Ed while she stood chatting with him, the folder clutched to her chest. All the time they were talking he must have known she had lied to him. Why had she done it? She didn't really know. It was just one of those stupid things that get people in trouble, she thought, hoping that by some miracle Ed hadn't noticed.

With more force than was necessary, she jammed the car into gear and reversed out of her parking spot, reminding herself to accelerate cautiously on the increasingly slippery road surface. Now, with a storm coming on, was no time to have an accident.

Chapter Twenty-four

*Many years went by and a thicket of briars
grew up and surrounded the Enchanted Castle.*

The snow was falling thickly by the time the older kids got home from school and several inches had already accumulated.

"No school tomorrow," crowed Toby as he unzipped his jacket.

"Don't be so sure," cautioned Lucy. "The forecasters have been wrong before."

"It was on the loudspeaker," said Sara. "The principal said no school tomorrow because of the snow emergency."

"Really?" Lucy had never heard of this happening before. She went into the family room and switched on the TV, flipping to the weather channel. She waited impatiently while weather conditions in foreign capitals were reported and a batch of commercials were aired. When the broadcast resumed an earnest young woman in a bright blue suit assured her that gale force winds, freezing temperatures, and a record snowfall were expected to batter the entire Northeast. Just in case she had any doubts, the satellite weather map showed an enormous swirling mass just offshore.

"The National Weather Service has announced a storm warning for Northern New England, and a storm watch is in effect for Rhode Island and Connecticut right on down to New York City," recited the weather girl. "This is a massive storm with serious destructive power and it is being watched closely. Flooding is expected in coastal communities and public safety officials are planning to evacuate some areas. Businesses and schools have been urged to close tomorrow and anyone whose job is not considered essential for public safety is encouraged to remain at home."

"Will we be okay?" asked Sara.

"Sure," said Lucy. "This old house has been through lots of storms."

"I bet we'll lose electricity," grumbled Elizabeth. "I hate that. It's so boring."

"It's not so bad," said Lucy. "What is it Daddy says? We'll have to watch TV by candlelight?"

Elizabeth rolled her eyes and groaned. "Right, Mom."

"In the meantime, you can all get to work bringing in some wood for the stoves. Fill all the woodboxes and stack as much as you can on the porch, okay?"

"Do we have to?" asked Toby.

"Not if you don't mind freezing to death—get to work, all of you. Now."

While the kids were busy with the wood, Lucy checked her food supplies. She had bought extra milk and bread that morning, and the freezer and pantry were full. A frozen turkey caught her eye, and she took it out of the freezer to thaw, planning to cook it tomorrow. The oven—thank goodness it was gas—would help keep the kitchen warm.

The flashlights all had fresh batteries, as did the radio, and they had plenty of candles and a couple of oil lamps. She set them all on the kitchen counter. Congratulating herself for remembering, she plugged her cell phone into the charger. After that there wasn't anything else to do so she went out to help the kids.

* * *

When Bill came home he had an enormous heart-shaped box of chocolates for Lucy and a bunch of flowers from the florist shop.

"You shouldn't have," exclaimed Lucy, throwing her arms around his neck and nuzzling his beard.

"I didn't want you to be disappointed. I know how much you were looking forward to going out to dinner, but it doesn't look as if that's going to happen. They're saying snow right through tomorrow."

"And then there's the digging out—that's going to take a while," said Lucy, pulling away from Bill and starting to arrange the flowers in a vase. "Oh, well, there's always next year. Besides, we've got everything we need right here."

"That's right," agreed Bill, stepping up behind her and wrapping his arms around her waist. "You're everything I need."

"And I do have the chocolates," said Lucy, leaning back against him.

"Tease," he whispered, biting her ear.

Lucy turned around and raised her face for a kiss, but thought better of it when she heard Toby clattering down the back stairs. She stepped away from Bill with a sigh.

"What's for dinner?" Toby asked, poking his head into the kitchen.

"Lasagna," said Lucy, opening the oven. "The lasagna of love."

Toby looked from his mother to his father, a puzzled expression on his face. Spotting the box of chocolates, he asked, "Hey, can I have some of that candy?"

"No! That's my present and I haven't even opened the box yet."

Seeing Toby's disappointment, she immediately felt bad. She always shared her Valentine's Day candy; it was a family tradition. "After supper—but I get the square ones," she added.

* * *

That evening, Lucy asked Bill if he would look at the library figures. He took the file, but never opened it, opting instead to play some computer games with the kids. "We're bound to lose power soon," he said, "and there's no telling how long it will be before we get it back."

But although the wind howled all night, occasionally slamming the house with such strong gusts that the walls shook and the pictures swayed on their hooks, the electricity was still on in the morning.

"It's because it's such light, powdery snow," said Bill, sipping his coffee and looking out the kitchen window.

"It's just a matter of time," said Lucy, stirring the oatmeal. "All it takes is for one tree to get blown down on the wires."

"Is the snow deep?" asked Zoe, rubbing her eyes sleepily.

"At least a foot, and there's more to come," said Bill, scooping her up for a hug. "Happy Valentine's Day!"

The storm was already being called the Valentine's Day Blizzard when Lucy checked the weather channel after breakfast. Toby and Elizabeth were sleeping the morning away but Sara and Zoe were busy making valentines out of construction paper and doilies.

Lucy had plenty to do, too. She had mixed up some cornbread for turkey stuffing and while it was baking had started a batch of cupcakes. Rummaging in a drawer, she found some paper liners printed with hearts and set them in the tins, carefully filling them with chocolate batter. The girls could ice them later—they'd love decorating them with candy.

Bill, however, was restless. Unable to go to work, he wandered from window to window, looking out at the storm. "No sense shoveling," he said. "It's drifting too much.

Might as well wait 'til it stops." Cooped up in the house, he flipped channels nervously. Regular programming had been cancelled; the stations were competing to have the latest news on the record-breaking blizzard.

Periodically, he'd give her a report. "The entire Northeast is shut down, even the stock market." A few minutes later: "Terrible flooding in Cape Cod. Houses gone in Chatham, terrific damage to the National Seashore beaches." Off he'd go, only to return with more news. "Fifty-foot seas—they say a Liberian tanker is in trouble off Nantucket. The Coast Guard's on the way, but they're not holding out much hope."

"You're making me nervous," said Lucy. "Can't you find something to do?"

"Sorry," he said. "You probably don't want to hear about the tragic fire in Fall River."

"You're right, I don't," said Lucy, tipping the cornbread out onto a wire rack. "How'd you like to chop up some onions? You know how they make me cry."

"Sure," he said eagerly. "How many? Ten? Twelve?"

"Two."

"I can do more."

"The recipe says two."

"Okay," he said, setting the chopping board on the counter. "Mind if I take a look at that recipe?"

While Bill made the stuffing, Lucy poured herself another cup of coffee. She sat down at the kitchen table to keep him company.

"Have you had a chance to look at those library figures yet?" she asked.

"Not yet," said Bill, who was carefully slicing the cornbread into cubes.

"Do you know what to look for?"

"Not exactly—I'm no accountant. But since the guy who was writing the checks has turned out to be a compulsive gambler, it seems logical to look for inflated costs. That might mean he was getting kickbacks."

"That would mean somebody else was involved—the subcontractors, right?"

"Yeah," agreed Bill, thunking a frying pan onto the stove and popping in a cube of butter. When it had finished sizzling, he added the onion and stirred it around. "When you think about it, this wasn't Gerald's first construction project. As president of the college he was responsible for several new buildings. I bet he's done this before, and knows just which subcontractors will play ball with him. That was one of the first things I was going to look for—see if he's been using the same contractors on a number of projects."

"But I thought Ed was in charge of the library addition."

"As I understand it, he was keeping an eye on the day-to-day progress. Making sure that the actual construction was being done right, that they were using the right materials. Gerald was in charge of the checkbook." He snorted, dumping the onions into the bowl of corn bread and mixing them together. "Kind of like putting the fox in charge of the chicken coop, when you think of it. Now you have to take it from here," he said, handing her the bowl of stuffing. "There's no way I'm going to get intimate with a turkey."

"Okay," laughed Lucy.

The storm continued through the afternoon. Toby and Elizabeth woke around one o'clock and immediately began fighting over who would get the first shower. Toby won and was making himself a fried egg, cheese, and bologna sandwich when Elizabeth appeared in the kitchen.

"That's disgusting—do you know what that does to your arteries?" asked Elizabeth, popping half of an English muffin into the toaster.

"I don't care," said Toby, setting the hot pan in the sink and filling it with water, creating a cloud of steam. "At least I'm not anorexic."

"I'm not anorexic—I eat plenty," insisted Elizabeth.

"Half of an English muffin isn't much of a breakfast," said Lucy. "How about some cereal or yogurt?"

Elizabeth exhaled noisily and rolled her eyes. "I can figure out what I want to eat for myself, thank you very much."

"Fine." Lucy looked out the window at the blowing snow, which had drifted against the shed, practically covering it. She wished she hadn't joined Toby's bandwagon by urging Elizabeth to eat more breakfast—she knew Elizabeth was terrified of getting fat and telling her to eat more would only be met with stubborn resistance. Lucy's plan so far had been to keep tabs on her daughter's daily intake and when it dropped too low, instead of nagging, she made one of her favorite foods. When even this didn't work she had a secret weapon: an imported chocolate and hazelnut spread loaded with fat and calories that Elizabeth couldn't resist.

"I made some cupcakes—maybe you could help Sara and Zoe frost them," she suggested.

"Okay." Elizabeth was finished with breakfast. She slipped her plate into the sink, whirled around, and tapped Toby on the shoulder. "Your turn to do the dishes," she crowed, beating a hasty retreat.

Toby sprang to his feet to chase her, but Lucy intervened. "Load the dishwasher. I'll make sure she does them next time."

"Mom," he wailed, beginning to protest, then changed his mind when Lucy gave him a sharp look. "Okay."

The house seemed to shrink as the afternoon wore on. Toby and Elizabeth couldn't be in the same room without squabbling, and even normally placid Sara and Zoe began to bicker. The wind and snow were still coming down at four, but Bill dragged Toby outside to shovel anyway. "Might as well get a start," he said. "Besides, you've been sitting at that computer all day. You could use some exercise."

"Aw, Dad," groaned Toby. "Do I have to? I'm doing re-search for a paper."

Bill looked over his shoulder. "What's your paper on? The MTV website? Get a move on."

Toby gave a huge sigh as he logged off, prompting Lucy to wonder for the millionth time why teenagers were so lazy. Given their druthers, he and Elizabeth would sleep well past noon every day; then they would shower for an hour or two before settling down with the computer or TV. They only showed signs of life when the telephone rang; otherwise they were content to recline and nibble—Toby on any sort of fatty snack food, Elizabeth on her nails.

Hearing high-pitched screams in the kitchen, Lucy went to investigate. She found Sara and Zoe at the kitchen table, which was littered with cupcakes, a bowl of pink frosting, and numerous containers of cake decorations. Zoe's face was red and she was crying.

"What's the matter?"

"Sara took all the silver ones!" Zoe was furious. Lucy had never seen her so upset.

"There were hardly any, Mom. See?" Sara held up a cup-cake with a few silver dragées on top.

"You and Sadie used them up on the cookies. Remember?"

"I hate Sadie."

"No, you don't," said Lucy, patting her littlest daughter's shoulder. "It's been a long day. I bet you're tired."

Zoe sniffed and gave a little shudder.

"How about some chocolate sprinkles instead?"

Zoe shook her head.

"I know—wait one minute." Lucy took the big heart-shaped box of chocolates down from the top of the refriger-ator, where she had hidden it after the family binge the night before, and opened it up. Inside, nestled among the remain-ing chocolates, was a heart-shaped piece of chocolate wrapped in red foil. She plucked it out and gave it to Zoe. "How about this?"

Sara gasped, suitably impressed and obviously jealous.

Zoe glanced at her and stuck the candy on top of one of the cupcakes. "This one is mine."

"You can have it for dessert," promised Lucy. "Where's Elizabeth? I thought she was going to help you."

"On the phone. She had to talk to Lance," volunteered Sara, spotting an opportunity to get her big sister in trouble.

She was doomed to be disappointed. "Oh, well," said Lucy. "Let's finish here and I'll help you clean up. You girls did a really good job—these cupcakes are beautiful. We're going to have a lovely Valentine's Day Blizzard supper."

Zoe giggled and licked her fingers.

Lucy was wiping off the table when Toby came in, covered with snow from head to toe.

"Look at you!" exclaimed Lucy, hurrying over to help him out of his snow-caked clothes. "Where's your Dad?"

"Mr. Bumpus came by and Dad went with him."

"He did?" Lucy was tugging at one of Toby's boots. "Why?"

"Something about the snow load on the library—he said they needed to shovel the roof."

"Shovel the roof?"

Toby ran his fingers through his damp hair. His face was red and flushed and little droplets of water were sparkling on his eyelashes. "It's something out there, Mom. There's a *lot* of snow."

Lucy peered out the window in the kitchen door. Because of the storm it was already starting to get dark, and the snow was still falling heavily, blowing this way and that. Everything was white. The car and truck were mounds of snow sitting in the windswept driveway. The wind had also cleared the front of the shed while covering one side with a huge drift. The same thing had happened to the house; some windows were half-covered with snow, others were bare.

"I wish he hadn't gone," said Lucy. "This isn't any sort of weather to be out in."

"Mr. Bumpus said the road isn't too bad, and he's got four-wheel drive."

"Four-wheel drive has its limits," said Lucy.

Toby was shocked at this heresy. "Don't worry, Mom. They'll be fine. That truck is . . ." He couldn't find words to adequately describe Ed's truck and sputtered. "Cool," he finally said.

"I hope he's back in time for dinner," said Lucy, opening the oven to check the turkey.

"Boy, that smells good," said Toby, spreading some peanut butter on a piece of bread.

"Save some room for dinner," said Lucy as she basted the turkey. "I don't get it—that roof is supposed to have steel beams. I remember people asked about the roof when they first presented the plans at the town meeting."

"Mmmph," said Toby, his mouth full of peanut butter.

Lucy closed the oven door and stood for a minute by the sink, tapping it with the turkey baster. Suddenly dropping it in the sink, she rushed up the back stairs, heading for Bill's little attic office under the eaves. There, she found the folder with the library figures on his desk.

Pulling out the chair, she sat down and opened it, slowly leafing through the pages. She wasn't sure what she was looking for—there were so many figures. After pages and pages of tightly noted columns, she turned with relief to the invoices for materials, neatly clipped together. One of the first was from A-B Steel, she noted with relief. That meant they did use steel beams, the way they were supposed to.

She was about to replace the invoices in the file when she noticed a notebook tucked among the papers—it was the journal kept by the clerk of the works. The clerk of the works, she knew, was responsible for logging in all the deliveries, and he had. Each page was dated and the time for each delivery was noted, as well as the materials. Perilli Excavating, Cove Readymix, Tinker's Cove Lumber, O'Brien Plumbing and Heating, Ashley Roofing, Flambeau Millwork—it was all there, a steady stream of deliveries by building materials dealers. But there was no mention of the company she was looking for: A-B Steel.

That didn't mean anything, she told herself. Maybe it was delivered by a hauler with a different name. So she began studying the lists of items. Cubic yards of concrete, squares of shingles, board feet of lumber, windows and doors, nails and wire and pipe, joist hangers, things she recognized and things she didn't. But nowhere was there mention of any steel beams. No I-beams, nothing. But there was a notation of eight forty-foot eight-by-eight beams from the St. Lawrence Salvage Company.

She thought of the open floor plan of the addition, how the circulation desk and the new books area seemed to flow right on into the children's area. There were no walls, no supporting beams. It was one huge, uninterrupted space, about forty feet from the front door to the back wall. Forty feet of roof, now covered with tons of snow, supported not by tempered steel I-beams but by wood beams from a salvage company.

Lucy was no engineer, but she could see why Ed was worried. If she'd known, she would have been worried, too. She reached for the phone, intending to call Chuck, when the lights went out.

That didn't necessarily mean the phone was out, too, she told herself. She lifted the receiver to her ear; there was no dial tone.

Sitting alone in the dark, she pictured Ed's face. The bristling eyebrows, the little piggy eyes. The smile that could seem friendly and open or vaguely threatening. What had he said at the funeral? "I want people to know that Bill Stone signed off on this project, that Bill Stone said it was okay."

She hadn't liked it when he said it then, and she liked it even less now. Bill, she knew, had taken Ed's word that everything was as it should be. He had signed the papers, but he hadn't been involved in the construction. But now, if something was wrong, he could be blamed.

Even worse, thought Lucy, what if something happened to him? Shoveling off a roof was dangerous. A knot formed in her stomach. What if he fell? She felt as if something was gripping her heart; she couldn't breathe. She forced herself to inhale and exhale.

That's why Bitsy died, and Hayden, too. They had made the same discovery she had—that Ed had substituted inferior materials in the library addition. Bitsy must have been working on the figures before the meeting, that's why she had to be killed. Ed hadn't gone to the men's room as he had claimed; he'd gone around the building, let himself into the workroom with his key, and shot Bitsy. He probably hadn't thought twice about it—as a hunter he was used to killing and he didn't think much of Bitsy anyway.

Hayden, also, had been worried about the library. His last words to Ralph had been that there was something he wanted to straighten out. If he had gone to Ed with his questions, Ed wouldn't have hesitated to kill him. He despised Hayden for being gay; he probably thought he was doing everybody a favor. Stealing the tankard and leaving it with Hayden's body had been cunning—it gave Hayden a motive for supposedly killing Bitsy and himself.

And that's why Ed had dragged Bill off to shovel the roof, thought Lucy. Now that Gerald had been arrested, the state police would certainly be taking a close look at the bookkeeping for the addition. Gerald was safe in jail—Ed couldn't get to him. Even worse, realized Lucy, Ed knew that she had the figures—he'd seen her with the folder. Furthermore, he knew that Bill would be taking another look at them. But if Bill died, Ed could blame him for the discrepancies and there'd be nobody to dispute his story.

Nobody but Lucy, and Ed had been doing his very best to frighten the wits out of her. He probably thought that between the sledding incident and the car fire she would be afraid of her own shadow. If he thought that was true, she decided, he didn't know her very well.

She jumped to her feet, banging her head on the slanted ceiling. Wincing at the pain, she clutched her head and groped her way to the door. If only she could get help for Bill. Damn the stupid phone. And the lights, too. Why did they have to go out now? Thank God she still had the cell phone, She could use that, she thought, grasping a knob. She pulled, intending to open the door, but discovered too late that she had instead opened the cabinet where Bill stored his rolled-up plans. Cardboard tubes rained down on her; she tried to turn away, toward the door, but her feet got tangled. The next thing she knew she was flat on her stomach in the pitch-black darkness, with a pounding headache.

"Dammit," she muttered, frustrated at the absurdity of her situation—helpless in the dark in her own house with her children only a few rooms away.

Chapter Twenty-five

*"I'll huff and I'll puff and I'll
blow your house in," said the Wolf.*

After a minute or two she cautiously felt around in the darkness with her hands, pushing the tubes out of her way and crawling toward the door. She found the knob, the right one this time, and pulled it open.

"Help!" she screamed down the pitch-black stairs. "I'm stuck in the attic." The effort made her head throb.

There was no answer. Alone in the dark, at the top of the steep stairs, she might as well have been in an empty house.

"Toby!" she yelled. "Bring me a flashlight!"

The house was silent.

"Kids," she muttered, feeling her way down the stairs backwards, on her hands and knees. What could they be doing? Were they sittting like idiots, staring at the blank TV screen? They knew better. They should be lighting the oil lamps and checking to see if everyone was okay. Especially their mother.

When she pushed open the door to the second-floor hall, Lucy was relieved to see there was still a little daylight filtering in through the windows. She groped her way downstairs to the kitchen. There she lit a lamp and looked for the cell phone, intending to call Barney at the police station to get help for Bill. But the place on the counter where she had left it, freshly charged next to the lamps, was empty. It was gone.

"Where's the cell phone?" she hollered, pushing open the door to the family room. There she saw Toby and the younger girls sitting on the floor, huddled around a lamp, playing checkers. Elizabeth was lounging on the couch, the cell phone in her hand.

"Give that to me," said Lucy, snatching it out of her hand.

"Okay—but it isn't working."

"What do you mean?"

"It was working fine, but then it started making a lot of static and I couldn't hear anymore."

"How long were you using it?" Lucy grabbed the phone and pushed the power button. The display panel read "Low Bat."

"A while, I guess. Not long."

"I charged it yesterday." Lucy was furious. "You must have been talking for hours. What were you using it for, anyway? This is for emergencies."

"It was an emergency," insisted Elizabeth indignantly. "Toby had the phone line tied up with the computer and I had to talk to Lance."

"How could you be so irresponsible?" Lucy's head was spinning. She glared at her daughter, her eyes glittering in the lamplight. "Do you know what you've done?" she began, then broke off. What was the point? Arguing with Elizabeth wasn't going to change the situation.

Her hands shaking with anger and blinking back tears of pain and frustration, Lucy carried her lamp into the bathroom and took three ibuprofen. Then she went back to the kitchen and sat at the table, her head in her hands. She could hear the turkey spitting and hissing in the oven; it must be almost ready.

She took a few deep breaths to calm herself and tried to analyze the situation. Had she overreacted? Was Bill really in danger?

Then she remembered Bitsy, lying on the floor of the storeroom, her lifeless eyes staring up at the ceiling. She thought of Hayden, his murder cleverly arranged to look like suicide.

She closed her eyes. Bill had gone to meet Bumpus, unaware that he was walking into a trap. Up on the roof it would be easy to rig an accident. One slip and Bumpus would silence Bill forever. Then he'd be able to shift the blame for the shoddy materials onto Bill. It would be his word against that of a dead man.

Lucy shuddered. It might already be too late.

No, she decided, looking out the window at the fading light. That's why Bumpus came along when he did. He'd wait until it was dark. There was still time if she hurried.

Lucy and Toby stepped off the back porch into a bleak wilderness of snow and wind. Clinging together, they hung on to the clothesline and struggled across the short distance to the shed. The snow was so thick that the porch light did little good; its soft glow served only to mark the warmth and safety they were leaving behind as they ventured out in the darkness and howling wind.

Reaching the shed, they scrambled into its shelter, knocking rakes and shovels aside.

"Mom—let me go," said Toby, already panting from the exertion of pulling the frozen door open. His jacket and snowpants were already coated with snow.

Lucy was beginning to doubt the wisdom of her plan. She hadn't realized the strength of the storm. She also wasn't sure of her ability to handle the snowmobile; until now she'd only been a passenger, riding behind Bill.

But Bill was out in the storm, alone with a murderer. She couldn't begin to explain it to Toby—this irrational, irresistible tug. She had to get to him.

"Help me get this thing out and we'll see what happens," she said, tugging at the machine's grab bar. "Chances are I'll meet one of the plows before I get too far."

They both knew the town trucks were equipped with radios; if she reached a truck they could radio for help.

"What makes you so sure the plows are out?" demanded Toby. "They're probably waiting 'til the storm's over."

Lucy knew he was probably right. The DPW superintendent wasn't going to put his men, or his trucks, in danger. Frustrated, she challenged him.

"Are you going to help me or what?"

Toby joined her and together they dragged the snowmobile to the door. He gave the cord a yank and it started right up. Lucy gave him a quick peck on the cheek before she pulled on her helmet and climbed aboard. Then, cautiously, she maneuvered the machine down the ramp and started across the yard to the road. She was halfway there when it sputtered and stalled.

She tried to restart it, but nothing happened. Tears sprang to her eyes and she pounded the useless hunk of metal with her fists.

Toby materialized out of the swirling snow, pounding on his chest to indicate that he would drive. Lucy obediently slid back and he climbed on in front of her. The machine sprang to life once more and she wrapped her arms around his waist and hung on as they hurled forward.

The headlight only showed a wall of whirling white snow but with Toby driving they moved ahead steadily and reached the road. There, Toby cautiously accelerated and they skimmed along the freshly fallen powder. The roar of the wind was muffled by the helmet, but the sudden crack of a falling tree made her start.

216 *Leslie Meier*

Out in the dark emptiness Lucy felt she and Toby were very alone. If anything happened to them it would be a very long time before help came.

She pushed those thoughts from her mind. They couldn't give up; they had to get help for Bill. She swallowed hard as Toby carefully maneuvered the turn at the bottom of Red Top Hill where her car had burned. How far was it to town? Four or five miles at most, a matter of ten or fifteen minutes.

Sensing the open road ahead, Toby accelerated the snow-mobile and they surged forward, speeding along through the wild night. Lucy's hands and feet were getting cold; she didn't have the benefit of the heated handles and the warmth of the engine as Toby did. She flexed her fingers and wiggled her toes inside her boots. A sudden flash of light made her jump. It was a broken power line giving off showers of sparks. Toby gave it a wide berth and pushed on.

They passed the Quik-Stop without realizing it. The familiar sign was covered with snow and the gas pumps were simply odd, snow-covered shapes. The first thing they recognized was the church, and next to it was the police station. It wasn't until they pulled up by the steps that they could see the faint blue light of the lamps by the door.

Lucy started to dismount but her legs wouldn't cooperate. They felt heavy and clumsy. She leaned heavily on Toby's shoulders and willed herself to move. Grabbing the railing, she pulled herself up the steps and yanked the door open, practically falling on the floor in front of the dispatcher's desk.

"Good God—what are you doing out on a night like this?" demanded Barney.

Lucy tugged at the helmet but couldn't get it off. Barney came around the desk and eased it off her head. "Easy now," he said. "Tell me what's the matter."

"I need help. Bill's in trouble."

"Jeez. What's happened?"

"He went with Bumpus. To shovel snow off the roof. Of the library." Lucy was struggling to be coherent. "He's the murderer."

Barney stared at her, trying to understand.

"You think Bill's in danger?"

Lucy nodded. "We have to help him."

Barney's face drooped. "Lucy—there isn't anything I can do."

"What do you mean? You can go over there with me!"

"I can't leave the station." Barney looked stricken.

"Well, call for help."

"I can't. There's nobody to call. We've had one emergency after another. You'll just have to wait until somebody gets back. And there's a coupla calls ahead of you." He looked down at the floor and studied the gray and white tiles. "Besides, if what you say is true, it's probably too late."

Lucy slowly blinked her eyes, then turned to retrieve her helmet.

"What do you think you're doing?"

"This is a waste of time. Toby's out there, freezing his ass off. We're going to the library." Lucy pulled the helmet over her head and turned to go.

"Please, Lucy. You're in no shape to go and I bet Toby's no better. Stay here where it's warm and safe. What do you think you're gonna do when you get there?"

She shook her head stubbornly. "I have to go," she said and staggered the short distance across the lobby to the door. She pushed it open and found herself once again in the storm. The wind had quieted, however, and the snow was falling less heavily. Moving stiffly, hanging on to the railing, she slid down the steps and staggered to the snowmobile. She grabbed Toby's shoulders and swung her leg over the seat. As soon as she sat down he was under way, zooming down Main Street to the library.

In minutes they were pulling up beside Bumpus's big black truck, the only one in the parking lot. Lucy tilted her head and raised her eyes to the roof.

There, a work light had been rigged, making an island of brightness in the darkness. She lifted her visor and gasped, seeing two figures struggling near the edge of the roof.

Toby followed her gaze.

She grabbed his arm with her hand as they watched the two dark shadows grapple with each other, locked in a life or death struggle. At first they seemed equally matched but gradually, the slighter, more slender man appeared to be losing ground. As they watched, he was pushed inexorably toward the edge of the roof by the bulkier one. She held her breath.

"No, no, no," she whispered.

She felt Toby tense, and she held his hand in both of hers. As they clung together they saw one of the figures topple off the roof.

Fueled by adrenaline, Lucy leaped off the snowmobile and ran through the snow toward the motionless figure crumpled on the ground.

"Don't let it be Bill," she prayed, kneeling beside the form in the snow. She tugged at the hood covering his face and moaned, recognizing Bill's beard. With her teeth she ripped her glove off and felt his neck for a pulse. It was there—she was sure she felt it.

Suddenly frantic, heart pounding, she looked for help and saw Toby running toward her.

"We have to get him to the hospital."

Toby pointed to the roof, where Bumpus was looking down on Bill's broken body in triumph.

"You'll pay for this!" Lucy yelled, shaking her fist at him. "I saw you. I know who you are."

Bumpus gave no sign of having heard her and turned away. Lucy brushed the snow from Bill's face. Hearing a moan, she leaned closer to his lips. It wasn't from him, she realized, as the sound grew louder. She froze.

"Listen," she said.

Alerted, Toby turned toward the building.

The sound was insistent, penetrating.

She followed Toby's gaze, realizing with horror that they were hearing the groan of overburdened timbers yielding to the weight of the snow.

"Get down!" she screamed and Bumpus turned to face her. His face was white in the spotlight and his mouth made an "O" as he realized the danger. He seemed to move in slow motion, stumbling as he scrambled across the snowy roof to the ladder that would lead him to safety.

He never reached it. There was a horrible crack, like an explosion. For a moment it seemed as if everything would be all right. Then, with a sudden sucking noise, almost like a huge intake of breath, the roof gave way. Lucy and Toby saw Bumpus teeter on the edge and then he was gone.

They heard a single, piercing scream and then it was quiet.

A few tiny snowflakes were still falling as Toby pointed to the sky. Lucy looked up, and saw faint pinpricks of light.

"Stars," said Toby, bending to help her with Bill. "The storm's over."

"I can't believe it," said Lucy, involuntarily clapping her hand to her head. "I forgot all about the turkey."

Chapter Twenty-six

*Thirsty and weighted down with stones, the
Wolf dragged himself to the well for a drink but
when he reached for the bucket he fell right in.*

As often happens after a storm, the next day dawned
bright and clear. The temperature was a balmy twenty
degrees, the sky was cloudless and bright blue. The sunshine
was dazzling against the fresh snow; you had to squint to
see.

Lucy and Bill were back at the library, ostensibly to survey the damage, but also drawn by the need to see the site of
Bill's near-fatal adventure.

"You fell from there," said Lucy, pointing to the corner of
the addition high above them.

"I was sure lucky I fell into a snowdrift," said Bill, with
the stunned amazement of one who has survived a close call.

"You sure were—especially if you think of all the stuff
that's under that snow—concrete blocks, scraps of wood and
pipe." She squeezed his arm. "I've never been so terrified."

He wrapped his arm around her shoulder. "It just wasn't my time, I guess."

They stood in silence for a moment, aware that Ed Bumpus hadn't been nearly as lucky as Bill. He was still inside the shell of the addition, trapped beneath tons of rubble. Searchers were combing through the mess looking for him, but no one expected to find him alive.

"That was some night," said Ted Stillings, joining them and opening his camera bag. "They're calling it the storm of the century, you know. Power's out over most of the state, there was a big accident on the interstate, and nobody knows yet how many fishing boats were lost." He raised his camera and began snapping photos of the damaged addition. "Have they found him yet?"

"No, they're still looking," said Lucy.

"You know, I never much liked that guy," said Ted. "But I never figured him for a murderer. Shoddy construction, yes, but not murder."

"One led to the other," said Lucy. "He let the contractor substitute cheaper stuff . . ."

"And probably got a handsome kickback himself," added Bill.

"When Bitsy started comparing the invoices with the estimates she realized what he'd done, so he killed her. Then when Hayden started asking questions he got the bright idea of killing him and making it look like suicide—everyone would naturally think he was stricken with guilt and remorse for killing Bitsy. Then when he realized it was all going to come crashing down literally—he tried to make Bill," she paused and smiled apologetically, "the fall guy."

"Can I quote you?" asked Ted, grinning wickedly.

"No!" exclaimed Lucy. "Absolutely not. I don't want to get charged with tasteless punning."

They were enjoying a shared laugh when a flurry of activity caught their attention. One of the searchers was waving to the ambulance crew that was standing by. They responded quickly, jumping out of the cab where they had been keeping warm and rushing into the wrecked building with a stretcher. It seemed like quite a while before they emerged, carrying a shrouded form. Bill and Lucy watched silently, but Ted hurried over to question the searchers.

"I can't say I'm unhappy he's dead," confessed Bill.

"Me, either," said Lucy with a little shudder. "He killed two people and he would have killed you, too, just to make some money. What was it for?"

"He wasn't the kind of guy who could ever say no—not to a supplier with a shady deal, not to a worker who found a shortcut. You can't run a business like that. Plus, he had to be a big shot—he liked living high on the hog. He had to have a big roll of bills in his pocket, he had to have the biggest truck, the hunting trips. If business wasn't good, and it hasn't been this winter because of the weather, he had to get his money somewhere else. He wasn't the kind of guy who would tighten his belt and wait for things to get better."

"I didn't like him at the board meeting but then I felt guilty when I saw him at the food pantry. I guess that was just another kind of showing off," said Lucy. "I don't think he really wanted to kill you, you know. He kept trying to warn me off—the near miss when the kids were sledding, the car fire. I guess he thought he had no choice when he saw me with that folder."

"The stupid thing is I never even looked at it. I didn't know what was going on when he started to fight with me on that roof. I thought he'd lost his mind."

"I'm sure glad you're okay."

"Me, too."

Arm in arm, they turned to go and encountered Chuck Canaday.

"This is one hell of a mess," he said, shaking his head.

Then he reached out and clasped Bill's hand. "How are you feeling?"

"Just had the wind knocked out of me—thanks to the snow and my down jacket."

Canaday nodded, then his gaze shifted to the library building. He sighed and shook his head. "What a shambles. All the work and planning that went into that addition, not to mention two lives. All because he was greedy."

"Do you have any idea how much Ed took?" Lucy had to know.

"I figured it out last night. I think it was close to $50,000. It wasn't just the roof, you know. He shaved something off everything. Carpeting. Light fixtures, everything. And this was a half- million-dollar project."

"What will happen now?"

"I don't know. I can tell you one thing, though. The board has plenty of work to do." He looked at Bill. "I don't suppose I could persuade you to fill one of the vacancies?"

Bill scratched his beard. "Sorry," he said. "I'm not much of a reader."

Epilogue

*. . . and they all lived happily
ever after.*

A year later, as Lucy poured herself a cup of punch at the dedication of the newly completed Julia Ward Howe Tilley wing of the library, the awful night of the Valentine's Day blizzard had already receded into the distant past. The reconstruction had gone smoothly, and standing in the rebuilt children's room, she found it hard to believe she had stood in the snow last winter and watched it collapse into a heap of rubble.

Once again there were sparkling windows and fresh, clean carpeting; the child-sized chairs and low bookshelves had all been replaced. In addition, several computer stations now provided access to the larger world beyond Tinker's Cove. And high above them, Lucy knew, strong steel beams properly supported the roof that provided protection from rain and snow and cold.

It would all be perfect, she thought, except for one thing: Josiah's Tankard was still missing from its glass case in the vestibule.

But this was no time to dwell on the negative, thought

Lucy, taking a sip of punch and looking about at the crowded library. Today was a day of celebration, and apparently nobody had wanted to miss it. In addition to the board members Lucy spotted many familiar faces: Barney had planted himself in a corner and was chewing the fat with the fire chief; Ted Stillings was snapping pictures and getting quotes for *The Pennysaver* from the librarian, Eunice Sparks; and both Edna and Edith Withers had come, enlivening the scene with their matching pink and orange plaid pantsuits. Juanita and a group of mothers had gathered in a circle, chatting and bouncing toddlers on their hips.

"Lucy, let's check out the food," invited Sue, leading the way to the buffet table. "I hear Corney has gone all out."

Lucy had to agree. The long table was filled with platters of tiny cakes and sandwiches; there were mounds of fruit topped with strawberries dipped in chocolate, and plates heaped with cookies for the children. Menus, handwritten in calligraphy, were placed at each end of the table.

"This Aunt Fannie's salmon spread is pretty good," admitted Sue, peering at the menu. "I wonder where she got the recipe?"

Corney beamed at her from her spot behind the table; these days she was only too happy to share the credit. "It's in the Fannie Farmer cookbook," she crowed. "I got the idea from Lucy—she told me how she always called the book 'Aunt Fannie' because it made her feel she had a helper in the kitchen." She bent closer. "In order to settle that awful lawsuit I agreed to provide attribution for my recipes and this seemed like a charming way to do it, don't you think?"

"I guess," said Sue, reaching for another sandwich.

"There's more to creating good food than a recipe, anyway," said Lucy. "It's the ingredients you choose, and the care you take in combining them."

"I couldn't agree more," said Corney, holding out a plate. "Try these cheese puffs."

"Mmm," said Lucy, reaching for another. "Terrific. Today I'm forgetting about calories."

Noticing a buzz of activity near the doorway, Lucy and Sue made their way through the crowd. Reaching the circulation desk, they found a pink and beaming Miss Tilley surrounded by a group of her cronies. She was waving a letter.

"I just got it today—it's from Lu Asquith—she's arranged to purchase Josiah's Tankard and is presenting it to the library!"

"But how can she do that?" asked Dot Kirwan, who was always up to date on the gossip, thanks to her job at the IGA. "Last I heard, the bank was taking the house. She was going to move in with her sister in Florida until Gerald gets out of jail next year."

"She was," nodded Miss Tilley. "In fact, she was packing to go. She was going through Gerald's things, deciding what to keep and what to give away, and she found a Lotto ticket. They're good for a year, you know, so she took it to the Quik-Stop. They punched it into the machine and you know what?" Miss Tilley paused, enjoying keeping everyone in suspense. "It was worth two million dollars!"

For a moment the room was silent, then there was an explosion of voices.

"Wow," said Sue. "That's some lucky lady."

"Yeah," nodded Lucy. "But it's kind of awful in a way. Just think how different things might have been for Gerald. I wonder if he just forgot it or . . ."

Her thoughts were interrupted by the sound of a spoon tapping against a glass.

"It's time to get started," began Chuck. "I promise I won't keep you from those delicious refreshments for long. But as chairman of the library board I need to acknowledge some very hardworking people. As you all know, we suffered a terrible blow last February when the original addition collapsed. Rebuilding would not have been possible without the cooperation of the Megunticook Insurance Company, and I especially want to thank Henry Howe, the vice president in charge of claims, for his guidance and under- standing."

He paused, indicating a gray-haired man in a suit, and there was a polite round of applause.

"A very big thank-you is also due to librarian Eunice Sparks, who managed to keep the library up and running throughout this difficult period."

Eunice bobbed her head and was greeted with smiles and more applause.

"I also want to thank our new board members, who weren't afraid to take on a challenge that sometimes seemed over- whelming: Juanita Orenstein, the Reverend Clive Macin- tosh, and Jack Mulroney from the Tinker's Cove Savings Bank."

He paused again, and there was another round of ap- plause.

"And, of course, great thanks is due to the faithful board members who held firm and did not flee from adversity: Lucy Stone and my lovely wife, Corney Clarke Canaday, who is responsible for the wonderful refreshments we are all enjoying today."

This was met with an enthusiastic outburst of clapping and even a few whistles from the men gathered in the corner, but Chuck held up his hand, asking for quiet.

"Finally, it is time to acknowledge the person who has given the most to the library throughout the years and the person in whose honor we are dedicating this fine new addi- tion: Miss Julia Ward Howe Tilley. To commemorate this occasion I have a plaque to present to Miss Tilley—where are you?"

There was a hush as Miss Tilley came forward, moving slowly and leaning on Rachel's arm. When she finally reached the front of the room, Chuck had to swallow hard before he could continue.

"I think everyone here agrees with me that if there is one

person who exemplifies the spirit of this library, it is Miss Tilley. As the librarian for many years and then as a board member, she has always maintained that our town's most valuable assets are the inquiring minds of its residents and has insisted that the library provide the information and inspiration needed to nourish those minds. In recognition of her life-long contribution to Tinker's Cove, I hereby dedicate this new addition the Julia Ward Howe Tilley Room."

He bent down, placing the plaque in her shaking hands and planting a kiss on her cheek.

"That's something I've wanted to do for a long time," he joked, prompting the crowd to erupt in a cheerful ovation. Lucy enthusiastically joined the clapping, blinking furiously to stop the tears that were filling her eyes.

When the noise finally began to subside, Miss Tilley took a step forward.

"This is truly a wonderful honor and I want to thank you all very much," she said, clutching the plaque to her chest. "But as marvelous as all this is, I have to admit that it's not quite enough."

There was a stunned silence. Chuck looked as if he'd been slapped. "What do you mean?" he asked.

"Well," she said, taking a step forward and lifting her chin in a challenge. "The one thing that would please me more than anything would be for Tinker's Cove to have the highest per capita circulation in the state."

"That doesn't sound too hard—what would it take to do that, Eunice?"

"Every card holder would have to borrow twelve books," answered Eunice, peering over her half-glasses from her post behind the circulation desk.

"That's just one a month—we can do that, can't we, folks?"

Chuck's question was met with nods and murmurs of assent until Corney stepped forward.

"I'd like to sweeten the challenge, if I may," she said, fluttering her eyelashes coyly. "I'll be happy to bake a Marvelous Mocha Cheesecake for the person who reads the most books in one year."

"Hear that, everybody?" announced Chuck. "The person who reads the most books wins a cake!"

Corney's offer was met with great approval from the crowd, who cheered and clapped. Lucy sneaked a peek at Sue, and caught her rolling her eyes. Sue didn't seem to like the new, kinder and gentler Corney any more than she had liked the earlier, pricklier version.

"Well, I've had enough of this," she said, setting her plate down on the table and brushing off her hands. "It's time to hit the road before all this sweetness and light sends me into insulin shock."

"I ought to get going, too," said Lucy. "But first I want to congratulate Miss Tilley. See you later."

She turned, intending to join the group that had gathered around Miss Tilley, but was discouraged by the large number of people. She wouldn't be missed, she decided, resolving to stop by for a visit tomorrow. If she didn't get home and get the pot roast started soon, it wouldn't be ready in time for supper.

Leaving the group, she headed for the computers, where Zoe and Sadie were playing an educational game.

"It's time to go, Zoe. Could you please turn off the computer and say good-bye to Sadie?"

"Aw, Mom," whined the little girl, sticking out her lower lip in a pout. "Can't I play just one more game?"

CHOCOLATE
COVERED
MURDER

For Abby

Chapter One

If the cold didn't kill her, the slippery ice on the sidewalk surely would, thought Lucy Stone as she stepped out of the overheated town hall basement meeting room into a frigid Monday afternoon. January was always cold in the little coastal town of Tinker's Cove, Maine, and this year was a record-breaker. The electronic sign on the bank across the street informed her it was five forty-five and nine, no, eight degrees. The temperature was falling fast and was predicted to sink below zero during the night.

Lucy hurried across the frozen parking lot as fast as she dared, mindful that a patch of ice could send her flying. Reaching the car, she made sure the heater was on high, and waited a few minutes for the engine to warm up. While she waited, she thought about the meeting she had just attended and how she would write it up for the local paper, the Tinker's Cove *Pennysaver*.

The topic under discussion was improving toilet facilities at the town beach and quite a crowd had turned out for the meeting. In her experience as a reporter, only dog hearings excited more interest than wastewater issues and this meeting had been no exception.

Of course, people had been complaining about the inadequate facilities for some time; a group of concerned citizens had even entered a float in the Fourth of July parade as a protest. The parade theme had been "From Sea to Shining Sea" and the float depicted the town beach strewn with sewage. The ensuing controversy had prompted the selectmen to address the issue, but there was little agreement on the solution. The budget-minded had favored continuing the present Porta-Potties, the cheapest option. Installing earth closets, the eco-friendly option, had brought out the tree-huggers; the business community, which depended on tourist dollars, had lobbied for conventional toilets, which would require digging a well and putting in an expensive septic system.

This was going to be fun to write up, she thought, as she shifted into drive and proceeded cautiously across the icy parking lot and onto the road. In addition to the cold, they had recently had a big snowfall, so the road was lined with high banks of plowed snow. It was hard to see around the piles of snow, so Lucy inched out into the road, hoping nothing was coming.

As she drove along Main Street, past the police station and clustered stores, past the Community Church with its tall steeple, she thought of possible opening sentences. She'd driven this route so often that her mind was wandering and she was halfway through her story when she cleared town and the landscape opened with harvested cornfields on both sides of the road. The winter sunset was fabulous, the sky a blazing red that took her breath away. She couldn't take her eyes off the gorgeous color that filled the sky and was barely paying attention to the road when a large buck leaped over a snowdrift, landing right in front of her. She slammed on the brakes and skidded, hanging onto the steering wheel for dear life and praying she wouldn't hit the animal, when the car fishtailed and slammed into the snowbank on the opposite side of the road.

Heart pounding, she caught a glimpse of brown rump and white tail bounding unhurt across the field, and sent up a little prayer of thanks. Then she shifted into reverse, intending to back out onto the road. Pressing the accelerator, she heard the dismaying hum of spinning tires. Climbing out of the car, she found the front end deeply imbedded in the snow and the rear tires sunk up to the hubcaps in soft slush and realized she wasn't going to get out without help.

The sun was now falling below the horizon, the sky was a deep purple, and the road was deserted. She got back in the car and reached for her cell phone, remembering she hadn't charged it lately. Indeed, when she flipped it open, the screen blinked BATTERY LOW and immediately went dark. She was only a bit more than a mile from home, but in this frigid weather she didn't dare risk walking. Her best option was to stay with the car and keep the engine running. Unfortunately, she'd been running close to empty for a day or two, too busy to stop and fill the tank.

It was just a matter of time, she told herself, before her husband, Bill, would wonder why she wasn't home and would come out looking for her. Or not. He might figure she was working late, covering an evening meeting, in which case they'd probably find her frozen body the next morning.

Perhaps she should write a note, letting her family know how much she loved them. Then again, she thought, perhaps not. What sort of family didn't come out and look for a missing member, especially on a night when the temperature was predicted to go below zero? She thought of Bill, who habitually watched the six o'clock news, and her teenage daughters, Sara and Zoe, probably texting their friends, all in the comfort of their cozy home on Red Top Road. Didn't they miss her? Weren't they worried? They'd be sorry, wouldn't they, when she was on the news tomorrow night. *Local woman freezes to death. Family in shock. "I should have known something was wrong," says grieving husband.*

A tap at the window startled her and she turned to see a smiling, bearded face she recognized as belonging to Max Fraser. She lowered the window.

"Looks like you could use a tow," he said.

"It was a deer," she said. "He jumped in the road and I swerved to avoid him."

"Doesn't look like the car's damaged," he said. "You were lucky."

"I'm lucky you came along," said Lucy. "I don't have much gas and my cell phone is dead."

"I'll have you out of here in no time," he said, signaling that she should close the window.

Max was as good as his word. In a matter of minutes, he had fastened a tow line from his huge silver pickup to her car. She felt a bump and heard a sudden groaning noise and all of a sudden her car popped out of the snowdrift. Max looked it over for damage and listened to make sure the engine was running okay, and when she offered to pay him for his trouble, he looked offended.

"Folks gotta help folks," he said. "Someday maybe you can help me, or pass it on. Help somebody else."

"I will," promised Lucy. "I certainly will."

Next morning, Lucy was writing her account of the meeting when Corney Clarke popped into the *Pennysaver* office, like a glowing ember leaping out of a crackling fire and onto the hearth. Her cheeks were red with the cold, her ski parka was bright orange, and her stamping feet sprayed bits of snow in all directions. "This is big, really big," she exclaimed, pulling off her shearling gloves.

Phyllis, the receptionist, peered over her harlequin reading glasses and cast a baleful glance at the melting puddle of snow. She drew her purple sweater across her ample bust and shivered. "Mind shutting the door? There's an awful draft."

"Oh, sorry," said Corney, pushing the door shut with difficulty and setting the old-fashioned wooden blinds rattling. "It's just I'm so excited about my big news." She paused, making sure she had the attention of Ted Stillings, the weekly paper's publisher, editor, and chief reporter.

"I'm listening," said Ted, leaning back in his swivel chair and propping his feet on the half-open file drawer of the sturdy oak roll-top desk he inherited from his grandfather, a legendary New England journalist. Like practically every man in town, he was dressed in a plaid shirt topped with a thick sweater, flannel-lined khaki pants, and duck boots.

Lucy typed the final period and turned around to face Corney. "This better be good," she said. Corney, an interior designer who wrote a monthly lifestyle column for *Maine House and Cottage* magazine, was always pitching stories, looking for free publicity.

"Oh, it is," said Corney. She took a deep breath and paused dramatically, then spoke. "Chanticleer Chocolate was voted 'Best Candy on the Coast.' "

It landed like a bombshell, and for a moment there was stunned silence in the newspaper office.

"You mean . . . ?" began Phyllis.

"What about . . . ?" murmured Ted.

"Talk about an upset!" exclaimed Lucy.

"That's right." Corney gave a self-satisfied nod. "It's the first time since the magazine began the Best of Maine poll that Fern's Famous Fudge hasn't won."

"Fern's Famous is an institution," said Phyllis.

Lucy nodded, thinking of the quaint little shop with the red-and-white-striped awning that had stood on Main Street in Tinker's Cove since, well, forever. The business was started by Fern Macdougal, who needed a source of income after her husband was killed in the Korean War. She started selling her homemade fudge through local shops, eventually buying her own place as the little business took off in the nineteen fifties when tourists began flocking to the Maine coast. Fern's Famous, with its big copper kettle and marble counters, was a must-see and nobody passed through town without picking up one of the red-and-white-striped boxes of fudge or saltwater taffy. Nowadays, Fern was in her nineties, but she still kept a sharp eye on the business, which was run by her daughter, Flora Riggs, who had added a catering service to the company, and her granddaughter, Dora Fraser, Max's ex-wife.

"Now, Ted," said Corney, turning to the reason for her visit. "You have to admit this is a big story. And it just happens to tie in very nicely with the Chamber of Commerce's *Love Is Best on the Coast* February travel promotion." Corney, as they all knew only too well, was chair of the Chamber's publicity committee.

"Whoa," said Ted, raising his hand. "February travel promotion? Are you crazy? This is Maine. I don't know if you've noticed, but there's two feet of snow on the ground, the temperature is fifteen degrees, and the forecast is for, surprise, more snow."

"Sleet," said Lucy. "We're supposed to have a warm spell. Global warming."

"Either way, snow or sleet," said Ted, "it's not exactly picnic weather."

"Maine is beautiful every time of year," said Corney, "but winter is my favorite time. The snow is so beautiful . . ."

"It's treacherous," said Lucy. "I barely made it home alive last night. If Max Fraser hadn't come along, I'd be headline news this morning. I got stuck in a snowdrift when a buck jumped in front of my car, out by those cornfields."

"There's a lot of deer out there," said Phyllis. "They eat the corn the harvester missed."

"You've got to be careful in the snow," said Corney, "but the town does an excellent job with the plowing. And you have to admit, on a day like today, when the sun makes the snow sparkle and the air is crisp, it's just a little bit of heaven here in Tinker's Cove."

Corney had a point, thought Lucy, thinking of her antique farmhouse on Red Top Road and how pretty it looked covered with snow, especially at night when the windows glowed with lamplight. Of course, the snow made it impossible to keep the house clean inside. Her daughters, Sara and Zoe, were constantly tracking in snow and mud, as did her husband, Bill. Even the dog added to the mess, rolling in the snow and shaking it off as soon as she came through the door. The kitchen floor was littered with boots and shoes; the coat rack was loaded with jackets and scarves and ski pants. Hats and mittens and gloves were spread on the old-fashioned radiators to dry.

It wasn't just the constant sweeping and tidying that got her down in winter, it was the way the house seemed to shrink in the bleak months after Christmas. The walls seemed to move in and the furniture grew larger. Every surface became cluttered with projects and busywork: the fishing reel Bill was repairing, the scarf Sara was knitting for the high school Good Neighbor Club, Zoe's rock display for eighth-grade science.

Going out for a meal or a movie, even a shopping trip, was the obvious cure for cabin fever, but it wasn't easy. It took a lot of determination to get anywhere. First you had to layer on all those clothes, then you had to shovel your way to the car, which might or might not start. Once you were on the road, you had to be constantly vigilant, watching for slick spots and creeping slowly through intersections made blind by enormous piles of snow, and you had to remember to start braking well in advance of every stop sign. Once you reached your destination, you had to hunt for a plowed parking spot and then you had to watch your step when you got out of the car because the sidewalks, even when shoveled, soon became slick with ice.

None of that seemed to bother Corney, who was listing

the advantages of winter. "Sleigh rides in the snowy woods," she said, prompting a snort from Phyllis.

"Endless shoveling," complained Ted. "Heart attacks— did you see the obits last week? Three old guys, in one week."

Corney ignored him. "We have all these romantic B&Bs with canopy beds and fireplaces. . . ."

"Fireplaces are awful messy. Wood chips, twigs, even leaves, and then there's the ashes. Filthy," said Phyllis. "And that stuff jams up the vacuum."

"Hot toddies and cocoa with tiny marshmallows," said Corney, as if she were raising the stakes in a poker game.

"The stink of wet wool," countered Lucy.

"Tree branches coated in ice, sparkling in the sun," said Corney, laying down a few more chips.

"Broken bones from falls on the icy sidewalks," said Ted. "The waiting time at the emergency room last week was three hours."

"We need to let the world know that Maine doesn't shut down in winter," declared Corney, ready to show her hand.

"It doesn't?" Lucy was skeptical.

"We have so much to offer," insisted Corney.

"Cabin fever. She's been cooped up too long and now she's hallucinating," said Ted.

"I'm sure that's it," said Lucy, laughing.

"Have your fun," said Corney, slipping off her fur-trimmed hood and giving her short, frosted blond hair a shake. "Let's face it: the economy sucks. Businesses are going bankrupt, people are losing their jobs, even their houses. Things are bad."

It was true, thought Lucy. Bill, a restoration carpenter, hadn't had a big job in over a year. He was making do, barely, with window replacements and repairs. Her oldest, her son, Toby, who was married and the father of little Patrick, now almost three, had become disillusioned with his prospects as a lobsterman and had taken out student loans to finish up the business degree he had abandoned. Even her oldest daughter, Elizabeth, who had landed a dream job with the Cavendish Hotel chain after graduating from college, was worried about looming layoffs.

"We have to do whatever we can to attract customers and get things rolling again," said Corney, "and that's what the *Love Is Best on the Coast* Valentine's Day promotion is designed to do." She smiled, as if explaining basic arithmetic to first graders. "Who cares if it's cold outside? That's better for business. The tourists will have nothing to do except shop and eat and drink. They'll have to spend money."

Ted was scratching his chin. "So what do you want? I can't write about Fern's Famous losing, they're one of my biggest advertisers."

"They didn't lose," said Corney, who always saw the glass as half full. "They came in second, just a hair behind Chanticleer. We have the two best candy shops in Maine right here in Tinker's Cove!"

"I suppose Lucy could do something with that," speculated Ted. "She can be pretty tactful, when she tries."

Lucy gave Ted a look. "Thanks for the vote of confidence."

"I know Lucy will do a great job." Corney turned her big blue eyes on Lucy. "You're going to love Trey Meacham. He's a fascinating guy, and a real visionary. Chanticleer Chocolate typifies the kind of success an enterprising entrepreneur can have in Maine. We're becoming a lot more sophisticated, it's not about whirligigs and fudge anymore. We have top-notch craftsmen and artists making beautiful things— oil paintings and handwoven shawls and burl bowls. And the local food movement is the next big thing: fudge and lobster rolls are great, but there are small breweries, artisanal bakeries, and farmers' markets with hydroponically grown vegetables, free-range chickens, grass-fed beef, all raised locally. That's the market that Trey has captured. His chocolates are very sophisticated, very unusual."

Phyllis raised one of the thin penciled lines that served as eyebrows. "I like fudge myself. With walnuts."

"I have absolutely nothing against fudge, especially Fern's Famous Fudge. This is a win-win situation. Two terrific candy shops. The old and the new. Something for everyone." Corney paused. "And believe me, Lucy, you're going to love Trey."

"I'm married," said Lucy. "I have four kids. I'm a grandma." She paused. "A young grandma."

"You're not blind, are you?"

Lucy laughed. "Not yet."

"Well, Trey is very easy on the eyes, and he's got an interesting story. He left a successful business career, got disillusioned with corporate life, and decided to break out on his own. It's been a little more than a year and he's already got several shops in prime spots on the coast. He's a marketing genius. In fact, the Valentine's Day promotion was his idea. He says all the merchants in town need to work together to attract business. Competition is out; cooperation is in. A rising tide raises all ships."

"Okay, you win," said Ted, holding his hands up in surrender. "I'm thinking we can maybe do a special advertising promo, a double spread, maybe even an entire special section, if there's enough interest."

"Now you're talking," said Corney. "The Chamber's going to have colorful cupid flags for participating businesses, radio spots; we're hoping for some TV coverage. I've got an appointment at NECN with the producer of *This Week in New England*."

"Sounds good," said Ted. "Keep us posted."

"You know I will," said Corney, flashing a grin. With a wave, she was gone, leaving the door ajar, swinging in the wind.

Phyllis heaved herself to her feet with a big sigh and went around the reception counter, shaking her head as she struggled to shut the door. "You've got to get this door fixed, Ted, before I catch my death of cold."

"I know a terrific carpenter," said Lucy.

"Cash flow's a problem," said Ted. "Can we work out a barter deal?"

Lucy was intrigued; Bill had a lot of time on his hands these days. "What do you have in mind?"

"I have an old guitar. . . ."

"Absolutely not."

Ted was making a mental inventory of his possessions. "A typewriter?"

"Donate it to a museum," said Lucy, laughing.

"A frozen turkey? We didn't eat it at Christmas."

Lucy was tempted. "It's a start."

"I'm pretty sure Pam's got all the fixings: stuffing, cranberry sauce, canned yams."

"Throw in a bag of frozen shrimp and you've got a deal," said Lucy.

"You're a tough woman, Lucy."

"I've got hungry kids at home."

"How soon can we do this?" asked Phyllis, as a gust of wind rattled the door in its frame.

"I'll call him right now," said Lucy, reaching for the phone.

"Might as well set something up with the chocolate guy, too," reminded Ted. "What's his name? Meeker?"

"Meacham, Trey Meacham," said Lucy, as she started dialing.

A sudden burst of static from the police scanner on Ted's desk caught her attention and she paused, finger in the air, waiting for it to clear. The dispatcher's voice finally came through, ordering all rescue personnel to Blueberry Pond.

Lucy looked at Ted. "Are you going or should I?"

"You." He paused. "I'd go but I've got a phone interview with the governor's wife in half an hour."

"Really?" asked Lucy.

"Yeah. She's calling for a renewed effort in the war on drugs."

"Stop the presses," said Lucy, sarcastically, as she began pulling on her snow pants, boots, scarf, jacket, hat, and gloves. She checked her bag and made sure she had her camera and notebook, also her car keys.

"You better hurry," said Ted. "You'll miss the story."

"Yeah, well, I don't want to be a frostbite victim," said Lucy, stepping out and making sure the door caught behind her.

A frigid blast of wind snapped her scarf against her face and she pulled her hood up over her hat, blinking back tears as she struggled across the sidewalk to her car. Inside, the air was still and cold, and she checked to make sure the heater was set on high as she started the engine. While the engine warmed up, she blew her nose and wiped her eyes, then dug a tube of lip balm out of her bag and smeared it on her lips. She flipped on her signal and cautiously pulled out into the snow-covered road.

The sun was bright and sparkling snow squalls filled the air as she drove down Main Street and out onto Route 1. There was little traffic, except for a police cruiser and an ambulance that passed her, lights flashing and sirens blaring. She followed them, eventually reaching the unpaved road leading to the pond, where a cluster of vehicles were scattered in the clearing that served as a parking area. She recognized Max's huge pickup among them, with his snowmobile in the back.

She turned the engine off, regretting the immediate loss of heat, and climbed out of the car into the icy blast blowing off the pond. She clutched her hood tight around her head and hurried down the path that had been trodden into the snow by booted feet. Ice fishing was a popular pastime this time of year, and several fishermen had even built shacks on the pond. Lucy had never quite understood the attraction of hanging out on treacherous ice waiting for a trap to spring, indicating a bite on the line, but then she didn't understand why people played golf, either.

Reaching the pond, she hesitated. She didn't like walking on ice; she didn't trust it. But there was a small group standing about a hundred feet from the shore, so it seemed safe enough. The temperature had been well below freezing since Christmas, she reminded herself, imagining the ice must be several feet thick. They used to cut huge chunks of ice from this pond, in the days before refrigeration. She'd seen photographs at the historical society of the ice cutters, with their horses and sleighs loaded with enormous blocks of ice that were packed in straw and stored in ice houses until needed in summer.

The ice was slippery underfoot and she walked carefully, leaning forward and making sure to keep her hands free for balance, resisting the urge to stuff them in her pockets. Approaching the group, she spotted her friend, Officer Barney Culpepper, and quickened her pace. That was a mistake, as she ended up sliding into him and would have fallen if he hadn't grabbed her by the arm.

"Whoa, Lucy. Take it easy."

Barney was dressed for the weather in an oversized, official blue snowsuit, his graying buzz cut concealed by a fur-lined hat that had flaps covering his ears. His eyes were watering, and his jowly cheeks were bright red, as was his nose.

"What's going on?" she asked.

"Somebody went through the ice."

"How can that be? It must be a couple of feet thick," she said, looking around at the little cluster of wooden fishing shacks.

"Dunno." Barney shrugged and wiped his eyes with a gloved hand. "Mebbe he made the hole too big, mebbe there's currents that make the ice thin in spots. I dunno. Seems like a terrible way to go."

There was a sudden surge of activity and Lucy pulled out her camera, thinking it wasn't going to be easy to get a photo in this weather, and with the group of rescuers and fishermen blocking her view. Then the crowd broke apart to make way for a stretcher and Lucy got a clear shot.

She yanked off her glove, stuffing it under her arm, and raised the camera to her eyes, automatically snapping several pictures of the blanketed victim. Then, when she'd lowered her camera, a stiff gust of wind lifted the blanket, revealing the drowned man's bearded face. Horrified, she recognized Max Fraser. Moving woodenly, she followed as the stretcher was carried to the waiting ambulance and was trundled inside. The doors were slammed shut and the ambulance took off, slowly, down the snowy track. There was no need to hurry.

Blinking back tears, Lucy turned to Barney. "Did you see what I saw?" she asked.

Chapter Two

"Yeah," said Barney, shaking his head sadly. "It was Max Fraser."

That was the trouble with living in a small town, thought Lucy. All the victims of horrible accidents were your neighbors and sometimes your friends, or your friends' kids. So were the petty criminals, for that matter. The police blotter, which was printed in the *Pennysaver* every week, was full of familiar names involved in minor tragedies: family quarrels that got out of control, drunk driving arrests, even petty thefts in these tough times. And drugs, always drugs—marijuana, OxyContin, and even heroin.

Of course, everyone knew Max. He was the divorced husband of Fern's granddaughter, Dora, and the father of their only child, Lily. But it wasn't simply the fact that she was acquainted with the victim and even owed him a debt of gratitude that was bothering Lucy.

"He was all tangled up in fishline," said Lucy. "And there was a lure . . ."

"A silver jigging spoon," said Barney.

"It was in his mouth," said Lucy. Max was gone, but she

couldn't erase the image of the glittering silver lure dangling from his blue lips and nestled in his ice-coated beard. She remembered how glad she'd been to see his smiling face in her car window just last night.

"He was hooked like a walleye," said Barney. "What a way to go."

Lucy thought of Max's blue eyes, wide open and crusted with ice, and for a moment felt the earth spin beneath her.

"Whoa, there," said Barney, grabbing her arm and steadying her. She took a couple of deep breaths and focused on the snow-covered mountain rising behind the frozen pond, as if the picture-postcard scene could erase the gruesome image of Max's death mask from her mind.

"He probably didn't feel a thing," said one of the bystanders.

Lucy turned and recognized Tony Menard, who she'd interviewed last winter when he won the Lake Winnipesaukee ice fishing tournament in New Hampshire. He was a short, slight man with a French-Canadian accent.

"The cold? Is that what you mean?" asked Lucy.

"More like the booze," said Tony, with a knowing nod. "He must've been blind drunk, eh? To get tangled up like that in his own line."

Lucy knew that drinking often went right along with ice fishing. You had to keep warm somehow and alcohol gave the illusion of warmth, for a while, anyway. "Even so," she said, "how'd he manage to fall through the ice?" She waved her arm. "Those shacks are standing, we're all out here. The ice must be a couple of feet thick."

Tony shrugged. "The current, maybe. You have to be careful and watch for thin spots."

"Snow ice," said Steve Houle, with a knowing nod toward the place where Max's body had been found. Lucy knew he was a volunteer fireman who organized the Toys for Tots campaign at Christmas. "See how it's white over there, not clear?"

Lucy looked and saw what he meant. "Yeah."

"Well, that happens when the ice melts and refreezes. It's not good."

Tony's head bobbed in agreement. "Punk ice. It's real dangerous."

"But wouldn't Max know about it?" asked Barney.

"Sure, but he could fish at night, and not see," said Tony. "Max was a big risk taker, no?"

"Yeah, his idea of testing ice was to zoom around the lake on his snowmobile," said Steve.

"You think it's down there?" asked Barney, pulling out his notebook. "Mebbe we should send in a diver."

"Could be," replied Tony, his voice rising on the last syllable. "He breaks through, tries to save himself, and his arms go ever' which way and somehow he gets tangled in his line. Could be."

"He wasn't on the snowmobile," said Lucy, remembering Max's competence as he towed her out of the snowdrift. "I saw it in his truck."

"He musta been blind drunk," said Steve.

"That, too," agreed Tony, shaking his head. "He was crazy."

"Yeah, like that old Steve Martin character," said Steve. "You know, the wild and crazy guy."

"That's him," said Tony. "Wild and crazy. We're gonna miss him."

The two drifted off to join their companions and Barney and Lucy headed back to shore together.

"Max was a good guy, and smart, too. Capable." She scowled. "I don't think this was an accident."

Barney gave her a sharp look. "The state police will handle the investigation. A lot depends on what the medical examiner finds."

Reaching shore, Lucy turned and looked out over the frozen lake, a white circle surrounded by bare trees and dark, pointed balsam firs. The place where Max fell through was a bluish patch, filled with bobbing chunks of ice; a handful of fishermen were gathered a respectful distance away. A column of smoke rose from one of the shacks, the metal smokestack glittering in the sunshine.

"It's a heck of a thing," said Barney, voicing her thoughts.

"Have you ever seen anything like that before?" asked Lucy. "I mean, with the fishing line and the lure."

Barney adjusted his thick navy-blue gloves and shook his head. "Can't say that I have."

"I don't buy the accident theory," she said. "It seems more like some sort of cruel joke."

Barney reached for her arm. "Lucy, don't go jumping to conclusions."

"I'm not," insisted Lucy. "But you have to admit it doesn't make sense. I interviewed Max last winter, when he won that snowmobile race. That race covers a thousand miles—you have to be a real survivor just to get to the finish line—and he won. I can't see how a man like that could get himself tangled up in fishline and fall through some punk ice."

Barney started walking toward his cruiser, parked like all the other rescue vehicles any which way in the clearing. "They said he drank a lot and I can tell you from experience that people can do some really weird stuff when they're drunk. And he had plenty of reason to drink lately."

"What do you mean?"

Barney rested his hip on the door of the cruiser, which sank a bit under his considerable weight, and looked her right in the eye. "This is off the record, right?"

"Sure," she said, always eager to get the inside scoop.

"He was having a run of bad luck. I happen to know 'cause he was involved in an altercation at the Quik-Stop, and I kept him overnight in the lockup at the station, just to dry out a bit. He was real chatty, like a lot of drunks, and was going on about how there wasn't any work and he needed money, his ex was after him. He also talked a lot about some woman. Tamzin this and Tamzin that. I didn't recognize the name, but he said she works at that new chocolate shop. He said she was trouble; everything was going fine until he met her." Barney paused, shaking his head. "It's always the same story with these guys; they're always blaming someone and it's usually a woman. You wouldn't believe how often I've heard it."

Lucy nodded. "Oh, yes, I would."

Barney opened the car door. "Remember what I said. Don't go jumping to conclusions." He paused a moment. "I've got some big news myself, but this is strictly off the record."

Lucy's eyebrows rose. "Sure."

"Eddie's coming home. Not just on leave, for good."

Lucy knew Barney's son, Eddie, was a marine and had served in both Iraq and Afghanistan. "That's wonderful news," she exclaimed. "I bet they'll have a parade."

Barney shook his head. "No way. Eddie doesn't want a big fuss."

Lucy thought she could understand. It must be hard to transition from war to peace, from the heat of battle to the chilly quiet of a Maine winter.

"Okay. We'll keep it off the record." Lucy squeezed his arm. "I'm really happy for you and Marge." She gave him a little salute and headed for her own car, her emotions in a tangle. What a day! Max dead and Eddie returning home. A loss and a gain, a minus and a plus. Life was crazy, she thought, noticing that the once sunny blue sky was gone; clouds had filled the sky and the temperature was dropping; Lucy's teeth were chattering when she got behind the wheel and started the car. She called Ted while she waited for the car to warm up and gave him the details of the story.

"Do you want me to come in and write it up?" she asked.

"You can do it tomorrow," he said. "Go on home. You must be frozen clear through."

"You know it," said Lucy, ending the call and dropping

her cell phone in her purse. Her breath was fogging up the window and she wiped it with her gloved hand, then pulled off her gloves and held her bare hands over the heat vent, rubbing them together. It helped, but there was no remedy for her feet, which were blocks of ice inside her boots. Shivering, she shifted into drive and headed for home.

It wasn't just the cold, she realized. Her emotions were ragged. She didn't know Max well, but she'd liked him. He could have driven right on by when she was stuck in that snowdrift; he didn't have to stop and help her, but he did. In his way, he was a bit like Eddie, who had enlisted straight out of high school to fight terrorists. He wasn't the sort to turn away from a problem. If something needed doing, Max would do it. She remembered a microburst last summer that had knocked out power, including the town's single traffic light. Max had parked his truck and started directing traffic. They'd run a photo of him—standing in the middle of the street, soaking wet and windblown—on the front page.

Cold sleet was falling when Lucy pulled into the driveway of the old farmhouse on Red Top Road. The windows were golden, beacons in the darkening afternoon, as she hurried inside. A delicious spicy, beefy, tomato smell hit her as soon as she opened the door. Sara, bless the child, was standing at the stove, stirring up a big pot of chili.

"Oh, it's good to be home," she said, sinking into a chair and pulling off her boots so she could prop her cold feet on the radiator cover. "I was out in the cold for most of the day and I never warmed up."

"What happened?" asked Sara, tapping the spoon on the side of the Dutch oven. A high school senior, Sara was tall and slender, dressed in a stylish chunky sweater, skinny jeans, and UGG boots. Her blond hair shone in the lamplight.

"Max Fraser fell through the ice at the pond. He's dead."

Sara picked up the boots Lucy had dropped on the floor and placed them in a tray by the kitchen door, then helped her take off her jacket. "That's horrible," she said, gathering up Lucy's hat and gloves and scarf and tucking them in the jacket sleeve before hanging it up on a hook, along with the rest of the family's coats and jackets.

Lucy wiggled her toes, trying to coax some warm blood into her frozen feet. "It seems there's one every winter. I don't know why they keep going out on the ice. I don't trust it."

"Do you want some tea?" asked Sara.

"No, thanks. I shouldn't be sitting here like a lump, letting you do everything."

"Take it easy, supper's under control. Zoe made corn bread, the salad's chilling in the fridge. I just have to set the table."

"Well, in that case, you can pour me a glass of wine."

Lucy had that glass, and another, before the family gathered at the dining room table. Sara had set the table with red place mats and chunky pottery plates and bowls; the silverware gleamed in the candlelight.

The chili was delicious and Lucy had seconds; the corn bread was crispy around the edges and hot enough to melt the butter she slathered on with abandon. Even the salad was a treat, dressed up with goat cheese and nuts. It was all so delicious that it seemed a shame not to have another glass of wine, so Lucy did. She didn't want to think about the scene at the pond, she was concentrating on counting her blessings.

"That was some dinner," declared Bill, leaning back in his chair and rubbing his stomach. His beard was streaked with gray, as was his hair, but his stomach was still flat, a fact that irritated Lucy no end. Of course, her job was mostly sedentary, she reminded herself, while his involved physical labor that burned calories.

"I've got news," said Sara, putting down her fork. "Renee and I got jobs at Fern's Famous Fudge. I've got the paperwork for you to sign."

Lucy knew Renee La Chance, Sara's classmate who lived with her mom, Frankie, on nearby Prudence Path. "I hope it's not going to interfere with your school work," she said.

"It's only until Valentine's Day," said Sara.

"What are the hours?" asked Bill.

"After school and weekends."

"That sounds like a lot," said Lucy, wondering if the dinner had been part of a plan to gain her approval of the job.

"Please, Mom." Sara was on her feet, starting to clear the table. "Like I said, it's only a couple of weeks and I could really use the money. The senior trip is coming up and I don't want to have to ask you and Dad for money."

Zoe, an eighth grader, nodded soberly. "We know about the recession, you know."

"Let's not kid ourselves, Lucy," said Bill. "They've got a point. A little extra money wouldn't hurt."

"They're going to New York and I really want to go," said Sara, carrying the plates into the kitchen. She returned with steaming cups of hot coffee for her parents.

"The whole class is going," said Zoe, rising to help her sister finish clearing the table.

"I guess a job is okay, as long as your grades don't suffer," said Lucy.

"Thanks, Mom. You won't be sorry. I promise I'll study extra hard."

"I wish I could get a job, too," said Zoe. "I'm fourteen now. I'm old enough."

"A job's a big responsibility," said Bill. "And Dora might be a tough boss."

"It's going to be hard for her, losing Max," said Lucy. "I know they're divorced, but they loved each other once."

"She seemed real nice at the interview," said Sara.

"She can be sarcastic, she makes everything into a joke. She was behind that float last summer, the one with the diapers and toilet paper strewn on the beach," said Bill. "You might have to develop a thick skin if you're going to work for her."

For a second, Lucy thought of Max and the silver lure hooked through his lip.

"We could have Mexican sundaes for dessert," said Sara. "Dora gave me a jar of fudge sauce and we've got ice cream and peanuts."

"I guess Dora's not so bad after all," said Bill, grinning. "Do you want me to scoop?"

"It sounds like this job may be dangerous," said Lucy, sipping her coffee. "Dangerously fattening."

Chapter Three

Next morning, Lucy woke up knowing she was facing a busy morning. Deadline was at noon on Wednesday, and Ted's favorite maxim was, "It's a deadline, not a guide-line." Much of the paper's content had already been written and edited and was ready to be sent electronically to the printer, but this week there were some last-minute news stories. Max Fraser's death was one; there were sure to be some late-breaking developments related to the drowning. And Lucy had an appointment with Trey Meacham at nine-thirty—it was the only time the chocolatier was free—which meant she had to write the story under pressure while the big old clock on the wall above Ted's roll-top desk ticked away the minutes to noon.

She had to get a move on, she decided, indulging in one final glorious stretch before getting out of bed. Bill's side of the bed was empty; he was already up. Lucy headed for the bathroom, passing through the upstairs hall. She could hear the girls' voices rising up the back stairs from the kitchen, telling each other to hurry, and then the slam of the door as they dashed for the school bus.

It was already past seven according to the watch she'd left on the bathroom vanity, so Lucy popped her vitamin, splashed some water on her face, smoothed on a dab of moisturizer, and ran a comb through her hair. Mindful of the interview, she took a few minutes to add a quick dab of mascara and a smear of lipstick.

Back in the bedroom, she pulled her favorite pair of jeans out of the closet. They were freshly washed, which was fortunate because she liked to look nice when she went out on interviews. And from what Corney said, it was worth looking nice for Trey Meacham—not that she wasn't happily married. She was. But there was something about meeting a reportedly good-looking man that seemed to require a bit of effort, an attempt to at least try to look good. As good as she could, considering she was in a hurry. So it was a very good thing that her favorite and best Calvins were clean.

Still in her nightgown, Lucy pulled on a pair of briefs and then stuck one foot into her jeans. She hopped a bit on that foot, sticking her other foot in the empty leg, and pulled them up over her bottom. Drawing the two sides together to fasten the waistband, she encountered a problem. What was the matter? She yanked her nightgown over her head and stood in front of the full-length mirror.

Goodness, when had that happened? She stood in shock, surveying the damage. A bulge of flesh, a roll, a muffin top, was spilling over the blue denim waistband, which was prevented from closing by a bulging, cotton-covered triangle of tummy. Guiltily, she remembered the seconds on chili, the three glasses of wine, the two pieces of buttery corn bread and, worst of all, the Mexican sundae.

It was clear she could not continue to eat like that, not if she ever wanted to wear these jeans again. It was time for action, so she threw herself flat on the bed and through sheer determination managed to button the jeans and zip them up. They'd stretch, she knew they would. If only she could get back up, onto her feet, despite her constricted middle.

Rolling onto her stomach, she used her arms to push herself off the bed, then marched stiffly over to her dresser, where she found a bra and a long, tummy-concealing sweater. The next challenge, she realized, was getting down the stairs.

"Are you all right?" asked Bill, as she shuffled into the kitchen.

"My jeans shrank in the wash," said Lucy, pouring herself a cup of coffee.

"Yeah, right," he said, laughing. "That's a good one."

"Are you saying I'm fat?" asked Lucy, turning to face him.

"No, no," said Bill, quickly backtracking. "You look great."

"I'm going on a diet," said Lucy glumly, seating herself with difficulty opposite him at the round golden oak kitchen table.

"I think we've all gained weight this winter," said Bill.

"You *do* think I'm fat!" exclaimed Lucy.

"Uh, is that the time?" Bill was on his feet, draining his coffee cup. "I've got to, uh, see somebody." He bent and kissed her on the top of her head. "Have a good day."

"I'm not counting on it," she said, sipping her coffee and watching him put on his outdoor clothes. Then he was gone, and she reluctantly went back upstairs to change into yesterday's comfortable, already stretched jeans.

Chanticleer Chocolate was just too cute, thought Lucy, steeling herself against temptation. The shop had a scalloped yellow awning and a handsome blue-and-yellow rooster on the sign that swung from a bracket over the door, and the mullioned windows were curtained with lace. Business must be good, thought Lucy, noticing a discreet HELP WANTED sign taped to the door.

Inside, a scattering of bistro tables were stacked with blue-and-yellow boxes containing three, six, nine, and twelve pieces of chocolate. An old-fashioned glass case containing trays of candies stood in front of the rear wall, beneath a large painting of the same rooster that was on the sign outside. Through a doorway behind the antique bronze cash register, Lucy caught a glimpse of a work area with a long, marble counter where, she assumed, the chocolates were made. The aroma of chocolate filled the air in the shop and Lucy reminded herself that smelling involved no calories and was almost as good as tasting, which did.

"Can I help you?" The speaker was a tall, slender woman with a remarkably large bust. Lucy didn't usually notice that particular feature, but there was really no avoiding it considering the woman's very low-cut black sweater dress. It was short and clingy, stopping some inches above the over-the-knee black stiletto boots that she was wearing.

"I'm Lucy Stone. I'm here to interview Trey Meacham."

"Right. I'm Tamzin Graves. I manage the shop," she said, with a toss of her long, wavy, bleached-blond hair. "Trey called, he's running a bit late, so maybe I can help you out and answer some questions."

She grinned apologetically and Lucy noticed some telltale crinkles on either side of her fire-engine-red lips, as well as a certain thinning of the skin beneath her heavily made-up eyes. Tamzin, she guessed, was well into her forties. Although, from a distance, you'd never know it.

"That would be great; I'm working on deadline," said Lucy, pulling her notebook out of her oversize handbag. "So I guess this is quite an honor, winning Best Candy on the Coast in the readers' poll."

Tamzin's bosom heaved with emotion and her hands fluttered, displaying impossibly long, painted nails. "It's fabulous! We had no idea! I mean, we consider these chocolates extraordinary, made with all natural ingredients and everything absolutely the finest, but still, you don't expect an honor like this, not in the first year, anyway."

"Right." Lucy was getting it all down. "And the chocolates are made right here, in the shop?"

"Oh, no. It's a quality control issue. Trey is a fanatic

about quality. No, all the chocolates are made in an old sardine factory in Rockland. It's all been cleaned, with steam and everything, there's no trace of the sardines anymore." Tamzin giggled. "In fact, Trey got an award for creative repurposing of an existing industrial space—I think that's right—from Keep Maine Green."

"But it smells so chocolatey in here," said Lucy.

Tamzin's shoulders popped up. "It's phoney. Well, I mean, the chocolates themselves do have a scent, but we amplify it with a gizmo; it's in the corner. Every few seconds it squirts out a little puff of chocolate scent." She paused, obviously having second thoughts. "I think that's off the record, a trade secret."

"Are you giving away secrets?" Lucy jumped a bit at the booming male voice, and turned to meet the fortyish man entering the shop.

"Not at all, Trey." Tamzin was all aflutter and Lucy briefly wondered if she was having some sort of respiratory problem from the way her amazing chest was rising and falling.

The guy was handsome; Lucy had to admit Corney was right. He had streaky sandy hair that fell over his brow, liquid brown eyes a girl could drown in, a square jaw, and a firm handshake.

"Trey Meacham," he said, grabbing her hand. "You must be Lucy Stone."

"Right," said Lucy, somewhat dazed herself. "Tamzin was just telling me about your commitment to quality. Congratulations on the award."

"We're deeply honored," said Trey. His voice was deep and his tone serious. "It's kind of like hitting a home run the first time you come up to bat. I never expected to be so successful so soon, especially considering the economy. But chocolate, you know, is an affordable luxury. I think that's the secret. And people are weight conscious, too. That's why we package them this way—you can buy three in a box for fifteen dollars."

Lucy's jaw dropped. "Fifteen dollars for three?"

"A terrific little gift, an indulgence." He paused, registering her shock. "Think about it, what other luxury can you enjoy for fifteen bucks? Or as little as five, actually, because we sell them singly, too."

Lucy was thinking that a Snickers bar, her favorite, cost eighty-nine cents, but she didn't mention it.

"I can see you're not convinced," said Trey, throwing in a charming chuckle. "You'll have to try a couple."

He nodded at Tamzin and she withdrew a tray of chocolates from the case and set it on the counter, fluttering over it like a Tiffany salesman displaying an assortment of jewelry. The counter, Lucy realized, was lower than usual and gave Tamzin an ample opportunity to display her remarkable endowment.

"No, no," said Lucy. "I'm on a diet."

Trey's brows rose in astonishment. "You? But you don't need to lose an ounce!"

Lucy knew this was pure flattery, because she was dressed in a puffy quilted parka that entirely concealed her figure. "Swimsuit season's coming," she said.

"Swimsuits . . . that's a good one," said Trey, with a nod out the window at the snow that had begun to fall.

Following his gaze, Lucy noticed his car, parked out front. It was an enormous green Range Rover, the current favorite gas-guzzling status symbol among the region's strivers and doers. She thought of Eddie, who'd risked life and limb in a war that was supposed to be about terrorism but just happened to be in a part of the world that contained enormous oil reserves.

"Really, you have to try them to appreciate the quality," said Trey, recapturing her attention.

"And the unique flavors," added Tamzin.

"That's right," agreed Trey. "And I'd like to mention especially that we're trying to overcome the male bias against chocolate."

"Chocolate's not just for the ladies," said Tamzin.

"Right. That's why we've got Mucho Macho. It's a manly blend with hints of beef jerky and German fingerling potato."

"In chocolate?" Lucy thought the mixture sounded repulsive.

Trey nodded. "Chocolate isn't just for sweets, you know. Think of chicken mole. In fact, we've got a chicken mole truffle."

"And lavender," said Tamzin. "So creamy and delicate. We call it Lovely Lavender."

Lucy was pretty sure she liked her lavender in a bar of soap. "Interesting," she said, suddenly remembering that time was fleeting and she had to meet a deadline. "Listen, I've got to wrap this up. Do you have a press release or something with the basic facts about the company?"

"Absolutely," said Trey, opening a slim leather portfolio and handing her a professionally produced PR packet.

"And I need a photo, too," she said, producing her camera.

Trey hopped around the counter and stood next to Tamzin, beneath the rooster. "Be sure to get Chanticleer," he said, grinning broadly. "Say chocolate!"

Lucy felt like groaning, but she snapped a couple of pictures instead.

"Well, thanks for everything. . . ."

"You can't leave without some chocolates," Trey said, grabbing one of the big boxes and forcing it into her hands. "Remember, a day without chocolate. . . ."

"Is a really crummy day," offered Tamzin.

"Well, yes," agreed Trey. "But I was going to say that a day without chocolate is like a day without sunshine."

"Oh, that's nice," Tamzin said, patting Trey's shoulder and straightening his collar. She turned slowly and regarded

Lucy, obviously making some sort of connection. "Did you say your last name is Stone?"

"That's right," replied Lucy.

"Are you related to Bill Stone? The carpenter?"

It was an instinctive reaction, a tightening of the gut and an increased awareness, as if a predator was heard snapping a twig. "Sure, he's my husband," said Lucy.

"Well, he's a really nice guy," said Tamzin.

Lucy's jaw tightened. "I know," she said. "Thanks for the chocolate."

Making her way out of the shop she wondered how Tamzin knew Bill, and why he'd never mentioned her. Walking carefully down the icy sidewalk to the *Pennysaver* office, she also wondered about the relationship between Trey and Tamzin. Was it purely business, or something more? And hadn't Barney said that Max was obsessed with Tamzin, repeating her name over and over when he spent the night in the town lockup? Lucy knew the speed with which news traveled in town; Tamzin must surely have heard of Max's death, but she hadn't seemed at all upset. Come to think of it, thought Lucy, pulling open the office door and setting the little bell to jangling, there hadn't seemed much of anything genuine about Tamzin, starting with her blond hair. And what about Trey? Wasn't he a bit too slick? Then again, she cautioned herself, she wasn't exactly Oprah or Barbara Walters herself, probing for shocking revelations. The interview was simply an opportunity for them to pitch their chocolates and her job was to write a flattering puff piece.

"Whatcha got there?" inquired Phyllis, pointing to the blue-and-yellow box.

"A small fortune in chocolate," said Lucy. "Want to try a Lovely Lavender, or a Mucho Macho?"

Ted was already opening the box. "Mucho Macho?"

"Beef jerky and some sort of potato."

Phyllis was studying the array of chocolates in their gold

foil compartments, trying to match them to the pictures on the inside of the box top. "Pretty small if you ask me. I like something to chew on. A mouthful."

Lucy shrugged. "I'm on a diet."

"That one," Phyllis told Ted, pointing with a finger tipped in Midnite Blue, "is Mucho Macho."

"Here goes," he said, popping it into his mouth.

The two women watched closely to gauge his reaction.

"It's different," he said, after swallowing. "Okay. I'm not rushing over there to buy a box."

"Good thing, 'cause this box costs something like sixty bucks."

"Sixty bucks!" Ted was running his tongue around his mouth, trying to extract every bit of expensive flavor.

"Five bucks a pop. Trey says it's an affordable luxury."

"I've got to try one," said Phyllis, picking a chocolate with a bit of crystallized violet on top. "I'm going for Purple Passion." She popped it between her coral lips and closed her eyes, concentrating.

Lucy watched, amused, as Phyllis sucked and rolled the chocolate around in her mouth before swallowing and opening her eyes. "Well?" she asked.

"I guess I'm not a goor-met," admitted Phyllis, pronouncing the final *t*. "I like Fern's Famous dark chocolate with walnuts a lot better. And you can get a half-pound for six bucks—that's what I call affordable luxury."

Leaving the chocolates on Phyllis's counter, Lucy went to her desk and started fiddling with USB cables so she could upload the photos. "How long do you want this story?" she asked.

"I've only got room for ten inches—and don't forget to mention Fern's Famous," said Ted. The fax went into action and he stood over it, pulling out the sheets of paper as they appeared. "It's the ME's report," he said.

Lucy's hand was on the mouse but she paused, finger poised. "What does it say?"

Ted was scanning the tightly packed medical jargon, looking for something he understood. "Ah, here, conclusion. Death due to drowning, indicated by presence of water in the lungs. Contributing factors: high blood alcohol level and cranial bruising . . ."

"A blow to the head?" asked Lucy.

"Yeah, but the ME points out that there is no way of determining if the injury was the result of an attack by person or persons unknown or an accident."

All three fell silent, imagining Max Fraser's final moments. "I hope he went quickly, didn't feel any pain," said Phyllis.

"That's likely, considering his blood alcohol level," said Ted, "and the knock on his head."

"There's always at least one tragedy every winter," said Phyllis. "I hope this is the only one."

Lucy nodded. It was true. Winter brought its own seasonal perils: people fell through the ice on frozen ponds, cars crashed on slippery roads, houses burned down due to the improper use of electric heaters, furnaces backed up and entire families died in their sleep of carbon monoxide poisoning. You tried to be careful, but accidents happened. That was life. Now, even though the image filling her computer screen was of Tamzin and Trey in the chocolate shop, she wasn't seeing them. She was seeing Max Fraser's ice-crusted face and that glittering silver lure dangling from his blue lips. An accident? She didn't think so, although the police certainly would. She was beginning to think Max's death was the work of a killer with a warped sense of humor. And it was up to her, she realized, to make sure the killer was caught. Max had helped her and she'd promised to return the favor. It was a promise she meant to keep.

Chapter Four

"**J**ust black coffee for me," said Lucy.

Norine, the waitress at Jake's Donut Shop, crossed out the notation she'd started writing on her order pad. "No hash and two eggs sunnyside up with whole wheat toast?"

Lucy shook her head, mourning the loss of her usual Thursday morning feast. "I'm on a diet."

"And about time, too," said Sue, with a prim nod.

"Nonsense. You look great and breakfast is the most important meal of the day," urged Rachel Goodman, a firm believer in the benefits of three meals a day. "I'll have a cranberry muffin."

Norine was way ahead of her. "Two black coffees, two regular coffees, one cranberry muffin, and one crunchy yogurt. That about it?"

"That's it," said Pam Stillings, Ted's wife, who was a bit of a health nut and always had the yogurt topped with granola. She turned to Lucy. "Rachel's right. If you starve yourself, your metabolism shuts down and it takes longer to lose. Look at Sue." She smiled at the fourth member of the group,

Sue Finch. "How do you think she survives on nothing but black coffee and red wine? She's got no metabolism at all."

"And if you ask me, the lack of nutrition is making her rather mean," said Rachel, unusually critical this morning.

"I eat." Sue tucked a lock of midnight black hair behind one ear. "I've found the perfect balance and I maintain it." She took a sip of coffee. "I simply don't see the point of eating calories I don't like, so I skip breakfast in favor of a glass of wine with dinner."

"More than one glass," sniffed Rachel. She'd majored in psychology at college, with a focus on addictive personalities.

"I had a cup of yogurt at home," said Lucy, sounding like a child announcing she'd tidied her room.

"Good girl." Pam nodded her approval and changed the subject, reporting on her work as a member of the Chamber of Commerce's publicity committee. "It looks like the *Love Is Best on the Coast* promo is really taking off." She paused, as Norine distributed the mismatched mugs that were a tradition at Jake's and filled them with coffee. "A lot of businesses are signing up."

"I suppose it's worth doing," said Lucy, in a doubtful tone. She was looking out the window at the frozen harbor and the parking lot littered with shrouded boats beneath a milk-white sky. Snow was falling but it wasn't serious, just what the TV weathermen called "ocean effect." It was funny, she thought, how you got to recognize different kinds of snow after you'd lived in Maine for a while. "I can't see why anybody would leave the comfort of hearth and home and spend a lot of money for this." She waved an arm at the bleak view, almost completely devoid of color.

"Are you kidding? Maine is beautiful in winter," declared Pam, as Norine set her bowl of granola-topped yogurt in front of her.

"I guess you've never been to the Bahamas," said Norine,

sending a plate with a muffin sliding across the table to Rachel. "*It's better in the Bahamas.*"

"No, no, no." Pam picked up her spoon. "It's best on the coast."

"You've been listening to Corney," said Lucy.

"That woman is trouble," said Sue, twisting her glossed lips into a scowl. "Somehow she convinced me to organize a Valentine dessert contest." She took a sip of coffee. "I'm counting on you all to enter."

"I'm awfully busy with the committee," said Pam. "I don't see how I'll have the time."

"Me, too," said Rachel, using her tongue to whisk a muffin crumb from her lip. "The Harbor Players are putting on A. R. Gurney's *Love Letters* and I'm directing."

"That's a first for you," crowed Lucy. "Congratulations."

"Yeah, I'm really enjoying it," said Rachel. "But the rehearsals are very time-consuming."

"That leaves you," said Sue, narrowing her eyes and pointing a perfectly manicured finger at Lucy.

Lucy shook her head. "I told you. I'm on a diet."

"You don't have to eat it," said Sue. "You just have to make it."

Lucy switched to Plan B. "I guess Sara and Zoe can whip something up." She drained her mug and signaled for a refill. "I bumped into Barney Culpepper the other day. He said Eddie's coming home. Permanently. He's done with the marines."

"That is a relief—now I won't have to worry about him." Rachel let out a big sigh. "They were so cute, weren't they? Those boys: Richie and Tim, Toby and Eddie. Remember how Eddie was the catcher, at Little League? That funny squat he had, with one leg stuck straight out?"

Pam nodded, smiling nostalgically. "They were so cute in those Cub Scout uniforms. Remember, Lucy?"

"I wish I could forget," said Lucy. "I was the den mother. They led me a merry chase. Those boys were a handful."

"They all turned out fine, though," said Pam. "My Tim's helping to rebuild New Orleans, Richie's going to make a big archaeological discovery. . . ."

Rachel smiled at the reference to her son. "We'll see."

"Oh, yes he is," said Pam. "Toby's a fine father. . . ."

"And someday he'll actually get that college degree," said Lucy, fretting about her son.

"He'll be a captain of industry," said Rachel. "And Eddie." She paused, thinking, while Norine refilled their mugs. "Do you think he'll become a cop like his dad?"

Lucy bit her lip. "You know, I think he may need some time to figure out what he wants to do. I said the town would probably have a welcome home parade and Barney said he doesn't want a fuss."

Rachel's face clouded. "Oh, dear. I hope he doesn't have post-traumatic stress syndrome like so many returning vets."

"And I hope he gets started on something pretty quick," said Sue. "It's no good for these kids to hang around aimlessly. Before you know it, they're in the court report for drunk driving or drugs."

"I know," said Lucy, with a grim nod. "We got one at the paper yesterday and I had to format it. I was shocked at the number of drug cases."

Rachel shook her head. "It's an epidemic."

"Where does it all come from?" asked Sue.

"That's a good question," said Lucy, checking her watch. "Gosh, I can't believe the time. It's back to the salt mines for me. I've got a budget meeting at ten."

The ten o'clock news budget meeting had been Ted's idea and Lucy didn't like it much. Deadline was noon Wednesday and the paper came out on Thursday mornings, which meant she used to have all of Wednesday afternoon and Thursday morning free. It was valuable time she used to catch up with her friends and polish off some errands. But Ted had come back from a recent productivity seminar full of ideas, one of which was the budget meeting. Lucy thought the meeting was actually counterproductive—she'd often gathered valuable news tips as she went about town with her list of errands, crossing off grocery shopping at the IGA, vacuum cleaner bags at the hardware store, wine at the liquor store, and mailing bills at the post office. Ted didn't see it that way, however, and now she had to come in at ten instead of twelve-thirty on Thursdays. She didn't even pick up any extra pay; in fact, her salary didn't begin to cover the time she actually worked because she often stayed late at the office on the days the girls had after-school activities and needed a ride home.

The new system had only been in place for a couple of weeks and Lucy wasn't in a good mood when she got to the office. Ted, however, was bursting with ideas.

"Good, you're here," he announced, turning his desk chair around so it faced the room and pulling over two more chairs to form a circle. "We can get started. Phyllis, that means you, too. Put the phone on voice mail, please."

Giving him an evil look, Phyllis punched a few buttons before pushing her chair back and getting to her feet. She hated leaving her comfortable area behind the reception counter, where her chair was just right and items like her enormous pump bottle of Jergens lotion and a big box of tissues were at hand, along with a photo of her husband. She perched uneasily on the chair Ted indicated, then shoved it aside and went back to her desk, wheeling her preferred chair across the office and seating herself.

Lucy was already in place, wrestling with the problem of Sara's job at Fern's Famous, which meant she would need a ride home at five-thirty.

"Let's begin," said Ted, rubbing his hands together. "Lucy, you have the usual selectmen's meeting. I'll take the school committee and the conservation committee, that should be a hot one because of the proposed toilets at the town beach."

"About time," said Phyllis. "Those Porta-Potties stink."

"APTC wants those ecological earth closets, composting toilets," said Ted. "They're up in arms over a septic system so close to the cove."

"That's not news," said Lucy, who knew the letters stood for the Association for the Preservation of Tinker's Cove. "They're always up in arms."

"I'll follow up on the Max Fraser investigation," said Ted, consulting his notebook.

Lucy started to protest but he brushed her objections aside. "I've got something else in mind for you, Lucy." He turned to Phyllis. "You handle the events calendar. Is there anything I should be aware of?"

Phyllis gave him a look. "How the heck am I supposed to know? It's only Thursday, I haven't even started."

"Oh." Ted looked disconcerted. "When you file the press releases, don't you read them?"

Phyllis sighed. "No. I don't have time. I scan them for the date, that's all. So I can file them."

"Well, in the future, perhaps you could just look them over and make copies for me of the important ones," suggested Ted.

Phyllis heaved her bust, a gesture that usually boded trouble, and Lucy pressed her lips together, trying not to smile. "I told you. I don't have time to read them or decide which is important. How do I know, anyway? Is a bake sale important? What about a roast beef dinner at the VFW? How do I decide?"

Ted wasn't about to give up. "Well, a production by the Harbor Players would be more important than a bake sale, for example."

Phyllis smiled in triumph. She knew she had him. "Just you try explaining that to the Junior Women's Club. They think their annual bake sale should be a first-page story."

"Right," said Ted, studying his list. "Moving along, we're going to do a special supplement for the *Love Is Best on the Coast* weekend. There will be special rates for advertisers, an events calendar, and a story. That's where you come in, Lucy. I want a big feature on a couple, an older couple, who've made love last. Don't be afraid to pull out all the stops—I want this to be over-the-top romantic."

"Like one of the fiftieth-anniversary couples?" They often ran stories about such couples, usually accompanied by then and now photos. "The Crabtrees were in the paper last week."

Phyllis was chuckling. "You mean the Crabby-trees? They were duking it out at the Quik-Stop the other day."

"Definitely not the Crabtrees," said Ted. "We want a cute, loving couple, not the Bickersons. Maybe even an old couple who fell for each other years ago but married other people, but then their spouses died and they found each other again. They reconnected." Ted was beaming, he really liked this idea.

Lucy didn't. "How in heck am I supposed to find this adorable couple?"

Ted shrugged. "Ask around. You'll turn up something, you always do."

Lucy chewed her lip thoughtfully, trying to come up with a suitable couple and, much to her surprise, coming up with a few names that she scribbled down.

"That's it, ladies," said Ted, with a satisfied nod. "I think we made some good progress this morning."

"Hold on," said Lucy, remembering the conversation at Jake's. "I'd like to do something about illegal drugs and youth. Have you seen the court report lately? There's a big uptick. We could follow up on your interview with the governor's wife."

Ted shook his head. "Trust me, Lucy. That's too big for us. We don't have the manpower or budget to do an investigative report like that." Before Lucy could protest, he swiveled his chair around and reached for the phone on his desk.

Disappointed, Lucy shoved her chair under her desk and stood, tapping her fingers on the chair back. She didn't want to write puff pieces, she wanted to tackle important issues, but she knew that Ted was struggling to keep the paper afloat. Maybe he was right to focus on promoting business, at least for now. She pulled out her chair and sat down, studying her list of loving couples.

She'd jotted down a few notes when Phyllis's husband, Wilf, came in, holding the door for Ted, who was leaving. Wilf was the mail carrier and he set the day's delivery, bound with a rubber band, on the counter. "Hi, sunshine," he said, with a wink.

Phyllis blushed and smiled at her husband as if they were still honeymooners. "Hi, yourself."

Too bad she couldn't write about them, thought Lucy, but she knew Ted would never go for it. He'd cite journalistic ethics, conflict of interest, or something. Lucy didn't buy it. She figured he just wanted to make her job harder.

"Hi, Wilf," she said, glancing at her list. "You know everybody in town, right?"

"And their dirty secrets," he said. "Only the trash haulers know more about folks than me."

"You're just the man I want," declared Lucy, explaining her assignment to him. "So tell me, do you think the Wilkersons, over there on Bridge Street, would be good subjects?" The Wilkersons had recently announced their fiftieth wedding anniversary and had even renewed their vows.

"I can't really say—people's mail is confidential. Postal regulations."

"How about a yes or no answer?"

"Okay. No to the Wilkersons."

"But why? They're so cute."

"Like I said, I can't elaborate. Regulations. But trust me. You don't want to look foolish, now."

"Okay." Lucy crossed the Wilkersons off her list. "What about the MacDonalds? The people with the farm stand."

Wilf shifted his weight from one sturdily booted foot to the other. "Don't think so."

"Oh." Lucy crossed off another name. That left her with the Sturtevants.

"Oh, gosh, no!" exclaimed Wilf, vehemently.

"What? They seem very happy," said Lucy, who often saw them walking their dog, an aged schnauzer.

"Too happy, if you ask me," said Wilf, with a leer.

"You can't make an expression like that without telling us more," said Lucy.

"That's right," added Phyllis. "Besides, you know you'll tell me later and I'll tell Lucy, so you might as well tell us both now and get it over with."

"Well," Wilf began, in a low voice, "they get a lot of mail in plain brown wrappers, if you know what I mean. And you didn't hear it from me."

"Eeuw," groaned Phyllis. "He's eighty if he's a day."

"And she's got more whiskers than that dog," said Lucy, crossing off the last name on her list.

The fax machine was whirring when Wilf left and Lucy got up to get the message, which she figured was one of the lunch menus that arrived around this time every morning. Instead, she found that the funeral home had sent Max Fraser's obituary.

It was written in the usual flowery style, announcing that "Maxwell Fraser has passed over to that distant blessed shore where he will be joyously reunited with his mother Andrea and father Phil, Gramps and Gran, Uncle Harry and Auntie Maude."

Taking it back to her desk, she passed the stack of new papers, with her photo of the rescuers carrying the stretcher with Max's body on the front page. She hoped he was enjoying the family reunion, but, personally, she had her doubts. She figured Max would rather be zooming from cloud to cloud on his snowmobile.

She started typing the text, editing as she went. When she

finished removing all the hyperbole and religious refer-
ences, she was left with two short sentences. She had to have
more so she reluctantly reached for the phone to call Max's
ex-wife, Dora. Dora had just answered when Bill arrived,
toolbox in hand, to fix the door.

"I'm so sorry to bother you at such a difficult time," she
began, after identifying herself, "but I need some information for Max's obituary."

"It's no bother, heck, I oughta be glad he's gone, right?"
Dora sniffed. "That man was nothing but trouble."

Lucy knew Dora had a reputation for cracking jokes so
she wasn't surprised at Dora's glib comment. There was
something in Dora's voice, though, that gave her pause.

"I know you were divorced," said Lucy.

"Right. Seven years ago. But I couldn't get rid of him. He
kept turning up, like a bad penny. Worse than that. Like one
of those coins you've got in your purse that you can't quite
tell what the hell it is, it's all stuck with candy wrapper or
something. Could be a penny, maybe a dime. You know you
should get rid of it, but how?" She sighed. "That was Max."

Lucy found herself nodding in agreement. "Do you happen to know his mother's maiden name? The funeral home
left it out."

"Gooch."

Lucy wasn't sure if this was a joke or not. "Really?"

"Yeah." Dora giggled. "She was a Gooch from Gilead."

Lucy suspected Dora was a bit hysterical and decided she
better wrap the interview up. "What about Max's education?"

"He graduated from Tinker's Cove High, did a year in
Orono at the university." She snorted. "He flunked out, of
course. I used to tell him he majored in partying."

"He was quite the sportsman," prompted Lucy.

"If you call drinking a sport," said Dora.

Okay, thought Lucy, we won't go there. "One child, Lily,
right?"

Dora's voice softened. "Lily, yeah. Max got one thing right."

"What about clubs he belonged to? Church?"

"Rod and Gun, o'course. That's all, I think."

"Awards?"

"Well, he won that snowmobile race, practically bankrupted himself doing it." Dora paused and Lucy heard her sniffling. "But if you ask me, I don't think his death was any accident. Max was smart about some things. He knew how to take care of himself."

"Do you think he was murdered?" asked Lucy. Bill, who was removing the pins from the door hinges, paused and gave her a look.

"I . . . I . . . I don't know what to think." And with that, Dora sobbed and hung up, leaving Lucy confused and wondering what she meant. She'd said she was glad Max was finally out of her life for good, but Lucy wasn't convinced. There'd been something in her voice that indicated real sorrow.

"You're awful quiet all of a sudden," commented Phyllis, who was filing press releases by date in an accordion file.

Bill was hanging a tarp over the empty doorframe in a feeble effort to keep out the cold while he planed the door. "I don't want you getting involved, Lucy," he said. "You better leave this up to the police. If Max was murdered, that means the killer could be right here in town. You don't want to get tangled up with any murderer."

"Of course not," said Lucy, deciding she could use some fresh air. "How about some hot coffee?" she asked. When Bill and Phyllis jumped at her offer, she got up and grabbed her anorak. Once she got outside, however, she had second thoughts. The snow was continuing to drift down and the sidewalk was slippery underfoot. She needed to move, though, so she started off in the direction of Jake's. Normally she would drive even that short distance, but walking would burn a few calories and clean out her lungs. If the sun came out, she'd get a bit of vitamin D, but a glance at the cloud-covered sky made that a dim possibility. But most of all she wanted to think over what Dora had said.

Max knew how to take care of himself.

He sure did, thought Lucy, walking past the hardware store with its display of snow shovels in the window. And he'd been ice fishing on Blueberry Pond for years. He would certainly know where the soft tricky spots were. The ME said he'd gotten a knock on the head. How did that happen? Did he slip and fall, hitting his head? She supposed it was possible, but she doubted it. She'd seen the careful, deliberate way Max had worked to free her car and remembered how he'd checked it over, making sure it hadn't been damaged. The more she thought about it, she decided as she reached Jake's, the more likely it seemed that Max's death was no accident.

She was just leaving the café with her cardboard tray of coffees, one regular for Bill, one black with skim for Phyllis, and plain black for herself, when she met Frankie La Chance on the sidewalk. Frankie lived with her daughter, Sara's friend Renee, on Prudence Path, off Red Top Road near the Stones' house.

"Lucy! I've been meaning to call you," exclaimed Frankie, in her charming French accent.

"Same here," said Lucy. "I understand Renee is working at Fern's Famous along with my Sara."

"Which means they will need rides," said Frankie. "I am hoping we can carpool. What do you think?"

"You're a lifesaver," said Lucy. "What is your schedule like?"

"It's all over the place, but I can commit to Monday, Wednesday, and Friday."

"That gives me Tuesday, Thursday, and Saturday," said Lucy. "Not good, but better than every day."

"Good." Frankie nodded. "I must run. I've got a couple who want to buy a house."

"Good for you!" exclaimed Lucy, who knew Frankie was a real estate agent. "Does this mean the market is turning around?"

"I wish," moaned Frankie. "They're older, a retired couple, I think they have money. Very cultured, they talk about art and music. Awfully particular. I've showed them a lot of places already, but nothing has been quite right. They have excellent taste; they're staying at the Queen Vic while they look."

Frankie started to go but Lucy caught her arm. "I have to write a story about an older couple who've made love last— do you think they'd be good subjects?"

Frankie broke into a broad grin. "Absolutely!"

"You say they're at the Queen Vic?"

"Yes. Roger and Helen Faircloth are their names. You can say I suggested them to you."

"Thanks," said Lucy, vowing to call them as soon as she got back to the office.

The heavy blue tarp was still hanging in the doorway when she arrived, as Bill had set the door on sawhorses and was working away at it with a plane. Phyllis, who was bundled up in her winter coat, took the hot cup gratefully, and so did Bill.

"I'm almost finished," he said, taking a long swallow and setting his cup aside.

"Can I help?" asked Lucy.

"Nope," he said, running the plane over the edge of the door a few more times and then rehanging it on its hinges. He pushed it shut, and the latch clicked easily. "All done."

"Good work," said Lucy, seating herself at her desk and sipping her coffee. "What are you doing next?"

Bill had settled in Ted's chair, enjoying his coffee break. "I'm going to see about a job on Parallel Street, a bathroom remodel. What about you?"

"I've got to set up some interviews," said Lucy. "And I've got to pick up Sara and Renee."

Bill nodded and began packing up his tools.

When he was gone, Lucy reached for the phone and called the Queen Victoria Inn. Helen Faircloth did indeed sound quite charming on the phone, but she and her husband were not available this afternoon or Friday since they would be house hunting. Lucy set up an appointment for Saturday afternoon, at the inn. Then she got to work on the birth announcements, one of the paper's most popular features, noticing a decided uptick in the number of unmarried parents. She sent an e-mail to Ted, suggesting they do a feature story on the trend, and at five o'clock she left for the day, heading over to Fern's Famous to pick up Sara and Renee.

Parking in front of the fudge shop, she had a clear view through the plate glass windows. There was no sign of Sara or Renee, who she guessed must be busy in a back room, but she saw Lily, Max and Dora's daughter, standing by the cash register, staring off into the distance. Then she turned and smiled and Lucy saw the girls, pulling on their jackets and coming toward the door, so she gave a quick honk to let them know she was waiting.

"How'd it go?" she asked, as they piled into the car.

"We got to make fudge," said Sara. "It's easy."

"We can eat as much as we want," said Renee.

"Better watch that," advised Lucy. "It's very fattening." She pulled out into the road. "Did I see Lily working there?"

"Yeah," said Sara.

"I thought she was at college in Rhode Island," said Lucy. "Did she come home because of her dad's death?"

"She's taking a semester off," said Renee. "She wanted to go back, but her parents weren't able to manage the tuition so she's working and saving."

Lucy sometimes thought she could drive the route home blindfolded, she'd done it so many times, so her mind was free to ponder this new information, wondering how Max's death would change Lily's situation. There might be a small estate; nobody died absolutely penniless. There might be a life insurance policy, a bit of property, even a stamp or coin collection. But even if Max didn't leave much behind, Lily would qualify for more financial aid now that she was fatherless and would probably be able to resume her education.

Lucy knew that money, especially the lack of it, was a frequent bone of contention between divorced couples. She'd never seen Max's name on the lists of deadbeat dads that the paper received from time to time, but Barney had said he was worried about money that night he'd spent in the lockup. No wonder; the recession was hitting lots of people, and Max was probably no exception. But if Max suddenly had had a reduced income, it could mean that he was worth more dead than he was alive. And that, she thought, as she braked for a stop sign, was a dangerous situation to be in.

Chapter Five

The Queen Victoria Inn was a survivor from an earlier, more gracious time, when the wives and children of prosperous Boston and New York businessmen would spend the entire summer at the coast, enjoying the cooling breezes and languid atmosphere. Back then the rocking chairs on the front porch would be filled with gossiping matrons, fanning themselves and keeping an eye out for their children's matrimonial prospects. Those days were gone and now most of the guests could manage to get away from their high-pressure jobs for only a weekend and spent much of their vacation barking orders into cell phones or pecking away at laptop computers.

The Faircloths were different, Lucy discovered, when she met them in the inn's spacious dining room for afternoon tea on Saturday. Unlike the handful of others scattered at the cloth-covered tables, they weren't hunched over any electronic devices whatsoever. They were simply sitting and chatting and obviously enjoying each other's company.

"Hi! I'm Lucy," she said, joining them.

Roger Faircloth immediately leaped to his feet and pulled

out a chair for her. He was tall and moved easily despite his age, which Lucy guessed must be close to seventy. His abundant hair was snow white, his face was tanned, and he was beautifully dressed in gray flannel slacks, tasseled loafers, and a camel cloth blazer. His blue oxford-cloth shirt was topped with a jaunty striped bow tie.

"Thank you," murmured Lucy as she lowered herself onto the chair Roger slid beneath her. She wasn't used to this sort of treatment and was frankly relieved when she found she'd succeeded in connecting with the moving chair.

"Allow me to introduce my wife, Helen," he said, taking his seat and signaling to the waitress.

"I'm so pleased to meet you," said Helen, who was every bit as good-looking as her husband. Her shoulder-length blond pageboy was streaked with gray, but her subtly made-up face exhibited only a few well-moisturized lines. She was wearing a blue twinset, which matched her eyes, a pearl necklace, and a tailored pair of slacks. A rather large diamond glittered on her finger, along with a broad gold wedding band.

"Well, I'm very grateful to you for agreeing to this interview. Tea is on me, of course," said Lucy, eager to get that detail out of the way.

"Absolutely not," said Roger, as the waitress, Caitlin Eldredge, appeared to request their preferences. Roger chose a hearty Lapsang souchong, but Helen and Lucy opted for Earl Grey. Moments later, Caitlin arrived with a steaming silver pot for each of them as well as a tiered silver stand containing scones, assorted cakes, and tiny sandwiches.

"Please, help yourself," invited Helen. "A young person like you must have a hearty appetite."

"Not so young," replied Lucy, "and I'm trying to lose a few pounds."

"It's a struggle, isn't it?" agreed Helen. She turned to her husband with a twinkle in her eye. "I'm afraid you're going to have to eat for both of us."

"I'll do what I can," he said, piling the little triangular sandwiches on his plate.

"Roger can eat as much as he wants and never gains a pound," said Helen. "It's so unfair."

"My husband, too," said Lucy, opening her notebook. "I understand you're here in town looking for a house."

"Yes," said Roger, polishing off a salmon sandwich and reaching for another. "We definitely are. Tinker's Cove is a beautiful town and we think, no, we *know* it will suit us perfectly."

"What prompted the move?" asked Lucy.

"Oh, we've lived in Connecticut for most of our marriage, that's over forty years."

"Remarkable," said Lucy.

"Not so remarkable. It's easy to stay married when you're in love," said Roger, beaming across the table at Helen. "She's every bit as pretty as the day I married her."

"Oh, Roger," protested Helen, her cheeks turning pink. "You're embarrassing me." She turned back to Lucy. "Isn't he impossible?"

"I think you're fortunate to have such a loving relationship," said Lucy, feeling she was in danger of losing control of the interview. "So why did you leave Connecticut?"

"Oh, our house burned down," said Helen, with a little shrug.

"That's right," agreed Roger, buttering a scone. "Total loss."

"Oh, my goodness." Lucy was shocked. "That's terrible."

"When life hands you lemons, you make lemonade," said Helen, brightly. "We decided to look at it as an opportunity. When you've lost everything, you see, at first it's very terrible. You're shocked. The photos, the artwork, the antiques, all turned to ashes."

"We were quite serious collectors," said Roger. "We had an early Warhol, a Basquiat. . . ."

"I never liked those much, dear. It was the Wyeths I hated to lose," said Helen.

"For me, it was the antiques. That Goddard highboy. . . ."

"Brown University had just made inquiries, too. They wanted to buy it."

"Buy it!" hooted Roger. "They wanted us to leave it to them."

"Doesn't matter now," said Helen, with a sad smile. "It's gone." She took a deep breath and straightened her back, taking a sip of tea. "It's all gone, but we decided not to look at it as a loss but to move on. We'd always wanted to live on the coast—I just love Maine, you see. And if I can't have a Wyeth landscape on my wall, I can have one right outside my window."

"That's a wonderful attitude," said Lucy. "Can you tell me how you met?"

"I was in London, modeling," said Helen. "It was the Swinging Sixties."

"I wasn't swinging, I was at the London School of Economics. I call it the Slogging Sixties."

"We met on a double-decker bus," said Helen. "The bus swerved 'round a corner and I lost my balance. I landed right in his lap!"

"Talk about luck! This beautiful girl lands in my lap. I took it as a sign that she was meant for me." Roger finished off his scone and reached for a tiny square of chocolate cake.

"So you married and came back to the U.S. and settled in Connecticut?" asked Lucy.

"More or less," agreed Roger.

"Any children?" asked Lucy.

Helen shook her head sadly. "It just never happened, it's my one regret."

Roger was looking over the remaining cakes, deciding between a lemon curd tart and a mocha mini-cupcake. "I know you feel that way," admitted Roger. "But I think—no,

I know—we were spared a lot of heartache. Think of the Westons."

Helen turned to Lucy, her blue eyes brimming over. "Their daughter was killed in a car crash."

"And even when there aren't any tragedies, children do tend to test a marriage," said Roger, choosing the mini-cupcake.

Helen dabbed at her eyes with a lace-trimmed handkerchief. "We've had good times, haven't we, Roger?"

"You betcha," said Roger, reaching across the table and covering her small pink hand with his larger speckled one. "It's like that old song: 'I Got You, Babe.' "

"You certainly do," said Helen, leaning toward him and smiling.

The two remained gazing into each other's eyes until Caitlin returned. "How's everything?" she asked.

"Just lovely," said Helen.

"Good, I'll be back with the check," said Caitlin.

Lucy reached for her bag. "This is on my expense account," said Lucy. "I can't thank you enough. . . ."

"Nonsense." Roger's voice was firm. "Call me old-fashioned but I couldn't let a lady pay for me. Besides, I'm the one who ate all the food!"

When Caitlin returned, Roger snatched the little plastic folder from her. "I'll just sign," he said. "We're guests here."

Caitlin pressed her lips together and leaned forward, whispering in Roger's ear. Suddenly Roger's face flushed beet red. "That's absurd. I never heard of anything like that. What sort of establishment is this?"

"I'm just following orders," she said, looking extremely uncomfortable.

"I'm sure it's a misunderstanding," said Roger, scribbling on the bill and snapping the folder shut. "Here you go. I'll take it up with the management later."

Caitlin shook her head, refusing to take the folder. "Cash only, those were my instructions."

"Can't you see I have guests," protested Roger. "I'll take it up with the manager later." He practically tossed the folder at her. "Now off you go, like a good girl."

Caught off balance, Caitlin snatched the folder out of the air and walked off, scowling.

"I'm so sorry about that," said Roger, turning to Lucy. "I don't know where they get their help these days."

"From right here in town," said Lucy, who sympathized with Caitlin's predicament and hoped she wouldn't get in trouble. "She's in my daughter's class at school."

"Well, I'm afraid she's going to learn a hard lesson. There's no tip for that girl."

"It wasn't her fault, Roger," said Helen. "It's just a mis-understanding. I'm sure you can straighten it out with the manager." She paused, beaming at him. "You always do."

Roger turned to Lucy. "You know what they say: Behind every successful man there's a good woman. I don't know what I'd do without my Helen. I don't deserve her."

"Of course you do, Roger. It's I who don't deserve you."

"No, dear, you are the glue that holds us together."

"No, Roger. You are. It's your strength. I'd be lost without you."

"And I without you."

Time for me to get lost, thought Lucy, feeling as if she'd eaten too many sweets. Which was funny, when you came to think of it, because all she'd had was tea. Plain tea with no sugar.

Back home, Lucy checked the mailbox that stood out by the road and found a couple of bills, a flyer from the hard-ware store, and a thick envelope like a wedding invitation. Intrigued, she opened it and found an engraved card from the Chamber of Commerce inviting her to the Hearts on Fire Ball scheduled for Valentine's weekend at the VFW hall. The part about the VFW hall was a bit discouraging, but the event was black-tie optional, which made her heart beat a little faster, imagining how handsome Bill would look in a tux. And she couldn't remember the last time she'd had a reason to wear anything dressier than a pair of slacks and a nice sweater.

Hurrying into the house, she debated how best to approach the subject with Bill, who declared himself allergic to neckties. A rented tux was a lot dressier than the all-purpose blue blazer he wore, most often with an open-necked shirt, when a jacket was absolutely necessary.

Lucy paused in the kitchen to slip off her boots and hang up her jacket, taking a moment to neaten up the coat rack. Why couldn't Bill and the girls manage to use the little loops for hanging that were sewn into their jackets? Instead, they tossed them on the row of hooks any old way, piling them one on top of the other until the whole mess slid off onto the floor. Catching herself in a negative train of thought, she resolved to try to think more positively, like Helen Faircloth. There was nothing she could do about winter, the weather was out of her control. She could control her thoughts, however, by concentrating on the positive aspects of the season. Like the ball.

The TV was on in the family room; Lucy could hear bursts of sound that indicated a sporting event of some kind. Maybe Bill would like a snack, she thought, popping into the powder room and applying a fresh coat of lipstick and a squirt of cologne. Thus armed, she advanced into the family room where she found her husband in his usual chair, a big old recliner, slapping his knee.

"A three-pointer," he declared. "You shoulda seen it. Right across the court. Wait, hold on, they're replaying it."

Trapped, Lucy perched on the sectional and watched as an abnormally tall man with many tattoos seemed to launch a basketball with an effortless flick of his wrist that sent it sailing from one end of the court to the other and right through the hoop.

"Amazing," she said.

"And they said he wasn't worth sixty million dollars," scoffed Bill.

"Fools," said Lucy, thinking to herself that nobody on God's green earth deserved sixty million dollars, not when other people were hungry and homeless.

"That's the quarter," said Bill, as a buzzer sounded.

Remembering her mission, Lucy jumped up. "Can I get you something? A beer? Would you like me to throw some popcorn in the microwave? There's a mini-pizza in the freezer I could heat up for you."

Bill looked at her suspiciously. "Did you smash up the car?"

"No. What makes you think that?"

"Dunno. You're not usually this nice. Are the girls okay?" He paused. "Don't tell me Sara's in trouble. Or Zoe?"

"Don't be ridiculous," said Lucy. "The girls are fine. And so is the car."

"Well, you obviously want something. What is it?"

Lucy plopped herself in his lap, giving him the full benefit of her cologne. "Don't I smell good?"

"You always smell good," he said, nuzzling her neck.

Lucy stroked his beard, noticing the gray. "You know what holiday is coming up?"

"Mother's Day?" he teased.

"No." She nibbled his ear. "Valentine's Day."

"Funny you should mention it. I noticed a bunch of red hearts in the windows at Fern's Famous."

For a moment, Lucy wondered if he'd also noticed something at Chanticleer Chocolate, or rather, someone, but pushed the thought from her mind. "No chocolate for me," said Lucy. "I'm on a diet."

You had to hand it to Bill, he could be amazingly prescient. "So what do you have in mind, *sweetheart*?"

Lucy handed him the invitation.

"A ball?"

"Wouldn't it be fun to get dressed up and dance? We could dance the night away."

Bill shrugged. "The VFW does a pretty decent prime rib."

"I could wear something with a low neck," she murmured in his ear. "And I haven't seen you in a tux since our wedding."

A shudder seemed to run through Bill's body. "A tux?"

Lucy knew the value of a strategic retreat. "It's optional." She sighed. "Of course, I'd look pretty silly all dolled up in lace and black satin if you're not dressed up, too."

"We'll see," he said.

"You mean we can go?"

"Yeah," said Bill, as she bounced in his lap and gave him a big hug.

"You can pick up the tickets at the Seamen's Bank," said Lucy, hopping off his lap. "Do you want popcorn or pizza?"

"Just a beer," he said, turning the volume up with the remote. "Whaddya mean, I can buy the tickets?"

"Well, it's ten dollars cheaper for men."

"Isn't that discrimination?" he asked, grinning. "I'm surprised your feminist ire isn't aroused."

"Sometimes even a feminist has to be practical," said Lucy, heading for the kitchen. "I think they want to encourage men to attend."

When she returned, Bill was frowning. "The Celts are behind," he muttered, taking the bottle of Sam Adams. "It's barely a minute into the second quarter and they're trailing by five points."

"Sixty million dollars isn't what it used to be," she said.

"You're telling me. The guy's a bum."

Lucy wanted to wrap things up before she started cooking dinner. "So you'll get the tickets?"

"I'll go, I'll think about the tux, but I'm not buying the tickets."

Lucy plunked herself down on the sectional and grabbed a magazine off the coffee table. "You're being ridiculous, you know," she said, flipping through the ads for beauty products and designer handbags.

"I hate writing checks," he said, groaning as a ball bounced off the rim.

"They take cash, even credit cards," said Lucy.

"Banks have weird hours." Bill leaned forward in his chair. "Damn."

Lucy knew it was counterproductive but she couldn't stop herself from arguing. "So it's okay for me to rearrange my schedule, but not for you?"

"I work hard," he snapped. "The least you can do is be supportive."

Lucy couldn't believe what she was hearing. "Like I don't work hard, too?"

"Yeah!" he exclaimed, as a ball made it through the hoop. "You have a part-time job, Luce. It's not the same thing as being the breadwinner."

Lucy threw down the magazine. "Men are so self-centered!" she declared, grabbing another.

"Hey, I'm a good guy," he protested. "I said I'd take you to that ball, didn't I?"

Lucy stared at the black-and-white photo of a nearly naked man and woman entwined in a steamy embrace on a beach; they appeared to be coated in baby oil.

"A funny thing happened when I was doing an interview at Chanticleer Chocolate. The woman who works there, Tamzin, asked about you."

"Did she?" Bill was staring at the TV, where two commentators in blue blazers were recapping a play. "I helped Max put in the shelves in the storeroom."

"You never mentioned it," said Lucy.

A commercial for an erectile dysfunction drug was playing on the TV; a man and woman were sitting in separate bathtubs, outdoors. "Who does that?" asked Bill, incredulous.

"Dora said Max was nothing but trouble. . . ."

Bill was flipping channels, pausing at a golf match. "You can say that again," said Bill. "He never paid me for that job." He was staring at the parched Arizona landscape that filled the screen. "Look at that, must be eighty degrees at least."

"How much did he owe you?" asked Lucy.

"We agreed on five hundred dollars, but I haven't seen a cent—and I'm not the only one he stiffed."

"Who else?" asked Lucy.

"Just about everybody," said Bill, watching as Phil Mickelson made a putt. "Nice."

"If he owed a lot of people money, a lot of people had a motive to kill him, didn't they?"

Bill looked at her. "I don't follow you. What would killing him accomplish? You still wouldn't get your money back."

"You'd get revenge," said Lucy.

"Pretty cold comfort, if you ask me," said Bill, draining the bottle of beer and switching off the TV. "What do you say to a 'matinee,' before the girls come home?"

Lucy was caught by surprise; she was wondering who else Max might have stiffed. "Now?"

He grinned wickedly. "Yeah, now. Like in that commercial. We can be spontaneous, right? And I don't need any pills, either."

Spontaneity didn't appeal to Lucy, who was newly self-conscious about her body, thinking of the tummy bulge she'd noticed the other day. "I feel fat," she said.

"Don't be silly," said Bill, taking her hand and drawing her into an embrace. "I love you just the way you are. You're perfect."

Lucy felt her resistance crumbling as he wrapped his arms around her.

"A little bit of extra flesh is sexy," he murmured, whispering into her ear.

Lucy felt as if she'd been slapped and pulled away. "I've got to start supper," she snapped, marching into the kitchen.

"What? What did I say?" demanded Bill.

Lucy grabbed a couple of onions and began chopping, furiously smacking the knife against the cutting board. How on earth did the Faircloths do it, she wondered, as her eyes filled with tears. It was the onions, she told herself. Onions always made her cry.

Chapter Six

Sunday morning, when the breakfast dishes were all cleared away and the dishwasher was humming, Lucy sat down at the round golden oak table with the newspapers. Bill was outside splitting wood, and the girls had gone over to Prudence Path to babysit little Patrick while Toby and Molly went to a christening.

Lucy always read the *Boston Sunday Globe* first, starting with the colorful magazine. She was turning the pages slowly, savoring this bit of quiet time, pausing to admire a mouth-watering photo of a red velvet layer cake. Perfect, she thought. Just the thing to make for the dessert contest.

Flipping the page over, she eagerly read the recipe but didn't find it all that appealing. It called for too much sugar—two cups—and two whole sticks of butter, as well as an awful lot of red food coloring. It also called for the addition of vinegar, which made the whole thing sound more like a science experiment than a cake.

No, red velvet wasn't the way to go. Maybe cupcakes, she thought. They were all the rage. Maybe she could work up a cupcake with a gooey chocolate surprise filling and a ganache topping. That sounded yummy, but she'd never had much luck getting ganache to set and she couldn't enter cupcakes with runny icing. And she had no idea how to get that chocolate filling inside the cupcake. Did you bake it in? Was there some sort of magic process involved like the Denver Chocolate Pudding in her Fannie Farmer cookbook that she sometimes made as a special treat?

Another specialty was the clafouti she often made in summer, when cherries and blueberries were in season. She'd found the recipe in her Julia Child cookbook and it was surprisingly simple. It was the only recipe in that book that she actually made. She was wondering if she could figure out a way to make a chocolate clafouti, perhaps with frozen raspberries. That would be really good, and original. She suspected all she'd have to do would be to add some cocoa powder to the recipe, but how much? Chances of getting it right the first time seemed slim—and would it also need a chocolate sauce? She rather thought it might, which made the project seem awfully ambitious.

She was leafing through her Paula Deen cookbook when she heard someone tapping at the kitchen door. Libby, never a very good guard dog, was giving mixed messages, simultaneously growling and wagging her tail, when Lucy opened the door. Discovering it was Frankie, the dog erupted into a joyful dance of greeting.

"Down," said Lucy firmly, pointing to the dog's bed.

The Lab settled down with a big sigh and Lucy took Frankie's coat. "Want some coffee? It's nice and hot."

"Sure," said Frankie, slipping into a chair. "I can't stay long, I've got another appointment with the Faircloths. I've been showing them everything from here to Portland and back."

"I meant to thank you for telling me about them," said Lucy, pouring two mugs and bringing them over to the table.

"They are every bit as cute as you said and I got a great interview."

Frankie sipped at her coffee. "I'm getting a bit sick of them, to tell the truth. Talk about picky!" She shrugged philosophically. "Of course, when you're spending the kind of money they are, I guess you can be picky. They have a lot of art and antiques and they want a house that will showcase their collections."

Lucy was puzzled. "I thought they lost everything in a house fire."

"You're right," said Frankie, knitting her brows. "I guess some of their stuff was saved—they must have it in storage." She wrapped her hands around the mug. "Actually, I was wondering about the couple at Chanticleer Chocolate. Do you think they're looking for a house?"

"You mean Trey and Tamzin? I don't think they're a couple," said Lucy. "Where did you get that idea?"

Frankie took a sip of coffee. "I saw them outside the store. They were arguing; I guess that's why I thought they were a couple." She giggled. "Maybe it's just their names. Trey and Tamzin. They sound like a couple, no?"

Lucy smiled. "I don't know much about Trey, but I do know that Tamzin is very flirtatious. She flaunts her assets, if you know what I mean."

Frankie's eyebrows went up. "Really?"

"Tight dresses, very low necklines, thigh-high boots. Stilettos."

"Not chic," said Frankie, who favored tailored pantsuits enlivened with colorful scarves.

"That's one way of putting it," said Lucy. "She's certainly not subtle. She's got 'em and she flaunts 'em."

"It's better to leave some things to the imagination," said Frankie, with a sly smile. "But as far as you know, Trey doesn't have a family?"

There was something in her expression that made Lucy

wonder if Frankie was interested in Trey for herself. If so, she thought, she wasn't the only one. "I don't think so, but I don't really know," said Lucy. "I know Corney said she finds him very attractive."

"Oh, Corney, she goes after all the single men, but she never catches one," said Frankie, looking at her watch and getting up. "I can't be late for the Faircloths. Roger gets very annoyed."

"He seems so formal, old-fashioned even," said Lucy, getting up and taking Frankie's coat off the hook where she'd hung it.

"He's very easygoing—as long as he's getting his way," said Frankie, pulling the coat over her shoulders and buttoning it. "But I told him, I can only give them the morning. I must go to the funeral this afternoon."

"I'll see you there, then," said Lucy, opening the door.

Funerals were always a big draw in Tinker's Cove, especially if there was reason to believe the sad observance would be followed by a generous spread. It was no surprise that Max's funeral, actually a memorial service since Max had been cremated, attracted a large crowd. Lucy figured most of the mourners were looking forward to the buffet lunch from Fern's Famous, which had a highly popular catering service run by Flora, as well as the candy business.

Lucy, who was sitting beside Bill in the crowded Community Church, was finding it difficult to concentrate on the eulogy as her thoughts kept straying to Flora's curried chicken puffs and beef satay. They also did a really tasty Greek spinach pie and truly amazing Swedish meatballs that Bill couldn't resist, and neither could she. Faced with all that delicious food, she knew she had to have a plan, so she intended to follow the suggestion in an article she'd read recently that advised limiting yourself to a single bite of high-calorie foods. "The second bite will taste just like the first," the author claimed.

Lucy was soon checking out the congregation, trying to judge the size of their appetites. The fishing crowd were undoubtedly big eaters and she hoped Flora had taken that into account. She was mulling over the best strategy for attacking the buffet, vowing to load her plate with crudités rather than cheese cubes, when the minister intoned the final benediction. Everyone stood as the chief mourners exited the front pew and began walking down the aisle. First went Lily, accompanied by her mother; she was holding tightly to Dora's hand. Flora walked behind them, beside Fern, who refused her daughter's offer of a supportive arm despite her advanced age.

Lucy was struck by the image this family of women presented: four generations, obviously sharing the same gene pool, all dressed similarly in black. Lily, the youngest with her fresh complexion and long blond hair and her mother, Dora, with her frosted bob. Flora, in her sixties, with salt-and-pepper hair, bore the same lines on her face as her mother, only less deeply etched. Fern was the smallest of the four, and the oldest, but was clearly the respected head of the family. Watching them, it occurred to Lucy that they made a complete unit in themselves and she wondered if there had ever really been a place for Max. How did he fit in with this tightly knit group?

The four women were followed by a scattering of Gooches from Gilead; at least Lucy supposed that's who they were. Max's parents had died years before and he was an only child, so she assumed these mourners were a loosely related collection of cousins, aunts, and uncles. They didn't have the same sense of unity about them that the four women had; they didn't resemble each other but came in a variety of shapes and sizes. A gawky, red-haired kid slouched along beside a very short, very fat woman who might or might not be his mother, a stocky man with a gray beard accompanied an attractive woman with streaked blond hair, a young man with a studious air and wire-rimmed glasses followed behind them.

The center aisle soon filled with people moving slowly toward the exit and Lucy was about to join them when Bill caught her arm. "Let's go out the side door," he said, whispering in her ear. "We don't want to be at the end of the procession."

Apparently Bill had also been thinking hard about the best strategy for getting first dibs on the buffet and was planning an end run around the crowd. The reception would take place at the Macdougal family homestead, a huge old Victorian that had been completely renovated and now sported an authentically gaudy paint job of brown, cream, and red. Lucy remembered how the house had looked when she first moved to Tinker's Cove; it had been practically bare of paint then and the sagging porch roof was held up with a couple of two-by-fours propped against cement blocks. That was before Fern's Famous had become the successful business it was today, of course.

Lucy and Bill weren't the only ones who'd avoided the crush at the church door. They found quite a number of people were already helping themselves to the buffet when they arrived, which Lucy thought was pretty rude. They should have waited for the reception line to form and murmured the usual platitudes to the grieving family before stuffing their faces, which would have been the proper thing to do. She noticed with alarm that the curried chicken puffs were disappearing fast, however, so Lucy decided there was nothing to do but abandon her principles. She did it reluctantly, fully aware that her extremely proper mother was probably spinning in her grave as she loaded her plate, careful to take only one of everything. Even so, the plate was filling up fast.

"Great food, but you can always count on Fern's Famous," said Corney, joining Lucy and Bill on the padded window seat in the bay window. Like Lucy and Bill, she was holding a plate piled high with finger food. "I don't know what it is about buffets, but I always eat too much."

"I think we'll have a light supper," said Lucy, talking with her mouth full. "Is that okay with you, Bill?"

"Mmph," said Bill, apparently in agreement.

"I'm feeling full and we haven't even gotten to the dessert table yet," confessed Lucy.

"Don't skip the desserts," advised Corney. "They've got something new—a Black Forest cake with brandy-cherry filling. It's absolutely delicious."

Lucy was surprised since she knew Corney was perpetually on a diet and avoided desserts. Come to think of it, she realized with a guilty pang, she was on a diet herself and had no business eating any dessert. "Maybe Bill can give me a bite of his," she said. "I'm trying to lose a few pounds."

"I normally don't eat sweets but that cake is worth the calories," said Corney. "Besides, when a guy takes you to dinner he doesn't want to hear you complaining about the calories. He wants to see you enjoy yourself."

"So you had the cake on a date?" said Lucy, picking up Corney's hint.

As she guessed, Corney couldn't wait to tell her all about it. "Trey took me out last night. We had a lovely meal at the Queen Vic—they get their desserts from Fern's Famous, you know."

"That does sound nice," said Lucy, noticing that Bill was wandering toward a group of men clustered in a corner. "Did you have a good time?"

"I did. Trey is everything a girl could want. Tall, handsome, wealthy. And he's fun, he's got a great sense of humor."

"Sounds like you're smitten. Has he asked you out again?"

"That's the thing," said Corney, scowling. "I'm not sure whether it was a real date or a business dinner. He spent an awful lot of time talking about his plans to expand the business and how the Chamber could help."

"That's tricky," said Lucy.

"You said it. I don't quite know how to play it. I called to thank him. I didn't want him to think I was chasing him, but I wanted to let him know I'm available and I really like him." Corney's face fell and she looked down at her empty plate. "He didn't suggest a second date. In fact, all he wanted to talk about was some kind of special chocolate that's going to revolutionize the confectionary business." She sighed. "I now know a lot more than I ever wanted to about chocolate."

"Bummer," said Lucy, chewing a meatball. "What's his relationship with Tamzin? Are they a couple?"

"I'm not sure." Corney lowered her voice. "It would explain why he doesn't fire her. Have you seen the way she dresses? That woman is sooo unprofessional."

"Men like that sort of thing," said Lucy, as a sudden silence fell in the room. All heads had turned toward the door where Dora and her family were entering; each woman was carrying a flower arrangement they'd brought from the church. A few friends rushed over to take the flowers and help them with their coats, and the noise level rose again.

The reception line formed and Lucy and Bill took their places along with everyone else, shuffling slowly along. Lucy wasn't sure what to say under the circumstances. "I'm sorry for your loss," was okay for Lily, but not quite the thing for Dora. "Terrific party, great food," came to mind and Lucy giggled, which made people look at her. When her turn finally came, she murmured something about a terrible loss, we'll all miss him, and was promptly passed along from Dora to Lily and then to Fern and Flora.

Duty done, Lucy and Bill made their way through the crowded rooms to the little study off the hall where they'd left their coats. Lucy's good black pants were feeling uncomfortably tight as she made her way to the door, and her conscience wasn't about to let her forget she'd over-indulged. That Black Forest cake was every bit as good as

Corney said, even though she'd only had a few bites, but she'd been unable to resist the mini-cupcakes with lemon filling and buttercream icing topped with coconut. All that delicious food made her sleepy and she was yawning and buttoning her good black coat when Fern herself approached her with a foil-covered plate.

"Lucy, I wonder if you'd do me a favor?" she said, placing a blue-veined hand on Lucy's sleeve. Her voice, usually firm and authoritative, was a bit quavery today and she looked tired.

"Whatever you want," said Lucy.

"You know my friend, Julia. . . ."

Lucy knew Fern was one of the few people in town who dared to call Miss Tilley by her first name. Of course, they had probably been schoolmates well before World War II. "I'm sure she would have come if she were able," said Lucy.

"Yes, she's getting over the flu. I absolutely forbade her to come," said Fern, with a flash of her usual bossiness. "But I put together a little plate for her and I wonder if you could deliver it for me."

"Sure," said Lucy, taking the foil-covered dish. "I'm sure she'll appreciate it."

"I happen to know she loves my Boston cream pie, so I gave her a big piece, and some other things, too."

"I'll take it right over," promised Lucy, making eye contact with Bill who gave an approving nod.

"It will be your good deed for the day," said Fern, patting her hand.

It was only a short drive to Miss Tilley's old Cape-style house and the car didn't have time to warm up. Bill stayed outside, keeping the engine running, while Lucy dashed up the path. She was chilled clear through when she knocked on the door, which was opened by Rachel.

"What are you doing here on Sunday?" Lucy asked, stepping inside.

"I was on my way home from the play rehearsal and

thought I'd stop by and check on Miss T," said Rachel. "She's had a touch of the flu."

The house was wonderfully warm and cozy. Miss Tilley kept a fire going all winter in the ancient keeping-room hearth that had once served for both heating and cooking. Nowadays, of course, the fireplace was supplemented with heat from a modern furnace and cooking took place in the kitchen ell that was added on sometime in the 1920s.

The house was generously furnished with antiques and Lucy always felt as if she were stepping back in time when she visited her old friend. Miss Tilley was sitting in her usual Boston rocker today, with a colorful crocheted afghan covering her knees. Cleopatra, her Siamese cat, was seated on her lap, a softly purring sphinx.

"How are you?" asked Lucy. "I hear you had the flu."

"Nonsense. It was nothing more than a head cold, but everyone made such a fuss I didn't dare show my face at the funeral."

"Your friend Fern sent along some Boston cream pie," said Lucy, handing her the dish.

Miss Tilley promptly lifted the foil and examined the cake, smacking her lips. "I'll have that for my supper," she said.

"You'll have chicken soup for supper," said Rachel, taking the plate and carrying it into the kitchen. "There's a pot all ready for you on the stove. You just have to heat it up."

"I'd rather have pie," said Miss Tilley.

"If you finish all your soup, you can have some for dessert." Rachel raised an eyebrow. "And don't think you can put the soup down the drain. I'll know."

Miss Tilley shifted in her chair, a guilty expression on her face. "I'm not a child, you know."

"Then stop acting like one," snapped Rachel.

"My goodness," said Lucy. "It seems you two need a break."

"You said it," said Rachel, laughing as she seated herself

on the sofa. "We are turning into a pair of bickering biddies."

Miss Tilley smiled and stroked the cat. "I don't know what I'd do without Rachel. I'd be in a pretty pickle, I'm sure."

"It's not easy keeping you on the straight and narrow," said Rachel, smiling fondly at her old friend. She'd started visiting regularly after Miss Tilley had an automobile accident years ago and now she was officially certified by the town council on aging as a home helper and even received a small stipend for her efforts.

"I would have liked to have gone to the funeral," said Miss Tilley. "For Fern. There aren't many of us old-timers left, you know, and she was so fond of Max."

"Was she upset about the divorce?" asked Lucy, perching on the sofa.

"She certainly didn't approve, divorce isn't something one approves of. But having said that, I don't think she was terribly surprised when the marriage didn't work out. She was never in favor of Max and Dora getting married; that was Flora's idea."

Lucy was puzzled. "How was it Flora's idea? Wasn't it up to Max and Dora?"

Miss Tilley pursed her lips. "Max had gone away, he wasn't the sort you could tie down. I remember him when he was a little boy, he'd come into the library and take out all sorts of adventure books. He read about all the explorers and astronauts and deep-sea divers. He wanted to see the world, he told me, and when he got out of high school he started traveling. I used to get postcards from him now and then. He went all over and somewhere he learned how to surf and he started competing and winning, too. There was quite a fuss about him when he came home for a visit, articles in the newspaper and all that. He was quite the hero, and Dora was his girl."

"And they decided to get married?" asked Lucy.

"Oh, no. He was only here for a short while before he had to leave for some surfing contest in Mexico or somewhere."

Lucy was puzzled. "So Dora followed him?"

"No. It was Flora."

"But she's old enough to be his mother."

"Oh, she wasn't interested in him for herself," said Miss Tilley, with a flap of her age-spotted hand. "It turned out he'd gotten Dora in the family way and Flora went down to wherever he was and made him understand his responsibility. She dragged him back and got them married before either of them knew what had happened. Fern told me she didn't think it was a good idea to force a marriage like that and it turned out she was right because the marriage didn't last." Miss Tilley's voice was fading and Lucy suspected she was growing tired. "And now poor Max is gone and he was much too young."

"Perhaps it was better that way," said Rachel, in a thoughtful voice. "I don't think he would have wanted to grow old."

"It's certainly not for everyone," said Miss Tilley, slapping her lap and causing the cat to leap onto the rug, where she began grooming herself.

"I've got to go," said Lucy, getting to her feet. "Bill's waiting for me outside. He's probably having a fit."

"I'd like to see that!" said Miss Tilley, giving her a little wave.

"Oh, no, you wouldn't," said Lucy, bending to give her a peck on the cheek. "Mind Rachel and eat your soup."

"I'll consider it," said Miss Tilley.

Chapter Seven

A few weeks later, the Tuesday before Valentine's Day, it was only ten o'clock and Lucy was starving. She'd had a piece of toast (whole wheat with a tiny sliver of butter) and a sixty-calorie pot of light yogurt for breakfast. Along with a glass of orange juice and black coffee, she figured it totaled about three hundred calories, which was apparently not enough to sustain life in Maine in February.

Her strict diet had resulted in the loss of six pounds, and her jeans were fitting better, but all she could think of as she made her way down Main Street was a big bowl of hot oatmeal, studded with raisins, sprinkled with sugar, and covered with cream. It hung before her eyes like a mirage in the desert, but she was about as far from any desert as a human being could be. Tinker's Cove in February was cold and wet and anybody with any sense was staying indoors, where it was warm and dry. Which was not possible for her because she was working on a man-in-the-street feature about Valentine's Day.

"What are your plans for Valentine's Day?" was the question she was supposed to ask five people. The replies would run in this week's paper along with head shots of the people she interviewed. It was a cute idea and the sort of thing she normally liked to do. The only problem was she couldn't find one person, much less five, and she was cold and wet and hungry.

Deciding to try the post office, she trudged down the empty street, sloshing through slush and telling herself the cold, damp mist that hung in the air was good for her complexion. She was just passing Chanticleer Chocolate when a huge SUV pulled up to the curb and Brad Cashman jumped out.

Brad was her neighbor. He lived on Prudence Path with his wife, Chris, who was Sue's partner in Little Prodigies Child Care Center.

"Hi!" she said, greeting him with a big smile. "Got a minute?"

Chris smiled back and cocked a wary eyebrow. "Maybe."

"I'm doing one of those man-in-the-street things, and I could really use some help. Just one quick question and a photo. Okay?"

Brad zipped his jacket, which had been open, and stuck his hands in his pocket. "Shoot."

"Say cheese." Lucy snapped the photo. "What are your plans for Valentine's Day?" she asked, pulling out her notebook and opening it to a fresh page.

"Funny you should ask," he said, nodding at the store. "I'm on my way right now to buy chocolates for my three beautiful ladies."

"That would be your wife, Chris, and the twins?"

"Pear and Apple," he said. "I can't leave them out."

"How old are they now?"

"Old enough to know about chocolate," said Brad, turning up his collar and moving toward the store. "See you around, Lucy."

"Thanks," she said, as he opened the door and vanished inside.

One down, four to go, thought Lucy, continuing down the street. She was just passing the police station when she spotted her friend, Barney, about to get into his cruiser. She couldn't help envying his official winter gear, the insulated blue all-in-one that covered him from chin to ankles, plus his fur-lined hat and sturdy boots.

"Barney!" she called, running to catch him.

"Hey, Lucy," he replied, turning to greet her. "What's up?"

"Got a moment for a man-in-the-street question? I just want to know what your plans are for Valentine's Day. Are you getting something for Marge?"

"Sure am. I always get her a big bunch of pink roses."

"Not red?" asked Lucy, snapping his photo.

"She doesn't like red. She likes pink."

"Because of the breast cancer?" Lucy knew Barney's wife, Marge, was a breast cancer survivor and pink was the color associated with efforts to raise money for a cure.

Barney's bulldog face crumpled, which Lucy knew was an indication of deep thought. "I don't think so. I think she just likes pink roses."

"Pink roses are lovely," said Lucy, writing it all down. "She's a lucky lady."

"No, Lucy." Barney was shaking his head. "I'm the lucky one. I don't deserve a wife like Marge."

"She must be thrilled to have Eddie home, safe and sound."

To her surprise, Barney's thoughtful expression deepened. "You know how it is with kids—you never stop worrying."

"I saw him at the Quik-Stop," continued Lucy. "He looks so handsome and fit."

"I'm just glad he's got all his arms and legs," said Barney. "A lot of these kids coming home are missing 'em."

"How's his mental outlook?" asked Lucy.

Barney shrugged. "It's hard to tell. He doesn't say much."

Barney looked so worried that Lucy didn't know what to

say and resorted to the usual cliché. "It's a big adjustment, it's bound to take time." She noticed Barney's eyes following Max's old pickup, driven by Lily with Eddie in the passenger seat.

"Are they dating?" she asked.

Barney shrugged. "Don't ask me. He doesn't tell me anything."

Par for the course, thought Lucy, remembering how sullen and uncommunicative Toby had been before he met Molly.

"She's a nice girl," said Lucy. "He could do worse. Which reminds me, how's the investigation going?"

Barney looked confused. "What investigation?"

"Max Fraser, of course."

"Oh, that," he said, adjusting his gloves. "That's over and done. The guy drank too much and got himself in a pickle. The surprise is it didn't happen sooner."

Lucy shivered, which was her usual reaction whenever she thought of Max drowning in the freezing pond water. "There must have been some sort of follow-up. The ME's report said he had been knocked on the head."

Barney shifted from foot to foot. "Yeah, but he said there was no way of telling if it was intentional or accidental."

"Which left it open for an investigation," said Lucy.

Barney sighed. "We questioned a few people, didn't come up with anything suspicious. The last person who admits seeing him alive is Dora, his ex, but she says that was in the evening, well before he went through the ice."

"Where did she see him?" asked Lucy.

"At home. She says she was having trouble with her car and he stopped by to take a look and see if he could help."

Lucy nodded. "He was like that, he got me out of a fix when I got stuck in a snowbank."

"Problem is, he never did look at the car. She admitted they got in a fight; she wanted money for Lily's schooling. Last she saw him, he was driving off in a huff."

"Bill says Max was up against it lately and owed a lot of people money. That could be a motive for murder."

"If you're saying Max had a lot of enemies, I'd say that's a lot of hooey. Like I said, he drank too much and got careless. We found an empty bottle of Southern Comfort in his truck." He paused, making eye contact. "And if he did have a falling out with somebody, and I'm not saying he did, well that somebody isn't anybody you want to tangle with, Lucy. You'd better stick to asking folks how they're going to celebrate Valentine's Day."

"Point taken," said Lucy, her teeth chattering. The mist was beginning to solidify, turning to sleet. "Have a good day."

"You, too, Lucy." Barney opened the door of his cruiser and Lucy dashed across the street to the liquor store.

Stepping inside, she gave a little shake.

"Pretty nasty out there," said the clerk, a fellow in his forties with oversize eyeglasses and a shock of graying hair that fell over his forehead. "What can I do for you?"

"I'm Lucy Stone, with the *Pennysaver*. I'm interviewing people about their plans for Valentine's Day."

"You want to know how I'm going to celebrate?" he asked, with a grin.

"If you don't mind." Lucy produced her camera. "And I have to take your picture, too."

He shrugged. "Well, as you might expect, I'm going to bring home a nice bottle of champagne and drink it with my wife."

"Say bubbles," said Lucy, snapping his photo. "What's your name?"

"Cliff Sandstrom."

"Any particular brand?" asked Lucy, noticing a display of Southern Comfort bottles by the cash register.

Cliff grimaced. "I wish I could go for the Veuve Clicquot but I think it's going to be Freixenet this year," he said. "Business is down, due to the economy."

"You'd think people would drink more, to forget their troubles."

"Oh, they do, but they buy the cheap stuff. Not much profit in that."

"Ahh." Lucy pointed at the Southern Comfort. "Do you sell a lot of that stuff? I drank it in college once and got really sick."

"Sportsmen like it. They say it helps them stay warm. Especially the ice fishermen."

"I heard Max Fraser liked a nip."

"Yeah." Cliff nodded sadly. "He was in here the afternoon before he died. He always took a bottle along when he went ice fishing."

"Was he a problem drinker?" asked Lucy.

"Let's say he was a regular customer," said Cliff. "Not one of my best customers, if that answers your question."

Lucy thanked him and turned to go, noticing that the liquor store was directly opposite Chanticleer Chocolate. Turning back to Cliff, she grabbed a bargain bottle of chardonnay and set it on the counter. "Is this stuff any good?"

"We sell a lot of it," said Cliff, ringing it up. "That's four ninety-nine."

Lucy handed him a five. "How's the new chocolate shop doing?" she asked. "They won the 'Best on the Coast' poll, you know."

"I saw that." He handed her a penny, which she put in the dish by the cash register. "We lost out to the Wine Warehouse in the outlet mall."

"Sometimes I think those polls are rigged to favor big advertisers," said Lucy.

"It wouldn't surprise me, though I gotta say there's a steady traffic across the way."

"Well, Valentine's Day is coming."

"It's a funny thing," he said with a leer. "The customers sure tend to linger, especially the guys."

"Maybe they can't make up their minds," said Lucy.

"The flavors are quite unique and Tamzin tends to go into detail, explaining them all."

"That must be it," said Cliff, chuckling.

Leaving the store with her purchase tucked under her arm, Lucy decided to stop in at Chanticleer Chocolate for a chat with Tamzin. The feature was a good excuse and she was sure Tamzin would jump at the chance for some free publicity.

Lucy looked both ways before crossing the street from habit, but she really didn't need to bother; there was no traffic on Main Street today. The road was beginning to fill with an inch or two of slushy sleet and she was grateful for her duck boots with their waterproof rubber bottoms.

A couple of musical chimes rang out when she opened the door, a marked improvement over the jangly bell at the *Pennysaver*. The shop was dimly lit with mood lighting and carefully placed monopoints that highlighted the boxes of chocolates arranged on little tables, but there was enough light for Lucy to see that Tamzin and Brad Cashman were standing very close. So close, in fact, that Lucy was certain she'd interrupted an embrace.

"Uh, two small boxes of strawberry blasts for the twins . . . ," he said, stepping away from Tamzin.

"*Bebe* or *petite?*" asked Tamzin, in a cool, professional voice.

"Bay-bay," said Brad. "And a *grande* for my wife."

"Assorted flavors?"

"Yeah," he said, avoiding making eye contact with Lucy.

Tamzin floated about the shop in her black boots with killer heels, gathering up the various boxes of chocolates, which she placed on the counter. Then, leaning over to display her décolletage, she began wrapping each box with the shop's trademark paper. It was a lengthy process involving a great deal of folding and tying, which took much longer than necessary due to the flirtatious chatter she was making.

While she waited her turn, Lucy began to understand

why customers, especially male customers, tended to spend a lot of time at the shop. Finally, Tamzin was bending down, yet again, giving Brad a generous view of her bosom as she reached for a chic little shopping bag. Slipping the wrapped chocolates inside, she slid it toward him. "That will be ninety-six thirty," she said, with a big smile.

Lucy's eyes grew wide as she watched Brad hand over his credit card; she couldn't imagine anybody spending that much on chocolates. Goodness' sakes, a bag of premium dark chocolates only cost three ninety-nine at the IGA.

Then, giving her a quick smile, Brad hurried out the door and Tamzin greeted Lucy with a big smile. "What can I get you? A little extravagance for yourself? A gift?"

"Actually, I'm working," said Lucy, explaining her mission. Tamzin was agreeable and posed for a photo, then told Lucy she had no special plans for Valentine's Day but was hoping that would change.

"I'd hate to spend Valentine's Day all by myself," she said, with a little pout, and Lucy remembered Barney saying that Max had been obsessed with Tamzin.

"I suppose you miss Max quite a lot," said Lucy.

Tamzin lowered herself onto a tall stool and hooked her heels over the bottom rung; she looked like she were about to break into song in a nightclub. "We had some fun," she said, with a shrug, "but that was all. It was nothing serious."

"But a death like that affects us all. And besides, there aren't that many available men in a town like Tinker's Cove."

Tamzin's eyes sparkled. "They're all available, honey."

Lucy was shocked at her bluntness, but had to concede she had a point. "I suppose they are," she said, deciding she'd better make one thing very clear. "Except for my husband. He's definitely off limits." She smiled when she said it, but it was a warning, a preemptive strike.

Not that Tamzin noticed; she was lost in her own thoughts. "Come to think of it, I was going to call you.

About your daughter, Zoe. Trey has given the okay for her to work here after school."

Lucy knew Zoe was eager to make some extra money, but she didn't know she'd gone so far as to apply at Chanticleer. She wasn't at all sure Zoe was mature enough to handle a job in addition to school, and furthermore, she was uneasy about letting her work with Tamzin. The woman was hardly a good influence. Lucy didn't like the way she dressed and she sure didn't like her attitude toward men, especially married men.

"I'm not sure Zoe has time for a job, and besides, she's just turned fourteen," said Lucy, hedging until she had a chance to talk with her daughter.

"Oh, she's already said she'd take the job. I texted her first thing this morning. She's going to start today, after school."

Lucy felt the blood rushing to her cheeks. She was furious about being sidestepped this way. Tamzin had no business getting a commitment from Zoe before she checked with her parents. After raising four kids, Lucy knew her rights and responsibilities as a parent and she wasn't about to relinquish them.

"She can't start today," said Lucy, narrowing her eyes. "Zoe's not sixteen, she needs a work permit from the Superintendent of Schools and it takes a few days to get it."

Tamzin rolled her eyes. "Are you kidding me?"

"No." Lucy looked her in the eye. "The child labor laws are quite clear and I will report any violations."

"Okay," said Tamzin, reaching for her phone, "but Trey's not going to like this."

"Then he can hire somebody else," said Lucy, turning on her heels and pushing the door open. This time she found the little musical chimes really irritating.

Chapter Eight

Lucy was so furious with Tamzin that she didn't even notice the sleet and slush as she marched back to the *Pennysaver* office. She plunked herself down in her chair and reached for the mouse, then proceeded to strip off her winter clothing, feeling unusually warm as she clicked away, Googling Tamzin Graves.

"Did you put the heat up?" she asked Phyllis, who was regarding her with amusement.

"I would if I could, but you know as well as I do that Ted freaks out if the thermostat is a hair above sixty-five," she replied.

Lucy shrugged and stared at the screen, but the only thing that turned up was an announcement that ran in the Portland paper a few years ago reporting that Tamzin had achieved black belt status in tae kwon do at the Maine Martial Arts Academy.

"Typical," snarled Lucy.

"What's got into you?" asked Phyllis.

"That witch at Chanticleer Chocolate, and witch isn't the

word I want to use," said Lucy, scowling at the computer screen.

"But it rhymes with witch, right?" asked Phyllis, chuckling.

"You said it." Lucy swung around in her office chair and faced Phyllis. "She hired Zoe behind my back, never even mentioned a work permit. She wanted Zoe to start this afternoon."

Just then Lucy's cell phone rang and she began digging in her purse for it. After a few more rings, she dumped the entire contents on her desk and snatched it up. "Zoe! I thought you might be calling."

"Mom, I can't believe you did this to me!"

Zoe's voice was so loud that Phyllis could hear her right across the room.

"I did what I thought best," said Lucy.

"And now I'm out of a job!"

Phyllis had turned back to her computer, but Lucy knew she was listening to every word.

"They were taking advantage of you," said Lucy. "You need my permission to work and I'm not going to let you work illegally. These laws are there for a reason. It's easy for employers to take advantage of underage workers."

"Mom, it's a chocolate shop, not some sweatshop."

"Then I don't see what the problem is. They can file the paperwork. . . ."

"Then you mean I can work there?"

Too late, Lucy saw she'd stumbled into a trap. "I guess so. If the permit's approved," she said, reluctantly. It wasn't really the work permit that was the issue, it was Tamzin. She really didn't want her daughter anywhere near the woman.

"You're the best, Mom. Tamzin's pretty sure they can have everything in order by tomorrow afternoon. She says Trey knows somebody in the superintendent's office."

"Oh, great," said Lucy, with a noticeable lack of enthusi-asm.

Looking over at Phyllis, she saw her shoulders shaking with laughter.

"It's not funny," said Lucy, flipping the phone shut.

"I know," said Phyllis. "It was just your expression. You looked so pissed."

"I've been advised not to play poker," said Lucy, already calling Sue. "Have you got a minute?" she asked, knowing that Sue was working and the needs of the kids at Little Prodigies took precedence. "Can you talk?"

Getting an affirmative, she continued, in a whisper. "I was over at Chanticleer Chocolate and I saw Brad Cashman in a, well, compromising situation."

"Hmmm," said Sue. "I'll have to check the invoice." A few moments later, she was back on the phone. "I'm in my office. Exactly how compromising was the situation?"

"I'm not sure," admitted Lucy. "I think I caught them kissing. They sort of jumped apart when I went into the shop."

"I've heard she's a real flirt."

"That's an understatement. She actually told me she thinks all men are available."

"They probably are," said Sue.

"How can you think that?" Lucy was shocked. "Does Chris seem upset or worried?"

"No. She's the same as always."

"Maybe she doesn't know," said Lucy. "Or maybe it's just the way Tamzin treats every man who comes in the shop. I saw her wrap a box of chocolates and it was about as subtle as a pole dance." She paused. "Maybe you can give Chris a heads-up."

"This is awkward—I'll have to think about it. I don't want to cause a problem if there's nothing there, if it's just a little flirting," said Sue.

"If she knows there's a potential problem she can take action," said Lucy. "She can cook his favorite dinner and wear a sexy nightie to bed."

"You think it's that simple?" Sue sounded amused.

Lucy bit her lip. In her experience, men were that simple. She and Bill had been married for over twenty-five years and there hadn't been much that a meat loaf dinner and a scented candle in the bedroom couldn't fix, but maybe she was just lucky. "It's worth a try," she said.

"I guess I can send up a test balloon and see if she's worried," said Sue.

"That's a good idea—but you better be careful. Use tact."

"Of course," said Sue, sounding a bit miffed. "By the way, have you been thinking about the dessert contest? It's just around the corner. Have you come up with any ideas?"

"Not really. Besides, I'm on a diet."

"And I told you to make a diet dessert," said Sue. "There's plenty of recipes on the Internet." Lucy heard a distant childish wail. "Gotta go," said Sue.

Lucy sat for a minute, holding her phone and scowling. Things were not going well. She sighed and looked out the window. It wasn't an inspiring sight. The street was filled with filthy snow, the sky was gray; it was so dark, in fact, that the street lights were still on and it was almost noon. She was thinking that if she had a gun she'd probably shoot herself, when she noticed Bill's red pickup truck going down the street. Impulsively, she punched in his cell phone number.

"Hey," he said.

"I saw you driving by."

"I'm done for the day. I thought I'd head home and have some lunch."

"Want some company?"

"Sure."

When Lucy got home, she found Bill was already heating up a can of soup on the stove and mixing up some tuna salad for sandwiches. A bowl of chips was on the table and she took one, then remembered her diet and put it back. "I hate myself," she said, collapsing in a chair.

"It's that sort of day," said Bill, unwrapping a loaf of bread. "Do you want a whole sandwich or a half?"

Despite herself, Lucy was smiling. "I can't believe you remembered."

"What? I noticed you've been skipping seconds and desserts and only been eating half-sandwiches lately."

She stood behind him, resting her cheek on his back and slipping her arms around his waist. "I've been trying to exercise, but it's hard this time of year."

Bill was about to pull some slices of bread out of the plastic bag but stopped. "I know how you can get some exercise," he said, with a wink.

"I might not have the right clothes, or the right equipment," said Lucy.

"Don't worry," said Bill, turning off the stove and taking her hand. "You don't need any clothes—and I happen to know you've got the right equipment."

"Oo-oh," said Lucy, following as he drew her upstairs.

An hour or so later, Lucy found her mood was much improved as she finished her one-hundred-calorie bowl of soup and half-sandwich lunch. "I'm not happy about Zoe working at Chanticleer Chocolate," she told Bill, putting down her soup spoon. "I don't think Tamzin is a good influence."

Bill grinned at her. "What have you heard?"

"It isn't what I've heard—it's what I saw. I caught her in a compromising position with one of our upstanding citizens."

"As long as he was upstanding, I don't see the problem." He smiled at her. "Come to think of it, you're no stranger to compromising positions."

Lucy still felt warm all over. "We're married."

"Good thing," said Bill, scratching Libby behind her

ears. The dog was hoping a few leftover scraps might come her way. "Otherwise what we just did would be very wrong."

"I'm no prude . . . ," began Lucy.

"I'll say," said Bill, with a leer.

"That woman's trouble and I don't want Zoe around her."

"From what I've heard, she's pretty harmless," said Bill, clearing the table and carrying the dishes over to the dishwasher. "You can't blame a fellow for looking, especially when you consider what most of the wives around here look like. Even if they've got nice figures, they hide them in baggy sweatpants. They don't even try to look good."

"That's no excuse for infidelity," said Lucy.

Bill closed the dishwasher door and leaned against it, crossing his arms. "She puts on a good show, but from what I've heard that's as far as it goes."

"What about Max? I heard they were seeing each other." Lucy gave him a look. "I bet you didn't know she's got a black belt in tae kwon do, did you?"

Bill rolled his eyes and grinned. "Don't tell me you think she's some sort of black widow killer?"

"I wouldn't be surprised. She's certainly able to overpower a man, especially a drunk one. And she seems to be morally challenged. Look at the way she went behind our backs to hire Zoe."

"That's hardly the same thing as committing murder. Besides, I don't think Max was interested in Tamzin. I heard he and Dora were seeing a lot of each other."

Libby gave a little yip, and Bill looked out the window as the mailman drove up to their box. "Mail's here."

Lucy watched as he went down the driveway, without his coat. Men were so silly. And blind. Didn't he see it? If Max had left Tamzin and gone back to Dora, Tamzin would have been hurt and angry. Maybe even angry enough to kill him.

That afternoon, instead of simply parking out front and waiting for Sara and Renee, Lucy went inside Fern's Famous, hoping to have a word with Dora about Max. The police might consider his death an accident, but she wasn't satisfied and she knew Dora had her suspicions, too. But instead of Dora, she found Flora behind the cash register. Her salt-and-pepper hair was cut in a neat bob, gold granny glasses perched on her nose, and she was wearing a red-and-white-striped smock with the Fern's Famous logo embroidered on the pocket. Her complexion was fresh and smooth, belying her sixty-odd years, and Lucy wondered if chocolate had something to do with it. Dark chocolate, anyway, was supposed to promote good health.

"The girls'll be out in a minute," she said, with a little nod. "Dora's got them packing up Valentine's Day orders."

"I'm not in a hurry," said Lucy, glancing around the shop. Unlike Chanticleer Chocolate, with its mood lighting and artful displays, Fern's was bright and white and the trays of fudge were kept free of contamination in a huge glass case. The atmosphere was almost clinical, and a vintage poster with two apple-cheeked children and a smiling Holstein nibbling a daisy declared, WE USE ONLY THE PUREST FARM-FRESH INGREDIENTS.

"Sara's a good worker," said Flora, pulling out a tray of penuche and realigning the little cubes with a gloved hand.

"That's nice to hear," said Lucy. "How's Dora doing?"

"About like you'd expect, I guess," said Flora. "Lily's the one I'm worried about. She really misses her dad. They spent a lot of time together."

"I didn't know that," said Lucy. "I guess I thought she'd be closer to her mom."

Flora slid the tray back in place. "Oh, she is. They had shared custody, so she spent time with both of them. I don't approve of divorce, but I have to say they were very amicable. They got along better after the divorce, really, and I have to give Max credit for being an excellent father. He taught Lily to fish and hunt and ski, turned her into a real outdoors person."

Lucy thought of the beautiful, ethereal girl she'd seen in the shop so often. "She looks so fragile," she said.

Flora laughed. "That fragile creature is a hell of a shot. We've been eating venison all winter, thanks to her. And she didn't just shoot it. Max made sure she hung it and dressed it proper."

Lucy figured her own girls' reaction to a job like that would be a big *Eeeuw*.

"She's a good cook, too," continued Flora. "Not only killed the beast but cooked it, too. Ragout, she calls it, but I think it's just a fancy word for stew."

"I saw her with Eddie Culpepper—do you think they're serious?"

"I hope not. She's way too young for that," snapped Flora, looking up as Renee and Sara came through the door from the rear of the shop. "Well, here're your girls. See you tomorrow."

For some reason that Lucy couldn't understand, Flora's words sent the two girls into paroxysms of laughter.

"What's so funny?" asked Lucy, as they all got into the car.

"Nothing," said Sara, giggling as she fastened her seat belt.

"Flora said you were packing up mail orders," said Lucy, starting the car and switching on the headlights. "Was it interesting?"

The girls didn't answer but started laughing again. Something was screamingly funny and Lucy couldn't help wishing she was in on the joke.

Chapter Nine

Sociologists estimate that forty to fifty percent of American marriages end in divorce and the numbers are even higher for second (sixty-seven percent) and third (seventy-four percent) marriages. Even couples who stay together tend to drift apart, according to a recent survey by the Association of Retired Citizens (ARC), which reported a marked decrease in romance among couples age sixty and older. Some lucky couples, however, defy the odds. Take, for example, Helen and Roger Faircloth, who insist they are still in love after more than forty years of marriage.

Interviewed recently at the Queen Victoria Inn, where the couple is staying while house-hunting in the area, Mr. Faircloth declared, "It's easy to stay married when you're in love." Beaming at his wife, he added, "She's every bit as pretty as the day I married her."

The couple met in London on a double-decker bus in the Swinging Sixties. Mrs. Faircloth was pursuing a modeling career and Roger was a student at the London School of Economics. In the years since. . . .

Lucy flipped through the notes she had taken during her

interview with the Faircloths but found them surprisingly thin. She should have written the story up immediately after talking with them, but she'd procrastinated, aware that the deadline for the *Love Is Best on the Coast* supplement was weeks away. Now it was Wednesday, deadline day, the story was finally due, and she couldn't remember what happened between their fabled meeting in London and the Connecticut house fire that prompted their decision to relocate to the Maine coast.

"If I can't have a Wyeth landscape on my wall, I can have one right outside my window." That was a great quote from Helen, and Lucy certainly planned to use it in her story, but where were the hard facts? What sort of career did Roger have? He certainly didn't spend forty years gazing at his beloved, like some lovesick swain.

And what about Helen? Did she continue to model? Lucy knew they didn't have any children; it was their "one regret," according to Helen. So what did she do for all those years besides dust the antiques and cook gourmet dinners for Roger? They said they'd collected art and antiques, they'd referred to a Goddard highboy, paintings by Warhol and Basquiat, all gone in the fire. "When life hands you lemons, you make lemonade." That's what Helen had said in a remarkable display of resiliency.

Lucy considered. They were resilient. Maybe she could do something with that. A quote from a marriage counselor would fill some space, she thought, but she still had a huge hole in the middle of her story. There was no way of getting around it, she had to call the Faircloths for more information. She knew they were still in town, she'd seen them just the other day, walking hand in hand on Main Street.

When she got Roger on his cell phone, he apologized profusely but said it wasn't a good time to talk.

"This will only take a minute," Lucy pleaded, glancing across the office at Ted, who was hunched forward, peering at his computer screen and pounding away on his keyboard.

"I'm on deadline. If you could just tell me a little about your career. . . ."

"Sorry. It's really impossible. I must go, I'm in the middle of a meeting with my realtor."

"I see. I'm sorry to interrupt," said Lucy, ending the call.

"That's no way for a reporter to talk," snapped Ted, glaring at her from his desk. "Call him back. Say the phone died and cut you off."

Lucy remembered the set of Roger's jaw at the Queen Victoria Inn; there was no way she was going to badger him. "He won't answer," said Lucy. "He's in a meeting."

"I need that story, I've got twenty inches to fill," said Ted.

"I know, I know." Lucy was already dialing one of her sources, a marriage counselor she'd quoted before. When she got through with him, however, she had only added an inch or two to the story. Maybe Frankie could help her out, she thought, dialing the real estate office. The phone was ringing when Lucy remembered Roger had said he was in a meeting with his realtor.

Much to her surprise, Frankie answered.

"Hi, it's Lucy. I'm sorry if this is a bad time."

"No, it's fine," said Frankie. "I was just working on some comps—but I'm glad you called. I've got a showing later. Can you pick up the girls?"

Sure, no problem," said Lucy. "So the meeting with the Faircloths is over?"

"What meeting?"

"I just spoke with Roger and he said he was in a meeting with his realtor."

"Well he wasn't meeting with me," said Frankie, "and he better not be meeting with any other realtor, because I have a signed contract with him."

"Maybe I misunderstood," said Lucy, who was pretty sure she hadn't. "You know how I'm writing about them and their amazing love story? Well, I've kind of run into a wall and I'm hoping you can help me out."

"Sure," said Frankie. "What do you need?"

"Some background. Roger's career, for example. Stuff like that."

There was a long pause before Frankie spoke. "Sorry, but all I know is that they used to live in Connecticut and their house burned down. I guess some stuff was saved because they're always saying they need room for the Duncan Phyfe sideboard and debating where they can hang the large Max Bohm seascape to best advantage." She sighed. "To tell the truth, I'm getting a little tired of the Faircloths. I have shown them every house in five towns and nothing is quite right. I told them maybe they should build, but they say they want to move into something right away, they don't want to wait a year while a house is built."

Lucy knew when she was beat. "Can you give me some warm and fuzzy quotes about how they are still in love?"

"Of course," said Frankie, "just give me a moment."

Lucy was listening to Frankie and typing in her flattering description of the Faircloths' relationship when she remembered that little awkward scene about paying the bill at the Queen Victoria Inn. When she'd finished, she found herself asking Frankie if she thought the couple were genuine.

"What do you mean?" asked Frankie.

"I don't know. They just seem a bit off. When we had tea at the Queen Vic, the waitress asked Roger to pay cash, something about his credit being cut off. And now, all of a sudden, he doesn't want to talk to me. It just makes me wonder."

"That's the trouble with being a reporter," said Frankie. "You don't trust anybody." She paused. "But they have left the Queen Vic; they said it wasn't quite up to their standards. They've moved to the Salt Aire."

"Oh," said Lucy, impressed. She knew the Salt Aire Resort and Spa was strictly top-of-the-line, the most luxurious—and most expensive—hotel in Tinker's Cove. "I guess I do have a suspicious mind, but it did seem odd for this guy who's got such very expensive tastes to argue over a restaurant tab."

"That's how the very rich are, Lucy," said Frankie. "Especially the ones with old money. They pinch every penny."

Lucy thought of some of the summer people who occupied the big shingled "cottages" on Shore Road—they ran up big bills at shops in town and were slow to pay. It was a common complaint among the local merchants. "I'm sure you're right," said Lucy. "Thanks for the quote."

"Uh, Lucy, talk about trust, I got a real unpleasant surprise last weekend."

"What happened?"

"I was doing an open house—they're an older couple, desperate to sell because he's got cancer and isn't expected to live long and she can't keep up the big old place on her own. You probably know them, the Potters."

"Oh, yeah. They've got that nice colonial on School Street."

"It's a steal. Needs a little work but a bargain for the right buyer. And they're such a nice couple, I really want to help them out and get it sold."

Lucy was wondering where this was going. Was it just a sales pitch? "Yeah, well, I'll keep it in mind." Then a thought came to her. "You know Eddie Culpepper is back and he might be looking for an investment. . . ."

"That's the weird thing, Lucy. He came, along with Lily Fraser."

Ah, young love, thought Lucy. It was enough to warm the cockles of your heart. "I guess they're getting serious."

"I'm not so sure that's a good thing. When the Potters came home, they discovered his OxyContin had been stolen, right out of the medicine cabinet."

Lucy's jaw dropped. "You don't think Eddie and Lily took it?"

"I don't know what to think," said Frankie. "I blame myself. I should have told the Potters to take the meds with them, it just slipped my mind." She paused. "And I should have kept a closer eye on those kids. I got distracted, an old client of mine came in and we got chatting. I think that's when it happened, Eddie and Lily were upstairs by themselves."

"Are you sure?"

"No, I'm not sure," admitted Frankie. "But I've been wracking my brain and that's the only time I think it could have happened. The bottle was in the upstairs bathroom medicine cabinet and they were the only people who were up there without me."

Lucy had a terrible sinking feeling. "Did you report it?"

"We had to; OxyContin is a controlled substance and Mr. Potter needed to get a new prescription. But I didn't name Eddie and Lily and I noticed they didn't sign in. The officer said it happens all the time. Kids steal drugs from their parents, home health aides steal from their patients, staff members steal from hospitals and pharmacies. And then there's the phony prescriptions, the people who go to a bunch of doctors and get multiple prescriptions."

Lucy had no idea. "For this OxyContin?"

"Yeah. Either they're hooked themselves, or they sell it. A single pill goes for eighty dollars."

That was a lot of money, thought Lucy. "Who buys it?"

"Addicts. It's very addicting, and once they're hooked they need three or four pills every day, or they start feeling sick. Withdrawal symptoms." Frankie paused. "When they can't afford the OxyContin they use heroin. It's much cheaper."

A year or two ago, thought Lucy, she would have been shocked. But not now. The police and court reports showed a big increase in drug-related crimes and the town had seen several violent drug-related deaths in recent years. Doc Ryder had expressed concern about the number of overdoses he was seeing in the emergency room. It wasn't just Tinker's Cove, either. Even the governor's wife was trying to raise awareness of the problem.

Still, Lucy resisted the idea that either Lily or Eddie might be using drugs. "They're both good kids. . . ."

"I know," agreed Frankie. "That's why I didn't name them. I wanted to give them the benefit of the doubt."

"That's exactly right," said Lucy. "I can't believe either one of them would do this awful thing, steal painkillers from a dying man."

"You're right, I'm sure you're right," said Frankie, but her tone of voice gave her away. She wasn't convinced and neither was Lucy.

That afternoon, Lucy ran a few errands before picking up Sara and Renee at Fern's Famous, and Zoe at Chanticleer Chocolate. The work permit had come through and today was Zoe's first day, but Lucy wasn't happy about it. She'd been in a bad mood as she went about town, making a stop at the town dump before picking up groceries and dry cleaning.

The rear of the Subaru wagon was full of green reusable grocery bags, dry cleaning hanging from the back of the front seat where she'd hooked the hangers around the headrest supports, and a couple of big boxes now empty of bottles she'd recycled, on the back seat.

"Gee, Mom, is there room for us?" asked Sara, when she opened the car door.

"Just stack up those boxes inside each other," said Lucy.

"They don't fit," complained Sara, struggling to jam one box inside the other. "This one's too big."

"Turn it sideways," said Lucy, wondering how a girl who got all A's in geometry couldn't figure out how to stack a couple of cartons.

"Got it," said Sara, succeeding in combining the two boxes and making room in the back seat.

The two girls jumped in and immediately began whispering and giggling.

"Can you let me in on the joke?" asked Lucy, accelerating into the road. "I had no idea chocolate was so much fun."

"It is at Fern's," said Sara, prompting a fresh round of giggling. "Especially around Valentine's Day."

"Come on, tell me," said Lucy, in a playful tone. "I've had a tough day and I could use a laugh."

"Well," began Sara. "Promise you won't tell?"

Lucy didn't get it. What was so funny and had to be kept secret, too? It didn't make sense, especially since you'd think the mood would be somewhat subdued at Fern's following Max's death. "Sure," she said. "I won't tell."

"Dora makes special chocolates that she doesn't sell in the shop. She calls them 'naughty chocolates.' "

Lucy braked hard at the stop sign. "Naughty?"

"Yeah." The girls were giggling again. "Like Hot Lips. Those are shaped like lips and are kind of spicy. They're real popular; we've been filling tons of orders from all over the country."

Lucy still didn't get it. You could buy lips wrapped in red foil at the local drugstore. They brought them out every year for Valentine's Day, along with boxer shorts printed with hearts. "That doesn't sound very naughty," she said, turning onto Route 1.

"It's not just lips," said Renee. "She has other, um, parts."

"Like boobs!" exclaimed Sara. "And, and, you know. . . ."

Lucy thought maybe she did. "Who'd 'a thunk it?" she exclaimed, chuckling to herself as she proceeded along Main Street toward Chanticleer Chocolate, where she had to pick up Zoe.

"You're not mad?" asked Sara. "Dora said you might not approve."

"I used to have standards, but motherhood has taught me to compromise." Lucy joked with the girls, but she fully intended to drop in at Fern's Famous first thing next morning to check out the naughty chocolates.

Pulling into a vacant spot in front of Chanticleer Chocolate, Lucy tooted the horn. Zoe was supposed to work until five, and it was now ten after, but there was no sign of her.

"Sara, just go inside and see what's holding her up," said Lucy.

A minute later Sara reported that Zoe would only be a few more minutes. "Tamzin's got her cleaning the display case and she's not done yet."

Lucy thought of the ice cream that was probably melting in the back of her car, not to mention other perishables like expensive winter lettuce and fresh fish. "How long do you think she's going to be?"

"A while," said Sara. "There were trays of chocolates everywhere and they've all got to be put back in the case."

Lucy wanted to go in and demand Tamzin let Zoe go for the evening, but she knew that wasn't a good idea. She'd already raised a fuss about the working papers and she didn't want to make things any harder for Zoe. But this was still darned inconvenient.

Finally, at thirty-five minutes past five, the door opened and Zoe appeared, zipping her parka.

"Sorry, Mom," she said, climbing in the back beside Sara and Renee. "Tamzin said I couldn't go until I finished."

"No problem," said Lucy, flicking on her signal and turning onto the street.

"I was afraid you'd be mad," said Zoe.

"Well, I'm pretty sure the ice cream has melted and twelve dollars' worth of fish is ruined, but it's not your fault," said Lucy. "It's Tamzin's."

"She was upset. I think that's why she made me do all that work," said Zoe.

"What do you mean?" asked Lucy, turning back onto Route 1.

"Everything was fine, she was all nicey-nice, showing me how to wrap the chocolates and tie bows and all this stuff. Not like a boss at all, like we were friends. But then Trey came in with Ms. Clarke and she was all smiley with them, but as soon as they left she turned into this really mean person. All of a sudden she was making me do icky stuff like cleaning the bathroom and mopping the floor." Zoe sighed. "I didn't think working would be so hard."

"Maybe tomorrow will be better," said Lucy, who was revising her thinking about Tamzin and Trey. Just because they weren't a couple didn't mean that Tamzin wasn't hoping to become one. Trey was awfully attractive, and wealthy, besides. Tamzin couldn't be making much more than minimum wage in the candy shop; it was probably barely enough to keep her in push-up bras and stiletto heels. Mentally slapping herself for being so catty, Lucy turned her attention to Zoe, who needed a bit of encouragement. "Was the shop busy?"

"Really busy. Valentine's Day is Sunday."

"With anybody you know? Did any of your friends come by?"

Zoe shook her head. "Tamzin took care of the customers."

I bet she did, thought Lucy, turning onto Red Top Road.

Thursday morning, Lucy met the girls at Jake's for breakfast. She couldn't resist telling them about Dora's naughty chocolates.

"There's a shop in Boston that has those sexy chocolates," Sue had told her, while Norine filled their mugs with Jake's high-test brew. "Some of them are pretty raunchy."

"I'm no prude," Pam had declared with a prim expression, "but I don't think it's appropriate to expect young girls to handle that kind of special order."

"Adolescents are very vulnerable," added Rachel, offering the insight she'd gained as a psychology major in college. "Their sexuality is just developing and is very fragile."

"Yeah," cracked Pam, "you don't want them thinking men taste like chocolate."

That sent them all into gales of laughter, including Lucy. But even as she laughed along with the others, she couldn't help feeling she didn't want her daughter exposed to such risqué products. She remembered how shocked she'd been as an impressionable girl when a catalog picturing trashy underwear had tumbled out of a pile of newspapers she was carrying out to the trash bins. She'd puzzled over the crotchless red underpants for years and, to tell the truth, the images still bothered her. As she matured and became more sophisticated, she came to believe that donning such garments turned you into a sex object, something she had no intention of becoming and which she certainly didn't want her daughters to become.

But when she stepped inside Fern's Famous, with its antiseptic white tile walls and the delicious scent of chocolate, her resolution wavered. She took in the smiling cow on the sign behind the counter and the scuffed wood floor, the ornate swirls on the antique bronze cash register and the collection of old milk cans that served as decoration, and wondered if the girls had been teasing her. All this old-timey wholesomeness seemed at odds with the production of sexy chocolates.

"Hi, Lucy," said Dora, pushing aside the red-and-white-striped curtain that separated the work area from the shop. "You should be real proud of Sara, she's a wonderful girl and a real good worker."

"Oh, thanks," said Lucy, feeling Dora already had her at a disadvantage. "That's what I wanted to talk to you about."

Dora blushed. "She told you about the naughty chocolates."

"Yeah." Lucy nodded. "I'm just not comfortable with that sort of thing."

"Come on back," said Dora. "I'll let you have a look."

Lucy followed her and was surprised to encounter Fern

herself, mixing up a big batch of penuche in a huge copper kettle with a gas flame underneath it. The tiny old woman was standing on a stool, wielding a huge wooden paddle.

"Goodness, that looks like quite a job," said Lucy, greeting her.

Fern brushed back a stray lock of gray hair that had escaped from the little bun on the top of her head and paused for a second. "I'm the only one does it right," she declared, resuming her stirring. "These young'uns are too impatient."

Dora smiled. "We let her think that, it keeps her out of trouble," said Dora, leading Lucy into the packing room and grabbing several boxes from the neat stacks arranged on industrial-style metal shelves. The boxes she chose were all shiny red, unlike the usual striped ones associated with Fern's Famous.

"This is kind of a sideline of mine," said Dora, opening one of the boxes and revealing half a dozen chocolates molded in the shape of lips. "I call these Hot Lips because the chocolate is quite spicy. Max got the recipe in Mexico. Want to try one?"

Lucy thought briefly of her diet, then nodded. Taking a bite of the creamy chocolate, she was amazed at the combination of flavors: the fiery hot pepper released flavor notes from the chocolate that she had never tasted before. "Wow," she said. "That is amazing."

Dora smiled and bit into one herself. "Of all the candy we make, this is the only one I don't get tired of," she said. "Every time, it's a new experience. An explosion of flavor, that's how I describe it on the website." She lowered her voice. "Fern doesn't approve, so I market them separately on the Web. I call them 'Sexsational Chocolates.' "

"Cute," said Lucy, determined to stick to her guns. "I assume some of the chocolates are racier than these?"

"Oh, yeah," said Dora. "I've got Bodacious Bods and Big Boobs." She opened two more boxes, revealing solid blocks of chocolate. One was shaped like a muscular man's torso, complete with six-pack abs, and the other was shaped like a breast with a dried cherry for a nipple.

In spite of herself, Lucy found she was laughing.

"I know," said Dora, with a shrug. "It's not the cleverest name but, believe me, I sell a lot of Big Boobs." She paused. "The truth of the matter is, if it wasn't for my naughty chocolates, we would have gone out of business years ago. Fern thinks everybody comes for that penuche of hers, but I actually throw most of it out. And she won't raise prices on the fudge, even though the price of sugar has gone through the roof. She won't admit it, but these shiny red boxes are the real moneymakers." Dora gave her a look. "And now that Chanticleer's in town, and getting so much attention, well, I'd be lying if I said they weren't cutting into our profits."

Lucy felt a stab of guilt. "Ted made me write that article about them."

"Sara said her sister's working over there." Dora tilted her head in the direction of Chanticleer Chocolate. "I'm surprised you let her. That Tamzin's a real floozy."

"I'm not happy about it." Lucy thought she'd better change the subject. "Somehow I was expecting something a lot racier," she said, finishing off her Hot Lips.

"That's Flora," said Dora, with a sigh. "She absolutely refuses to let me make anything, um, below the waist." She scowled. "I could make a lot of money with Size Matters lollipops but she won't let me go there."

"That's probably just as well," said Lucy, thinking back to the days when you only had to worry about warning kids not to run with lollipops in their mouths.

"So it's okay if Sara keeps working here?" asked Dora. "I really need the help. This is our busiest time of year."

"Oh, sure." Lucy's thoughts turned to Lily. "I suppose you'll be shorthanded when Lily goes back to school."

"Who told you that?" asked Dora, replacing the red boxes on the shelves.

"I just assumed. . . ."

Dora turned and shook her head. "I loved Max, I did, and I'll miss him. But I learned early on not to count on him. He'd promise the world, but there was never enough money to pay the rent. That's what I told Lily when he said he had money coming and she'd be able to go back to school. 'Don't worry,' he said. 'It's under control.' Now he's gone and there isn't any money, there isn't even any life insurance. All he left behind is an old truck and a snowmobile that doesn't run. It's gonna cost more to fix it than it's worth—and that's the story of Max's life." She sighed. "And now that she's been seeing a lot of Eddie Culpepper, she's not so eager to go back to school. He's just back from Afghanistan, you know, and he's pretty eager to settle down. I wouldn't be at all surprised if they got married."

"But Lily's so young," said Lucy.

"I know," said Dora. "I'd like her to wait but, well, I remember what it's like when you're young." She smiled and for a moment the years dropped away and she looked like the girl who'd fallen in love with Max.

"Have you heard anything more about Max's death from the police?" Lucy asked.

Dora shook her head. "Case closed. Accidental drowning."

"Do you believe that?"

"I didn't at first, but now I guess it must be true. Who would kill Max? Sure he had his faults, but everybody loved him, he'd give you the shirt off his back if he thought you needed it. You saw the turnout at the memorial service. He was a real popular guy."

"Yeah," agreed Lucy. "He helped me that night—the night he died—when I got stuck in the snow."

Dora smiled. "That was Max all over. I really miss him."

"You're not alone," said Lucy.

But as she left the shop and made her way to the *Penny-saver* office, Lucy's thoughts turned to Eddie and Lily. She knew Barney was worried about Eddie, saying he was hav-

ing trouble adjusting to civilian life. Barney hadn't elabo-
rated, so she didn't know if he was suffering from a full-
blown case of post-traumatic stress syndrome, or just the
normal sense of dislocation that accompanies major life
changes like moves and new jobs. Either way it was worrying, especially in light of Frankie's suspicions. Lily had
been through a lot, including her parents' divorce and her father's tragic death, and Lucy hoped this relationship with
Eddie wouldn't bring her more grief.

Chapter Ten

Phyllis had raised the old-fashioned wooden venetian blinds and was taping big red paper hearts on the plate glass windows when Lucy got to the *Pennysaver* office. She paused, tape in hand, and cocked her head.

"What do you think?"

"It's very festive," said Lucy, studying the scattered arrangement. "Maybe a few more up in the left there? And what about the door?"

"One big one? A cluster of small ones?"

Lucy took off her jacket and hung it on the sturdy oak coat stand next to the door, tossed her bag on the floor next to her desk, and turned, one hand on her hip. Lifting the blinds had made the whole office brighter, she realized, and the red hearts were a cheerful counterpoint to the snowy street. "I think a scattering of small ones on the door. And maybe we should keep the blinds up." Her eyes were wandering around the office, noticing cobwebs in the corners and the shadowy shapes of insect corpses in the glass globes of the light fixtures. "This place could do with a cleaning," she said.

"That's why the blinds are coming back down," said Phyllis, yanking a cord and bringing the slats down with a clatter.

Lucy laughed, flicking on her desk lamp and booting up her computer. When the humming and whirring stopped and her desktop icons appeared, she paused. "Where's Ted?" she asked.

"Dunno. He called and said he'd be in after lunch."

Hearing this, Lucy went straight to the Internet and Googled "low calorie dessert recipes."

"We have a lot of listings this week," said Phyllis, slapping a thick pile of press releases down on the reception counter. "I guess Corney's been busy twisting arms for this *Love Is Best on the Coast* promotion."

"I promised Sue I'd enter her dessert contest," grumbled Lucy, scrolling down the list of recipes that had magically appeared. "It's not fair. I'm trying not to think about food."

"Have the girls do it." Phyllis was filing the press releases by date in an accordion file that was rather the worse for wear.

"They're busy with their jobs." Lucy's eye was caught by a recipe for low-fat cheesecake when the phone rang; it was Sue. "Funny you should call. I was just surfing the Web looking for a dessert recipe."

"Quiet day at the paper?" asked Sue.

"You could say that," said Lucy. "Phyllis put up some Valentine's decorations."

"Well, I have some news but it's not for publication," said Sue, in a low voice.

"Do tell," said Lucy, perking up.

"You're not gonna believe this," began Sue. "Remember how you saw Brad Cashman messing around with that woman in the chocolate shop?"

Lucy's eyes widened. "Tamzin?"

"Yeah. That's her. Chris said the phone was ringing all night. It was this Tamzin calling Brad."

"That's kind of pushy," said Lucy.

"According to Chris, it got so bad that Brad wouldn't take the calls. He actually turned off the phone."

"How did he explain it to Chris?" asked Lucy.

"He told her he'd flirted with Tamzin at the shop but that was all there was to it. He didn't understand why she was acting like this and he certainly didn't want anything to do with her."

"I think it was a bit more than flirting," said Lucy.

"I think you're right," said Sue, "because when she couldn't get through on the phone, Tamzin actually went to their house and made a terrific scene."

Lucy's jaw literally dropped. "What did she do?"

"Oh, she was screaming and crying and running around trying to grab Brad and kiss him, literally throwing herself at him while Chris and the girls watched."

"No!"

"Yes. She wouldn't stop. They couldn't get her to leave. They had to threaten to call the police."

"Did that work?"

"That—and a Xanax."

"So how is Chris taking it? Are they talking divorce or anything?"

"She's pretty upset. She doesn't know what to think. Brad's being a model husband—he made waffles for them all for breakfast and sent a big bouquet of flowers to her here at the school this morning—she says it's kind of making her crazy. She'd like it better if he wasn't quite so apologetic."

"I can see that," said Lucy. "I guess time will tell."

"Maybe they should talk to somebody, like a marriage counselor." In the background, Lucy heard a child crying.

"And get a restraining order," said Lucy, but Sue was already gone.

"What was that about?" asked Phyllis, raising one of the penciled lines that were her eyebrows.

Lucy considered. She didn't want to spread gossip, but

Phyllis had heard most of the conversation and it seemed rude not to tell her the rest. And besides, nothing stayed secret very long in Tinker's Cove. "Tamzin from the chocolate shop has a thing for Brad Cashman and she went to his house last night and made a big scene in front of his wife and kids."

Phyllis clucked her tongue. "That woman's trouble. Do you know she gives Wilf a truffle every day when he delivers the mail?"

"Just as long as it's only a truffle," said Lucy, with a wry smile.

Phyllis scowled at a press release. "She better not mess with me, that's all I have to say."

"Me, too," said Lucy, closing out Google and opening the file for events listings. "Give me some of those press releases," she said, with a sigh. "I might as well get started."

Lucy tried to concentrate on the task at hand, but she found her mind insisted on wandering. For one thing, she'd written up these same announcements about children's story hours at the Broadbrooks Free Library and ham and bean suppers at Our Lady of the Harbor Church and free Friday night movies at the community center so many times that she could type them from memory. Of course, there was always the remote possibility that the movie time would change from 7 P.M. to 7:30 P.M. or that the price for the ham and bean dinners would rise from five dollars to six, which was why she really needed to pay attention.

But the harder she tried to concentrate, the more unruly her thoughts became, following their own path. And that path led straight to Tamzin Graves. What a nerve that woman had, flaunting herself at every man she met. She was practically a public menace; somebody ought to petition the selectmen to write a preservation of marriage act banning her from town. And it wasn't just husbands she was after— she went after your children, too, she realized, thinking of Zoe. They needed a family preservation act.

Lucy was chuckling at this idea when she noticed that the Newcomer's Club was canceling a planned talk by Dora Fraser until further notice. No wonder, thought Lucy, Dora probably didn't feel up to speaking before a crowd so soon after her ex-husband's death. Max's death was especially sad, thought Lucy, since he and Dora had seemed to be reconciling. At least that's what Bill had told her and she didn't doubt it. She'd known other couples who had gotten back together after divorce. Maybe it was like slipping on a pair of worn sandals you'd put away for the winter; when you strapped them on, you found they'd been molded to your feet and fit perfectly.

In the past, Dora never hesitated to criticize Max, but now that he was gone she seemed to have found good points that outweighed his faults. Or maybe she'd simply come to accept him, warts and all, realizing that she still loved him in spite of everything. Most of their trouble seemed to involve money, that was the factor that broke up most marriages, at least according to the surveys in women's magazines. But now that the recession had arrived, everybody was having money trouble. All of a sudden people were reevaluating their priorities and discovering that relationships and family mattered more than their adjusted gross income. Maybe, she thought, that's what happened with Max and Dora. Or maybe once you loved someone, you always did—a sort of vestigial emotion.

But what about Tamzin? Lucy was sure she'd heard that Tamzin and Max were an item, even though Tamzin insisted they were only friends. Of course that's what she would say if Max had left her to return to his wife. A femme fatale like Tamzin would hardly broadcast the fact that she'd been rejected in favor of a heavier, plainer woman. She had an image to maintain.

Here Lucy had to admit she was letting her emotions get the better of her. She didn't like Tamzin, in fact, she was beginning to hate her. The woman was a predator, she stole people's husbands. She was self-centered, she thought the world revolved around her. She was blithely unaware of other people's concerns. She even thought she was above the law, if the incident with Zoe's working papers was anything to go by.

That's when Lucy decided she had to put the brakes on. Okay, so Tamzin hadn't bothered about the child labor regulations, she was hardly the first employer to ignore them. Like dog licenses and leash laws, the requirements for work permits were frequently ignored. And failing to apply for a work permit for an underage employee was a far cry from murdering someone, even someone who had jilted you.

Still, thought Lucy, the fact remained that Tamzin did have a black belt and could have overpowered Max, especially if he was drunk.

Was Tamzin a murderer? Lucy didn't know. The one thing she did know for sure was that she didn't want her daughter anywhere near the woman, who was clearly unstable. Zoe was at an impressionable age and Tamzin was a terrible role model. Lucy had high hopes for her daughters: Elizabeth had graduated from college and was successfully embarked on a career with the Cavendish Hotel chain; Sara had scored well on her SATs and was waiting to hear from the colleges she'd applied to; and Zoe was in the top of her class. All three were serious, responsible high achievers and Lucy wanted them to stay that way. She didn't want Zoe to become a sexpot like Tamzin.

Lucy came to a decision: Zoe had to quit working at Chanticleer Chocolate. Since she was at school, there was no way Lucy could discuss the matter with her and convince her to quit. The best she could do was to send a text saying something had come up and she should call in sick this afternoon.

Moments later she got a reply: **R U CRZ? T WL KL ME!**

Lucy stared at the glowing letters, wondering if Zoe was on to something. Of course not, all she meant was that

Tamzin was an abusive boss. She decided it was time to appeal to a higher authority and picked up the phone, dialing Trey's office at the converted sardine factory in Rockland.

"Bit of a problem," she began. "The job's not working out for Zoe. Tamzin kept her late yesterday and, well, frankly, she was really mean to her."

"Tamzin? Mean?" Trey couldn't believe it. "She's such a sweetie."

"Zoe was really upset when I picked her up."

"I'm sure she overreacted. She's very young, this is her first job, right?"

"I'm her mom and I don't like the way Tamzin treated her. That's the bottom line."

Trey immediately backtracked. "That's your prerogative, of course. But I pride myself on the company's employee relations. We value all our workers, they're our most important resource."

Lucy felt as if she were listening to a public relations spiel. Like the layoff notice Pam had received from Winchester College notifying her she'd been chosen for a special program and would be able to collect unemployment insurance. Lucky Pam!

"How about this?" Trey was continuing. "Give me a chance to talk to Tamzin. In the meantime, we'll put Zoe on leave. No pay, of course. . . ."

"Of course," said Lucy.

"But we'll keep the job open for her in case she changes her mind."

"I wouldn't hold my breath," said Lucy.

The next step, she realized with a sinking feeling, was to let Zoe know. She sent another text and braced for fireworks, a cell phone screenfull of stars and other symbols. Instead she got a phone call.

"I'm in the girls' room, I'm not supposed to phone at school."

"I know."

"Mom, I just want you to know I'm really glad. Thanks."

Lucy thought she'd misunderstood. "You're glad you're not working today?"

"I don't want to ever go back."

"You don't have to."

"Good. I think I'll stick to babysitting."

"Good choice," she said. "Take the bus home. I'll see you later."

Relieved, Lucy let out a big sigh just as Ted walked in the door. "Glad to see you're working hard," he said.

Lucy glanced at Phyllis, who ran her fingers across her lips in a zipping motion. "That's us," Lucy said. "Busy little bees."

Chapter Eleven

Ted tossed his jacket, hat, and gloves in the direction of the coat tree and made a beeline for the bathroom, causing Lucy and Phyllis to exchange amused glances. Unable to resist tidying up, Lucy picked up Ted's things, stuffed the hat and gloves in the jacket pocket, and hung it up.

"You know, Lucy, I couldn't help overhearing," said Phyllis. "I think you did the right thing, getting Zoe away from Tamzin."

Lucy turned and leaned her elbow on the battered Formica reception counter. Phyllis wasn't getting any younger, she thought, noticing the way her neck had developed crepey folds. And anxiety only served to emphasize the lines around her mouth.

"She's trouble," said Lucy, with a sympathetic nod. "One of those two-faced women who's nice to men. . . ."

"Wilf can't stop talking about her, he loves those truffles."

"As long as it's only a truffle, you don't have to worry."

"I do, though. She's prettier and sexier than I am," said Phyllis. "He doesn't see through her like a woman would, he doesn't understand why I don't like her."

"Don't be silly," said Lucy. "Wilf waited until he was practically fifty to get married and that's because he wanted to find the right woman, and that woman is you."

"I can't help worrying." Phyllis was chewing on the end of a ballpoint pen. "She's got him doing special favors, bringing her coffee from the shop next door. And not just regular coffee, skim milk lattes or some such thing. That Tamzin's got Wilf wrapped around her little finger."

Ted had emerged from the tiny toilet tucked behind the morgue looking much relieved, until he noticed Lucy standing by Phyllis's desk. Then he furrowed his brow and scowled. "Haven't you got anything better to do than gossip?"

"Actually, Ted, I was hanging up your coat," said Lucy, scowling right back at him.

"Uh, oh, sorry." Ted was momentarily shamefaced until he thought of a fresh avenue of attack. "I wish you wouldn't bad-mouth our advertisers. Chanticleer took out a six-month contract, so no more grumbling about them, okay?"

"We weren't grumbling about Chanticleer, we were talking about Tamzin," said Lucy.

"And you should be ashamed of yourselves," said Ted, self-righteously. "You should welcome her. The poor little thing is new in town and wants to make friends."

Lucy and Phyllis both laughed. "Only men friends," said Phyllis.

"That's right, Ted. You're not qualified to talk on this particular subject. Tamzin's got you under her spell, like all the other men in town."

"Right," agreed Phyllis. "We women have a special sense that warns us about husband stealers like Tamzin. It's like when chickens know a storm is coming, or the wildebeests stampede because a lion's on the prowl."

"Heaven help us if the women in this town stampede," muttered Ted. "Considering their average weight is two hundred pounds, there'd be nothing left. The place would be flattened."

"Not funny, Ted," said Lucy. "Besides, the fact that Tamzin's a man-eater isn't all that I object to. She hired Zoe without getting a work permit and then she treated her badly and made her work extra time. It's Zoe's first job—and she's a rotten boss."

Ted shook his head. "You know what kids are like. . . ."

"So don't hire a kid," snapped Lucy. "She hired Zoe because she thought she could exploit her."

"That's a reach, Lucy. Put yourself in Tamzin's shoes. . . ."

"Ha! I'd break my neck in those stilettos!"

"See! That's what I mean. What's really bothering you is pure female jealousy of someone who's more attractive. . . ."

"Watch it, Ted," warned Phyllis.

Lucy decided she'd better not say what she was thinking and instead marched over to the coat tree and pointedly lifted Ted's jacket off the hook and dropped it on the floor, in the exact spot it had been before she'd picked it up for him. Then she stomped over to her desk, plopped herself into her chair, and clicked on the solitaire game.

"I'm sorry, Lucy," said Ted, stooping to retrieve his clothing.

Lucy was staring at the screen, clicking her mouse and moving cards.

"I'm really, really sorry. I don't know what I was thinking."

"Hmph," said Lucy, starting a fresh game.

Ted seated himself in the spare chair next to Lucy's desk. "The thing is, Lucy, I need you to do something for me. I need you to take some photos at Chanticleer Chocolate for the ads."

Lucy was moving cards, pretty sure she was going to win this game. "Why can't you do it?" she asked.

"Uh, this is embarrassing."

"I knew it!" crowed Lucy. "Pam won't let you!"

Ted was staring at the scuffed floor. "That's right."

The little cards were dancing around on the computer

screen, celebrating Lucy's win. She smiled at Ted. "Can't do it today. I left my camera home."

"You should always bring it," said Ted, unable to resist putting Lucy in the wrong. Lucy cocked an eyebrow in his direction and he backtracked. "Tomorrow will be fine."

"Good," said Lucy, reaching for the phone. Darn it, she'd called the place so often in the past few days that she'd memorized the number, which was taking up way too much precious brain space. She winced, hearing Tamzin answer with "Chanticleer Chocolate" in a phony French accent.

"Hi, Tamzin, Lucy Stone here at the *Pennysaver*," she began, in a tone that was all business. She certainly didn't want to get into a discussion about Zoe's need for a leave of absence after only one day on the job; she'd leave that to Trey. "Ted wants me to take some photos for the ad campaign."

"Great!" From her enthusiastic tone, Lucy guessed Tamzin was also eager to avoid the subject of Zoe. "When do you want to come?"

Lucy considered her schedule. She sure didn't want to go out of her way for the woman. "Maybe tomorrow morning, on my way to the office. Eight-thirty?"

"We don't open until nine." Tamzin made it clear she was doing Lucy a favor. "I'm happy to come in early for you, though."

"Well, thanks, Tamzin," said Lucy, happily. She was on a winning streak today. "See you then."

Friday was the sort of day that would send any sensible person diving back under the covers. It was well after sunrise when Lucy drove down Main Street, but the streetlights were still lit, which meant the sun was not providing enough light to trip the sensors that turned them off. In other words, it was dark as night at eight-thirty in the morning.

The gloom wasn't the worst of it, though. Sleet, frozen

rain, whatever you wanted to call it, was coming down hard, plopping on the windshield of Lucy's car faster than the wipers could get rid of it. The road was filling with the slushy stuff, too, and every now and then the rear wheels would start to fishtail. The car's automatic all-wheel drive caught it every time, but it was still unnerving and Lucy's stomach lurched when she felt the car start to slip.

Maybe, she thought, swallowing down the coffee and bile taste that filled her mouth once again, maybe she should have had something more than black coffee for breakfast. Of course, she reminded herself, she hadn't had time to eat anything because she'd put off getting out of bed to the very last minute. Behavior like that wouldn't win her the mother-of-the-year award, or the wife-of-the-year award, either. She usually got up and made breakfast for Bill and the girls, but this morning she simply hadn't had the energy. Even now she had to resist the urge to turn the car around and go back home and back to bed, just like the snoring old man in the nursery rhyme *who went to bed and bumped his head and couldn't get up in the morning.*

Really, there was something to be said for opting out, especially on a day like this when she had to photograph Terrible Tamzin. Talk about adding insult to injury. If there were ever a day she'd like to skip, a day she'd like to pretend never happened, it was this Friday, actually the twelfth, but it felt like an unlucky Friday the thirteenth. There was nothing to look forward to even after the photo session. When she finished at Chanticleer she had to go back to the office to write up the water commission's meeting, the highlight of which was the superintendent's assurance that the town had plenty of water.

Sure they did, thought Lucy, remembering last summer's floods and casting her eyes at the dark clouds filling the sky. Water in all its forms—ice, snow, rain, sleet, salty ocean, freshwater ponds, and streams—was one thing they had plenty of and, frankly, she could do with less of it.

She remembered a commercial for Aruba she'd seen on TV last night and pictured the sunshine, the sandy beach and turquoise Caribbean water. Boy, what she wouldn't give to be there. Now, that would be a great way to celebrate Valentine's Day: in a swimsuit, pale white skin slathered with sunscreen, sipping a piña colada, while Bill nibbled on her toes.

Not that Bill would ever do such a thing, she thought resentfully. Some men had foot fetishes, but Bill could truly be said to have a foot phobia. He didn't even like to see her barefoot. And instead of her being the focus of his adoring attention on Valentine's Day, this most personal of holidays had turned into a marathon. She had a to-do list that was a mile long. She had to make a dessert for the contest, pick up Bill's suit, jolly him into wearing it, and somehow find a way to stuff herself into her tight black skirt. Maybe skipping breakfast hadn't been such a bad idea after all, she decided, patting her now almost-flat tummy.

There was no problem finding a parking spot today. Main Street was practically deserted and Lucy thought of her old friend Miss Tilley's assertion that there was so little traffic when she was a girl that she and her friends used to play tennis in the road right in front of Slack's Hardware. Lucy parked in front of Chanticleer Chocolate and sat for a minute, lost in thought.

She was thinking of how things had changed even in her lifetime. When she and Bill first came to Tinker's Cove, the town had been more self-sufficient—you could get everything you needed right in town. There was a grocery store, drugstore, post office, liquor store, hardware store, a five and dime, and even a small department store with household linens and clothes to fit everyone in the family from newborn babies to grandmas. Through the years many of those old, established businesses had vanished, one by one, replaced by national chains. Now, if you wanted a new set of sheets or some pot holders, good luck to you. You had to travel to one of the big box stores that had sprung up out by the interstate or else you had to take your chances and order from the Internet.

Holidays were simpler, too. They were primarily family events, nobody thought of capitalizing on a holiday to bring tourists to town. Lucy remembered the kids making valentines for friends and family out of lace doilies and red construction paper. She'd make cupcakes for dessert, with pink icing and conversation hearts on top. Bill would bring home a box of Whitman's chocolates for her, which she shared with the kids after she'd plucked out her favorite caramels (easily identified from the chart on the inside of the box top), and that was that.

Sighing, she decided she'd put it off long enough, it was time to face the music. Or rather, Tamzin, with her fake boobs and false eyelashes, the glistening lips and the jeans that were so tight you wondered how she ever got them on, not to mention tucked inside those thigh-high boots.

Lucy pulled the fur-lined hood of her parka over her head and climbed out of the car. Ducking her head to avoid the sleet that pelted her face, she ran around the car and onto the sidewalk, seeking the shelter of the yellow Chanticleer awning. She was reaching for the door handle when the door flew open and Roger Faircloth barreled into her.

The man was obviously upset. He grabbed her by the shoulders with shaking hands and Lucy grabbed his sides, afraid he would fall. Noticing his pale face, shiny with sweat, and his panicked expression, Lucy thought he was having a heart attack.

"Roger, what's wrong? Shall I call the rescue squad?"

He couldn't manage to speak but nodded. Lucy needed to be able to reach inside her purse for her cell phone but she was still supporting Roger, she couldn't let go of him for fear he would fall. She decided the best thing would be to go inside the shop, where they would be out of the weather, Roger could sit on one of those oh-so-cute café chairs, and Tamzin could make the call.

But when she suggested going inside the shop to Roger he became frantic, shaking his head and saying no over and over. Lucy didn't know what to do, all that came to mind were those old black-and-white westerns where the cowboy hero was always slapping some hysterical woman. She couldn't slap Roger, she had to get help for him.

"Come on, Roger," she said, "we can't stay out here in the weather."

The man was sobbing and shaking, but he finally allowed her to guide him toward the door. Pulling it open, she heard the musical chimes ring once again and her nostrils were filled with the heavy scent of chocolate. Chocolate and something else. But what?

"Tamzin, I need help," she yelled. "Call nine-one-one."

There was no answering cry from Tamzin, which Lucy figured was typical. The woman was so self-absorbed, she was probably putting on fresh lip gloss or something and was too busy to make the call. She looked around the shop, past the tables stacked with blue-and-yellow boxes of chocolates and behind the counter, searching for the phone. It was then Lucy suddenly understood why Roger was so upset. At first, she thought it was just some sort of promotion, a giant chocolate displayed on the marble table behind the counter. A giant chocolate in the shape of a naked woman, a "Sexsational Chocolate" bigger and fancier than anything Dora ever dreamed of. But when she took a closer look, she realized it was Tamzin; her naked body had been stretched out on the table and coated with chocolate.

Lucy's stomach heaved and, dragging Roger with her, she ran out of the store and stood on the sidewalk, gasping for fresh air. Tamzin was dead, somebody had killed her. Somebody with a wicked sense of humor.

Chapter Twelve

Lucy's car was parked right outside the shop so she helped Roger across the slippery sidewalk and opened the door for him. He made no attempt to seat himself, but stood, obviously in shock, leaning heavily on her arm and unaware of the globs of icy sleet that were falling on their heads and sliding down their faces. Lucy wasn't feeling too good herself. She was shaking and nauseous and realized a dark shadow was falling across her vision. She knew she had to sit down and lower her head or she'd faint and then she'd be no good to anyone.

"Come on, Roger," she said, coaxing him. "You've got to get in the car. We'll sit here and I'll call nine-one-one."

A glimmer of understanding flitted across his blank, staring eyes. Lucy turned him 'round and, imitating the maneuver she'd seen Rachel use with Miss Tilley, she guided him into the seat and lifted his legs one by one until he was properly seated. Bending down to seat him cleared her head, but she still felt dizzy and queasy when she took the driver's seat and started rooting in her big purse for her cell phone.

Finding it, she rested her head on the steering wheel and

pressed the numbered keys. The dispatcher answered right away and Lucy told her she'd found Tamzin Graves's body at Chanticleer Chocolate.

"Is the victim conscious?" asked the dispatcher.

"No."

"Is the victim breathing?"

"No."

"Can you perform CPR?"

"Yes, I can," answered Lucy, who'd taken a course soon after her grandson Patrick's birth. "But there's no point. She's been dead for a while."

"Are you sure?"

Lucy was losing patience. "She's covered with chocolate!"

"Like she fell into it?"

"I don't know, but I've got an elderly man here who discovered her and he's in shock and we need some help."

"That's the thing—because of the sleet we've had a bunch of accidents and I don't have any units available. And if she's already dead, there's really no hurry."

Lucy couldn't believe what she was hearing. She glanced at Roger, who was breathing heavily, his face pale and waxy. "I've got an elderly man here in shock, he needs help."

"Maybe you could drive him to the ER?"

Give me a break, thought Lucy. "That would mean leaving a crime scene and I don't think I should do that."

"Are you sure it's a crime? Maybe it was an accident."

Lucy pictured Tamzin's body in her mind, neatly arranged on the marble table with her hands crossed over her stomach and completely covered with shiny dark chocolate. Her killer must have spent most of the night creating the macabre scene. This was no hit-and-run killing. The murderer wasn't content to simply eliminate Tamzin; he, or maybe she— Lucy conceded the killer could have been a woman—went to a lot of effort to humiliate her. It was on a par with Max's murder, she realized with a start. The two had most likely been killed by the same person. But why? And why did the killer feel the need to arrange the bodies so dramatically? First it was Max, found trussed in fishline with a lure hooked to his lips, and now it was Tamzin, turned into a giant chocolate bar.

"Hello? Are you still there?" It was the dispatcher breaking into her thoughts.

"Yeah."

"You're in luck. I've got an available unit and I'm sending it right over."

"Good," said Lucy, noting with alarm that Roger was reaching for the door handle.

"No, Roger. You have to stay here and talk to the police."

"I'll buy chocolate for Helen another day," he said, sounding like he'd just happened to find the store closed and needed to adjust his schedule. If he remembered finding Tamzin's body, it seemed he was determined to forget it. "I want to see Helen."

"You'll see Helen soon," said Lucy. "But first you have to talk to the police and tell them everything you saw."

Roger was quiet for a few minutes, staring straight ahead at the icy drops plopping onto the windshield, following their descent down the glass. "I was only there a minute or two before you arrived," he said. "I could go and you could tell them what you saw."

"I could do that," she said, "but they'd want to talk to you eventually."

"You wouldn't have to mention me at all. They don't need to know I was here," said Roger.

"No, Roger. You need to stay here. I think you might need medical attention."

"I'm fit as a fiddle," declared Roger, reaching once again for the door handle just as a police cruiser pulled up and parked at an angle, neatly blocking the Subaru.

"We're not going anywhere, Roger," said Lucy, watching as Officer Todd Kirwan stepped out of the cruiser and approached them; when he was beside the car she lowered the window. Inside the cruiser she could see Barney calling in to headquarters on the radio. At least that's what she thought he was doing.

"What's the problem?" asked Todd, leaning on the door. He was a tall, good-looking kid with a crew cut, one of Dot Kirwan's brood.

"We found a body in the shop," said Lucy, pointing at Chanticleer Chocolate. "And I'm a little worried about Roger here, it was a terrible shock for him."

At that point Roger seemed to pass out, his head dropped forward and his whole body slumped against the car door. Todd quickly called for an ambulance on his walkie-talkie, then reached across Lucy and felt Roger's neck to check his pulse. "Strong and steady," he said, with a shrug. He'd barely finished extracting himself from the car when they heard a siren. Lucy saw Barney get out of the cruiser and make his way to the shop. He went inside at the same moment the ambulance arrived. Her attention turned back to Roger and she was sure she saw his eyelids flicker when the ambulance crew approached the car; for a brief second she wondered if he was faking unconsciousness to avoid being questioned. Then the door opened and the emergency medical technicians began the process of extracting him. Seeing nobody was paying attention to her, Lucy joined Barney in the shop.

He was a big man, bulky in official cold-weather blue from head to foot, and was standing with his legs planted far apart and his hands on his hips, studying the situation. Lucy could tell he was thinking hard because he'd drawn his eyebrows together and had lifted one hand to his face to scratch his chin.

"Somebody's got a mean sense of humor," she said.

Barney scowled at her. "You shouldn't be here. This is a crime scene."

"I know," said Lucy. She heard the doors of the ambulance slam and the wail of the siren as Roger was carried off to the emergency room. The musical chimes on the little door rang and she turned to see Todd Kirwan enter.

Spotting Tamzin's body, he stopped in his tracks and gave a low whistle. "That's one hell of a chocolate tart," he said.

Barney started to reprove him when the chimes sounded once more and the police chief, Todd's brother, Jim Kirwan, arrived, accompanied by State Police Detective Lieutenant Horowitz.

Horowitz's glance raked the shop, taking in the body and landing on Lucy. "Did you find the body?" he snapped.

"No. Roger Faircloth found her. . . ."

"He went into shock," said Todd. "The ambulance just left with him."

"I got here a minute or two after Roger," said Lucy.

Horowitz cocked a pale eyebrow. "You're losing your touch," he said.

Lucy had worked with the lieutenant for years but she still never knew if he was joking or serious, whether he liked or disliked her. He never seemed to change; he'd looked gray and tired the day she first met him and that's how he looked today, with his long upper lip, grayish eyes, and sardonic smirk.

"I was supposed to photograph her for an ad," said Lucy. "I set it up yesterday; we agreed to meet at eight-thirty this morning, before the shop opened."

"So what was that other guy, Faircloth, doing here?"

"I think he wanted to buy some chocolate for his wife. He said something like that before he passed out."

Horowitz was writing it all down. The chief, meanwhile, had ordered the other officers to set up crime-scene tape across the sidewalk where a small knot of curious townsfolk had gathered.

"So you came here with your camera . . . ," prompted Horowitz.

"Yeah, I'd just got to the door when Roger ran out, all upset. I thought he was having a heart attack so I brought him inside and yelled for Tamzin to call nine-one-one and that's when I saw her body. I took Roger outside to my car and called from there on my cell."

"Did you know the victim?"

It was the question she'd been dreading. "It's a small town and I work for the newspaper. I know everybody."

Horowitz sensed he was on to something. He lifted his pen, waiting for her to continue.

"My daughter Zoe, the youngest, had an after-school job here for one day." Lucy shrugged. "It didn't work out."

Horowitz wasn't about to let it go. "How come?"

"She's just a kid, she just turned fourteen. She wasn't ready for a job."

Horowitz looked skeptical. "I think there's something you're not telling me."

"I didn't want Zoe working here but Tamzin went behind my back and hired her but didn't bother to get the work permit. . . ."

"And why didn't you want Zoe working here?"

Lucy didn't want to be the one to tell Horowitz about Tamzin's reputation, it was bad enough the woman was dead. "Like I said, I thought she was too young. She should concentrate on her schoolwork."

"Oh, right, and the moon is made of green cheese," said Horowitz.

"Okay, okay. I saw Tamzin in a compromising situation with a neighbor of mine, a man who happens to be married."

Horowitz didn't actually exclaim ah-ha; it was there but unspoken. "Name?"

Lucy sighed. She didn't want to involve Brad and Chris but she knew Horowitz wouldn't give up. "Brad Cashman," she said. "But he wouldn't have anything to do with something like this."

"That's for me to decide," said Horowitz. "Anything else you don't want to tell me?"

"No, but I have some questions I'd like to ask you," said Lucy, as the crime-scene workers began arriving, shouldering her aside.

"No comment," snapped Horowitz. "I may need to talk to you some more, so don't leave town."

"Darn," said Lucy. "You mean I'll have to cancel my Caribbean vacation?"

Horowitz grinned. "If I don't go, you don't go."

Released from questioning, Lucy left the store and headed for her car, only to discover strips of yellow crime-scene tape were fastened to the antenna.

"Uh, what's going on?" she asked the nearest officer, who happened to be Todd Kirwan. "Why can't I drive my car? It's not connected to the crime."

Kirwan looked down at her from his lofty six-feet-plus. "It's just temporary," he said. "There wasn't anything else to attach the tape to."

The sleet was still coming down and Lucy was half soaked and cold. She wanted to get into her car, crank the heat up as high as it would go, and drive home where she would hop into a steaming hot bath. Instead she sighed and reached for her camera, snapping a few photos of the crime-scene techs going into the store. Then she walked on down the street to the *Pennysaver* office.

Phyllis looked up when she entered. "What's going on down the street?" she asked.

Lucy noticed immediately that Ted's desk was empty. "Where's Ted?" she asked.

"He's at some conference or other in Portland, he told me but I don't remember." Phyllis bit her lip, coated in Tangerine Tango. "Might be the Freedom of Information Act, or maybe wind power. He's gonna be gone all day."

"Figures," muttered Lucy. "He's here when you don't want him and he's gone when you need him."

"Why do you need him?" Phyllis and Lucy had long ago come to the conclusion that Ted was mostly a nuisance, except for signing their pitifully small paychecks. "Whatever's going on down there," she tilted her head in the direction of Chanticleer Chocolate, "you can handle it. What is it? A gas leak?"

Lucy plopped herself into her desk chair and swiveled it around to face Phyllis. "Somebody killed Tamzin Graves."

Phyllis's orange mouth got very small and her turquoise-shadowed eyes got very large. "No!"

Lucy nodded and pulled off her hat and gloves. "Yes. I saw the body."

"I can't say I'm sorry," admitted Phyllis. "For one thing, I didn't really know her and for the second thing, well, now I don't have to worry about her stealing Wilf." She tapped her lip with a finger tipped in matching Tangerine Tango nail polish; her diamond wedding set glittered, catching light from the antique gooseneck lamp on her desk. "Come to think of it, I bet a lot of wives and girlfriends had a motive for killing her. Do you think a woman did it?"

Lucy had unzipped her jacket and pulled off her boots; she shoved her feet into the battered boat shoes she kept underneath her desk and shuffled over to the coat tree, where she hung up her parka. The hat and gloves she arranged on top of the cast-iron radiator.

"Maybe," said Lucy, going back for the boots. "She was coated in chocolate." Lucy bent down to set the boots in front of the radiator and shove the toes beneath it.

Behind her she heard a crash. The sudden noise made her heart jump and she whirled around, adrenaline pumping. "What was that?"

"Nothing. I dropped my Rolodex." Phyllis was on her knees, picking up scattered index cards. "What do you mean, coated in chocolate?"

Lucy heard her but her mind was busy adding up this and that and coming to a conclusion she didn't like. "She was naked and coated with chocolate," she said, thinking that was clue number one. "It made me think of Max, the way he was found. The killer was making a statement." That was the second thing she didn't like, because she could only think of one person who had a motive for killing both Tamzin and Max.

"I wonder," mused Phyllis, who was now seated at her desk and putting the cards back on the Rolodex. "How would you even go about coating somebody in chocolate? I mean, I can barely get the stuff to stick to strawberries. Coating an entire body would be a huge project." She paused, whirling the Rolodex. "And messy, too."

"There was no mess," recalled Lucy, thinking that there was only one person in town who knew enough about chocolate to manage such a trick. And that person, the same person who had a motive for killing both Tamzin and Max, was known for her wicked sense of humor.

Chapter Thirteen

Lucy went back to her desk, sat down, and opened a new file. She typed, slowly, recording her recollections of the crime scene. She made no attempt to write sentences, she simply wrote down her recollections as they occurred to her: the cloying scent of chocolate, her frustration with the dispatcher, the detached professionalism of the crime-scene technicians. She felt it was important to make a record while it was all still fresh in her mind and she could remember everything exactly the way it happened. She typed almost automatically, finding herself emotionally detached. It was as if she were seeing it all through a thick glass. It didn't seem like something that had really happened, it was more like a lurid scene from a TV show or a movie.

Oddly enough, she discovered, it was Roger she found most puzzling. Not his original reaction; the unexpected discovery of a body would unsettle anyone. It was later, when he attempted to leave the scene. Why didn't he want to talk to the police? And did he really lose consciousness due to shock, or was it feigned? Why did she think there was something dodgy about Roger?

She was sitting there, hands poised above the keyboard, when the door opened and Corney breezed in, clutching an armful of red-and-white Valentine's banners. "What's going on at Chanticleer Chocolate?" she demanded.

"Tamzin's been murdered," said Lucy.

"Coated in chocolate," added Phyllis, with a prim nod.

Suddenly, the banners clattered to the floor and rolled every which way, followed by a fluttering cascade of brochures. "Oh . . . my . . . oh!" exclaimed Corney, at a loss for words.

"Yeah," said Lucy, stepping carefully over the scattered banners and coming to her side. "Are you okay?" she asked, reaching for a chair and sliding it toward Corney. "Maybe you better sit down."

"Thanks." Corney lowered herself onto the chair and watched while Lucy gathered up the flags, with their big red cupids against a wavy pink-and-white background, and propped them against the reception desk. "I don't know what came over me." She clutched her purse to her chest and turned to Phyllis. "Did you say she was coated in chocolate?"

"That's right." Phyllis couldn't wait to tell the rest. "Naked, too."

Corney's jaw dropped. "How?"

"I have no idea. The crime techs are there, I suppose they'll figure it out," said Lucy, who was on her knees, gathering up the brochures.

"Maybe it was some sort of weird sex thing that went wrong," said Corney. "Like dabbing whipped cream here and there."

"Weird is right," sniffed Phyllis.

"I don't think so," said Lucy, wondering if Corney had a rather interesting sex life. She stood up and set the stack of brochures on the reception counter. "I think the chocolate must have been applied after she was dead. It was all very neat and tidy."

Corney gave her a curious look. "Really," she said.

"Can I get you something? A cup of tea?" asked Lucy. She was in caregiver mode, going through the motions.

"No." Corney shook her head. "I should get going. I have all these *Love Is Best on the Coast* banners and calendars to distribute." She gasped, suddenly grasping the implications of Tamzin's murder. "The weekend! Valentine's Day weekend! All our work and planning! Now it's ruined!"

"Yeah." Phyllis gave a sympathetic nod. "I know I'll never think of chocolate the same way again."

"Don't say that!" protested Corney.

"Why not?" Phyllis shrugged. "Better face facts. Chocolate's not sexy anymore. It's over."

"I'm not so sure," said Lucy, slowly. She still had that odd feeling of distance, as though she were watching herself from a far-off point. "It's certainly sensational. This is going to be all over the news—think of the free publicity. Tamzin's murder is going to attract a lot of interest."

Hearing this, Corney seemed to revive a bit. "Media will come, for sure," she said, brightening.

"And thrill-seekers," said Lucy. "People are ghouls. Trust me, they'll want to see the place where it happened."

"You're right, Lucy." Corney was on her feet, gathering up her flags and brochures. "I've got no time to waste. I better get these delivered right away!" She paused at the door. "Poor Trey! He'll be devastated." She reached for the knob. "I'll give him a call," she said, "but not just yet. Better give him a little time to let it sink in, get over the shock." Then Corney was gone. They could see her through the plate glass window, chatting away on her cell phone as she marched purposefully down the street.

Lucy sat back down at her computer, intending to continue working on her memories of the crime scene, but found the well had gone dry. She couldn't concentrate, she discovered, as her thoughts darted all over the place: Had she remembered to take the chicken she intended to cook for dinner out of the freezer? Thank heavens Zoe hadn't been the one to discover Tamzin's body. Good thing she nipped that problem in the bud. What about Sara? The news was going to be all over town. Would the girls be frightened? Maybe they should all be frightened—was there really a serial killer loose in town? Or did the killings have something to do with Tamzin and Max's relationship? How many lovers had Tamzin really had? Would they be upset? Would it be obvious? Would the male population of Tinker's Cove be wandering aimlessly around town, sniffling and dabbing their tears with handkerchiefs? Was that why Roger was so upset? Was he really in the shop to buy Valentine's chocolates for Helen? And what about dinner? What could she cook, instead, if she hadn't remembered to thaw that chicken?

She was suddenly startled out of her thoughts by Ted's booming voice. "Why didn't you call me?" he bellowed, slamming the door behind him. "A woman is killed and covered in chocolate and you don't think it's news?"

"I thought you were at a conference," said Phyllis. "I wasn't sure I could reach you."

"I have a cell phone," said Ted, glaring at her.

"I didn't want to disturb you," said Phyllis.

"This is news! This is what I do! Disturb me!" Ted was jumping around like Rumpelstiltskin, stamping his feet on the scuffed plank floor and rattling the wooden venetian blinds hanging over the plate glass windows.

"Calm down," said Lucy, in the tone she used for her children. "It's under control. I was on the scene minutes after Roger Faircloth found her body. I'm the one who called nine-one-one."

"Oh," said Ted, momentarily losing steam, then rallying to defend himself. "I didn't hear that part."

"How did you hear about it?" asked Lucy.

"It was all over the conference. People were asking me

about it, since they know I'm from Tinker's Cove." Once again his temper flared. "I felt like an idiot, I was the last to know what was happening in my own town."

"Somebody must've called somebody," mused Lucy. "Darn cell phones. Thanks to Twitter, everybody knows everything the minute it happens." She paused, considering the ramifications of instant news. "We're obsolete, aren't we?"

"Not while I've got breath in my body," declared Ted. "We're going to find an angle, something nobody else has. And we've got five days before deadline to do it."

"Well, I was there," said Lucy. "I actually saw the body. Here, I'll send you the file."

"That's a start," said Ted, pulling out his chair and sitting down at his desk, still wearing his coat and boots. Slowly, he began unwinding his scarf, which he tossed on the chair he kept for visitors, and unbuttoned his coat, shrugging out of it. Little puddles formed around the boots, which remained on his feet. He switched on his computer and opened Lucy's file, leaning forward to read it. When he finished, he leaned back in his chair, shaking his head. "I hope you girls are sorry about all the mean things you said about that poor woman."

Lucy and Phyllis exchanged puzzled glances. Was this a typical male reaction? Was Tamzin now a blameless victim?

"Well," said Phyllis, in a judgmental tone, "it does seem to me that her behavior might have had something to do with her death."

"Blame the victim," said Ted, angrily. "She didn't kill herself, you know."

"I know that," said Phyllis. "But maybe she contributed to it."

"I think you're on the wrong track here," said Lucy, thoughtfully. "Don't forget Max Fraser's murder. What I think we've got here is a single killer who likes to make a statement."

Phyllis took in a sharp breath. "A serial killer."

Ted was rocking in his chair. "A real sicko." His expression brightened. "This is going to be a hell of a story." He drummed his fingers on his desk. "If only I can get somebody official to confirm your theory. . . ."

The wooden blinds rattled again and Lucy looked up to see a big white satellite truck rumbling down the street. "NECN is here," she said. "You're going to have plenty of competition."

"Yeah," said Ted, rising to the challenge. "But we've got a big advantage. We know the lay of the land." He reached for his phone. "Have you called Trey Meacham for a comment yet?" Receiving a no from Lucy, he proceeded to make the call.

Phyllis and Lucy were all ears, listening as he probed for a comment.

"Really sorry to hear the sad news," Ted began. "When did you hear? Oh, so the police have already contacted you? They just left? What did they tell you? Well, I understand. Once again, just want to say how sorry I am."

Scowling, Ted put the phone down rather harder than necessary.

"The police told him not to talk to the media?" ventured Lucy.

"How'd you guess?"

"Par for the course. Did he say anything you can use?"

"He's terribly shocked and Tamzin was a stellar employee who will be greatly missed."

The blinds rattled again; this time it was the WCVB truck from Boston.

Watching it drive by, Ted came to a decision. He was on his feet and putting his jacket back on. "I guess I'll head on over to the police station and see what's going on."

"Sounds like a plan," said Lucy, wondering what her next step should be.

"No sense you hanging around here," said Ted, who kept close tabs on her hours and didn't want to pay her for doing nothing. "Phyllis can handle the listings. I've got your stories on the finance committee and selectmen's meetings. I can call you at home if I have any questions."

Lucy wasn't pleased, she didn't want to miss out on a big story, and it showed in her expression.

"But, Lucy, thanks for everything you did," he added, wrapping the scarf around his neck. "That was good work."

Watching as he hurried out the door, Lucy had the urge to grab the ends of that scarf and strangle him. "You know," she said to Phyllis, as she logged off her computer, "sometimes I understand what drives people to kill."

Phyllis adjusted the harlequin reading glasses that had slipped down her nose. "We might want to, but we don't. It's a big difference."

Driving home and thinking about lunch, Lucy realized she'd only worked four hours, which didn't amount to much money at all. Certainly not enough to compensate her for what she'd been through. She'd found a body, she'd been physically sickened and emotionally ravaged, and how much would she actually clear after taxes? It was enough to make you think about signing on to work nights at the big box megastore that had recently opened out by the interstate—if they'd have her.

Pulling into the driveway, she climbed out of the car and sloshed through the slush, noticing that the paint on the porch trim was peeling, revealing gray patches. Now that she was really looking she noticed the entire house could use a coat of paint. Oh, well, she told herself, as she climbed the steps, if the economy didn't pick up by spring, Bill would have plenty of time to paint. There was a bright side to everything.

Libby certainly thought so, greeting her with ecstatic wiggles and tail wags. Lucy gave her a handful of dog treats and considered her lunch options while she took off her coat and boots. It was definitely a day for comfort food, she decided, scuttling her diet and reaching for the peanut butter and jelly.

After polishing off a huge sandwich and a big glass of milk, she decided she'd better get cracking on the dessert she had promised to make for Sue's contest. Chocolate was obviously out of the question. Just the smell would make her sick, not to mention the look of the stuff. Shiny and brown and fragrant, no, she wasn't going there.

Opening the fridge and standing there, just like the kids did when they were looking for a snack, she noticed a tub of cottage cheese and a couple of bars of cream cheese. Cheesecake! Why not? She had an easy, delicious recipe. And, suddenly inspired, she remembered the blueberries she'd frozen last summer. What if she topped the cheesecake with blueberries, cooked with a little maple syrup for sweetener? Soon she was busy, happily mixing and stirring and remembering sunny summer days when she and the girls had picked the tiny blueberries that grew at the far end of the yard, where the woods began.

Looking out the window now, she saw a dismal view. The yard was filled with gray slush, the sky was gray, the trees were bare of leaves. Even the pointed balsams were black in the dim winter light. But here in her kitchen, the dog was snoozing on her plaid cushion, yipping every now and then as she chased rabbits in her dreams. The refrigerator door was covered with colorful photos of friends and family; many were of little Patrick, her grandson. The curtains were blue-and-white check, her beloved regulator clock was ticking, and the gas hissed as the oven heated. She was warm and busy and all around her was evidence she was loved and appreciated: a colorful pottery pitcher Elizabeth had sent from Florida "just because I knew you'd love it," the wooden bread box Bill had made for her, the KEEP CALM AND CARRY ON tea towel Sue had given her after their trip to England last year.

Suddenly she seemed very fortunate and she thought of

Tamzin, killed and laid out in a gruesome display, objectified and ridiculed. Lucy hadn't liked her, but she didn't deserve that. Nobody did, she thought, stirring an egg into the cheese mixture, not realizing she was crying until a hot tear fell on her hand. And then another and another, as her body was wracked with tears of rage and regret. First Max and now Tamzin, both killed so horribly. It was more than she could stand.

Chapter Fourteen

Saturdays sure weren't what they used to be, thought Lucy, as she loaded the dishwasher with last night's snack dishes and this morning's breakfast crockery. She remembered lazy mornings when she and Bill slept late, then made plans for the rest of the day over a leisurely breakfast. Later, when the kids were little, they used to let them watch Saturday morning cartoons while they lingered in bed until the kids got bored and came in for a midmorning romp. That all ended, however, when the kids became teenagers. Now she and Bill were at the mercy of sports schedules and coaches, AP exam coaching sessions, and part-time jobs. This morning she not only had to make sure Sara got up and was fed and dressed, but she had to drive her and Renee to work because Frankie usually had open houses on Saturdays. Revising her original thought, she added realtors. Like all the parents of teenagers, they had to adjust their schedules to accommodate the demands of others.

Now that Sara had her driver's license, she could drive herself except for the fact that Lucy needed the car later to take Zoe to her volunteer job at the Friends of Animals shelter. And there was always the possibility that Ted would call with a last-minute assignment, which often happened when a big story like Tamzin's murder was unfolding. It would be nice if they could afford a third car for Sara, she thought, straightening up and stretching her back, but that wasn't possible these days. Simply adding Sara as a driver had pushed their insurance premium so high that it was straining the family budget.

Glancing at the clock, Lucy realized they were running late. "Sara!" she yelled up the steep back stairway that led from the kitchen to the upstairs bedrooms. "I'm going out to start the car!"

Sara yelled back. "I'm almost ready!"

Lucy checked the thermometer that hung on the porch post and learned it was ten degrees outside. A mite nippy, she thought, but at least the sun was shining. Yesterday's slush had frozen solid overnight, so she put on her boots, reminding herself to watch her step and to expect icy patches on the road. She'd have to drive slowly and leave plenty of time for braking.

"Sara!" she yelled once more, pulling her knit beret over her ears and pulling on her gloves. "We've got to go!"

There was a huge clatter as Sara crashed down the stairs and landed in the kitchen, where she paused to pull her hair back into a ponytail. "No sense fussing with my hair since I have to wear those ugly shower cap things."

"Dress warm, it's freezing," Lucy advised, picking up the carefully wrapped cheesecake she intended to drop off at the contest and going out to warm up the car. Moments later, Sara popped out of the house, coat and scarf flapping.

"Brrrrr," she said, hopping into the car beside Lucy. "You weren't kidding."

"The sun's out, I think it will warm up," said Lucy, switching on the radio. "Might even get up to twenty."

"I think Elizabeth had the right idea," said Sara. "While we're freezing up here, she's working on her tan in Florida."

Lucy was backing out, humming along to a Beatles tune. "I don't think she gets too much time to lie around the pool—she's not a guest, she's the hired help."

"She gets plenty of time off," said Sara, in a sour tone. "And she doesn't have to wear a shower cap when she's on the job!"

Lucy chuckled, picturing her oldest daughter in the tailored Cavendish uniform with an embroidered "C" on the blazer pocket, as she made the turn into Prudence Path and pulled up at the La Chance house. She gave the horn a little toot and looked over at her son Toby's house, hoping to catch a glimpse of Patrick. "I thought Toby and Patrick might be playing outside but I guess it's too cold," she said, disappointed.

"I bet they're watching cartoons," said Sara. "I used to love Saturday mornings."

Lucy smiled, remembering how she and Bill took advantage of the kids' passion for cartoons to indulge in a little passionate activity of their own.

The song had changed and the Rolling Stones were singing "Gimme Shelter" when Renee ran out of her house and hopped into the back seat.

"Wow, it's cold," she complained, fastening the seat belt.

"I don't know why you girls refuse to zip your jackets," said Lucy. "They put zips and buttons on them for a reason."

Sara rolled her eyes. "We don't want to look like dorks."

"So you look like Popsicles instead," retorted Lucy, as the song ended and commercials began to play. Lucy was driving slowly, wondering who could possibly be interested in an adjustable mortgage after the recent financial crisis and how exactly did Dr. Myron Bush reverse baldness, at the same time keeping an eye out for that tricky black ice. She'd made it to the end of Red Top Road when the news came on.

Police have made an arrest in the Chanticleer Chocolate murder case. Dora Fraser, 38, of Tinker's Cove, was arrested late yesterday, according to state police. Fraser, who works at a rival chocolate shop, is accused of strangling Tamzin Graves and then coating her nude body with chocolate in what police have termed "a bizarre ritual slaying." In other news. . . .

The newscaster continued his report but nobody in the car was listening. They were sitting, silent and stunned, trying to absorb what they'd heard.

"Do we go to work?" asked Sara.

"I can't believe it," said Renee.

"I was afraid of this," said Lucy.

Sara's head snapped around. "You were?"

"Do you think she did it?" asked Renee, leaning through the gap between the two front seats.

"No. Of course not. I wouldn't let you work for a murderer, now would I?" said Lucy, cautiously making the turn onto Main Street. "It's because of her wicked sense of humor, the way she's always joking."

"The police must have more than that," said Sara. "You can't be arrested for making jokes."

"You're right," said Lucy, wondering what evidence the cops had found that incriminated Dora. She also wondered how long it would be before they charged her with murdering Max, too.

"Mom, do you really think the store will be open?" asked Sara.

"Only one way to find out," said Lucy, hoping she'd learn more about Dora's arrest at the shop.

When they pulled up in front of the familiar storefront, with its red-and-white-striped awning and curtained windows, the OPEN sign was prominently displayed on the door. Lucy led the way, marching right in, followed by the girls, who hung back reluctantly.

"Come on in! I won't bite!" said Flora, in her usual bossy tone. She looked the same as always, with her short salt-and-pepper hair and pink poly pantsuit. Her eyes didn't have their usual sparkle, however, and she looked pale and drawn.

"We heard the news about Dora," said Lucy. "The girls weren't sure. . . ."

"It's business as usual," said Flora. "I'm manning the counter and you girls can go on back and start filling the mail orders."

When they stood in place, she made a little shooing motion with her hands. "Go on. I'm not paying you to stand around gaping."

The girls shuffled off through the curtained doorway and Lucy approached the counter, adopting a sympathetic expression. "I can't believe the police suspect Dora," she began.

"It's nonsense," said Flora.

"I know Dora likes a good joke but she'd never kill anybody," prompted Lucy.

"Of course not."

Flora was known for being close-mouthed, but Lucy was hoping distress would make her a bit more talkative. So far this was tough going. "Did they say what sort of evidence they've got against her?"

"Nope."

"They just came and arrested her?"

"Yup."

"When was that?"

"Last night, around eight o'clock. They came to the house." Flora paused. "Good thing she hadn't put on her pajamas like she usually does to watch TV."

Lucy could just imagine the scene. Police rushing into the cozy old Victorian, guns drawn, upsetting potted plants and knocking over tables. "That must have been terrible."

"They were very polite, I'll say that for them."

Lucy realized she'd let her imagination run away with her. "Even so, it must have been very upsetting. How are Lily and Fern?"

"They're not crying into their milk, that's for sure. They're checking out lawyers; we want to get the best for our Dora."

"Of course," said Lucy, struck with the woman's brisk efficiency and determination. The police probably hadn't gotten Dora into the cruiser before Flora was organizing the family and assigning jobs. "Let me know if I can do anything."

Flora gave her a look. "Lucy Stone, I've known you forever and I like you fine, but I know you work for the paper so don't be thinking I'm going to tell you anything I don't want to see in print."

Lucy felt as if she'd been slapped across the face, but she had to admit the woman had a point. "I understand," she said, turning to go. At the door, she paused and turned. "The offer to help still stands, and I won't print anything you tell me is off the record."

Flora narrowed her eyes and crossed her arms across her chest. "Hmph," she said.

Typical Mainer, thought Lucy, leaving the shop.

The dessert contest was taking place at the Community Church so that's where Lucy went next. The parking lot was a slick sheet of glass so she walked slowly, keeping her weight forward and praying she wouldn't slip and drop the cake. Sue was inside the basement fellowship hall, instructing her husband, Sid, where to set up tables.

"After the judging we'll be selling portions of the desserts, as well as coffee and tea," she was saying, when she spotted Lucy. "Hi, Lucy. You're the first." Sue waved a hand at the large, empty room with a stage at one end and a kitchen at the other, separated by a serving counter. "We're not ready yet. You can put your entry on the kitchen counter. What did you make? Can I have a peek?" she asked, crossing the room.

Sid, a dark-haired man with a mustache, was lifting one of the big folding tables off the wheeled rack where they were stored. "Hi, Lucy," he called. "How's the family?"

"Everybody's fine," she replied, setting the cake on the counter. "It's cheesecake," she told Sue. "With blueberries."

Sue frowned, picking at the foil with one finger. "Cheese-cake?"

"Yeah. What's wrong with cheesecake?" Lucy asked, defensively.

"Somehow blueberry cheesecake doesn't say Valentine's Day to me. It says summer, maybe at a clambake."

"Too bad," snapped Lucy. "Cheesecake's what I felt like making. . . ."

"Yeah, I can see how you didn't want to mess with chocolate, after finding Tamzin's body," admitted Sue. "I'm just telling you because I don't think the judges are going to love cheesecake."

"I like cheesecake just fine," said Sid, flipping one of the tables over and unfolding its legs. His tight T-shirt revealed his muscular build; he worked as a closet installer and stayed fit, carrying heavy prebuilt components upstairs and down and wrestling them into place.

"Did you hear the news?" asked Lucy. "Dora's been arrested for Tamzin's murder."

Sue put the cheesecake down. "Are you sure?"

"Yeah. It was just on the news."

Sue was silent for a moment, absorbing this news. "Well, if you ask me, she did us all a favor. That woman was nothing but trouble."

"Meow," said Sid, grabbing another table.

"If it wasn't for the heavy lifting—and his spider-killing ability—I wouldn't keep him around," said Sue. "What about Max? Do they think she killed him, too?"

"The radio didn't say, but I wouldn't be surprised." Lucy leaned her back against the counter and pulled off her gloves. "The killings were similar, bizarre, and Dora does have an odd sense of humor."

"I can't say I miss Max, myself, and I bet I'm not the only one," volunteered Sid. "He'd beg you to help with a job and then if he paid you at all, he paid late."

"I dunno," said Lucy, thoughtfully. "From what I've

heard, he was pretty popular, in spite of his money problems. And if there's one person in town I'd expect to really miss Max, it would be Dora. There was something going on between them, even if they were divorced."

"And Lily," added Sue. "He loved his daughter, and she loved him. You've got to give him that." She gave Lucy a look. "Why don't you take your coat off and help us out here?"

Lucy looked at the vast empty room and the waiting racks of tables and chairs; just looking made her back ache. "Uh, thanks for the irresistible invitation but I've got a bunch of errands to do."

"Be like that," muttered Sue.

Lucy ignored her. "How's Chris? Are she and Brad okay?" Lucy was feeling guilty about mentioning Brad to the police.

"I think they'll be just fine, now that Tamzin's out of the picture."

"I wonder," mused Lucy. "Did the cops question Chris? She had a motive, after all."

"They did," said Sue. "But she had an alibi. We were together Thursday night, working late, writing up student reports."

"How late did you work? She could've gone to the shop afterwards and knocked off Tamzin."

"No way. Brad took the SUV that day because of the weather, so she didn't have a car. He dropped her off in the morning and I drove her home that night." She paused, clearly remembering something. "In fact," she said slowly, "the lights were on at Chanticleer when we drove by and I remember thinking it was awfully late for anybody to be in the store, especially since they don't actually make the chocolates there. I even looked at the clock in the car. It was a little past nine." She shuddered. "Do you think that's when the murder took place? Isn't that creepy?"

"Yeah," said Lucy, wondering if the police had established a time of death for Tamzin's murder.

Sue's eyes widened. "Oh my gosh, I saw. . . ." She immediately turned toward Sid. "Don't forget the mike, okay?"

He nodded and continued arranging chairs.

"What did you see?" asked Lucy. "Or should I say, who?"

Sue was looking down at the floor. "Dora. I saw Dora," she whispered. "She was right in front of Chanticleer."

"Are you sure? What was she doing?"

"Nothing, really." Sue was hugging herself. "For all I know, she was just walking down the street. But I did say something to Chris about it. Like, how come she wasn't walking on the other side of the street, some stupid crack like that."

"And Chris probably told the cops."

Sue nodded. "I feel sick about it."

"It's not your fault." Lucy squeezed her lips together. "I'm sure the police have other evidence."

"I don't think Dora is a murderer," said Sue, "but we did see her near the scene of the crime."

"Poor Dora. This explains a lot—it seems she had means, motive, and opportunity," said Lucy, realizing a little seed of doubt was sprouting in her mind. "Well, I gotta run. See you later, Sid," she called, heading for the door.

Outside, in the car, she thought about what Sue had said. It certainly didn't look good for Dora. She was probably the only person who had the skill to paint a body with chocolate, and witnesses had seen her at the shop the night of the murder. But as Sue had said, they didn't actually make the chocolates at the Tinker's Cove shop. The copper bowl and the marble-topped table and the other candy-making equipment were just for show. If Dora was the killer, she would have had to bring the chocolate that was used to paint Tamzin's body. How did she do it? And why did she bother? And what happened to Tamzin's clothes? When you thought about it, there were a lot of unanswered questions about the murder.

When she parked in front of the dry cleaners she noticed Trey's Range Rover was also parked on the street; maybe she'd get a chance to ask some of those questions. She hurried inside, hoping to catch him before he left, but there was no need. He was waiting patiently at the counter for the clerk to find his clothes.

"Hi," said Lucy, standing next to him and digging in her purse for the little green receipt. "I'm awfully sorry about Tamzin."

"Thanks, Lucy," he said, in a solemn voice.

"Three-three-oh-four-five, here it is," proclaimed the clerk, a gray-haired woman in her fifties, coming around the wall of hanging, plastic-bagged clothes. "Misplaced," she said by way of explanation, setting Trey's boxed shirts on the counter. "I didn't realize you wanted them boxed." She made it sound like an unreasonable request. "That'll be eight dollars and forty cents."

Trey handed over a ten dollar bill and turned to Lucy. "I'm still in shock, if you want to know the truth. Poor Tamzin. She didn't deserve this."

"Shocking," said the clerk, counting out his change. "I told my boss, there's no way I'm staying here after dark. I'm closing the shop at three-thirty. Folks'll just have to come early."

"It's hardly the sort of thing you'd expect in a little town like this," said Trey.

"It's outrageous! We've had two murders, right here in town." The woman's chin shook with indignation as she shut the cash drawer. "You can't be too careful these days."

"That's for sure," said Lucy, handing her the green slip of paper and turning to Trey. "I know they arrested Dora Fraser—did the police tell you why they suspect her?"

"Pretty obvious, don't you think?" replied Trey. "Tamzin

was dating her ex, and then there's the fact her business was suffering due to Chanticleer's success. . . ."

"Those don't seem very compelling to me," said Lucy, as the clerk hung Bill's suit on the rack. "You're not really in competition with Fern's Famous. You attract an entirely different clientele." She paused, remembering how he'd touted the truffles as an affordable luxury, a status symbol. "I mean, you're selling a lot more than chocolate."

Hearing this, Trey's expression hardened, but Lucy didn't give it much thought. She was digging in her purse for her wallet.

"If you ask me, anybody who kills somebody else must have a screw loose," the clerk was saying. "I won't rest easy until she's locked up for good. That'll be eight seventy-five."

Lucy was thoughtful, handing over a twenty. "I suppose the police think she killed Max, too."

"I wouldn't be surprised," sniffed the clerk.

"Dora's sure made a lot of trouble for me. I don't know when the cops are going to let me reopen," said Trey. "And I have to find a new store manager."

Lucy couldn't believe it. Was the man out of his mind? A woman was dead and he was complaining about losing business. "What about Tamzin's family? Have you been in touch? What are the funeral plans?"

For a moment, Trey seemed at a loss. "I haven't really . . . I mean, I don't actually know. I'll have to check with HR." He pulled out his iPhone and began texting. "It's early days yet, of course, but the company will help any way we can."

Lucy didn't know what she expected. Sure, there had been rumors about Trey and Tamzin having a relationship, but that didn't mean it was true. Maybe he really was nothing more than her employer. She took Bill's suit off the rack where it was hanging and turned to go, discovering that Trey was holding the door for her.

"Hey!" called the clerk. "Don't forget your change!"

"Oh, right," said Lucy, embarrassed at her mistake. She went back to the counter and Trey continued on his way; she heard him slam the door of the Range Rover before speeding down the street.

The clerk handed Lucy her money. "You know, I thought he and that woman were real close. He was at the shop a lot, and sometimes they left together, when she closed."

"Really?" Lucy was tucking the cash into her wallet.

"Yeah. I have a clear view from here," said the clerk, nodding toward the plate glass window.

Lucy turned and discovered it was true. The WCVB truck was parked directly opposite, blocking her view of the drugstore, and a reporter was being filmed standing on the sidewalk in front of Chanticleer Chocolate.

"They seemed awfully affectionate," continued the clerk. "She'd be holding his arm and he'd open the car door for her, like a real gentleman. I even saw them kiss a couple of times."

"Not to speak ill of the dead, but I heard Tamzin was a very affectionate girl," said Lucy.

"That sort always gets in trouble," said the clerk, clucking her tongue.

Leaving the store with Bill's suit, Lucy wondered about Trey and Tamzin's relationship. They had seemed quite friendly when she'd interviewed them, but she hadn't really thought anything serious was going on between them. Now it seemed she may have underestimated their relationship. Or maybe the clerk had overestimated it. Two good-looking people, single, working together. It wasn't like they were kids or anything, they were a man and a woman and these things happened. It didn't necessarily mean they were truly intimate and involved in each other's lives.

And Tamzin wasn't shy about making her availability known. She might even have been using her sexuality to advance professionally. She certainly wouldn't be the first woman who'd slept her way to the top. And, to his credit, Trey had seemed shaken by her death.

Maybe he was still in shock, she thought, carefully hanging Bill's clean suit inside the car. A sudden loss could make your mind play tricks, make you forget details. She remembered how she'd struggled to remember appointments and keep the family on track after her mother died. Come to think of it, she was still struggling, but now it was just due to an overpacked schedule.

Lucy slid behind the wheel and consulted her list. Next stop: the post office. She had a box of books and clothing that Elizabeth had asked her to send to her in Florida.

Lucy was thoughtful, wondering if some small choice might have changed the direction of Tamzin's life and saved her from her terrible fate. If her mother, perhaps, had insisted she dress more modestly, or if her father had encouraged her to study harder and become a professional. What if she'd become a doctor instead of a chocolate shop manager? What if she'd taken another path and become a famous actress? Could she have changed her destiny? It was impossible to know; she didn't really know anything about Tamzin's background. She didn't know if she'd slipped down the social ladder, or if working at Chanticleer Chocolate was a step up; she had no idea what obstacles Tamzin had faced.

Lucy was wondering what information Tamzin's obituary might provide when she rounded the corner by the Quik-Stop and saw an ambulance with its lights flashing parked by the air machine. Slowing for a better look, she saw her friend Barney sitting on the raised concrete slab that protected the gas pumps, with his head in his hands. What was going on? She pulled off the road and parked, then hurried to his side. As she approached she saw he was crying; tears were rolling down his crumpled bulldog face.

"Barney! What's the matter?"

He looked up, blinked, and brushed at his eyes with his gloved hands.

"It's Eddie," he said.

Lucy looked around and spotted Marge's car, which Eddie had been borrowing, parked by the Dumpster, apparently undamaged. A sudden wail of the siren indicated the ambulance was leaving; she watched as it departed, lights flashing. A police cruiser remained, and Officer Todd Kirwan approached with a sympathetic expression.

"They're taking him to the hospital," he said, leaning down and touching Barney's shoulder. "They think he's going to make it."

Barney nodded, but made no effort to move.

"What happened?" asked Lucy.

Todd turned to her, speaking softly. "It's his kid. Just back from Afghanistan. He OD'd."

"Eddie? On drugs?"

Todd nodded. "Heroin. He was shooting up, we found the needle."

Lucy's eyes widened. Now Frankie's suspicions about Eddie and Lily didn't seem so ridiculous. But what a terrible waste. She knew drugs were a problem everywhere, Tinker's Cove included. She'd seen the number of arrests rising, she'd written a number of obituaries for young people who didn't seem to have much going on in their lives but had loved animals, had lots of friends, and died unexpectedly of unexplained causes. She'd had her suspicions but somehow she'd managed to insulate herself. She'd been in denial, thinking drugs were something that happened to other people. She had never been personally affected, until now.

"It's everywhere," said Todd.

"Come on, Barney," she said, taking his huge hands in hers. "I'll give you a ride to the hospital."

He looked up at her. "I've got to get Marge." He shook his head. "How am I gonna tell her?"

"We'll go together," she said. "Where is she? Home?"

Barney seemed to be struggling to remember, trying to

see through his fogged emotions. "She was taking a cake to that dessert contest."

Good heavens, thought Lucy, thinking of the now-crowded church hall, filled with happy, busy volunteers getting ready for the contest. Poor Marge! She'd just gotten her son back, safe and sound, from the war and now she might lose him. It was too cruel.

"Come on," she said, tugging at Barney's hands. Slowly he rose to his feet.

"You go back to the station, file the report," he told Todd.

The young officer nodded. "I hope, uh, I hope Eddie's okay."

"Yeah," said Barney, straightening his shoulders. He turned to Lucy. "Let's go."

It was only a short drive to the Community Church, where Marge was just coming out of the door, an empty pie basket slung over her arm. She was wearing a flattering knit hat and scarf that matched her green eyes and smiled as they pulled up, recognizing Lucy's car. When she noticed Barney in the passenger seat, her brow furrowed in concern.

Lucy braked and Barney got out, slowly, and lumbered clumsily across the sidewalk to his wife's side. He lowered his head, speaking to her, and Lucy saw Marge's face crumple. Then, taking Barney's arm, she hurried to get in the car.

"Let's go, Lucy," she said, taking charge. "As fast as you can."

In a matter of minutes Lucy reached the small "cottage" hospital that served the town's basic medical needs; the ambulance was parked outside the ER entrance. Lucy dropped Marge and Barney off at the door and parked the car. When she joined them in the waiting room, they were talking to Doc Ryder.

"He was lucky," the doctor was saying. "A few minutes later and, well, this story would have a different ending."

"He's going to be okay?" asked Lucy.

"Well, let's just say his chances are good at the moment,"

said the doctor. He took Lucy's elbow and guided her to a corner of the waiting room, apart from Marge and Barney. "We've got a real problem on our hands," he said, shaking his head. "This is the third overdose this week."

Lucy's jaw dropped. "Third?" She knew that Tinker's Cove was a small town, with a population of less than five thousand. Three overdoses in one week constituted an epidemic.

"It's out of control," said Doc Ryder. "We've always had a problem with drugs here in town but I've never seen it this bad. The stuff is pouring in from somewhere."

Lucy knew that illegal drugs had long been available to those who wanted them, but it wasn't terribly obvious. There were plenty of secluded areas in town where deals could be conducted; plenty of places where a user could get a fix unobserved. Police occasionally made a bust and sometimes the illicit traffic erupted in violence, as it had last year when Rick Juergens and Slash Milley were murdered. But most people in town had little or no contact with drugs except those they bought with a prescription.

"People need to know what's going on," said Doc Ryder, peering at her over his half-moon glasses.

"I'll see what I can do," said Lucy. "I'll check with Ted and give you a call next week."

"You know how to reach me," said the doctor, giving her a nod before going back to Marge and Barney. They made a tight little circle and Lucy felt it was time for her to go; she wasn't needed here. She suddenly felt an overwhelming need to make sure the girls were okay, to reassure herself that they were safe and sound and straight.

Chapter Fifteen

Lucy was leaving the hospital when she saw Max's big old silver pickup truck speed into the icy parking lot, taking the turn too fast. She held her breath, watching as the driver zoomed into a vacant spot and braked hard. The door opened and Lily jumped out, still wearing her red-and-white-striped apron with the FERN'S FAMOUS FUDGE logo.

Lucy waited inside the doorway and grabbed the girl's arm as she hurried in.

"Eddie's going to be okay," she said. "You can slow down."

Lily whirled around. "Let me go," she said, pulling her arm away. The girl was a nervous wreck, twitching and shivering.

"Take it easy," said Lucy, in mother mode. "Everything's going to be okay."

Even as she spoke she realized how ridiculous her words were. Things weren't okay for Lily, far from it. Her father had been murdered, her mother was in jail, and her boyfriend had just overdosed.

"Where's Eddie?"

"In the ER," said Lucy, pointing down the hall.

Lily started to run off and Lucy called after her. "His mom and dad are already there."

Lily stopped in her tracks and suddenly hunched over, as if in pain. "They are?"

Concerned, Lucy approached her. "Are you okay?"

"Yeah, yeah, I'm fine." Lily was nodding like a bobble-head doll. "What are they doing here?"

"They're his parents, they love him." Lily was clearly in some distress, trembling from head to toe. "Do you want me to take you to them?"

"No!" she shouted. "No, no, no!"

"Okay," said Lucy, who was completely confused. "Let me buy you a cup of tea," she suggested. "It will warm you up and help you relax."

"Tea." Lily said the word slowly, as if she'd never heard of it.

"Yes. Tea. We'll have a cup of tea in the cafeteria and you can pull yourself together and then you can see Eddie." Lucy had to admit her motives were mixed. She wanted to help Lily, who was obviously in trouble, but she also hoped to ask her a few questions about her mother.

Lily was staring at her warily, as if she sensed a trap. "Who are you, anyway?" she demanded.

"I'm Sara's mom. You know, Sara works at the shop with you."

"Right." Lily bit her lip. "Mom's gonna be mad. I better get back to the shop."

Lucy's jaw dropped. Dora was in jail, awaiting arraignment for murder, and had bigger things to worry about. But before she could say a word, Lily disappeared back through the door. Lucy started after her, but by the time she got outside, Lily was in the truck and speeding out of the parking lot.

Shaking her head, Lucy headed for her own car, pulling the list of errands out of her pocket. Post office. Right. She checked her watch and discovered she just had time to make it before it closed at noon. But as she drove along the familiar roads, she struggled to figure out what was going on with Lily. The poor girl was clearly an emotional mess, but who could blame her? Considering everything that had happened to her, it was no wonder she was struggling. Thank goodness she had her grandmother and great-grandmother, Flora and Fern, to take care of her.

Leaving the post office, Lucy noticed the lights were on in the *Pennysaver* office and decided on impulse to stop in. As she suspected, Ted was there, hunched over his desk.

"Hi," she said. "What are you doing here on a Saturday? You should be getting ready for the ball tonight."

Ted laughed. "I won't need much time, but Pam is making a day of it. She's getting the works at the Salt Aire Spa."

"Lucky her." Lucy felt a twinge of jealousy but resolutely ignored it. "Did you hear about Dora?" she asked.

"That's why I'm here. The cops had a press conference this morning. Horowitz was unusually chatty."

"Really?" Lucy had taken off her hat and gloves and was loosening her scarf. "What did he say?"

Ted stopped typing and looked at her, twisting his mouth into a scowl. "I don't know. Maybe I'm hallucinating or something, but I got the feeling something was going on. It's all circumstantial, there were no witnesses. . . ."

"You'd hardly expect a witness."

"It's more than that. They didn't have a weapon, no concrete evidence. Just a theory."

"That she was a woman spurned?" Lucy's voice was dramatic.

Ted nodded. "Yeah. She killed Tamzin out of jealousy, and they're reopening the investigation into Max's death, figuring to charge her with that, too."

Lucy sat down, mashing her hat, gloves, and scarf together in her lap. "I expected as much." She sighed. "What about Tamzin? Any family?" She paused. "How old was she, anyway?"

Ted laughed. "You women are all alike—that's what Pam wanted to know, too."

"And?" prompted Lucy.

"Forty-six."

"I knew it!" crowed Lucy. "I knew she was no spring chicken!"

"She was well preserved, you've got to give her that," said Ted. "And there's a husband. . . ."

"A husband?"

"Well, an ex. Career army, in Afghanistan. They stayed in touch, there were letters and photos in her apartment."

"I had no idea." Lucy suddenly felt ashamed of her uncharitable opinions of Tamzin.

Ted shrugged. "Nobody did."

When Lucy returned to the church basement later that afternoon for the judging, she found the air was heavy with the scent of sugar and chocolate. The tables Sid had arranged under Sue's instructions were now covered with white cloths and packed with desserts of all kinds, arranged by category. There was a table with nothing but pies and fruit tarts, another with cookies and cupcakes, and several others devoted to all sorts of chocolate treats. Smaller tables with red balloon centerpieces and chairs were scattered around the room, ready for the customers who would buy the treats after the judging, and then consume them along with tea and coffee. Just looking at all the goodies was enough to cause a diabetic coma, but nobody was interested in checking them out. Instead, everybody was talking about Dora's arrest. That was fine with Lucy, who was relieved that news of Eddie Culpepper's overdose hadn't reached the grapevine yet.

"She was always a prankster," recalled Franny Small, her face unnaturally smooth and tight thanks to a recent face-lift. Franny owned a wildly successful jewelry company and could afford anything she wanted; her Lexus was parked outside. "I remember she got in trouble when she was in high school—something about an effigy of the principal."

"It wasn't an effigy," offered Luanne Roth, who had recently contacted Lucy about publicizing the twentieth reunion of her class at Tinker's Cove High School. "We were in the same class, you know, and there was quite a fuss. It was a sign. A bed sheet they hung from the roof that said something bad about Mr. Wilkerson; he was the principal then. I can't remember exactly what it said but it was insulting."

"They let her graduate but they kicked her out of the National Honor Society," said Lydia Volpe. Now retired, Lydia had taught kindergarten to all four of Lucy's kids. "It was quite a scandal at the time. The police prosecuted and she was on probation and had to perform community service and couldn't go to college right away. They postponed her admission until her probation was completed." She paused, her huge brown eyes momentarily unfocused as she dredged her memory. "I don't know if she ever did go, now that I think about it."

"I think she went right to work in the shop," said Luanne.

"She got pregnant," said Franny, with a little sniff.

"That's right," agreed Lydia. "We had quite a little flurry of teen pregnancies around then."

"Well, I know Dora has a unique sense of humor, but getting in trouble for a high school stunt is one thing and murder is another," said Lucy.

"A double murder," offered Dot Kirwan, joining the knot of gossipers. They all looked at her expectantly, knowing she was the police chief's mother and most likely had the latest information. "They're most likely charging her with Max's murder, too."

"Now that I don't believe," said Luanne. "They've been on and off ever since junior high school. I mean, even though they're divorced, I still think of them as a couple. I think everybody who was in school with them does. They were always fighting and making up. The girls would side with Dora and the boys with Max; it was high drama in the cafeteria. A real soap opera, a new installment every day."

"Well, if it was a soap opera, this was the final episode," said Dot. "They've got witnesses who saw Dora on the ice, arguing with Max, the evening before he was killed."

If that was true it was bad news for Dora, thought Lucy, who remembered Barney telling her that Dora said the last time she saw Max was at the house, when he came to help her with her car. Did she lie, or were the witnesses mistaken? Was it Dora, or someone else?

"Max had been seeing a lot of Tamzin," said Luanne, who worked at the Irish pub by the harbor. "They came in for drinks quite a few times."

"A classic love triangle with a tragic ending," said Lydia, welling up with tears. "I remember Max and Dora, they were in some of my first classes. I had such high hopes for them—especially Dora. She was such a bright little thing."

Lucy gave her a hug. "Well, she's innocent until proven guilty."

"That's right," said Dot, with a smart nod. "If you ask me, I don't think Dora would hurt a fly."

"You know she makes those dirty chocolates," said Franny, pursing her lips with disapproval. "She sells them on the Internet."

"I've seen the chocolates—they're not offensive," said Lucy. "My own daughter works there, packing them, and I certainly wouldn't let her handle anything I didn't approve of."

"Dora's always marched to her own drummer," said Dot, "but that doesn't make her a murderer."

"Is the case against her strong?" asked Lucy. "They must have evidence. . . ."

"Circumstantial," said Dot. "And she's a smart girl. Last I heard, she's refusing to talk to investigators—you know most perpetrators are only too happy to incriminate themselves. My Jim says if it wasn't for the fact that the bad guys aren't too smart and love to talk, they'd hardly convict anybody."

"I saw Flora this morning," said Lucy. "She said they're looking for a lawyer."

"Smart," said Dot, with an approving nod. "That's the other thing in Dora's favor. She's got a lot of support from her family."

"That's for sure," agreed Lydia. "Flora was always there for every conference, every school event. And Fern, too. And then when Lily came along, all three of them would show up."

Sue was tapping on a glass with a spoon, so conversation ceased as everyone focused on the panel of judges gathered beside her. Sue then made the introductions, but Lucy wasn't listening because she recognized them all: Roger Wilcox, chairman of the board of selectmen; Hildy Schultz, who owned a bakery; and Fred Farnsworth, executive chef at the Queen Victoria Inn. They were nodding and smiling and saying nice things about all the entries, but Lucy's mind was miles away, thinking of Dora, sitting in the county jail. As a reporter Lucy had been there numerous times, covering various stories. It was one of her least favorite assignments; she hated the moment the door clanged shut behind her, even though she knew she could leave whenever she wanted. Nevertheless, she always sympathized with the inmates, who couldn't.

Of course, Dora was tough. She was probably better able to withstand the indignities of imprisonment than most. And, as Dot had mentioned, she had plenty of support from her family. If anybody could successfully conceal a saw in a cake and smuggle it in to the jail, it would be Flora, she thought, as a little smile flitted across her lips.

Thinking about that tight family of women, who all lived and worked together, she wondered if perhaps Dora was protecting somebody else. Not Fern, she was too old to manage such elaborate murders. She could probably bash somebody on the head or shoot them, but staging the bodies the way the murderer had was a big job and Lucy doubted she had the strength. Flora, however, was a big woman with a lot of determination. And she'd been handling heavy sacks of sugar and other ingredients her entire life. Flora was also judgmental, and used to getting her way, according to Miss Tilley, and had forced Max to marry Dora when she got pregnant. Perhaps Flora didn't approve of the divorce and would rather see Dora as a widow than a divorcée with an ex who kept hanging around. Lucy was wondering if Flora wasn't a likelier suspect for the murders than her daughter when Dot elbowed her in the ribs.

Lucy was recalling her strange encounter with Lily and wondering if she wasn't an even likelier suspect—after all, Flora had bragged about Lily's skill at hunting and dressing deer—when Lydia poked her in the ribs.

"Lucy! They called your name!"

Lucy blinked. "What?"

"Once again," Sue was saying into the microphone, "our first-prize winner is Lucy Stone for her Maple-Blueberry Cheesecake!"

Stunned, Lucy made her way through the crowd toward the judges. When she was in place behind the table, Sue continued, reading from a card.

"The judges all agreed that this cheesecake showed an imaginative and original use of local ingredients. It was refreshing and light and surprisingly low in calories, the perfect end to a coastal dinner."

"And I might add, absolutely delicious," said Fred Farnsworth, leaning in to the microphone.

Everybody laughed and applauded, except for Sue, who looked rather annoyed as she handed Lucy an envelope.

"The grand prize is a dinner for two at Chantarelle. Congratulations and bon appétit, Lucy."

"Thank you," said Lucy, still not quite comprehending her triumph. "This is a real surprise."

"I'll say," muttered Sue, under her breath, as there was another round of applause. She held up her hand for silence. "And now, I encourage everyone to sample the delicious entries—the five dollar per plate cost goes to support the Hat and Mitten Fund, which provides winter clothing for local children. Tea and coffee are also available."

Putting the mike down, Sue thanked the judges while Lucy tucked the envelope into her handbag. Then she asked Sue if she could help with the serving as people started to mob the tables where the desserts were displayed.

"It looks like they could use some help with the pies," said Sue, scanning the crowd, which was thickest around the table displaying that category of entries. Cupcakes were also popular, as were the cookies, but Lucy noticed that few people had gathered at the table with brownies and chocolate cakes.

"Chocolate's gotten some bad press lately," said Lucy.

"Absolutely," declared Sue. "If that poor woman hadn't been coated with chocolate, I'm sure my Better-Than-Sex Brownies would have won. The entries were blind, you know, so they could have picked mine. But right now it's hard to think about chocolate without picturing Tamzin's body and it takes your appetite away."

"I'm sure that's it," said Lucy, before heading over to the pie table.

"People are sick of chocolate," added Sue, in a parting shot.

When Lucy picked up Zoe at the Friends of Animals shelter, she discovered the news about Eddie was finally out.

"Mom! Did you hear? Eddie Culpepper overdosed at the Quik-Stop. He's in the hospital."

"I know." Lucy scowled, waiting for Zoe to fasten her seat belt. "How did you hear about it?"

"I got a text from Sara."

Hearing the click, Lucy shifted into drive. "How did she know?"

Zoe gave her a patronizing look. "From Lily, of course. At the shop. She and Eddie have been dating."

Lucy braked at the road. "You know about that?"

"Yeah." Zoe's tone implied that everybody knew this, everybody except her stupid mother.

"Does Lily use drugs?" Lucy kept her tone offhand, as she turned onto Oak Street.

"No way. She's anti-drug, anti-alcohol."

Lucy was beginning to think this was a bit of protective camouflage. Now that she thought about it, it seemed that drugs might explain Lily's odd behavior at the hospital. "How do you know all this stuff?"

Zoe shrugged. "I dunno. I hear stuff. Sara and her friends talk." She paused. "I guess they think I'm deaf or something." She laughed. "I'm the little sister. It's like I don't exist."

Lucy thought she had a point. "What else have you heard?"

Zoe's tone was serious. "Plenty, but you'll have to pay."

In spite of everything that had happened, in spite of Dora's arrest and Eddie's overdose, Lucy found herself chuckling as she turned into the driveway. But her emotions were ragged and she was on the verge of tears when she entered the warm and homey kitchen. Determined to distract herself, she got busy making supper for the girls.

Lucy saved the news of her prize until they were dressing, hoping to present it to Bill as a sweetener before she dragged him off to the Hearts on Fire Ball. She knew he was less than enthusiastic about wearing a tie, much less an entire suit, and he hadn't danced in years. Probably not since their own wedding reception, come to think of it.

"Guess what?" she said, leaning into the mirror and brushing mascara onto the back of her upper lashes, the way she'd read about in a magazine at the dentist's office. It seemed impossibly difficult and required a great deal of concentration, but whoever wrote the beauty column insisted it was important to first coat the lashes, then to use the tiny brush to lift them.

"What?" growled Bill, straining to button the collar on his starched shirt.

"I won the dessert contest and the prize is dinner for two at Chantarelle."

Bill wasn't impressed. "What's Chantarelle?"

"It's fabulous, everybody raves about it."

"It's not here in town," he said, warily. "Is it in Portland?"

"Actually, it's in Portsmouth."

The collar was flipped up and Bill was looping a tie around his neck. "New Hampshire?" he demanded, his tone verging on outrage.

Lucy sensed her plan was not working. "That's where Portsmouth is, last time I checked," she said.

"No need to get all sarcastic," he said, scowling at his reflection in the full-length mirror behind the bedroom door and undoing the knot.

"Let me do that," said Lucy, screwing the cap on the mascara and setting it on her dresser.

"That's a heck of a drive for dinner," he said, surrendering the tie to her.

"The food is supposed to be well worth the trip," said Lucy, sliding the knot up to his chin. "There. You look very nice."

She was only wearing her bra and a half-slip and Bill

slipped his hands around her waist. "You should go like this," he said, pulling her close.

"Whoa, boy," she cautioned, stepping away from him. "We're running late."

He sighed and reached for the hanger with his pants. "The portions in those fancy places are always so small," he said.

"That's so you can savor the flavors," said Lucy, applying lipstick. "After a few bites you don't really notice the taste anymore." She pressed her lips together and examined the effect, then added a slick coat of gloss. "At least that's the theory."

Bill was fastening his belt. "And you can't relax, there's always some waiter fussing around, trying to grab your plate."

"Well, for your information, Sue was very put out when I won the prize. I think she wanted it." Lucy was fastening the waistband of her good black skirt, pleased to discover it fit easily. The diet was working.

"Maybe you should give the certificate to her, then," said Bill, adjusting his jacket on his shoulders.

Lucy was pulling her lace blouse over her head, so Bill didn't hear her reaction, which was just as well. When she emerged, her hair was tousled and her eyes were blazing.

"You look amazing," said Bill. His expression was a combination of surprise and awe, as if he were seeing her anew and liked what he saw.

Lucy was about to ask if she didn't look too fat but bit her tongue. Moments like this didn't happen very often, especially when you'd been married for more than twenty-five years and had four kids. "So do you," she said, smiling and smoothing his lapels.

She wasn't just saying it, she realized, he really did look great. He still had plenty of hair, mostly still brown but gray at the temples, and he wore it a bit long, so a lock fell over his brow. His beard also had a touch of gray, but it made him look distinguished. He was slim and stood tall and straight in the suit, which still fit even though he'd had it for years.

"Thanks for doing this," she said. "I know you're not really keen on dress-up occasions."

"It's good to break out of a rut, once in a while," he said, offering her his arm. "Shall we go?"

Chapter Sixteen

The VFW was decorated to the hilt for the ball, but it was still, unmistakably, the VFW. All the red crepe paper streamers and heart-shaped balloons in the world couldn't disguise the scuffed wood floors and the walls that needed a fresh coat of paint, scarred as they were by all the notices that had been taped up and removed through the years. There was also that VFW smell, a combination of stale cigarette smoke, booze, and pine-scented cleaning fluid.

The organizers had done the best they could—the round tables were covered with floor-length white cloths, topped with smaller red ones, and a single red rose in a chunky milk glass vase served as a centerpiece on each table. The colored cloths set off the VFW's basic white china to advantage, and a red cloth napkin was tucked in each industrial-strength wine goblet.

When Lucy and Bill entered, the DJ was playing classic Beatles tunes and a disco ball was throwing spots of light around in the darkened room. Lucy had the déjà vu that she'd been in the same place before and realized she was thinking of her high school prom.

Smiling at the recollection of her awkward self, dressed in four-inch heels and the ridiculous slinky black dress she'd insisted on wearing despite her mother's objections, she was pleased when Bill took her hand and led her to the table where their friends were sitting.

There was a flurry of greetings as air kisses and hand-shakes were exchanged, and soon Lucy was seated at the table while Bill went to get drinks from the bar. It was odd to see everyone dressed to the nines, since dress in Tinker's Cove tended to be extremely casual, especially in winter when everyone clomped around in duck boots and bulky down coats and jackets.

Sue was especially gorgeous, dressed in the lace cami-sole she'd bought last spring in London and a pair of skin-tight black satin pants. Her bare arms were golden, evidence she'd spent some time at the tanning salon. Lucy was tempted to warn her about the dangers of tanning, but bit her tongue. Sue would just laugh at her. It was definitely annoy-ing that Sue managed to look fabulous, always had tons of energy, and was never sick despite a diet that consisted of little but black coffee and alcohol, with the occasional indul-gent gourmet dinner.

"You look great," said Lucy, remembering the day they'd gone shopping together in London. "That camisole was a terrific buy."

"I barely had time to get dressed," said Sue. "The dessert contest didn't wrap up until almost six and the clean-up committee didn't show. Poor Sid got pressed into duty when he came to pick me up."

Sid ran his finger around his neck, trying to loosen his collar. It was too small and his ruddy cheeks made him look as if he were about to burst and pop a button. "It was a big success, though," he said, beaming proudly at Sue. "Tell them how much it made for the Hat and Mitten Fund."

Sue leaned forward. "Believe it or not, over a thousand dollars."

"That's a lot of cookies," said Pam, who'd recently given up Nice 'n Easy and her ponytail for a neat, silvery cut that hugged her head. Her day at the spa had refreshed and rejuvenated her; her complexion was glowing, and she looked gorgeous in an electric blue sari she'd probably picked up in a vintage clothing shop. It was the sort of thing I would feel ridiculous wearing, thought Lucy, but it looked great on Pam.

"It's a lot of hats and mittens," said her husband, Lucy's boss, Ted. He was seated beside Pam, nervously stroking his tie, as if he needed to check that it was still in place and hadn't slithered off somewhere.

"That fund does so much good—you should be really proud of yourself, Sue," said Rachel. "You made the contest a big success."

Rachel had gone to the beauty salon where they'd clipped and curled her long black hair, which she usually wore pinned up in a loose knot. Sensible as always, she was wearing a burgundy cashmere sweater dotted with sparkly beads that was warm as well as flattering, and a long black skirt.

Her husband, Bob, was the only one of the men who seemed comfortable in his suit. He was a lawyer and often wore a jacket and tie. "I've got a scoop for the *Pennysaver*," he said, with a nod to Ted. "I've been hired to defend Dora Fraser."

"I knew they were looking for a lawyer. Flora said she wanted the best and I guess she got it," said Lucy. "What do you think her chances are?"

"I really haven't had time to look at the case," he said, as Bill returned with a beer for himself and a glass of white wine for Lucy. "They called me this morning. I'll know more next week, after I talk to her."

Ted fingered his napkin and Lucy figured he was adding up column inches in his head, working out whether the story was worth the expense of adding a page. "Lucy, you can follow up on that, right?"

"Sure." Lucy didn't want to think about work or murder or Eddie's drug overdose; she wanted to enjoy herself. She took a sip of her wine and reached for Bill's hand.

"I went to the hospital today to visit Joyce Rennie—her husband is in the play and they just had a baby girl—and I ran into Barney and Marge," said Rachel. "They said Eddie was in the ER, but then they hurried off. I hope it's nothing serious."

Darn it, thought Lucy. Here we go. "It was drugs," she said. "He OD'd. . . ."

Everyone fell silent for a moment.

"Poor Marge and Barney," said Rachel.

"Is he going to be okay?" asked Pam.

"Doc Ryder said he'd make it, but he almost died," said Lucy.

"PTSD, post-traumatic stress disorder," murmured Rachel. "It's not unusual after what these kids go through over there."

"That's true, as far as it goes," said Lucy. "But Doc Ryder told me there's been a recent epidemic of overdoses. He wants us to do a story about it."

"We already ran that interview with the governor's wife," said Ted, in a defensive tone. "I'd like to give it a rest, maybe revisit the issue in a month or so."

Lucy struggled to hold her temper. "Sooner would be better than later," she argued. "We could save lives." She felt a nudge on her ankle and realized Bill was signaling her that she'd said enough on this particular topic.

"Drugs are a fact of life these days," said Ted. "They're everywhere. It's hardly news."

"Sadly, that's true," offered Rachel, with a sad smile.

Recognizing defeat, Lucy glanced around the room. Chris and Brad Cashman were seated at a nearby table, along with Frankie and the Faircloths, as well as some people she didn't recognize. It seemed a lively group, however, and there were frequent bursts of laughter. She looked around for

Corney but didn't see her; maybe she was busy with some last-minute details.

Lucy had only had a sip or two of wine before the high school–student waiters began serving the fruit cup appetizers that preceded the VFW's famous rib roast dinner.

"Canned fruit!" exclaimed Sue, picking out the tiny bit of maraschino cherry and popping it in her mouth. "I haven't had fruit salad since I was a kid." She cautiously speared a bit of pear and tasted it. "Now I know why I haven't had it—it's gruesome."

"I kinda like it," said Sid.

"Me, too," said Lucy, digging in as the DJ started playing a Four Tops tune. "It takes me back—in fact, this whole thing is like a trip down memory lane."

"I wonder if that's what Corney had in mind," said Rachel. "Somehow I think she was going for something more glamorous."

Lucy glanced around the room, but once again didn't see any sign of Corney. "There was a committee, wasn't there?"

"The activities committee is pretty square," admitted Pam, who was an active Chamber member and served on the publicity committee.

"Old guard," agreed Ted, cocking his head at a table of older men and their tightly permed wives. "Insurance, insurance, real estate, and banking."

They were laughing at his joke when the waiters took away the chunky glass compotes that had held the fruit salad and brought plates loaded with huge slabs of beef, mountains of mashed potatoes topped with craters of gravy, and haystacks of grayish French-cut green beans amandine.

Sue's eyes widened in horror as her plate was set in front of her. "This explains a lot," she said, pushing it away and reaching for her wine.

"What do you mean?" asked Pam, who was busy cutting her meat.

"The fat epidemic!" explained Sue. "Huge portions, tons

of salt, it's no wonder Americans look the way they do if this is how they eat."

"Oh, you're right," said Rachel. "You know I prefer organic food and Bob and I mostly eat grains and veggies, but once in a while," she said, taking a bite of beef and savoring it, "I just love a big piece of juicy red meat."

"Amen," said Bob.

By the time the dessert plates—cherry pie à la mode—and coffee cups were removed, Lucy was feeling guilty about slipping off her diet and was uncomfortably aware of her control-top panty hose. The DJ was playing a slow dance so she begged Bill to take a turn on the dance floor. "I've absolutely got to move or I'll burst," she said, grabbing his hand.

He got up reluctantly, earning sympathetic looks from the other guys, and followed Lucy onto the dance floor where a handful of couples were moving to the music, mostly swaying back and forth. Lucy had endured cotillion dance classes when she was in seventh grade, letting repulsive pimply boys in button-down shirts and sports jackets that smelled of cleaning fluid put their arms around her so they could learn the waltz and fox-trot, and she found it frustrating that nobody, including Bill, seemed to know how to dance anymore.

Still, it was nice to slip her right hand into his and feel his other arm around her waist, and Bobby Darrin sure knew how to melt a girl's heart. She tried to keep her toes out of his way as they moved around the patch of parquet that served as a dance floor, trusting him to keep her from colliding with the other dancers.

The Faircloths, she noticed, danced beautifully together and made a lovely picture as they glided smoothly, perfectly in step with each other. Frankie and her partner, fellow real estate agent Bud Olsen, were having a good time, laughing as they struggled to keep time to the music and each other. When the inevitable happened, and they crashed into Lucy and Bill, there were giggles and apologies all round. Frankie just had time to tell Lucy the Faircloths had finally made an offer on a Shore Road house before Bud swept her away in a dramatic twirl.

"Did you hear?" she asked Bill. "Frankie sold a house to the Faircloths."

Bill was interested; real estate had been at a virtual standstill for months. "Where?" he asked.

"I think she said Shore Road."

"The only place for sale out there is the old McIntyre mansion," said Bill. "It's listed for a million and a quarter."

"I wonder what they offered," said Lucy.

"Check with Frankie," urged Bill, as the song ended. "Maybe they'll be looking for a contractor."

Lucy noticed that Frankie was making her way across the room in the direction of the ladies' room, so she followed and eventually joined her in front of the mirrored counter, and began to refresh her lipstick.

"So the Faircloths finally found a house they liked," said Lucy.

"Finally is the word," said Frankie, with a huge sigh. "I must have showed them fifty or more houses. I swear we covered the coast from Kittery to Camden several times over. Then they decided to make an offer on the very first place I showed them."

"The McIntyre mansion?"

Frankie nodded, leaning forward and running her finger along her eyebrow. "It needs work, but they said they're excited about remodeling."

"How much did they offer?" asked Lucy.

"Just under a million," said Frankie, screwing up her lips. "It's a low offer, but the place definitely needs updating. The wiring and plumbing are last century, the kitchen is a nightmare. I don't know if the McIntyre kids—well, they're all in their forties, not really kids—it's a question of how much they want the cash. If they don't need the money, they could decide to wait for the market to improve."

"It must be hard for them to let it go," said Lucy. "They've spent every summer there since they were kids."

"They told me they don't get to use it much, now that their folks are gone. One is in Turkey, works for some bank; a couple of others are out on the West Coast. It's a big responsibility and they can't keep it up. It needs a roof; just keeping the lawn mowed is a big expense."

Lucy nodded. It was a familiar story. "Well, I hope the sale goes through. It would be a nice commission for you—and maybe a job for Bill."

"And I could use it," said Frankie, dropping her lipstick into her purse and clicking it shut.

Lucy was following her out the door when her cell phone rang, so she sat on the droopy, slipcovered sofa to take the call, afraid it was one of the kids. That whole awful episode with Eddie was stuck in her mind. No matter how well you thought you knew your kids, how much you trusted them, there were always surprises and experience had taught her that trouble always came when you were least expecting it. Wasn't that always the way? When she and Bill finally got a rare night out together, some emergency invariably seemed to come up. But when she glanced at the phone, she saw it was Corney who was calling.

"Hi!" she said, wondering what had kept Corney from the ball. "Where are you? I thought you'd be dancing the night away."

"I wish," whispered Corney. "I think I'm being held against my will."

"What do you mean?"

"Trey suggested we have a little, you know, before going to the ball and I foolishly agreed. I read in a magazine that sex gives you a terrific glow, much better than makeup."

"I read that, too," said Lucy.

"It didn't exactly work out."

"What do you mean?"

Corney's voice got even lower. "He suggested handcuffs, said they'd be fun."

Lucy resisted the temptation to laugh. "And?"

"Well, here I am, stark naked and handcuffed to my bed. Thank heavens the cell phone was on the night stand. I could just manage to reach it, kind of shoved it along with my nose until I could grab it."

"Where's Trey?"

"That's why I'm calling. He left me here. I need you to come and free me."

"He left?"

"Yes."

Lucy didn't understand. "He handcuffed you and then left? Left the house?"

"Yes! I begged him to unlock them but he just laughed and walked out."

"What a bastard!"

"Yeah." There was a pause. "So will you come?"

"What he did is against the law," said Lucy, primly. "This is a matter for the police."

"Are you crazy? I'm naked. This is Tinker's Cove! Do you think I want the Kirwan kids and Barney Culpepper seeing me like this?"

"You have a point," said Lucy. "But what can I do? I don't have the keys."

"They're right here. They're on the dresser. I can't reach them."

"Okay," said Lucy, finally accepting the fact that she was going to have to leave the party to help Corney. "I'll be there in ten minutes."

"I'll be here," said Corney. "I'm sure not going anywhere."

Chapter Seventeen

When Lucy returned to the ball she found Bill standing with a group of friends near the bar. They were all holding glasses of beer and were engaged in a loud, play-by-play discussion of the Super Bowl. Lucy didn't want to interrupt them, they were all in high spirits with plenty of laughing and backslapping and she didn't want to be a ball-and-chain sort of wife. Instead she caught Bill's eye and held up her car keys, then tapped her watch. She hoped he'd take her sign language to mean she was leaving the party for a few minutes.

He didn't. Looking puzzled, he left the group and crossed the room. "What's going on?"

"I have to leave for a few minutes . . . ," she began.

"Why? Is one of the kids in trouble?"

"No, no," she hurried to assure him. "It's Corney." She paused, trying to come up with a reason why Corney needed her. "It's her car. It won't start and she needs a ride."

"Want me to come? I've got jumper cables, maybe I can get it started."

What was it with men? she wondered. She'd been after Bill for weeks to replace the toilet seat in the powder room. She'd even bought a new seat and tried to do the job herself but wasn't strong enough to loosen the bolts that held the broken one in place. Somehow he wasn't interested in a little job that would take him two minutes, but now when she didn't want his help he was suddenly Dudley Do-Right.

"Don't be silly," she said. "You're having a good time with your buddies and I'll be back in no time."

"Are you sure?" he asked. "I don't mind going. It's cold and you're not really dressed for it."

Lucy realized he had a point. Unused to walking in heels, she'd had to hang on to his arm just to cross the icy driveway. She hadn't wanted to mess up her hair by wearing a hat and her good black coat wasn't nearly as warm as her parka.

Lucy was about to give up and confess the truth when Sid, who had loosened his collar and stuffed his tie into his jacket pocket with one end dangling out, joined them and punched Bill in the arm. "Whassup, buddy?" he asked.

"Lucy needs me. . . ."

"No, I don't," said Lucy, interrupting him with a smile. "I can handle this."

"Well, that's good because the Bruins game is on the TV in the bar and Montreal's got two players in the penalty box."

Bill was clearly torn. "Go on," she said. "I'll be back before those Canadiens are back on the ice."

"Okay," he said, as Sid clapped an arm around his shoulder and dragged him off to join the crowd of men gathered in front of the TV.

Buttoning her coat as she stepped outside, Lucy had second thoughts about her mission. The temperature had dropped while they were inside, and a stiff breeze had blown up. The cold air hit her like a slap in the face and she hurried to pull on her gloves. Her ears were already burning from the cold and she covered them with her hands as she slipped and slid across the icy parking lot. She almost fell when she reached out to open the car door but saved herself by grabbing the roof.

Finally in place behind the steering wheel, she realized the car wasn't any warmer than the parking lot. At least she was out of the wind, she told herself, as she started the engine and cranked the heat up as high as it would go.

The roads were deserted as she drove along under the star-filled sky. There was no moon but the stars were very bright. Orion was hanging so low she felt as if she could reach out and touch the archer's belt; the Big Dipper pointed to the North Star, just as it had in the days when escaping Southern slaves followed it to freedom in the North. In fact, a number of houses in town were said to have been stops on the Underground Railroad that led to Canada.

Corney had recently moved into a brand-new house on Shore Road and Lucy remembered how she'd proudly showed off all the modern advances—gas fireplaces that turned on with the touch of a remote, jacks in every room for phones, TVs and computers, a dream kitchen with granite countertops and energy-saving stainless steel appliances, even a heated toilet seat.

Lucy wasn't jealous; she loved her antique home with all its quirks. But at this moment, driving through the dark and silent streets, she wouldn't mind a heated car seat. She was shivering in her short silky skirt and lace blouse—even under her coat they felt cold against her skin. Why hadn't she dressed like Rachel, in a long skirt and sweater? She suspected Rachel had worn warm boots under that long skirt, too. Which reminded her, she kept an old pair of boots in the car for emergencies, along with a blanket.

Warm air was finally beginning to blow from the vents when she turned onto Shore Road and approached Corney's house, which sat on a double lot overlooking the ocean. It was a gorgeous spot in summer, when you could sit on the porch and watch the sailboats tacking back and forth, but winter was a different story. Tonight, the ocean was angry and she could hear the waves rhythmically pounding the rocks below. Lucy was wondering if Corney regretted her choice of location when she noticed that Trey's Range Rover was parked in the driveway.

What did this mean? she wondered, as she braked and came to a stop in front of the house. All the windows were dark but Lucy knew Corney had expensive, custom-built window coverings that blocked the light. Inside, every light could be on and you'd never know it from the outside if the shades were drawn.

Lucy sat there a minute, wondering what to do. Corney had said Trey was gone, but if he had left, he was back. Or maybe he'd just left the bedroom and was lurking inside. Perhaps he'd even gone back to the bedroom and picked up wherever he'd left off with Corney. Lucy was tempted to leave; she certainly didn't want to interrupt the pair in a romantic moment.

Maybe romantic wasn't exactly the word, she thought, considering the handcuffs, and maybe Trey was a kinky guy who got off by abusing women. Sometimes that sort of thing went too far. Corney had called for help, she couldn't drive away without making sure everything was okay.

She couldn't just walk up and ring the bell—what should she do? Time was passing, pretty soon Bill would start to worry. She had to do something and do it fast, she decided, turning into the driveway opposite Corney's. Nobody was there this time of year; the Whittleseys were summer people.

Bracing for the shock of cold air, she opened the door and went around to the back of the car, where she opened the hatch and found her emergency stash. She draped the blanket over her head and wrapped it around her shoulders and shoved her feet into the boots; then she clomped across the street feeling like a Muslim woman in a chador. Except that she doubted any devout Muslim woman would be out alone at night trying to peep into her neighbor's windows.

Reaching Corney's porch, Lucy looked for a gap in the blinds or curtains, without success. That meant she'd have to walk around the house, on the lawn, where the snow wasn't shoveled. She stepped off the porch, expecting to sink into deep snow, but found instead that a crust had formed that supported her, though it occasionally broke through. Even so, her feet went down only a few inches when that happened, so she soon reached the rear porch, where a patch of light on the snow revealed an uncovered window. She hurried across and peered inside, discovering the kitchen.

It was empty, and so was the adjoining dining area and family room. Lucy stood there, noticing that nothing was out of place. The counters were bare, the farmhouse sink was empty, only one pot, a large cast-iron frying pan, was sitting on the stove. There was no sign of a struggle, no evidence that anything was wrong.

There was also no sign that anything was right. If only she could catch a glimpse of Corney, alive and well. Opening a bottle of wine, perhaps, or settling down on the couch to watch TV. Snuggling up beside Trey, even.

The silence was beginning to worry her. She decided she had to find out what was going on inside the house, even if it meant discovering Corney and Trey in an embarrassing situation. Corney had called her for help and hadn't canceled the request, she reminded herself, reaching for the doorknob. She had a responsibility to make sure her friend was safe.

To her surprise, the door opened, and she stepped inside. She'd been there many times and knew the layout. A formal dining room was just beyond the kitchen and a central hallway led to the living room and study, which were separated by another hall that led to the guest bath and the master suite beyond. There was no sign that anyone was in the house besides her; it was absolutely quiet. The windows were shut tight against the cold; you couldn't even hear the roar of the ocean waves.

The warm air inside the house was making her nose run so she reached for a paper towel from the roll on a decorative black wirework holder. She was just blowing her nose, as quietly as possible, when she heard a piercing scream.

She stopped, frozen in place as adrenaline surged through her body, ready to fight or flee. Fleeing definitely seemed the best option but she couldn't leave Corney. She remained in place, trying to decide if the scream was one of pain or pleasure, fear or delight. Unsure what to do, she considered calling for help. But Corney had specifically said she didn't want the police. Too embarrassing, she had said.

You couldn't die of embarrassment, thought Lucy, only too aware that a double murderer was still on the loose. Before she could change her mind, she dialed 9-1-1 and told the dispatcher there was an intruder at Corney Clarke's on Shore Road.

No sooner had the dispatcher said she'd send a unit right over than Lucy regretted making the call. She decided the best thing would be to go outside and explain the situation. It would be awkward, but she knew all the officers on the force and they knew her. They'd probably just think it was a big joke and everyone would have a good laugh. If they insisted on checking out the house, well, the flashing lights and radio noise would give Corney and Trey time to make themselves decent. And if Corney was angry with her, well, darn it, she shouldn't have called her in the first place. She was supposed to be dancing the night away, not standing in somebody else's kitchen, listening to the hum of the refrigerator and waiting for the cops.

She was about to go outside when another scream ripped through the nighttime silence.

This time Lucy was sure. That was a scream of pure terror. She looked around for a weapon, anything, but Corney's counters were bare. She yanked a drawer open, but all she found were rolls of wrap. Another drawer held silverware.

Where were the knives? Her eyes fell on the stove where that hefty black cast-iron frying pan was sitting on a burner. Better than a knife, she decided, grabbing it. She could use it as a shield, too.

Holding the pan in front of her with two hands, she started down the darkened hall, toward the bedroom. As she proceeded she heard muffled sounds, moans and whines that could have come from a cat. She reached the door and paused, listening, trying to figure out what was happening on the other side. She reached for the knob, then decided it was too risky to go into a situation blind, and withdrew. What if it was a home invasion like the recent one in nearby Gilead, and Trey was a captive, too? Those guys, two strung-out drug addicts, had been armed with a gun and a machete. She was simply not prepared to face something like that. She'd be better off going back outside, where she could try to peek through a bedroom window.

Hurrying back down the hall to the kitchen, she stepped outside onto the porch. The cold hit her like a hammer and she drew the blanket more tightly around herself. Clutching the frying pan to her chest, she stepped off the porch into knee-deep snow. Scrambling awkwardly, as quickly as she could in the snow that clung to her boots, she headed for the one window where she saw a crack of light. Her teeth were chattering and she was shivering as she peered inside the bedroom, all aglow from the pink lightbulbs Corney insisted were most flattering to her skin.

The gap in the curtains was small and Lucy didn't see much skin, only Corney's bare pink legs, only one leg really. Trey Meacham was kneeling, fully dressed, between her legs and it looked as if she was trying to kick him.

Just then, Lucy was caught in a bright light and a male voice ordered, "Police! Drop it and raise your hands over your head."

Lucy whirled around, squinting against the powerful

beam of light and trying to decide who was holding the flashlight. "He's—he's killing her!" she yelled, pointing at the window.

"I'm armed. Drop the frying pan and raise your arms over your head."

"Okay, okay," said Lucy, complying. "I made the call. I'm not the intruder. Corney called me. She's in trouble."

"Walk slowly." The flashlight beam indicated the direction he wanted her to take, around the side of the house to the front yard. "Keep your hands above your head."

"For Pete's sake!" declared Lucy, frustrated beyond belief. "I'm Lucy Stone. I'm not a peeping Tom. There's a murder going on inside . . . at least I think it's a murder."

"What's going on here?" Lucy recognized Todd Kirwan's voice, coming from behind whoever was holding the flashlight.

"What's going on is this guy thinks I'm a peeping Tom and meanwhile Trey Meacham is attacking Corney inside the house."

"Uh, sorry, Lucy. This is Will Martin, he's new to the force, he's filling in while Barney's on leave," said Todd, striding past him and stepping onto the porch, where he banged loudly on the door with his flashlight. "POLICE! OPEN UP!"

Noticing that young Officer Martin had joined Todd on the porch, Lucy decided discretion was definitely the best part of valor. She sure didn't want to face Trey and Corney if she'd misunderstood the nature of their encounter. Picking up the frying pan, she placed it on the porch and then slipped away, as quietly as she could.

She'd reached the corner of the house when the door opened and she heard Trey asking, "What's the trouble, Officer?" His voice was calm and cool, polite.

She ran, as fast as she could, to her car.

Chapter Eighteen

The car had cooled down while Lucy had tried to figure out how to help Corney, but she didn't notice. She was burning with embarrassment and exertion—fleeing the scene through the snow had taken a lot of energy. Now she was trying to catch her breath as she fumbled with the keys and started the car. It took a great deal of restraint not to floor the gas pedal, but she knew it would be foolish to speed on the icy roads, and she sure didn't want to attract attention by peeling off down the street at high speed.

As she drove along the dark, empty roads she tried to figure out what to do next. The clock in the car said it was already nearly ten. The ball was probably in full swing and she knew she ought to go back, although she was hardly in the mood. How was she going to join her friends in the festivities when her mind was across town, worrying about Corney? They would be joking and laughing and probably drinking a bit too much and she'd be wondering what was happening on Shore Road.

She replayed the scene she'd glimpsed through the curtains, trying to figure out what was going on. If it was sex, it wasn't like any sort of sex she'd ever been involved in, though she was pretty sure her experience in this department was rather limited. But if it wasn't sex, but an attempted murder, why would Trey want to harm Corney? He might be a bit kinky but he hardly seemed like some psycho who got off by killing women. Could he have killed Tamzin? That murder had some sexual overtones, the way the killer stripped the victim and covered her with chocolate. But what about Max? His death didn't fit that mold at all. He was a guy, for one thing, and emphatically heterosexual. The police thought Dora was the killer, and maybe they were right, which meant that if Trey was a killer, then there were two murderers operating in Tinker's Cove. Considering the town's small population, that seemed a statistical impossibility. Although Lucy knew that lightning sometimes did strike twice, she couldn't believe that was the case here.

She believed Dora was innocent, so maybe Trey was the real killer, but that also seemed a stretch. He was successful and admired—what would he possibly have to gain by killing Max? And if he was the murderer, why would he have risked discovery by attempting to kill Corney? She admitted to herself that she might not like Trey very much, but that didn't mean he was a murderer.

Reaching the VFW, where the lights were all ablaze and the thumping beat of rock music could be heard even in the parking lot, Lucy resolutely put thoughts of murder in the back of her mind. A handful of smokers were shivering on the porch as Lucy entered; inside she sniffed a heady mix of perspiration, perfume, and booze. The DJ was playing "Y.M.C.A." at top volume and a few serious party animals on the dance floor, including Pam and Sue, who were dancing together, were waving their arms in the shapes of the letters.

Bill was sitting at the table with Rachel and Bob, swirling his half-full glass of beer and staring at the dwindling foamy head. She slipped into the empty seat next to him and he snapped to attention. "Where were you?" he asked, his voice thick.

"I told you. Corney had car trouble."

"Right." He looked around. "Where is she?"

"In the end she didn't feel well and decided to stay home."

"That's a shame," said Rachel. "She worked so hard to organize this shindig and now she can't enjoy her success."

Bob, clearly a bit tipsy, raised his glass. "To Corney!"

Rachel shook her head. "I can see I'm going to be driving the car home tonight."

Bill nodded and leaned toward Lucy, putting his hand on her knee. "Speaking of which, I'm ready to go anytime you are."

Lucy found she was disappointed. The DJ was playing a new song, "Heard It Through the Grapevine," and Lucy was itching to dance. "Oh, come on, let's just dance a couple of songs."

"You know I feel like an idiot on the dance floor," said Bill, draining his glass. "Another round, Bob?"

"Sure," said Bob, getting a look from Rachel.

"All these guys want to do is drink," she said. "I'll dance with you, Lucy."

Lucy grinned and hopped up. "When we first got here I was reminded of my high school prom, but now that the girls are all dancing together it's more like middle school."

"Yeah," agreed Rachel, as they joined the twisting and writhing dancers. "Except in middle school the guys were interested enough to stand on the sidelines and watch the girls dance."

"Now they don't even watch," said Lucy, staking out some dance floor territory next to Pam and Sue.

"They watch . . . sports," said Sue, cocking her head toward the bar where a crowd of men had gathered to stare at the basketball game on the TV.

"They're missing out on a lot of fun," declared Pam, as

the song ended. "Let's do the Macarena," she yelled to the DJ. "And the Chicken Dance!"

Rachel caught Lucy's eye. "You know, I think I better get Bob home or he'll have a heck of a hangover tomorrow. And he's got that case. . . ."

"Right," said Lucy, her thoughts turning back to Corney's predicament. "I should get home, too."

Pam and Sue were already crossing their arms and slapping their hips, keeping time to the music, so Lucy wiggled her fingers in a little wave and followed Rachel back to their table. When she got there, she realized her phone was ringing. She picked up her purse and drew it out, heading for the quiet of the ladies' room. It was Corney, again.

"Are you all right?" asked Lucy.

"I'm scared." She paused. "And confused."

"What happened?"

"I'm not sure. That's why I'm scared. What if he comes back?"

"You've got an alarm system, don't you?"

"Yeah," said Corney. "He could disable it, couldn't he? I've seen it on TV. A snip of the wire, they open the window. . . ."

"Lock all the windows, and the doors, too. Anyway, he's not going to come back. Not after the cops came."

"I told you not to call the cops," hissed Corney. "Talk about embarrassing—and they weren't any good at all. Trey wrapped them around his little finger. He got all chummy with Todd Kirwan, told him it was just sex play and Todd, sweet lad that he is, just wanted to get away as fast as he could. That young one, on the other hand, was sure fascinated with my predicament. Couldn't take his eyes off me while Trey was unlocking the handcuffs. He did that first— then gave me a sheet so I could cover myself, the bastard."

"I'm sorry," said Lucy. "But I couldn't see through the door and I was worried it was a home invasion. That's why I called the cops. I was scared, too," admitted Lucy. She dropped her voice as a couple of women entered the ladies' room. "Do you think he really wanted to hurt you?"

"I honestly don't know. I'm so confused. He had his hands on my neck, but I think that's supposed to make everything more intense or something. A lot of men like it rough, remember what those girls said about Tiger?"

Lucy did. It had been quite a revelation. "Trey's got a big ego," ventured Lucy. "Maybe that's something these Type A guys need."

"Well, I'm done with him, that's for sure. I don't care how successful he is, I don't need to be treated like that."

"Absolutely," agreed Lucy. "How did it start? I mean, weren't you all dressed up for the ball?"

"Yeah. I was dressed to the nines. I spent the entire day getting ready. Manicure, pedicure, hair, facial, the works. I had a new dress, Valentine red, fabulous shoes. And he was in a tux when he arrived, gave me a box of truffles. The big one. The *grande*. I offered him a drink, I had a bottle of champagne on ice. We were sitting in the living room, in front of the fire. It was lovely. We chatted, light stuff, you know. I was in a great mood, I felt flirty, you know?" She paused. "Maybe I went too far."

"I don't think you should blame yourself. I don't think you had control of the situation," said Lucy.

"I did in the beginning," said Corney. "I invited him in, I had the champagne ready."

"When did it change? Did he drink a lot of the champagne?"

"No. He hardly had any."

Another dead end, thought Lucy. "What were you talking about?"

"I think I said I was going to Mexico in a week or two. I asked if he was going to get away someplace sunny this winter."

"That sounds innocent enough."

"I know. It's not like it was personal or anything. Just small talk, cocktail party chatter."

"Maybe he couldn't get away himself this year," said Lucy. "The economy is still pretty bad, a lot of people are cutting corners."

Corney's tone was thoughtful. "I don't think that was it. It was more about me, something I said. I just had this feeling the atmosphere had changed."

"What did you say?"

"I think I said I was looking forward to drinking *sangria* and using my high school Spanish!"

"And what happened then?"

"He put down his glass and stood in front of me and put his hand under my chin and sort of pulled me up and kissed me and said there was no hurry about getting to the party."

Lucy shook her head. "Speaking Spanish is a turn-on for a lot of men. Bill loves to see those Almodovar movies just to hear Penelope Cruz do that lispy thing."

"I do have a Castilian accent," said Corney. "Maybe I said *thangria* instead of *sangria*."

"That's probably it," said Lucy, realizing she'd been talking too long and Bill was still at the bar. "I've gotta go. Take a sleeping pill and I'll see you in the morning."

"Thanks, Lucy. You've been a pal."

Chapter Nineteen

Lucy took the wheel for the drive home, and Bill immediately fell asleep, snoring loudly as she followed the familiar route home. She was left to her own devices, and her thoughts followed their own meandering track. So Corney was going to Mexico, and she spoke Spanish. A lot of people went there. James Taylor had a song about it. Mexico. What was it with Mexico?

Chocolate was discovered in Mexico, at least she thought it was. The Aztecs drank it in their religious rituals, but it was a bitter, unsweetened drink. One of the explorers—Cortez, Magellan, Columbus—she wasn't sure who, but she did know one of them brought it back to Europe, where it created a sensation when some genius came up with the idea of adding sugar. The rest was history. And now the health experts were saying that dark chocolate was good for you, so she didn't even have to feel guilty about that secret stash of chocolate bars she kept in her night stand.

But the popularity of dark chocolate was a relatively recent phenomenon. Lucy remembered how the kids would refuse to eat it and the little miniature bars would linger in the bowl of Halloween candy until she finally finished them off. Until then, in fact, she'd always chosen milk chocolate but after eating those few, spurned bits of dark chocolate, she came to prefer it.

Now, of course, dark chocolate was just the beginning of a chocolate revolution. Trey had been proud of his unusual flavors and she knew he was part of a larger trend. Even Dora was mixing up hot-pepper-flavored chocolates for her Hot Lips, which, come to think of it, she'd learned from Max. Hadn't Dora said something about Max picking up the recipe in Mexico?

Okay, so maybe both Max and Trey had gone to Mexico, and Corney was planning to go there, too. A lot of people went to Mexico. Even Bill's parents, in fact, had a time-share in Cancun. They loved it and spent a few weeks there every winter. They didn't speak Spanish, they said they didn't need it. They had little contact with actual Mexicans, except for the time-share employees, but spent their time with other Americans. Lucy figured that was probably the case with most English speakers in Mexico, who lived in a sort of parallel universe to the natives, encountering them only when they bought something in a shop or ate in a restaurant. Bill's parents, however, stuck to the time-share's own restaurant, fearing the native food would make them sick. And they never drank the water without boiling it first.

Lucy chuckled to herself, remembering Bill's mom Edna's hilarious account of how the first thing she did upon arrival every year was to fill every pot with water, bring it to a boil for ten minutes, and then load all the pots into the refrigerator. Lucy doubted it was really necessary but you couldn't convince Edna, who wouldn't even make coffee with unboiled water.

"What's so funny?' asked Bill, waking up when she turned into the driveway.

"I was thinking about your mother," said Lucy, braking.

"My mom is funny?"

"Sometimes," said Lucy. "It's been a while since you spoke with her. Why don't you give her a call tomorrow?"

"I will," said Bill, stumbling on the porch steps.

"Take it easy," said Lucy, taking his arm and guiding him inside. She doubted he'd remember much about the evening tomorrow morning, least of all his promise to call his folks.

Bill wasn't the only one with a thick head on Sunday morning—Corney complained of a hangover when Lucy called to check on her.

"I couldn't sleep, so I had some brandy," confessed Corney. "I finished the bottle."

"It wasn't full, was it?" asked a horrified Lucy.

"I don't remember," admitted Corney. "All I know is that it's empty now. It's sitting on the kitchen counter, mocking me."

"My father used to swear by something called a prairie oyster," said Lucy. "I think it's a raw egg with Worcestershire sauce and something else. Maybe tomato juice."

"That sounds disgusting," said Corney.

"The hair of the dog, that's the thing," said Bill, pulling a beer out of the refrigerator.

"Try a beer," advised Lucy. "That's what Bill is doing."

"I think I'll just throw up and go back to bed," said Corney.

"No sign of Trey?" asked Lucy.

"No." Corney paused. "You know, I think I probably over-reacted. It's just been so long since I was with a man I think I forgot how they are."

Lucy didn't think using handcuffs and trying to strangle your partner were typical male behaviors, but she didn't say anything for fear of upsetting Corney. She'd been through a traumatic experience and it would take time for her to process it. In the meantime she would need sympathy and support. "I'll stop by later," promised Lucy. "Just to make sure everything's all right."

"Thanks, Lucy," said Corney, her voice a bit shaky.

Hanging up, Lucy dialed Fern's Famous, where Flora answered the phone.

"How's Dora?" she asked.

"About how you'd expect, if you were innocent and accused of killing two people and sitting in a stinky jail cell," said Flora, in her matter-of-fact tone.

"I heard you hired Bob Goodman," said Lucy. "He's the best."

"He's charging enough," said Flora, adding a little *humph*.

Lucy knew Bob's rates were extremely fair, but doubted Flora knew that many lawyers charged hundreds of dollars per hour. "Maybe they'll catch the real murderer before it goes to trial," said Lucy. "I'm following up on something that might help. Do you know when Max was in Mexico?"

"Well, it was when Dora got pregnant with Lily. He got her pregnant and hightailed off. I had to go down and bring him back and make him do the right thing."

"So that was about twenty years ago, something like that?"

"That'd be about right."

"There's another thing," said Lucy. "Do you know anything about the tuition money Max promised for Lily?"

"Promises, promises," snorted Flora. "Max was always making promises."

"Do you have any idea where he was going to get it?"

"I do not," said Flora. "As far as I know, he was broke, he was always broke." She paused. "Maybe his rich old uncle died and left him a bundle. Maybe he was blackmailing somebody. Maybe he won the lottery. I really don't know. What I do know is that if he got a dollar, he spent it."

Lucy was thoughtful. Flora had meant it as a joke, sort of, but blackmail could be a motive for murder. "Do you really think Max was blackmailing somebody? Where'd you get that idea?"

"Same place I got the idea about the rich uncle and the lottery ticket. Where do people get money if they don't work for it? Trust me, Max wasn't much of a worker. Maybe he was going to sell something, maybe he had a buyer for that snowmobile of his. Like I said, I really don't know where Max thought he was going to get twenty thousand dollars for Lily. All I know is that he never did."

"Right. Well, thanks, Flora. Say hi to Dora for me. Let her know I'm thinking of her and doing everything I can to catch the real killer."

Flora didn't reply immediately and Lucy suspected she probably didn't think much of her investigative abilities, so she was surprised when Flora finally spoke. "You be careful, Lucy."

"I will," promised Lucy, touched by Flora's concern. "I surely will."

Turning to her morning chores, Lucy loaded the breakfast dishes into the dishwasher, wiped the counters, and swept the floor. She was just finishing running the vacuum around the family room when the girls appeared, looking for rides.

"Can I take the car?" asked Sara.

"What for? I thought your job ended with Valentine's Day."

"I've got a study group meeting at Jenny's house. It's a group project on women's suffrage."

"And I'm going to Friends of Animals," added Zoe. "I'm filling in for Laurie—she went on that ski trip."

Lucy thought for a minute. Bill was under the weather now, but he'd probably want his truck later. Besides, he didn't like anyone to drive it except himself. She could let Sara take the Subaru, but that would leave her without transportation and she had promised to stop in at Corney's. "No. I'm going to need the car," she said.

Sara wasn't happy with her decision. "What about the truck?"

"Don't push it," said Lucy, laughing. "Your father's not in a mood to share this morning." She wrapped up the vacuum cleaner cord. "I'll take you."

Lucy made the familiar trip, first dropping Zoe at Friends of Animals and then letting Sara off at Jenny's house. She went on to the Quik-Stop for gas, feeling guilty about adding to the nation's thirst for foreign oil and resentful that she didn't really have a choice, and picked up a sports drink for Bill's hangover. When she was leaving the store, a man with a buzz cut and a decided military bearing held the door for her. She thanked him and hurried to her car, but when she started the engine a little hunch popped into her head. She waited until the man left the store and watched as he strode off down Main Street, observing that he appeared to be in his early fifties and extremely fit. She was certain she'd never seen him in town before.

Acting on the hunch, she drove slowly until the car was alongside him, then rolled down the window. "You're new in town, aren't you?" she asked. "Can I help you with anything?"

He turned, an amused expression on his face. "I know this is a small town but. . . ."

Lucy interrupted him. "I'm Lucy Stone. I'm a reporter with the local paper. I really do know everybody in town," she said, handing him her card. "And I'm thinking you might be Tamzin Graves's ex-husband."

"You must be a really good reporter," he said, raising an eyebrow. "I'm Larry Graves and I was married to Tamzin for a couple of years."

"I'm very sorry for your loss," said Lucy, in a serious tone.

Graves's expression hardened. "She didn't deserve this."

"I know." Lucy paused, thinking that survivors often wanted to talk about their lost loved one. "You know, I'm going to have to write an obituary for her and I don't know much about her. Maybe you could help me?"

Graves hesitated a moment, then nodded.

"How about a cup of coffee?"

"Sure," he said, reaching for the car door.

When he was seated, Lucy continued driving down Main Street, toward Jake's. Graves sat beside her, large and silent, and she remembered hearing he was in Afghanistan.

"You must have some case of jet lag," she said. "How long is the flight from Afghanistan?"

"Actually, it was only a short hop, from Cape Cod. There's a training facility at Camp Edwards—a little village and a lot of sand—it's to give the troops a feeling for what they'll encounter in the Middle East. I'm one of the instructors."

"Oh." Lucy pulled into a parking spot in front of Jake's and braked. "But you were in Afghanistan?"

"Yeah." He fell silent, climbing out of the car. "I've been back stateside for six months or so," he said, as they climbed the steps and went inside the coffee shop.

The morning crowd had gone and Norine, the waitress, was busy clearing tables and tidying up. "Sit anywhere you want," she said.

Lucy chose a booth at the back. "This is on me," she said, as Norine set two menus down in front of them. "Have whatever you want."

"Just coffee, regular," he said, pulling off his hat and shrugging out of his jacket. His buzz cut was sprinkled with gray, Lucy noticed, and the skin was stretched tightly over his cheekbones. His eyes were very blue.

Lucy ordered a black decaf for herself, then pulled out her notebook. "I hope you don't mind if I take notes?"

Graves shrugged.

"First of all, I need your full name and rank. . . ."

He raised an eyebrow and slid a business card across the table. "Not my service number?"

She smiled back, taking the card. "That won't be necessary."

"It's major. Major Lawrence Graves, United States Army, currently stationed at Camp Edwards in Massachusetts." Norine set the coffees in front of them and he busied himself adding cream and sugar.

"And you were married to Tamzin?"

"Yeah." He nodded, stirring his coffee. "For three years, back in the nineties. She was in her early thirties. Beautiful. I never knew such a beautiful woman."

Lucy nodded, wondering how to broach her next question. "She made quite an impression here in town. . . ."

Graves laughed. "I bet she did—especially with the male half of the population."

"Well, yes," said Lucy. "Was she always so . . . ?"

"Promiscuous?" Graves took a long drink of coffee. "She was."

"Is that why you divorced?"

"Yeah."

"But you stayed in touch?"

"Sure. It was a lot easier being her friend than being her husband."

"So what was she really like?"

"She grew up in Troy, it's one of those towns in New York State that have fallen on hard times. She couldn't wait to get out and joined the army; that's where we met. She's the only person I ever heard say she loved boot camp, but she thrived on physical challenges, she just loved the workouts, the obstacle courses, the runs. And she really liked being with all those guys."

"How come she left?"

He shrugged. "She was stuck in Texas and didn't like it much, so when she got twenty years—enough for a pension—she didn't reenlist. She always loved New England so she came up here to Maine. She loved this town, she said she'd never been happier."

Lucy felt the pull of a great sense of guilt. "I'm so sorry. . . ."

"It's not your fault," said Graves. "You didn't kill her, did you?"

"I could have been nicer to her."

"It's okay. She never had a lot of girlfriends," he said, signaling Norine for a refill. When she'd filled his cup and he'd gone through the rigmarole of tearing open the little paper pouches of sugar and poured in the cream, he made eye contact with Lucy. "So what do you know about this guy she was working for? This Trey Meacham?"

Lucy shifted in her seat, uncomfortably aware that the situation had changed and she was now the interviewee instead of the interviewer. "I don't know him very well," she said, feeling that the incident with Corney was something she shouldn't talk about. Corney deserved to have her privacy protected.

"But you told me you know everybody in town," he said, challenging her.

"I may have exaggerated," she said, attempting a chuckle.

Major Lawrence Graves was not amused and Lucy had the feeling she was up against a skilled questioner, someone who was able to get information from toughened Taliban fighters. "How big is this chocolate operation of his?"

"Oh." Lucy was relieved. This was something she could talk about. "There are four stores: Kittery, Camden, Bar Harbor, and here. The chocolates are made in Rockland, in a converted sardine factory, and there's a shop there, too. I haven't seen the corporate balance sheet, but Trey himself seems quite prosperous—he drives a Range Rover—and the chocolates have won prizes."

"Is he a local guy?"

"You mean, did he grow up here?"

"Yeah."

"No. He left a high-powered career in public relations, I think, and started Chanticleer Chocolate about a year ago."

"Did he and Tamzin have a relationship?"

"That's open to debate," said Lucy. "They certainly seemed friendly."

"What about this woman they say killed her? Dora Fraser?"

"She's a local woman, her family owns a fudge shop so she was a competitor with Chanticleer. Also, Tamzin had a relationship with Dora's ex-husband and she may have been jealous."

"I don't buy it," said Graves. "I don't think a woman could take Tamzin. She was into martial arts, she taught hand-to-hand combat."

Lucy brightened. "That's what I think, too. I don't see Dora as a double murderer."

Graves's eyebrows shot up. "Double?"

"Dora's ex-husband was killed last month when he was ice fishing. Knocked on the head and tangled up in fishline and shoved through the ice. They're charging Dora with that, too. Or trying to. I'm not sure of the status of the investigation."

"Wow, this is some nice town you've got here."

Lucy decided not to respond. "Are there any funeral arrangements yet for Tamzin?" she asked.

He drained his cup and set it down. "Her family is still back in Troy. They'll have a service and she'll be buried there."

"Thanks for your help," said Lucy. "I guess you'll be heading off to Troy?"

Graves caught her in his gaze. "Oh, no. I'm staying right here until I find the bastard who killed her."

The cool, calculated way he said it took her breath away. "Oh," she said, her voice a whisper. "Good luck."

"Luck will have nothing to do with it," he said, reaching for his jacket and pulling his watch cap over his head. "I have a mission and I intend to complete it. Thanks for the coffee."

Lucy watched as he left the coffee shop, feeling a bit like a bystander in a superhero movie. Graves, it seemed, was no ordinary mortal, he was battle ready and itching for a fight. She was convinced he had the skills and the mental preparedness to fight his enemies and even kill them.

Reaching for her purse, she picked up the check and went over to the cash register. "Who was that guy?" asked Norine. "He looks like one tough customer."

"That was Tamzin's ex-husband," said Lucy, handing her a five-dollar bill. "He's a soldier."

"Well, I'm glad he's on our side," said Norine, giving Lucy her change.

But as Lucy left the coffee shop and hurried to her car, she wondered if Graves was really the avenger he said he was. As a reporter she'd covered a number of murders and the sad fact was that most of the victims were women who'd been killed by their husbands or lovers. Graves said he wanted to find Tamzin's killer but was that nothing more than a smoke screen to hide his own guilt?

She climbed into the car and started it, thinking that the more she knew about Tamzin, the less she knew. Here she'd thought she was nothing but a trashy sexpot and now she had learned she was a soldier for twenty years and even taught hand-to-hand combat. It seemed crazy. Yet in spite of all that, somebody had overpowered her and killed her. Who could have done it? And why? This was one story she couldn't wait to write; it was going to upset a lot of people's preconceptions about Tamzin, that was for sure. And it was going to blow a very big hole in the case against Dora.

Lucy was already composing sentences as she headed for home, detouring along Shore Road to stop by Corney's place.

When Corney opened the door, Lucy saw that Corney had definitely had a tough night. Her eyes were puffy, her face was blotchy, and there were faint bruises on her neck and wrists. Her short blond hair hadn't been brushed and was sticking out all over her head. "Oh my goodness," Lucy exclaimed, wrapping her friend in her arms and giving her a hug.

"I feel awful," said Corney, "and I look worse."

"You had a bad time," said Lucy. "Trey's bad news."

"You can say that again." Corney sat on one of the stools at the breakfast bar. "A lot of it's my own fault. I never should've drank all that brandy. I always try to sleep on my back, but when I woke up this morning my face was squished into the pillow."

"Don't blame yourself," said Lucy. "You're the victim here. Those are terrible bruises on your neck You're lucky to be alive."

"No, Lucy, you've got it wrong. He's just a big guy. He doesn't know his own strength—and I bruise easily." She got up and went over to a mirror that hung on the wall, examining her face and running her fingers beneath her eyes, smoothing out the bags. "Do you happen to have any Preparation H?"

This was the last thing Lucy expected to hear. "Not on me," she said.

"It's the best thing for bags under your eyes." Corney flipped up the collar of her blue fleece robe, holding it beneath her chin with two hands and hiding the bruises. "You know, I think he really likes me."

Lucy had done a couple of stories on the rape crisis center in Gilead and knew that Corney's reaction wasn't unusual. The counselors there said one of the most difficult obstacles to getting rape convictions was the victims' tendency to blame themselves for causing the incident in the first place, believing it was something they did that made their partner become violent. She knew she had to use a gentle approach if she was going to convince Corney that she hadn't deserved to be assaulted.

"I'm sure he does like you," said Lucy, seating herself on

one of the rustic stools that were lined up at the island. She was recalling Larry Graves's interest in Trey and wondering if he suspected Trey had killed Tamzin. Now that she knew about his assault on Corney, it seemed possible, but what about Max? Was there some link between Trey and Max?

"Last night, you said something about how Trey's mood changed when you mentioned you were going to Mexico."

"Yeah." Corney took a big gulp of coffee. "I said I was going to this little town on the Baja coast. A lot of surfers go there and I know he likes to surf, at least he did when he was younger. He was always talking about surfing."

Somewhere in Lucy's brain a connection formed and she felt a mounting excitement. "Max surfed, too. In Mexico. What's the name of the town?"

"Playa del Diablo."

"Devil's Beach?"

"I didn't know you knew Spanish," said Corney.

"I don't," said Lucy, slipping off the stool. "Mind if I use your computer?"

"Not at all. It's down the hall, next to the guest bath."

Lucy followed Corney's directions and found a small, very messy office. The desk was covered with stacks of papers, the bookcase was crammed with cookbooks and design books, and a bunch of Valentine's flags were propped in a corner. A box of promotional brochures was sitting on the desk chair, and Lucy couldn't find anyplace to put it except on the couch, where stacks of newspapers and magazines were already taking up most of the space. She sat down and booted up the computer; she was waiting for the Internet connection when Corney joined her, plunking herself down on the couch amid all the piles of print media.

"You've found my secret," said Corney, crossing her legs and revealing a fuzzy blue slipper that matched her robe. "I can organize other people's stuff but I can't get a handle on my own."

"Like the shoemaker's barefoot children," said Lucy, typing PLAYA DEL DIABLO in the search box. A few moments later she was rewarded with colorful pictures of a pristine beach and muscular, tanned surfers with very white teeth. "Looks like you're going to have a fantastic time in Playa del Diablo."

"Oh, that's just PR. I bet they're all eighty years old and toothless. And the beach is probably covered with globs of tar and oil." Corney propped her feet on a storage box marked TAX RETURNS. "That's the trouble with being in public relations—you never believe anything."

Lucy chuckled and began a search for Mexican newspapers. Playa del Diablo didn't have its own paper, but nearby Cabo San Lucas did and its archives were available for a small fee. "Corney, I need your help here."

Corney groaned as she got up and shuffled over, kicking a pair of high-heeled shoes out of her way. She leaned over Lucy's shoulder to read the screen, then opened a desk drawer and pulled out a credit card. "It's my shopping card," she said. "I keep it handy, in case I want to order something."

Lucy vacated the chair and Corney plopped down and began typing in the numbers. It took a couple of tries but she finally got it right and was inside the archives. "It goes by year. What year do you want?"

Lucy told her and she entered the date. "What now?"

"Just keep scrolling through. I'm looking for anything about Max or Trey."

"Talk about a needle in a haystack," complained Corney. "How do you think we're going to find . . . uh, whoa! Here we go!"

"What is it?" asked Lucy, spotting a photo of several surfers and recognizing youthful versions of both Max and Trey. "What does it say?"

"*American killed in surfing accident*," translated Corney, reading the accompanying story. "*Wes Teasdale drowned yesterday when hit by a loose board . . . his companion Trey Meacham was tragically unable to save him.*" Corney leaned back in the chair. "Poor Trey. That must have been terrible. Imagine seeing your friend drown in a horrible accident."

Lucy had a different take. "Maybe it wasn't an accident," she said. "And maybe Max knew it."

Chapter Twenty

Excited about finding a connection between Max and Trey, Lucy dialed the state police barracks and asked for Lieutenant Horowitz, half expecting her call to be transferred to voice mail. He was there, however, and took her call.

"You're working on a Sunday?" she said, in a surprised voice.

"And so, apparently, are you," he replied.

"I guess I am," said Lucy. "I'm actually with Corney Clarke. She was involved in a very unpleasant situation with Trey Meacham last night."

"Umm," said Horowitz, sounding bored.

"Well, I've found some evidence that casts doubt on Dora Fraser's guilt. It points instead to Trey Meacham."

Horowitz sighed. "Go on."

"It's a connection between Trey and Max that goes way back, about twenty years ago, when they were both in Mexico. A friend of theirs, Wes Teasdale, was killed in a surfing accident, but I don't think it was an accident at all. I think Trey actually murdered Wes. And when Trey showed up here in Tinker's Cove, I think Max may have attempted to blackmail him."

"Whoa," said Horowitz. "This was twenty years ago?"

"Yes. You see, I knew there was a connection between Tamzin and Trey, of course, but I couldn't figure out why he would kill Max. But Max told Dora he was going to come up with the money for Lily's college—and how else would he get twenty thousand dollars if he wasn't blackmailing Trey?"

There was a long pause before Horowitz spoke. "You've really done it now," he said. "Off the deep end. Completely crazy. My advice is to take two aspirins and call a psychiatrist."

Lucy was disappointed, she'd really expected a bit more enthusiasm. "I'm probably not explaining it well. I'm sure I'm on to something."

"It's more like you're *on* something," said Horowitz, ending the call.

"What did he say?" asked Corney, as Lucy pocketed her phone.

"He told me to seek professional help," said Lucy, chagrined.

Corney laughed. "I think you may be making a mountain out of a molehill. According to the newspaper article, the Mexican authorities were convinced Teasdale's death was an accident."

"I doubt they really conducted any sort of investigation," said Lucy. "Bill's mom and dad have a time-share in Mexico and they say the police are notoriously corrupt. They make phony traffic stops and threaten to arrest you, but if you give them fifty bucks they let you go." She chewed her thumbnail. "Don't you see? Max and Trey knew each other, there's a connection. They have a shared past in Mexico and I think they were involved in more than gathering chocolate recipes."

"That doesn't necessarily mean that Trey killed Max," said Corney, yawning. "I'm beat."

"Oh, sorry," said Lucy, hopping to her feet. "I'd better let you get some rest."

"Thanks for everything, Lucy," said Corney, giving her a hug.

"Make sure you lock the door after me," advised Lucy, reaching for her coat. She had zipped up and was digging for the car keys in her purse when she found the card Larry Graves had given her.

Should she call him? she wondered, as she left the house and made her way to the car. He had seemed very interested in Trey Meacham, she remembered. Of course, Tamzin had probably mentioned Trey to her ex-husband. The two were friends, he said. They probably communicated regularly. It was natural to talk about your job and your boss. But Graves had particularly asked about Trey, as if he had a special interest in him. Jealousy? Maybe, but he seemed to have put that behind him. It was easier to be her friend than her husband, that's what he said, and Lucy took it to mean he wouldn't be hurt when she went with other men.

In the car, Lucy waited for the engine to warm up and fingered the card. Graves was a tough guy and she wasn't sure what his reaction would be to this new information. She didn't want him to go off half-cocked and do something he would regret. On the other hand, she didn't feel she had a right to withhold information he might find valuable. He had loved Tamzin, after all, and clearly felt a need to resolve her death. Lucy didn't think he was motivated by revenge as much as the desire to achieve justice. Somebody had killed Tamzin and desecrated her body and he wanted to make sure that person paid for the crime.

And, face it, she told herself, she didn't owe Trey a thing. His behavior to Corney was inexcusable—and suspicious. Trey might seem like a nice guy but his treatment of Corney had revealed another side to his personality. There was definitely something a bit off about Trey. Coming to a decision, she dialed his cell phone but Graves didn't answer; the call went straight to voice mail.

Disappointed, she shifted into drive and headed for home. Today was Valentine's Day and she couldn't help hoping there might be something special waiting for her; Bill usually had some little surprise for her. She had a card for him—one of the big, expensive ones—and was planning a special dinner, his favorite meat loaf, with butterscotch brownies and ice cream for dessert.

Pulling into the driveway, she stopped the car by the mailbox, irrationally hoping to find some red envelopes. She smiled, finding one, hand-delivered and signed with a crayon scrawl, from Patrick.

When she went inside the kitchen, she found a vase filled with a dozen perfect red roses in the middle of the kitchen table, with a note from Bill. It was one word: ALWAYS. She pressed the card to her chest and bent down to inhale the flowers' scent, savoring the moment. He loved her, he really, really did. He'd remembered. She felt as if she were floating on air as she took off her winter jacket and danced around the kitchen, humming a little tune. "Love, love, love," she sang, gathering butter and brown sugar and walnuts to make the brownies. She was just about to grease the pan when her cell phone rang.

She half expected it to be Bill, checking to see if she'd found the flowers, but it was Larry Graves.

"I found a link between Trey Meacham and Max Fraser," she said. "They were in Mexico about twenty years ago."

"Tamzin called me, terrified, just before she was killed," said Graves. "A big package from Mexico came to the shop and when she opened it she found cocaine. She was going to take it to the police, but she never made it."

Of course, Lucy thought, drugs. The chocolate business was a perfect cover. Suddenly, an image popped into her mind. It was Trey, standing in the dry cleaner's shop. She'd said something about how he was selling a lot more than chocolate. She'd meant that the chocolates were something special, a luxury item that implied the discriminating consumer deserved only the very best. But his expression had implied something very different; he'd looked shocked and had hurried out of the shop. It was as if she'd hit a nerve, and she was pretty sure exactly what that nerve was. He was selling more than chocolate; he was selling drugs. And she was willing to bet he was making a lot more money from the illegal drug operation than he was from his overpriced chocolates.

"I called the police but they didn't believe me," said Lucy.

"I don't want to go on record with this, it's just between you and me, but I'm on my way to Rockland, to the factory," said Graves. "Could be quite a scoop for the town's best reporter."

Lucy was suddenly energized; she felt like a racehorse waiting for the gate to open. "I'll bring my camera," she said.

This was better than roses, thought Lucy, as she followed the road up hill and down dale to Rockland. She felt exhilarated, chasing down a story that wasn't some stupid puff piece assignment from Ted but one she developed herself, following her hunches and taking the initiative. And what a story it was! Everything was coming together. She was not only solving two murders, and clearing Dora in the process, but nailing Trey would cut off the supply of drugs that was pouring into the region. Not forever—she wasn't naïve enough to believe that—but long enough that a lot of users would have time to go to rehab and get themselves straightened out. She couldn't wait to see Ted's face when she presented him with the story of the year, complete with photos. And best of all, it was her story.

They'd know soon enough, of course. NECN and CNN and the Boston stations and newspapers would be all over it, but that would be later. She was breaking this story, a story that was going to be big, really big. Maybe they'd even interview her. She could just see herself chatting with Deborah Norville. "How did you break this story?" Deborah would ask. "Well, it was nothing more than good investigative reporting and a little bit of luck, Deborah," she'd say. "I followed a hunch and learned the luxury chocolates were a front for illegal drugs from Mexico."

But when she arrived at the old waterfront sardine factory, the parking lot was empty. She wasn't sure what she'd expected, Larry Graves had been pretty vague, but she'd definitely gotten the feeling that something was going to come down. A raid maybe? She drove around the building, looking for the major, but there was no sign of life at all and she was beginning to wonder if she'd misunderstood and jumped to the wrong conclusion.

The five-story building was handsome; she had to admit Meacham had done a terrific job restoring the classic nineteenth-century factory. The brick had been cleaned and pointed, and the windows, which were lined up in symmetrical rows, had been repaired. Even the tall bell tower that once called workers to their shifts had been restored. The plowed parking lot was freshly paved and lined, dotted here and there with hardy young trees, and a handsome carved wood sign with the trademark rooster identified the former cannery as the home of Chanticleer Chocolate.

Somewhat frustrated that Graves had turned out to be a no-show, Lucy decided that rather than waste her time, she might as well snap a few photos of the factory. She found the structure surprisingly photogenic in the slanting afternoon sunshine: the ranks of windows offered an interesting visual, the tall bell tower made a dramatic image shot from its base, and the original doors, now freshly painted, featured elaborate hand-forged hinges. She was just focusing her camera when the door opened and Trey stepped out.

"What are you doing here?" he demanded. His tone wasn't exactly pleasant and Lucy felt uneasy.

"Just taking photos," she said, with a big smile. "I can't believe what you've done with this old place. It used to be such an eyesore, all covered with grime, most of the windows cracked or broken. Ted wanted a photo for the paper, for an article on repurposing older buildings."

"Oh," he said, sounding mollified. "Why don't you come in? The machinery is pretty interesting, too, especially the big copper kettles."

Considering her suspicions about Trey, Lucy didn't think that was a good idea. She made a show of glancing at her watch. "Actually," she said, stepping backwards, "I'm running late. Maybe another time."

"It will only take a few minutes," he said, wrapping an arm around her shoulders and drawing her toward the door. "Believe me, it's worth the time. You're going to get some great photos."

Every instinct told her to run, but Trey had maneuvered himself so that he was beside her and was exerting pressure on her back, pushing her through the door. She tried to pull away but his arm tightened around her shoulders when he felt her withdrawing. It was extremely awkward; Lucy wasn't sure if Trey really wanted to show her the machinery or if he was abducting her. Looking over her shoulder for some means of escape, she saw a number of police cars arriving with lights flashing and realized the raid had finally materialized. The timing couldn't have been worse; now she was in the middle of it. She made a desperate effort to escape, shoving Trey and pulling away, but he only tightened his grip on her.

"Don't move or I'll shoot," he said.

Lucy felt cold metal pressed against her temple.

The police cruisers—there were four of them—came to a

stop about thirty feet away, where a row of evergreen bushes provided some cover. A door on the first one opened and Lieutenant Horowitz stepped out.

"Stop!" yelled Meacham. "I've got a gun and I'll use it."

Horowitz's arms went up. "We can work this out," he said. "There's no need to shoot."

"I've got a hostage. You make any moves and I'll shoot her."

"Nobody's moving," said Horowitz.

Caught in Trey's grip, Lucy's teeth were chattering. She noticed that he was shivering, too, and the hand holding the gun was shaking. The next thing she knew he had dragged her inside the building and the thick wooden door had closed behind them.

"Did you call the cops?" he demanded.

Lucy shook her head. "No! I only came to take pictures."

He jabbed the gun into her back. "Move. We'll go in the office."

Lucy obeyed, walking woodenly in the direction he indicated, toward a door with a frosted glass panel painted with the word OFFICE. Once they were inside the large room, which was filled with old-fashioned wooden desks and had big windows overlooking the parking lot, he pushed her into a chair and snapped a handcuff on one arm. Lucy wondered if they were the same pair he'd used on Corney.

He looped the other cuff around the arm of the chair and when he snapped it shut she realized how helpless she was and a huge shudder ran through her body. She was a hostage, entirely at the mercy of a twisted killer, and she could only hope the police outside knew what they were doing. Trey gave the wheeled chair a shove, placing her in front of one of the big windows, where she was a sitting duck. She had a clear view of the parking lot, where a steady stream of police vehicles was arriving and a group of black-clad SWAT team members were taking up positions surrounding the building.

If shooting broke out, Lucy decided, her only chance would be to try to tip the chair over and fall to the ground. That plan was flawed, however, because she'd have to survive the first volley of shots and her exposed position made that unlikely. Mind whirling, she remembered hearing somewhere that if you ever found yourself in a hostage situation you should try to develop a friendly relationship with your captor. It was worth a try, she thought. "I'm supposed to be making brownies and meat loaf," she said, trying to keep her voice steady.

"This wasn't exactly on my agenda," muttered Trey, sounding nervous.

She decided to keep up the small talk. "Do you have a date for tonight?" she asked. "It's Valentine's Day."

Trey had positioned himself behind a heavy oak filing cabinet, probably a relic from the sardine cannery, and was staring out the window.

"I was going to call my mom."

This whole situation was surreal, thought Lucy, and getting even weirder. "That's nice," she said, feeling a bit more confident. "I was going to make meat loaf for my husband, it's his favorite. With mashed potatoes and gravy. And I was going to have ice cream for dessert. We have two daughters. . . ."

"I have a bad feeling about this," said Trey, just as the phone rang. "Answer it," he said. "Put it on speakerphone."

Lucy slid the chair closer to the nearest desk and reached for the phone with her free hand, getting it on the fourth ring. "Hello," she said.

"I'm Brian Sullivan. I'm a trained negotiator." A warm, relaxed voice filled the room.

"I'm Lucy Stone," she replied, looking at Trey for permission to continue. When he nodded, she said, "I'm the hostage. I'm handcuffed to a chair."

"We're going to get you out of this, Lucy. Are you the only hostage?"

Getting a shake of the head from Trey she replied. "I don't know."

"Who is with you?"

Lucy looked once again to Trey but this time he drew his finger across his throat. "I have to go," she said, and hung up.

Develop a relationship, she reminded herself. "He sounded nice," she said.

"Nice!" barked Trey. "They want to put me in jail for life."

"Not for life," said Lucy. "You don't get life for dealing."

He looked at her. "I think we both know I did more than that."

"There were mitigating circumstances," said Lucy. "Max tried to blackmail you, didn't he? He knew what happened in Mexico, with Wes Teasdale."

"Wes? Wes drowned. He was a lousy surfer." Trey scratched his chin with the gun. "No, Max wasn't blackmailing me. He wanted in on the drugs."

"He knew about the drugs?" asked Lucy.

"Yeah. From Mexico. We did some stuff together a long time ago. He knew the chocolate business was a good front—I used the cocoa shipments to smuggle in coke, heroin, even oxy; you can get it cheap down there."

The phone rang again, but Trey shook his head, signaling she shouldn't answer it. The rings continued for a while, and Lucy could hardly stand it. She felt panic rising in her chest with every ring and tried to concentrate on breathing, just breathing. Finally the rings stopped. "That was annoying," she said.

"Yeah," agreed Trey.

"It was really clever, the way you killed Max. The cops thought it was an accident."

"Max helped, he was really drunk. It was easy."

"Did you plan it?"

"No. We'd set up a meeting on the ice, he liked to fish at night. Said he'd show me how it was done. One thing led to another. He got mad, took a swing at me. I swung back and he went down, fell on his gear, and got tangled up. That's what gave me the idea to kind of embellish his body."

"The thing I wondered about is how you got him through the ice—how'd you do that?"

"I knew there was that punky spot and I just slid him over—the trick was not to go through myself. It was a near thing, I almost did."

Lucy wished he had, she wished it more than anything she'd ever wished, but she wasn't about to let him know that. "That was lucky," she said, trying to sound as if she meant it.

"I don't think you really mean that," he said, with a crooked smile. Lucy almost liked him, she realized, wondering if this was that Stockholm syndrome she'd heard so much about.

"What about Tamzin?"

"She opened a package of cocoa beans and found a brick of coke. She said she wouldn't tell anyone but I didn't trust her, she was always talking about that ex-husband of hers and what a hero he was. I couldn't risk it."

"Why the chocolate coating?" she asked.

"I wanted to make it look like Dora did it," he said.

"Very clever," said Lucy, as the phone started ringing again.

Trey was looking out the window, where the parking lot was filling up fast with official vehicles with red and blue flashing lights. "It's like Christmas out there," he muttered. Then, in a tone of amazement, he added, "Look at that sky."

A spectacular winter sunset had tinted the overarching sky a gorgeous shade of pink and a handful of fluffy white clouds were rimmed with gold. It seemed as if God Himself could reach down and touch the earth, making everything right.

"I'm not going to jail," said Trey. His voice was low and decisive. "If I'm going out, I might as well do it in a blaze of glory."

Then he was gone and Lucy was left alone with the ringing phone. She answered it. "He's left. I don't know where. . . ."

Just then a dark shape tumbled past the window, landing with a heart-stopping thud.

She sat, absorbing what had happened, and waited for the SWAT team to release her.

"He was up on the tower," one of the officers told her, as he unlocked the handcuffs. "He climbed up on a ledge and stood there, facing the sun. Then he stretched out his arms and just stepped off."

"Is he dead?" asked Lucy.

"Oh, yeah."

She stood up and stretched, then, feeling woozy, thought better of it and sat back down.

"Do you need a medic?" the officer asked.

"No, I'll be okay," she said, noticing Larry Graves standing in the doorway. "Where were you?" she asked. "You were supposed to meet me here."

He shrugged, a sheepish expression on his face. "I got lost. The GPS didn't work." He paused, studying her face. "I'm really, really sorry."

Lucy tried standing again and this time she didn't feel dizzy. She felt good, she decided. It was definitely good to be alive.

"Don't be," she said. "You were right. I got a hell of a story."

Chapter Twenty-one

The police had set up a temporary crisis management headquarters in a trailer in the parking lot outside the chocolate factory, and that's where Lucy was taken to be debriefed. Brian Sullivan, the negotiator with the warm voice, interviewed her, and she was surprised to find he was short, slight, and balding, a complete contrast to the mental picture she'd built based on his voice.

"I just want to go over the video with you," he said. "We had a very sensitive listening device, but it didn't pick up everything and I need you to fill in the blanks."

He pointed to a video monitor and when the snow cleared she saw a grainy picture of the office, shot through the windows. Meacham was a shadowy figure, never seen in full as he remained partially hidden behind the file cabinet. She, on the other hand, was front and center, handcuffed to the chair. It was an unsettling image.

An audio technician arrived and was soon able to match his recording with the video and Lucy was able to see and hear the worst hour of her life all over again. It went excruciatingly slowly, however, because the process was halted frequently so Lucy could supply missing scraps of dialogue. She tried her best to be accurate, but oftentimes the technician would determine that her memory didn't match the fragments of sound on the tape and she'd have to try all over again. She was completely exhausted when they finally said she could go.

She wasn't sure how she was going to get home and was trying to decide if she could manage to drive herself when the door opened and Bill arrived. She rushed into his arms and he held her tightly, smoothing her hair and covering her face with kisses, and that's when she burst into hysterical tears.

"It's all over, you're safe, you're safe," he said.

"I know," she blubbered, unable to stop sobbing.

"The cops said you were amazing, really cool, did everything right."

"I want to go home," she finally said, wiping her eyes with her hands.

Bill gave her one of his big white handkerchiefs and just seeing it and holding it made her start crying all over again. "I love you," she said, sputtering.

He gave her a big squeeze. "You can show me later. But for now, you owe me a meat loaf dinner."

"Okay," she said, letting him take her hand and lead her out into the night.

On Monday morning Ted was already at his desk when she arrived. "How are you?" he asked.

"Kind of shaky," she said.

The door opened and Phyllis came in, wrapped in a colorful poncho with matching hand-knitted hat and gloves. She was carrying a big bouquet of flowers. "These are for you," she said, engulfing Lucy in a multicolored hug.

It was all too much for Lucy, and the tears began flowing again.

"Oh, for Pete's sake, the story of the year and my ace reporter is too emotional to tell it," muttered Ted, as the bell on the door jangled furiously and Frankie blew in, all in a dither.

"The story of the year—that's what I've got for you!" she exclaimed, waving a sheaf of papers in her gloved hand.

"We've got it. Lucy was there when Trey committed suicide."

"Trey? Suicide?" Frankie was puzzled.

"Haven't you heard?" asked Ted.

"Renee and I spent yesterday *chez ma mère*; she lives in Portsmouth. Why? What happened?"

"It's a long story," said Lucy. "What's your news?"

Frankie couldn't wait to tell them. "It's the Faircloths. They're gone!"

"But I thought they were buying the McIntyre place," said Lucy.

"Yeah, so did I." Frankie waved the papers. "I've got a purchase and sales agreement right here, but when I went over to the Salt Aire to get them to sign it, the desk clerk told me they'd left sometime in the night without paying their bill. It's over five thousand dollars."

Lucy wasn't sure she'd heard right. "They skipped out on their bill?"

"Yeah. When housekeeping went in this morning, they were gone—and they even took the bathrobes!" Frankie paused. "But they did leave a twenty for the maid, along with a note thanking her for excellent service."

"Classy," said Ted.

"Not really," muttered Frankie. "I devoted every waking moment to those people and now I'm out a hefty commission. I was counting on that money."

"They seemed so nice," said Lucy. "I saw them dancing Saturday night at the ball and they made a lovely couple."

"*Seemed* is the operative word here," said Phyllis.

"You said it," agreed Frankie. "It turns out they're a pair of scam artists. They've been doing this for months, maybe years. They lost their house to foreclosure so they've been moving around to inns and B&Bs, living it up in the style to which they're accustomed and leaving a trail of unpaid bills. The clerk at the Salt Aire said they got an e-mail from the innkeeper's association just this morning, warning about them. They left a big bill at the Queen Vic, too."

Ted was reaching for the phone. "I'm calling the printery," he said. "I think we're going to need some extra pages this week."

Lucy was nodding. "And people say nothing happens here in the winter!"

Punxsutawney Phil had predicted six more weeks of winter on Groundhog Day and for once he seemed to be right. March roared in like a lion, but this particular lion turned out to be a pussycat, bringing bright sunshine and warm temperatures. When Elizabeth came home for a long weekend before starting her next assignment at the brand-new Cavendish Hotel on Cape Cod, the snow was gone and buds were swelling on the forsythia bushes. Lucy had cut some branches a week or so earlier and they were already in bloom, a yellow explosion on the dining room sideboard.

Lucy was putting the finishing touches on her table, laying out the silver serving spoons, and the scent of cooking turkey was heavy in the air. A series of sharp barks from Libby announced the arrival of her dinner guests, Marge and Barney Culpepper and their son, Eddie.

"It's like Thanksgiving," declared Zoe, when they were all sitting at the table.

"We have a lot to be thankful for," said Lucy.

"You can say that again," said Barney, with a nod to Eddie.

He was fresh out of rehab and looked great, thought Lucy. He was letting his military brush cut grow in and the slightly longer, curly hair softened his appearance. He smiled often, paying special attention to Elizabeth. Lily, he said in answer to Lucy's pointed inquiry, was away in Switzerland, apprenticing with a master chocolatier.

Elizabeth seemed to be enjoying herself, which was a big change from her returns home during college breaks, when she complained about there being nothing to do and couldn't wait to get back to Boston. Now that she was working and fending for herself she had a new appreciation for home, where Mom took care of the cooking and cleaning and even did her laundry.

When they'd polished off the shrimp cocktail and turkey with stuffing and gravy and all the fixings—Bill's payment for fixing the door at the *Pennysaver*—Lucy suggested moving into the living room for coffee. Sara and Zoe were delegated to clear the table and load the dishwasher; Elizabeth and Eddie went off together to hear a local band and catch up with high school friends at the Irish pub down by the harbor.

"Eddie looks terrific," said Lucy, pouring a cup of decaf for Marge.

Bill lit the fire he had laid earlier. When he was satisfied that it had caught, he produced a bottle of brandy and, receiving a nod from Barney, poured two glasses. "What's his legal situation?" he asked.

Barney took the snifter and raised it to the light, admiring the golden liquid, then took a sip. "Mmmm," he said. "Well, he took my advice for once and agreed to cooperate with the DA. He got a good deal, no jail time, probation for a year with random drug and alcohol tests, and of course rehab. You never know, but it looks like he's staying clean."

"He's thinking about going to college," said Marge, holding her saucer with one hand and lifting the cup with the other. "He's looking into physical therapy. Maybe because of the guys he knew who got wounded. He says he wants to help people."

"I guess he already has," said Lucy, sitting down on the couch with her coffee. "He's named some of the dealers Meacham was supplying. The drug task force is finally making real progress." She paused. "I didn't realize that they'd been working on making a case against Meacham for months."

Barney nodded. "Nobody did. Those guys work undercover, way undercover. Even Horowitz didn't know what they were doing. He was convinced Dora was the killer, and there was a lot of circumstantial evidence. But when Graves showed up with his story about Tamzin discovering the drugs, he contacted the task force and they set up the raid." He took a sip of brandy. "Meacham had quite an operation, bringing the stuff in from Mexico with the cocoa beans and using the factory to distribute it. It turned out that Chanticleer Chocolate's most popular flavors were heroin and OxyContin, along with pot, coke, and ecstasy. He had something for everyone, whatever their preference and budget."

"Who knew?" mused Marge, biting into a cookie. "He seemed so nice. I never would have guessed. And the scope—I couldn't believe the amount of drugs they found in his warehouse."

Lucy nodded, remembering the photo Ted ran in the *Pennysaver* showing huge bottles of pills and hundreds of plastic bags of marijuana and cocaine, laid out so they completely covered the big conference table at the police station. "Ted said Trey was going to be the Chamber of Commerce's Businessman of the Year."

"Some businessman," snorted Bill. "It was all a big lie."

"What's happening to all his drug customers?" asked Lucy. "They can't all be in rehab."

"They've found other dealers," said Barney, draining his glass. "Or they steal. There was a pharmacy break-in last night, over in Gilead."

Lucy shook her head. "What's the solution? How do we stop this?"

Barney set his empty glass on the mantel and stood studying the flames dancing in the fireplace. "I wish I knew," he said. "I wish I knew."

Much has happened since Leslie Meier first introduced her beloved sleuth Lucy Stone with Mistletoe Murder. *Many holidays and bake sales have come and gone, Lucy's children have all grown up. But even after twenty-four books into the bestselling series, murder is never out of the picture. . . .*

As Tinker's Cove, Maine, buzzes over a town-wide silver wedding anniversary bash, Lucy is reminded of her nuptials and ponders the whereabouts of Beth Gerard, her strong-willed maid of honor. Lucy never would have made it down the aisle without Beth's help, and although the two friends lost touch over the years, she decides to reach out. It only takes one phone call for Lucy to realize that a reunion will happen sooner rather than later—at Beth's funeral.

Beth, who was in the process of finalizing her fourth divorce, had a reputation for living on the edge—but no one can believe she would jump off a penthouse terrace in New York City. The more Lucy learns about Beth's former husbands, the more she suspects one of them committed murder.

Summoning her friend's impulsive spirit, Lucy vows to scour New York from the Bronx to the Brooklyn Bridge in search of the killer. With each ex dodgier than the last, it's not long before Lucy's investigation leads her to a desperate criminal who will do anything to get away—even if it means silencing another victim. . . .

Please turn the page for an exciting sneak peek of
Leslie Meier's

SILVER ANNIVERSARY MURDER

now on sale wherever print and e-books are sold!

Chapter One

"Honestly, I'm surprised he hasn't killed her," whispered Harry Nuttall, leaning over the deli counter at the IGA in Tinker's Cove, Maine. He was speaking to one of his regular customers, Lucy Stone, who was doing her weekly grocery shopping.

Lucy was a part-time reporter for the *Pennysaver*, the local weekly newspaper, and had developed the habit of shopping after the paper's Wednesday noon deadline, taking advantage of the free afternoon, which also happened to be a time when the usually crowded super-market had few customers.

"So is it the usual?" Harry pulled on a fresh pair of plastic gloves. "A pound of ham, sliced thin, and a half of Swiss?"

"I guess I'll live dangerously," said Lucy, turning to watch Warren Bickford, Harry's potential murderer, presenting his wife and likely murder victim, Sylvia, with his wrapped cold cuts. Then remembering the task at hand, she turned back to Harry. "Throw in a half pound of turkey breast, too."

"Do you want it sliced like the ham?" asked Harry. Lucy's attention had returned to the Bickfords; Warren's deli purchase had clearly not satisfied Sylvia. She glared at the label on the package through heavily made-up eyes, ran her red-tipped nails through her obviously bleached blond hair, pointed at the label, then roughly thrust the packet back to Warren. "Black Forest, Warren. I told you Black Forest! Honestly, how many times do I have to repeat myself?"

Warren bent his head and seemed to offer an apology, then trotted obediently back to the deli counter.

"Same thickness as the ham?" Harry asked again, the grin on his face revealing his amusement at Lucy's fascination with the Bickfords.

Lucy considered asking him to slice the turkey a bit thicker than the ham, but aware that Warren was under the gun to deliver the correct order, changed her mind. "Same," she said, turning to give Warren a big, warm smile. It seemed the least she could do for the poor, henpecked husband. "Nice day," she said, referring to the lovely, mild, May weather that was such a treat after the bitter cold Maine winter, which this year had been followed by an especially blustery March and extremely muddy April.

"Sure is," replied Warren, unzipping his jacket. Lucy guessed he was in his early fifties, and like most middle-aged men in Tinker's Cove, he was wearing khaki pants and a sports shirt topped with a light sweater. His thinning hair was combed in the standard left-parted barbershop cut and he was developing a bit of a paunch. That growing tummy was probably the result of an occupational hazard; as owner and operator of a limo service, he spent a lot of time sitting behind the wheel. "Sorry to bother you, Harry, but I got the wrong ham. I should've asked for Black Forest. I hope it's no problem."

"No problem," said Harry, placing Lucy's three packages on the counter. "It's already wrapped. I'll save it for the next customer who wants Virginia ham."

Warren let out a relieved sigh. "Thanks, Harry." It seemed he was about to say something more, perhaps a reference to his wife, but thought better of it and bit his lip instead, rocking slightly from one sturdy Timberland shoe to the other while waiting for Harry to slice his Black Forest ham.

Lucy put her packages in her cart and pushed it along, heading for the meat counter, which ran along the back wall of the supermarket. She paused at an island displaying English muffins—buy one get two free, a deal that was hard to pass up—and witnessed Warren rejoining his wife and presenting the correct ham, rather like a little girl offering flowers to the queen.

"Warren, you always do this. You don't speak up and people take advantage of you. Just look—this ham is sliced much too thick. Not that I blame Harry. He isn't going to shove that slicer back and forth any more times than he has to, if people don't speak up and ask for thin slices."

Warren stood like a statue, letting his wife's criticisms rain down on him. "Do you want me to take it back, *dear*?" he asked, with the slightest note of sarcasm in his voice.

Sylvia expelled a large sigh. "No, Warren. We don't have time. We have a big order this week." She flourished her shopping list. "Do you think you could manage a simple task like getting the coffee while I look over the meat? Beef chuck is supposed to be on sale, but I'll be amazed if they have any left this late in the week. They probably sold it all on the weekend. Not that they'll get away with it, not with me. I'll insist on a rain check."

"You do that, dear," said Warren. "Quite right. Now,

do you want decaf or regular, and what brand? Or should I go for price?"

"It never ceases to amaze me, Warren. How long have we been married? Twenty-five years next month, and you don't know what brand of coffee we drink?"

"Well, it's usually the one in the red package, but sometimes it seems to me we have the blue kind."

"*The red kind? The blue kind?* Honestly, Warren, you sound like a child." She rolled her eyes. "Get the Folgers, unless Maxwell House is on sale for half price. And don't fall for that foul French roast stuff. Can you do that for me?"

"Yes, dear." Warren trotted off in the direction of the coffee aisle, and Sylvia, as promised, attacked the meat counter. Lucy, hoping to avoid witnessing any more of Warren's humiliations, slipped off into the cereal aisle. Distracted by a special on canned soups on the end cap, where she was searching for chicken noodle but only finding minestrone and vegetarian vegetable, she wasn't quick enough to miss Warren's presentation of a green can of coffee.

"Green is decaf, Warren; everybody knows that," declared Sylvia, in a voice that could probably be heard on Metinnicut Island, ten miles across the bay.

"But it's Folgers, like you said." He attempted a weak defense. "They could have changed the package, you know."

"No, Warren, they haven't changed it." Sylvia paused to sniff a cello-wrapped piece of chuck, then replaced it. "Now, take this back and get the red Folgers. And do hurry. We've got a lot to do and I'm going to have the butcher cut me a fresh piece of chuck. The nose knows— you can't fool my nose. This meat has probably been sitting out here since Sunday."

"Right, dear," said Warren, obediently hurrying back to the coffee section to complete his assignment. Watching him go, Lucy thought Harry might have a point. Some day, maybe some day soon, Warren was bound to snap.

Diverting as that thought was, Lucy had a long shopping list that demanded great concentration as she frequently consulted the weekly ad for specials, checked prices, and thumbed through her coupon file. From time to time she heard Sylvia's strident voice berating Warren for something or other, but she didn't actually encounter the Bickfords again until she reached the checkout counter.

Warren was busy bagging their order when Dot Kirwan, the cashier, announced the amount due. "A hundred and forty-seven dollars!" exclaimed Sylvia. "We don't want to buy the store, do we, Warren? We just want to eat for a week."

"Should we put this back, dear?" suggested Warren, who was holding a large bottle of expensive olive oil. "We could get a smaller one."

Sylvia shook her head. "The larger one is a better value, Warren. You ought to know that. It's cheaper per ounce. Now pay the bill and stop grumbling."

"Yes, dear," said Warren, pulling his wallet out of his back pocket and handing a credit card to Dot.

"Let me see that!" demanded Sylvia, snatching the card out of Dot's hand. "Just as I thought. It's the wrong card!"

Dot's eyes met Lucy's, and they both struggled to maintain neutral facial expressions while Warren fumbled with his wallet. The two women were of like minds and Lucy had great respect for Dot, who was the widowed matriarch of a large family. Most of her kids and grandkids worked for the town, filling positions in the fire and police departments, which made Dot a valuable source of inside knowledge for Lucy.

"Oh, give me that wallet!" demanded Sylvia, losing

patience. He obliged and she flipped it open, pulling out a wad of plastic cards. "My word! What is all this? Exxon, Sears, Shell, Visa, Plenti . . . Ah, finally! This is the one that gives us rewards, Warren." She waved the colorful bit of plastic underneath his nose. "Only use this one, from now on, only this one. You don't need the rest. You might as well cut them up and throw them away."

"I'll do that, dear," said Warren, who had continued packing the groceries and was holding the disputed can of Folgers coffee.

"Just slide the card on the keypad," urged Dot, and Sylvia complied, signing with a flourish. Warren carefully placed a plastic bag containing their eggs on the child seat and pushed the cart toward the door, followed by Sylvia, who was checking the register tape as she walked.

"Thank you and have a nice day," said Dot. Unable to stifle her laughter any longer, she burst into a fit of giggles. "I call them the Bickersons," she whispered to Lucy, as the automatic door opened and the Bickfords exited the store.

Lucy felt a certain sympathy for Sylvia as Dot finished ringing up her order, which amounted to nearly two hundred dollars despite her coupon clipping. Sylvia was right about one thing, she decided, as she pushed her heavily loaded cart out to the parking lot, and that was the price of groceries. The sun this afternoon was very bright, and she paused in the shady overhang to put on her sunglasses only to find they were missing. They weren't in the usual pocket on the outside of her purse, and they weren't inside, along with her wallet, granola bar, numerous pens, phone, and reporter's notebook, either. Sighing, she gave the cart a shove and stepped into the sunlight, squinting. She'd almost finished loading everything into her trunk when it came to her: she'd pulled the sunglasses off when she got to work earlier that day and set them down on her desk. They were most likely still there, so she'd have to swing by the *Pennysaver* office to retrieve them.

Lucky for her, there was a vacant parking spot right in front of the weekly newspaper's Main Street office and Lucy swooped right in, then dashed into the office, setting the little bell on the door to jangling. Somewhat to her surprise, she was greeted not only by the receptionist, Phyllis, but also by her editor, Ted, who didn't usually stick around the office after deadline. The two were standing at the reception counter, heads bent over a press release.

"What's up?" asked Lucy. "Breaking news?" Late-breaking news was a problem for a weekly, which had to wait an entire week before printing stories that by then had become stale.

"Not hardly," said Ted, chuckling. He was not only the editor, but also the publisher and chief reporter for the paper, which he'd inherited from his grandfather. That celebrated New England journalist's rolltop desk still dominated the old-fashioned newsroom and was Ted's most prized possession.

"You've got to see it to believe it," said Phyllis, laughing so hard that her sizable bosom was jiggling as she handed the press release to Lucy. Phyllis was celebrating spring's late arrival by wearing a pink bouclé sweater that matched her pink reading glasses and her hair, also dyed pink.

Lucy quickly scanned the press release, which announced in bold capitals that Sylvia and Warren Bickford were soon to celebrate their twenty-fifth wedding anniversary in June by renewing their vows, that joyous ceremony to be followed by a reception to which the whole town would be invited. And that was not all, promised the press release, which went on to invite all the ladies of the town to participate in a fashion show of wedding gowns from the past by modeling their own dresses. All those interested should contact Sylvia at her shop, Orange Blossom Bridal.

"This is so funny," said Lucy, when she'd finished reading. "I just saw the Bickfords, who Dot Kirwan calls the Bickersons, at the IGA. She picked on him mercilessly; the poor guy couldn't do anything right. Harry, the deli guy, said he was surprised Warren hasn't murdered Sylvia. A divorce would be more appropriate than renewing their vows. The whole town is going to be laughing at them."

"It's pretty smart, if you ask me," said Ted. "It's great publicity for her bridal boutique, and also for his limo company."

"It could backfire," said Lucy. "Everybody knows it's an unhappy marriage. Nobody'd be surprised if Warren bailed out, or worse."

"Oh, I don't know," said Phyllis, in a thoughtful tone. She was a bit of a romantic, having found her great love, Wilf Lundgren, rather late in life. "There must be something that keeps them together, despite outward appearances. I think it's kind of sweet."

Lucy spotted her sunglasses, exactly where she had left them, and grabbed them, perching them on top of her head in Jackie Kennedy style. "Speaking of sweets, I gotta run before my ice cream melts—see ya tomorrow!"

Lucy thought about marriage as she drove the familiar route through town, down Main Street, and out to Route 1, then turning onto Red Top Road and up the hill to the handyman's special she and Bill had restored and in which they'd raised their four children. Sometimes the glue held, even for couples like the Bickersons, who didn't seem terribly happy, and sometimes that glue dried up and crumbled, like the stuff she'd spent hours scraping off the back of an antique picture frame she'd recently picked up at an estate sale. There had been rough spots in her marriage to Bill—she remembered fights but not exactly what caused them—but she'd never seriously considered divorce. Maybe, she admitted to herself, that was because she was far too practical to attempt to raise four children by herself, especially considering the mostly low-wage jobs available to women like her in coastal Maine. She didn't want to spend her summers juggling a couple of jobs, chambermaiding by day and waitressing by night as many local women did.

That wasn't quite fair to Bill, she thought with a smile, pulling into the driveway. She loved him. She'd been distant at first, when he began chatting her up in college, but through sheer persistence he'd gradually won her over. Now, after the house and the kids and grandson Patrick, he was so much a part of her that she couldn't imagine life without him.

Though, she admitted to herself as she began toting the heavy recyclable bags of groceries into the house, she could use a little help from him right now. What was it her mother used to say, when her father was nowhere to be found? Something about wishing she could put on her hat and walk out the door, though that didn't quite take into account the fact that Dad was just going to work. She knew that Bill, who was a restoration carpenter, was hard at work on a big project, transforming an old, abandoned church into a vacation home for a successful Portland restauranteur and his family.

Still, it was a big job, toting all the groceries that would feed herself and Bill, and their two daughters who hadn't yet flown the nest. The fact that Sara, now a graduate student at nearby Winchester College, was a vegetarian, and Zoe, an undergraduate at the same institution, was avoiding gluten, didn't make things any easier. Her grocery list was now filled with the special foods the girls demanded: quinoa, kale, organic yogurt, free-range eggs, hormone-free milk, on and on it went. She dropped two heavy bags on the kitchen table and went out for more, eventually making three trips to get everything inside. And then there was the unloading, the sorting and the storing.

When she'd finally folded the last bag and tucked it away with the others in her bag of bags, she sat down at the round, golden oak kitchen table and considered making herself a cup of tea. Entirely too much work, she decided, opting instead for a glass of water. She sipped it thoughtfully, thinking of Sylvia's challenge: could she possibly fit into her wedding dress? Setting down her glass, she decided she had to find out.

The dress, shrouded in a garment bag, hung in the back of her closet. She hadn't looked at it in years, had almost forgotten about it. Like most mothers, she had a vague hope that one of her daughters might wear it for her wedding, but so far that hadn't happened. Even Elizabeth, her oldest, who worked for the tony Cavendish Hotel chain and was currently living in Paris, hadn't shown any interest in marriage, much less in wearing her mother's dress. It probably wouldn't suit her, thought Lucy, climbing the steep, back stairway that led from the kitchen to the bedrooms on the second floor. She would surely want something more high fashion.

Entering the bedroom she shared with Bill, Lucy opened the bifold closet doors, which stuck a bit and which Bill kept meaning to fix. She slid the clothes along the rod until she came to the long garment bag, which she pulled out and laid on the bed, then unzipped it to reveal the white dress.

It was a simple design with short sleeves and a jewel neckline. The bodice was made of Alençon lace, ending in a slightly raised waist. The full skirt was heavy satin ending in the slightest suggestion of a train, and fastened with a wide ribbon sash at the waist. It was slightly crushed from hanging in the closet all these years, and the veiled headpiece, which she had tucked into the bottom of the garment bag, was flattened.

She took it out, reshaping it with her hands, and set it on her head, fluffing out the white tulle veil, and looked in the mirror. She was much older now, but if she brought the veil forward, over her face, she almost looked like the young woman in the wedding picture that stood on Bill's dresser. But not quite, she decided, snatching the coif off and tossing it on the bed.

Picking up the dress, she held it at arm's length and studied it. It was a pretty dress but nothing like the strapless sheaths the girls wore these days, and not like the heavily beaded and hugely skirted cream puffs that had been fashionable for a while. Turning to the full-length mirror on the back of the bedroom door, she held the gown against her body and sighed. It was obvious, without even trying it on, that she could never fit into it. She wasn't fat, not by a long shot, but she'd given birth to four children, and she'd breast-fed them all. Her body had changed and she was no longer the little slip of a thing who had worn that dress.

Standing there and studying her reflection, she thought it wasn't just her body that had changed; she had changed, too. She was much more confident these days and much more assertive than she had been as a young bride. She was more open-minded, too, and less opinionated. Back then, she thought, she'd been a bit of a prig, convinced there was a right way to do things and a wrong way. Nowadays she was no longer convinced that food colorings were poison, that childbirth had to be natural, and all plastic should be banned.

She realized now that her strongly held beliefs had

been a defense against an uncertain world. That had become obvious when she stepped inside the church vestibule on her wedding day and panicked, completely terrified to take that first step down the aisle to the altar where Bill was waiting for her.

"Ready, sweetie?" her father had asked, cocking his elbow and inviting her to take his arm.

Not at all, she'd realized, wanting only to turn tail and run right out the door. She would have fled, she remembered, except for the fact that everything was going black and she was about to faint. It was Beth Gerard, her best friend and maid of honor, who had produced from somewhere a brown paper lunch bag, which she gave to Lucy, instructing her to breathe into it.

Dad had held her up as Lucy breathed in and out, deep breaths, into the paper sack. "I thought this might happen," said Beth.

"I can't do this," said Lucy. "The wedding's off."

"It's rather late for that," said her father.

"Look, if it's no good, you can get a divorce or an annulment. But today, you have to get married," said Beth.

"It's not Bill, it's me. I can't go down that aisle."

"Oh, yes you can," said Beth. "Just imagine they're all naked."

Standing there, in front of her mirror, Lucy smiled, just as she had on her wedding day when she followed Beth and the other bridesmaids down the aisle on her father's arm. Afterward, everybody said they'd never seen such a radiant, happy bride.

It was time, thought Lucy as she replaced the dress in the garment bag, to call Beth. She hadn't spoken with her in a long time, and she knew Beth would love hearing about the Bickersons and reminiscing about the wedding. No time like the present, decided Lucy, knowing that unless she made the call immediately the moment would pass and she would be distracted and forget. She perched on the side of her bed and picked up the phone from the bedside table, punching in the number she knew from memory.

The voice that answered wasn't Beth's; it was male.

"Is Beth there?" asked Lucy, puzzled.

"I'm afraid not. Who's calling?"

"I'm an old friend, Lucy Stone. Could you please tell her I called?"

"I'm afraid not, Lucy," said the voice, which was close to breaking. "This is Dante."

Lucy knew Dante was Beth's son, whom she remembered as a skinny, mischievous kid. Now, from his deep voice, it was clear he was all grown up. And it was also clear to her that something was wrong. "Is everything all right, Dante?"

"No. It's not. Oh, Lucy, everything's wrong." He gasped, letting out a sob. "My mother is dead."

Connect with

Visit us online at
KensingtonBooks.com
to read more from your favorite authors, see books
by series, view reading group guides, and more.

Join us on social media

for sneak peeks, chances to win books and prize packs,
and to share your thoughts with other readers.

facebook.com/kensingtonpublishing
twitter.com/kensingtonbooks

Tell us what you think!

To share your thoughts, submit a review,
or sign up for our eNewsletters, please visit:
KensingtonBooks.com/TellUs.